I0627753

Lost Chances

The Redstone Chronicles Book Three
J. T. Bishop

Eudoran Press LLC

Copyright © 2022 by J. T. Bishop

All rights reserved. No part of this publication may be reproduced, distributed or transmitted in any form or by any means, without prior written permission.

Eudoran Press LLC

6009 W. Parker Rd. #149-913

Dallas, TX 75093

www.jtbishopauthor.com

Publisher's Note: This is a work of fiction. Names, characters, places, and incidents are a product of the author's imagination. Locales and public names are sometimes used for atmospheric purposes. Any resemblance to actual people, living or dead, or to businesses, companies, events, institutions, or locales is completely coincidental.

Author Photos by Nick Bishop and Mayza Clark Photography

Book Editing by P. Creeden, G. Enstam, C. McGuire and C. Marquis

Updated Cover Design by J.T. Bishop

Lost Chances/ J.T. Bishop -- 1st ed.

ISBN Paperback 978-1-955370-17-2

ISBN Hardback 978-1-955370-32-5

To my friends and the stories they inspire...

You know who you are. Here's to more fun meals with lots of laughter and tasty rum drinks.

Other Books by J. T. Bishop

Detectives Daniels and Remalla standalones/novellas
The Girl and the Gunshot (subscribers only)
A Hamburger Christmas
The Magic of Murder (subscribers only)
Murder Unveiled—a prequel to Haunted River

Detectives Daniels and Remalla
Haunted River
Of Breath and Blood
Of Body and Bone
Of Mind and Madness
Of Power and Pain
Of Love and Loss
Dominion
Illusions
Vendetta
Black Bird

The Redstone Chronicles
Lost Souls
Lost Dreams
Lost Chances
Lost Hope
Lost Lives
Lost Time
Lost Love

Chapter One

MASON REDSTONE CLUTCHED AT his bedsheets. His body trembled, and he wiped the sweat from his eyes. He did his best to focus on how far he'd come, but a chill lanced through him, and he cursed. A week into his stay at the drug rehabilitation center, his withdrawal symptoms were less intense, and the nausea and vomiting had abated, but his body still craved the drugs, and he'd often wake in the night, sweaty and desperate for a pill.

He wondered how he'd suffered through this on his own when he'd gone cold turkey the first time he'd kicked the pills. It was a pain he'd forgotten or had chosen to wipe from his mind. He didn't recall it being this difficult but realized this time he'd been addicted for longer and his body was fighting back.

Forcing himself up, he pushed back the covers. With shaky fingers, he reached for the glass of water beside his bed. He picked it up and took a sip, studying his quiet space, grateful he had it all to himself. After being admitted, he'd learned that all the residents had their own personal room. Apparently, Mallory, the woman who'd arranged his stay, had admitted him into a posh and exclusive rehabilitation center typically reserved for the rich and famous. When he'd questioned how he'd qualified, the woman who'd greeted him when he'd arrived had explained that many residents gained entrance on scholarships. If they met certain criteria, they wouldn't have to pay a cent. Apparently, he'd met the requirements and had received the benefits of a free ride.

At the time, he'd been too anxious and terrified to ask questions. He'd just done what he was told, followed the instructions and started his detox. They'd allocated two weeks to allow for the withdrawal from the drugs. He figured it would take a week at most, but now, after a week in, he'd changed his mind. Based on how he was feeling, he was going to need the full two weeks.

Blinking and still shaking, he set the water down, grabbed the blanket at the edge of the bed and wrapped it around him. He'd kept the lights off because he hoped after a few minutes, the shaking and sweating would abate, and he could go back to sleep. He thought of Mikey and Trick and wondered how they were coping with his absence. He couldn't help but worry. Would they be able to keep SCOPE afloat without a paranormal investigator at the helm?

Mikey had assured him they would handle it. He could still recall her face when he'd told her of his addiction. She hadn't believed him at first, but then the shock and denial had set in. It had quickly transformed to worry and uncertainty and then resolve and determination. She'd taken his hand and had told him he'd been there for her when she'd needed him, and she would do the same for him. All she wanted was for him to get better. Assuring him she and SCOPE would be fine, and, like him, fighting back tears, she'd hugged and held him.

His brother, Max, and girlfriend, Valerie, had done the same. They'd showered him with support, told him they would help Mikey while he was gone, and were proud that he was getting the help he'd needed.

After suffering serious injuries from their previous case, Trick had still been recuperating in the hospital, but he'd reminded Mason that SCOPE needed a healthy P.I. at the helm and Mason's well-being mattered more than any client, and as soon as he was back on his feet, he would be there for Mikey and not to worry about anything.

Sitting in his dark room, Mason wished he could talk to them, but family visits weren't allowed in the first thirty days. He hadn't seen or spoken to them since arriving, and while he understood the reasons behind it, he would have welcomed hearing their voices more than once this past week.

The blanket wrapped around him, his shaking eased, and his chills slowed. He did his best to quiet his mind as the counselor had recommended. Sometimes it helped, but often it didn't. This time though, he had more success. Sitting back against the headboard, he relaxed, telling himself in soothing words to take it easy. This battle would take time, and there were no overnight fixes. He was in a better place, and while it would be difficult, he'd get through it. His muscles relaxed, and his thoughts slowed. The chills stopped, and although he was still sweating, he felt calmer.

Giving himself time to sit and be still, he felt a slight tingle run up his arm. The tingles grew until the hair raised on his skin. Recognizing the presence of more than just himself in the room, he opened his eyes, and saw the faint outline of a woman standing in the corner.

Seeing her, his whole body prickled. It was his first spirit encounter since entering the facility. It was possible he'd had other visits, but Mason doubted he would have recognized them as such due to the effects of the withdrawal. This time though, he was well enough to realize that this was a spirit who wanted to communicate.

Waiting to see if she'd speak, he stared at her. She stood quietly, with her straight brown hair running down her back and her eyes wide. She wore a knee-length black dress with long sleeves, and a trickle of blood ran from her nose.

Mason didn't move. His heart thumped, and he wondered why she'd chosen to appear to him. He wasn't in much condition to help anybody.

When she made no attempt to communicate, he decided to break the ice. "How can I help you?" he asked.

She didn't react but continued to stare.

"You should know," he said. "I'm in rehab right now. Kicking pain pills. It sucks." He considered if perhaps she'd been a patient. "Were you here once?"

No answer.

"Do you know someone who is here?"

She jerked at the question, and her mouth opened.

Mason shivered, but not from withdrawal. "What do you want?"

The woman began to whisper.

Mason leaned in. "I can't hear you."

She spoke louder. "You should have listened," he heard her say.

"Listened?" he asked.

"You should have listened to me. You should have listened to me," she repeated.

"Listened to what?" He leaned back as her voice raised.

"You should have listened. You should have listened." She started shouting. "You should have listened."

Mason shook his head. "I don't understand."

Restless, she moved closer. The blood streamed from her nose, and blood droplets dripped and streaked down her dress. "You should have listened."

She approached, and Mason pushed back against the headboard. "To what?"

At the edge of the bed, she pointed at Mason, her bony finger sporting a red-polished nail. "You should have LISTENED." Her voice bounced off the walls, and Mason held his ears. She reached forward and touched Mason on the arm.

An electric pulse sizzled through him, and Mason jumped. She continued her mantra, her eyes turned milky white, and she aimed an ugly glare at him.

Scared, Mason tried to get away. He scooted back toward the edge of the bed and slid off onto the floor. He wriggled away into a corner of the room.

The woman followed, still yelling that he should have listened.

Unable to go anywhere and powerless to stop her, Mason opened his mouth and screamed.

Chapter Two

MIKEY REDSTONE STUDIED HER laptop. Her head pounding, she eyed the clock and wondered for the thousandth time how Mason was doing. Checking the calendar, she saw he'd been in rehab for two weeks. It was the longest they'd ever gone without talking. Mikey had called more than once to check on her brother, and the facility had told her each time that he was fine, and as soon as family visits were allowed, they would contact her.

Closing the laptop, she stood from Mason's desk, grabbed her phone and went to sit on the couch. Laying her head back, she reflected on the last fourteen days. Mason's paranormal P.I. agency, SCOPE, which stood for The Study of Cryptids or Paranormal Entities, was hanging on, although without Mason at the helm, business had suffered. With his absence, and Trick still recovering, Mason's girlfriend, Valerie, who was also a private investigator, had stepped in to help with the non-paranormal clients. Not that there had been many, but she'd helped to locate a lost family dog and had tracked down a missing woman after her family had contacted SCOPE, believing she'd been the victim of foul play. Luckily, Valerie had located the woman on a beach in Mexico after learning she'd taken off with her boyfriend.

Mikey had managed to push back the paranormal inquiries, telling clients that Mason was on an extended leave of absence and, when he returned, would follow up on their cases. She hoped they'd stick around long enough for Mason's return, but Mikey knew they'd lose a few. There wasn't much to be done, though, since nobody else could handle Mason's caseload and Mikey couldn't fake his abilities. She'd considered it but knew it wouldn't be ethical.

She thought of Kyle, the man she'd met while banishing Mason's evil spirit, Mr. Dark, just before Mason had gone into the treatment center. She and Kyle had met for coffee and dinner since that first meeting, and he'd offered to assist with SCOPE's paranormal work. He shared similar skills to Mason, and he'd told her he'd be happy to jump in during Mason's absence. Mikey had thanked him, told him she'd consider it, but had yet to take him up on his offer. She couldn't deny, though, that they needed the help, and if SCOPE was going to stay afloat for the next two and a half months, they'd need someone to pick up the slack. Kyle met all the requirements, but she still resisted.

Sighing, she thought of Aaron Remalla, the detective she'd grown close to over the last several months. Their traumatic experiences with Victor D'Mato and his cult had brought them together, and they'd become close. The problem was, Mikey didn't know how or if that would translate into romance. Some part of her wanted it to, but another part wanted to run from it. It scared her to think of Remalla as more than a friend. She'd never been good at relationships, and if she screwed it up, she'd get hurt and so would he. While Mikey appreciated vulnerability in others, she wasn't good at it herself.

Despite those issues, which were difficult enough, the one that loomed over everything had her even more concerned. Because of it, the last two weeks had been hellish, and it had affected not just her, but also Remalla, and Mikey had no idea what to do about it.

The day Mason had left for rehab, she'd talked to Rem about her coffee date with Kyle, and it had been an awkward conversation. When Rem had called back, Mikey had figured he wanted to talk about it, and she'd steeled herself for the conversation, but what he'd said instead had stunned her. Margaret, her psychopathic sister, whose unique abilities and taste for evil had guided her toward Victor and had lured Mikey down the same path, had escaped from the psychiatric hospital where she'd been held since Remalla's assault and near death. And it wasn't just that her sister was ill and dangerous, although that was bad enough—she had almost killed Mikey, too.

She'd gone mute with disbelief. Remalla had offered her police protection and a stay at a safe house. Mikey had taken him up on both at first. With Mason gone, Mikey expected Margaret would contact her, and the thought of being home alone scared her. Mason could not be reached, but the facility had been notified and had assured Mikey that they would keep him safe. Trick had offered to let her stay at his place, but there was barely enough room at Trick's for Trick.

Mikey had chosen the safe house, but after five days, realized that it was silly to remain there. If Margaret wanted to come after her, then no safe house would prevent it. Rem had argued, but Mikey didn't relent and had chosen to go home, although the police protection continued. A patrol car remained outside SCOPE while Mikey was at the office, and it followed her home at night.

Despite his objections, Rem had come to the same conclusions as Mikey. Since he was also a target, he'd tried a safe house for a few days, then had stayed with Daniels, his partner, for a short time, but then had ultimately returned home. Neither of them could hide forever. Their only hope was to find Margaret and return her to the psychiatric facility. But until then, they'd have to live their lives and pray they'd remain safe.

Since hearing the news, Mikey had seen Rem only once. She suspected he was keeping his distance in case Margaret was watching. He didn't want to rile Mikey's sister up, which Mikey understood, but she also had to wonder if he was just as hesitant to discuss Kyle as she was. Was Remalla the reason she hadn't contacted Kyle for help?

Trying to relax and not overthink, she debated lying down and taking a nap. She hadn't slept well since Mason's departure and Margaret's escape, and she wondered if she would ever sleep again.

Starting to doze, she heard the click of a lock and the squeak of the outer office door. Opening her eyes, her heart thudded, and she thought of her sister. "Hello?" She sat up. "Who's there?" She heard footsteps and waited, half-expecting to see Margaret walk into SCOPE, her blue eyes blazing, and cackling loudly. Mikey wasn't close enough to the desk computer to see the cameras. Gripping the edge of the coffee table, she called out again. "Hello?"

The footsteps approached, and Trick stuck his head into the inner office. "Mikey?" He raised his hands. "Don't scream. It's me."

Mikey blew out a relieved breath and considered again whether to keep a weapon at SCOPE. Rem had recommended it, but she wasn't a fan of guns. She knew Mason would agree with Rem and would be furious when he learned she'd been unarmed with Margaret running around.

"Trick," she said, holding her stomach. "You scared me."

Trick walked in. His face was thinner than usual, but Mikey could tell he'd gained some weight since leaving the hospital and starting physical therapy. "Sorry," he said. "I should have called first."

"What are you doing here?" she asked. "You're not supposed to be back at work for another week."

He walked carefully to his desk and sat in his chair with a sigh. "Mikey, if I sit another day at my place, I'm going to end up joining Mason in therapy. I'm capable of coming into the office and helping. You shouldn't be alone, anyway."

"I'm okay. There's a patrol outside."

Trick scoffed. "That's bullshit protection. Your sister could get past those guys faster than it takes them to eat a donut."

Mikey didn't doubt it. "Well, Batman has yet to respond to my bat signal, so they'll have to do for now."

"Mason would be pissed as hell if he knew about Margaret. Thank God he didn't hear about it before he went into rehab, or he never would have gone."

Mikey nodded. "I just hope he's safe. I worry about him."

"That place has more security than the bake shop those officers frequent. He's the safest of all of us. It's you I'm worried about. I don't like you staying at your place by yourself."

"What choice do I have? The safe house Remalla put me in wasn't any better." She paused. "If Margaret wants to get to me, she will."

"What about Rem? Where's he staying?"

"He's doing what I'm doing. He's back at home. We can't live like hermits. We've both got jobs to do and lives to live."

Trick put his hand on his desk. "Then that decides it. I'm officially back at SCOPE."

"Trick," she said, rubbing her temples. "You're not ready."

"Ready for what? Sitting in an office, talking, and doing nothing?" He waved a hand. "I'm getting the feeling we don't have a lot of clients."

Mikey moaned. "You're not wrong. Valerie's helping where she can, but we need the paranormal assistance. That's our bread and butter."

"Did you talk to Kyle? Didn't he offer his services?"

Mikey pursed her lips. "He did, but I haven't spoken to him yet."

Trick studied her. "Because you think he won't be a good fit or because of the whole romantic triangle thing?"

Mikey narrowed her eyes. "Don't start, Trick."

Trick stood with a groan, came over to the couch and sat beside her. "Listen," he said. "I get it. You like Remalla, and you like Kyle. You can't pull the trigger on either because Remalla scares the hell out of you and Kyle is just safe enough to like, but if you get to know him better, maybe do more than just like. It's a fascinating conundrum, but it's time to get over it."

"Trick—"

"Bottom line, Mikey. I can't do the paranormal stuff, and neither can you. I can try to fake my way through it, but I think most people will see through my psychic Trick charade. Not that it wouldn't be amusing." He shifted to face her. "If you want SCOPE to make it these next two months, then we need Kyle." He paused. "You know it, and I know it."

Mikey hung her head.

"You can tell Remalla exactly what it is. Kyle's helping us out of a jam. And you can tell Kyle that for now, it's better to be friends while you're working together. That will allow you to keep them both at a distance until you figure out what to do. Hopefully, Rem and Daniels will find Margaret before Mason gets out of rehab. Because if they don't..." He stared off and sighed. "Well, I don't want to think about that right now."

Mikey ran her hands through her long hair and rested her forehead in her palm. "I don't want to think, period," she said. She studied the floor. "It's been a hard two weeks."

Trick remained quiet for a second. "Then let me take over for a while. Where's your phone?"

"On the couch beside you."

Trick found it and held it out. "You want to call Kyle, or do you want me to do it?"

Mikey closed her eyes and knew Trick was right. They needed the help. She hoped Rem would understand. "Fine." She held out her hand. "I'll call."

Chapter Three

MASON SQUIRMED IN HIS seat, staring out the large picture window. Dr. Hamlish sat across from him in a cushioned seat; a side table with a folder and a pen was beside him. Mason eyed the large trees and manicured lawn, wishing he were anywhere else but sitting in the chair across from the doctor.

Dr. Hamlish swiveled in his seat. His narrow grey eyes and thick reddish-brown beard made Mason think of his paternal grandfather. Mason hadn't liked him either.

"Any more hallucinations?" asked the doctor.

Mason recalled the woman in the black dress with the bloody nose who'd yelled at him a week earlier. The doctor didn't believe Mason's explanation that she was a spirit who'd come to communicate, confident she was merely a figment of his imagination.

Mason picked at the armrest. "No." A part of him wondered if maybe Dr. Hamlish was right. The woman had not reappeared since that night.

"How are you sleeping?" asked the doctor.

"Better."

"No more chills or night sweats?"

Mason shook his head. "No."

"Good. That's a big step." Dr. Hamlish paused. "You were quiet in group yesterday."

Mason shrugged. "Not much to say."

Hamlish swiveled some more. "It takes time. It's not easy being vulnerable. I think once you get to know everyone, it will be less difficult."

Mason recalled one of the patients, Barry, a small man with big ears, bursting into tears after talking about his mother's death. "I suppose."

"You want to talk about anything now?"

"Like what?"

The doctor's narrow eyes narrowed further. "Anything. We can discuss how you're feeling after your first two weeks. The facility. The other patients. Your family." He picked up a paper and read from it. "We can talk about your brother, sister, or rather sisters. Your business partner." He read some more. "Or your paranormal work."

Mason caught the slight edge in Hamlish's voice when he mentioned paranormal. "You have a problem with what I do?"

Hamlish set the paper down. "No. Not at all. It's just a first for me."

Mason scratched a hole in the armrest with his fingernail. "It is for most." He smoothed the leather to conceal the hole.

"When did you first realize you could talk to...for lack of a better term...dead people?"

Mason almost chuckled. The movie *The Sixth Sense* had done wonders for his business but not so much socially. When people met him, they either thought he was a joke or were fascinated by his talents and wanted to know more. He figured Dr. Hamlish was a member of the former group. Thankfully, his girlfriend Valerie was part of the latter. Thinking of Valerie and missing her, he sighed. "It started when I was a kid."

"How did you feel about it?"

Mason recalled his youth. "I don't know. I would see spirits at night when I woke up, some of them with nasty wounds, and most of whom wanted to talk to me. It was terrifying."

"How did you handle it?"

Uncomfortable, Mason shifted in his chair. "I tried to ignore them at first, but that failed. So, I told my parents." He squirmed again, anticipating the next question.

"What did they say?"

Mason fiddled with his handlebar mustache. He needed a haircut and a shave, but they wouldn't give him a razor and certainly not scissors. He wondered if the facility provided a barber. With the rates they charged to their non-sponsored patients, he figured they could afford a stylist to the stars. "Mom understood. She'd had her own similar experiences. She explained what was happening and helped me figure out how to handle it. She got me through it."

"And your father?"

Mason stared off. "He...uh...didn't say much."

"Why not?"

"My father...he was a man of few words." He started picking at the hole again.

"Did he believe you?"

Mason tensed. "No. I don't think he did."

"What makes you say that?"

Mason watched the tree branches beyond the window blow in the wind. "Probably because he suggested my mother take me to a shrink and put me on medication."

"How did that make you feel?"

Mason remembered his parents' arguing after his revelation. "Not very good." His mother had called his father a 'damn fool' and his father had called his mother a 'witch who needed medication of her own.' His older brother Max hadn't been home at the time, but his sister Margaret had listened at the closed door and laughed. Mikey had hidden in a closet. Mason had found her and gone to sit with her until the yelling stopped, his father left, and his mother had found them huddled together in the dark.

"Were you angry with him?" asked Hamlish.

Mason took a deep breath. "At first, but then I felt sorry for him."

"Why?"

"He...uh...I don't know. He's a lost man."

"What do you mean?"

Mason leaned forward and put his elbows on his knees. "He comes from a very conservative family. Having a wife and kid, or should I say kids, who could do crazy things that did not fit into the typical expectations of the perfect family, was hard for him. He prefers to blend in, not stand out."

"How is your relationship with him?"

"Strained."

Hamlish eyed his folder. "You don't mention him in your paperwork."

"We're estranged. I haven't spoken to him since Mom's funeral. I doubt Mikey and Max have either. And before you ask about that, it's for the best, so don't ask me to reconsider."

Hamlish made a note on a piece of paper. "Understandable. Sometimes it's better to maintain healthy boundaries." He set his pen down. "Going back to your early years and your father, was your relationship with him strained before or after you told him about your spirit contact?"

"Both." He paused. "But worse after."

Hamlish sat forward. "Why was it strained before?"

Mason studied his hands, recalling a past he'd rather forget. "My dad is a man's man. He likes sports, drinking and talking tough. I was none of those things. My older brother is more like him, though, and they got along better, at least for a while."

"What happened after a while?"

Mason interlaced his fingers. "Dad liked the ladies. Once Max found out...well...that Dad wasn't faithful, their father-son relationship soured."

Hamlish nodded. "How's your relationship with Max?"

Mason considered the hectic days leading up to his stay at the rehab center. "Strained, too, but since I helped prove his innocence after a murder charge, they're improving."

"I heard about that on the news. Your brother was lucky to have your help."

"He wasn't thrilled at first, but he came around."

"Does your brother have gifts, too?"

Mason nodded. "He does, but he's like Dad. He doesn't like to rock the boat. He prefers to keep his head down and run his business. He'd rather follow the crowd than break away from the herd."

Hamlish tipped his head. "Does that bother you?"

"It was always a point of contention with me. I never shied away from my gifts. I embraced them. Max didn't want to have anything to do with them. I think he was, and is, embarrassed."

"Does that make you feel judged, like your father judged you?"

"Sure as hell does."

"You think Max feels judged by you?"

Mason shrugged. "Maybe."

Hamlish smoothed his beard and sat back. "You think Max also felt judged by your dad?"

Feeling the beginning of a headache, Mason massaged his temples. "What do you mean?"

"You said when you 'came out,' so to speak, that your dad didn't like it. Did Max ever confess his gifts the way you did?"

"No."

"Why not, do you think?"

Mason remembered Max confiding in Mason when they were kids that he'd been seeing similar things at night, but he wouldn't tell Mom or Dad, and he refused to let Mason say a word, either. Mason clutched his hands together when it occurred to him why. "I guess he was scared."

"Of what?"

"Of Dad and his disapproval."

"He'd seen what had happened to you, and he didn't want to go through that. So he buried his talents to satisfy his father."

"Yeah. I guess."

"Then he carries a wheelbarrow of crap around, too." Hamlish tapped his fingernail on his knee. "He just expresses it differently."

Mason sighed heavily. "He's not popping pills."

Hamlish pursed his lips. "He buries himself in his work? Makes a lot of money? That's just another way to gain approval. Popping pills is one way to cope, but it isn't the only way."

Mason rubbed his face and sat up. "I always took the hard road."

"That's something else for us to discuss." He made another note on the paper. "Maybe in our next group."

Mason groaned.

Hamlish raised the side of his lip. "I promise. By the time you leave Windhaven, you're going to miss your group meetings. You'll form bonds you'll wish you could have with others outside of here."

"I have great bonds with others outside of here."

Hamlish scribbled some more. "We'll talk about that, too."

Mason squeezed the armrest. "Great. When do I get to see my people?"

"After thirty days. Until then, I want you to settle in. Get to know other patients. The social aspect is important here. Plus, get involved. We have art classes, pottery, painting, horseback riding. And I want you to go to the meditation circle every day. It'll do wonders for you."

"I'm not sure meditation is such a good idea."

"Why not?"

"It tends to conjure more than just happy thoughts."

Hamlish stared for a second. "You mean...?"

"Dead people? Yes."

Hamlish sighed. "Have you seen any recently?"

"No. Not recently."

Hamlish shrugged. "Then why not give the circle a try? Let's see where it leads. You may be surprised."

You might be surprised too, thought Mason. He looked out the window and spotted a young woman who Mason guessed was a patient, walking across the grass. Her light-brown hair blew in the wind. "Whatever you say."

"Good." He wrote something else. "I'll tell Candace you'll be joining starting tomorrow."

"Great." Mason thought of another issue. "While you're at it, tell Candace the food here could use a little upgrade. A place like this should have a five-star chef."

Hamlish frowned. "You don't like the food?"

"The selection is fine, but it's bland. I get why you don't let us have sharp objects, but I think it's safe to add a little salt. That won't kill us anytime soon."

Hamlish straightened. "Have you thought about killing yourself?"

Mason did groan then. "That was a bad joke." He fiddled with his mustache. "And no. I'm not thinking about killing myself. At least not since my first week of detox." He brushed the stubble on his face. "I have been thinking of a barber, though. You guys have one?"

Hamlish's expression remained unchanged, and Mason wondered what he was thinking. "I'll tell Candace you want a haircut, too. She'll set you up."

"Candace does a lot."

"She's our patient liaison. You need anything, Candace is your gal." He clicked his pen and put it in his pocket. "I'll mention the food."

"I can't wait to meet this magical Candace, the liaison." He bit back a laugh.

"You met her when you arrived. She showed you to your room and gave you a brief tour."

"She did?" Mason recalled his arrival. He'd been signed in by a solemn receptionist at the front, and then a petite woman with bouncing blonde hair and pretty blue eyes, who was way too perky for his mood, had taken him back. "That was Candace?"

"It was." Hamlish closed the folder. "You'll see her around. She likes to get to know the patients to better fulfill their needs."

"I don't suppose she could get me a hamburger and a beer?"

"How about a turkey burger and a soda?"

"Put some salt on the burger and you got a deal."

Hamlish finally smiled. "I think you're going to do very well here, Mason. Just stick to the program, be willing to open up, and I think after ninety days, you're going to be happy with the results."

Ninety days, thought Mason. "Actually, it's now seventy-six days, but who's counting?"

Hamlish stood. "There's a reason we're expensive. Our behavioral therapy approach has proven time and again to be highly successful. We're quite proud of our track record. When you leave here, you'll be prepared for the outside world and how to handle its various pitfalls."

Mason stood too. "I hope you're right. I'd hate to spend the next seventy-six days in group therapy and meditation, with a fabulous liaison, and end up the same."

Hamlish's smile became a grin. "Trust us, Mr. Redstone." He adjusted his sleeve and smoothed his shirt. "After you leave, you won't be the same man."

A tingle ran up Mason's arm, and the hair on his neck raised, just as a form took shape behind Hamlish. Mason froze a flat stare on his face as a Black man came into view behind the doctor. He wore a white hospital gown, his gray frizzy hair was matted, and a trickle of blood ran from his ear down to his neck.

Staring at Mason, he raised a finger and pointed at him. *You won't be the same man*, Mason heard in his head.

"Something wrong?" asked Hamlish.

Mason swallowed, but then shook his head. He eyed the man, who slowly drifted away and vanished. "Uh, no. Nothing." He stepped away from the chair and toward the door. "See you tomorrow, Doc."

Chapter Four

Trick sipped from his coffee cup and relaxed back in his chair. He sat at a four-top table at the coffee shop and waited for Mikey. She'd suggested they meet outside of the office for once, and Trick had agreed that a change in scenery would be good for them. They'd both either been at SCOPE or at their homes for the better part of three weeks because it was safer for Mikey, and Trick was still recuperating.

He'd been doing his best to follow the physical therapy regimen and was getting stronger, although he still tired easily, not that he would tell Mikey. She already worried enough about Mason. She didn't need to worry about him, too.

Taking another sip, he eyed the shop. Margaret Redstone was always on his mind, and although he felt comfortable Mason was safe, he didn't feel as confident about Mikey. He knew Margaret well enough to realize that her instability made her dangerous, and a police patrol would not thwart her. If something happened to Mikey, Mason would never forgive Trick and, worse, Mason would blame himself. Trick wouldn't feel too great about it, either.

Relieved he didn't see anything suspicious, he told himself to ease up, but caught the gaze of a woman who sat by herself on the other side of the shop. She had long, thick, wavy black hair and dark wide eyes. Her eyebrows and lipstick were as thick and full as her hair, and when he made eye contact, she looked away and sipped from a mug.

If he'd been more of himself, he would have approached her, but the last month had been a doozy, and the thought of meeting anyone added to his weariness. His last date night had almost killed him, and he figured waiting a little longer would be wise.

The bell above the door chimed, and a tall man with shiny hair as lustrous as the woman's entered. He looked around and waved and then approached the woman

Trick had just noticed. She smiled, stood, and hugged him, and the man sat with her.

Trick shrugged. *So much for that,* he thought to himself.

The door chimed again, and Mikey entered. He raised a hand, and she headed over, wearing her usual black jeans and fitted black t-shirt. A small diamond stud glittered in her nostril, and her shoulder-length reddish-brown hair sported new purple highlights. Adjusting the knapsack across her shoulder, she approached the table.

"Hey," she said, sitting across from him.

"Hey," he said. "You want a coffee?"

She slid off the knapsack and placed it in the chair beside her. "I'll get some in a minute. How are you?"

Trick sighed. "You know, you don't have to ask me that every time you see me."

She studied him. "You look pale. Did you sleep?"

He noted the dark circles under her eyes. "I could ask the same of you."

"I slept fine."

"Sure you did." He eyed her highlights. "You've gone back to purple?"

She ran a hand through her hair. "I figured I needed the change."

"Looks good. Did you actually go to a salon?"

She shifted and looked around.

"We're safe," he said. "No Margaret. You sure you want to meet here?"

"I do. I can't keep living like the bogeyman is going to jump out at every turn." She swiveled back toward him. "And yes, I went to a salon. And survived."

Trick didn't like that she'd taken the risk but also couldn't blame her. "No news from Remalla about Margaret?"

"Nothing. It's like she's vanished from the earth."

"Maybe she has."

"You actually believe that?"

"No."

"Neither do I."

Trick set his cup on the table. "Have you considered what will happen if they never find her?"

Mikey shook her head. "No, because that's not Margaret's style. Right now, she's biding her time, knowing she's driving us all nuts wondering when she'll strike. She's relishing our worry and fear, but when she gets bored…"

Nodding, Trick knew she was right. "You shouldn't be home alone."

"We've had this conversation."

"I know. But in light of what you just said, let's discuss it again."

"Trick, what do you want me to do?" Mikey closed her eyes. "Marge has got us right where she wants us." She groaned and opened her eyes. "I wish I could talk to Mason."

"Red's got his own problems to deal with. We can't interrupt that. Once he's done with therapy and he's home, then we can—" An idea popped into his mind.

Mikey raised an eyebrow. "Then we can what?"

Trick cursed. "I'm such an idiot."

Mikey narrowed her eyes. "Are you expecting a debate?"

"Listen," he said, "I don't know why the hell I didn't think of this sooner. Mason's house is empty. You and I should both stay there until he's back. You take Mason's room; I'll take the guest room. That way you're not alone, and I can keep an eye on you."

Mikey opened her mouth, and he waited for her to argue with him. "That's actually not a bad idea," she said. "I have keys to his place. Mason certainly wouldn't care. He'd probably be pissed if we didn't do it." She met his gaze. "You don't mind?"

He groaned. "Mind? Hell, Mikey. Half the time I don't sleep it's because I'm worried about your crazed sister. This way, we can both keep an eye on each other."

"I can help you out while you continue to recover and make you decent food to eat, too."

"And I'll be in the house with you at night." Satisfied, he smiled. "It's a win-win." He pointed. "I'll warn you, though, I do eat the occasional Taco del Fuego with a few beers."

"It's not any different from hanging out with Rem." She picked at a scratch in the table.

"You talk to him at all? About anything besides Margaret?"

She straightened and reached for the knapsack. "Not really. No."

"You tell him Kyle's helping us out at SCOPE?"

"I mentioned it." She pulled out her laptop and a notebook. "He said it was a great idea."

Trick nodded. "Have you seen him? Any plans to go out?"

Her gaze sharpened.

"Not like a date," he said. "But you two used to go to the movies, grab lunch or dinner, and just generally hang out."

"The Margaret situation has dampened that. Rem thinks that might set Marge off."

"So, he's trying to keep you safe."

"He's trying to keep us both safe. He's a target as much as I am."

Trick wondered if Remalla's distance was due to more than just safety issues. Was Remalla holding back because of Kyle?

Trick rested his elbows on the table. "That sister of yours is sure putting a wrench into everything."

"That's her specialty. She's good at it." Mikey opened her laptop and notebook. "Maybe we should talk about work."

Trick checked his watch. "You want to wait for Kyle? He should be here soon."

Her face fell. "You invited Kyle?"

Trick almost rolled his eyes. "He's working with us. He's taken three cases so far. Don't you think he should be here?"

She fiddled with the pages in her notebook. "No. Of course. You're right. He should join us. It's fine."

Trick watched her, doing his damnedest to figure her out. "What's going on? Why don't you want to see him?"

"I didn't say I didn't want to see him. You're right. He's helping us."

"Then why the hesitation?"

She flipped through the blank sheets in her notepad. "Can we talk about something else?"

Trick leaned in. "Mikey. Listen. If it's difficult to—" The door to the shop chimed and Trick saw Kyle step inside. He spotted Trick and waved. "We'll talk more later," he whispered to Mikey.

Mikey found a pen. "Great. Can't wait."

Kyle strode over. His tall, lean frame, long braided black hair and chiseled cheekbones attracted more than a few looks from various women in the coffee shop. He carried his own knapsack and smiled as he walked up. "Hi, Trick." He eyed Mikey. "Mikey."

"Hey, Kyle," said Trick. "How are you?" Mikey's knapsack was still in the seat beside her, so Trick scooted out the chair next to him. "Have a seat."

"I'm terrific." Kyle set his knapsack down.

"Hi, Kyle," said Mikey.

Kyle grinned at her. "You have any coffee?"

"Not yet," said Mikey.

"You want the usual?" he asked.

Mikey raised a hand. "You don't have to get me any."

"It's on me. Don't worry about it." He regarded Trick. "You good?"

Trick raised his cup. "Fine. Thanks."

"Be right back." Kyle pointed at Mikey's bag. "I like it."

Mikey eyed her knapsack. "I like it, too. Thanks again."

"You're welcome." He turned and headed to the counter.

Trick eyed Mikey's and Kyle's bags. "You two shop at the same store?"

Mikey turned on her laptop. "He bought mine."

"Really? That was nice."

"And now he's buying me coffee. Again."

Trick pursed his lips. "Is that a problem? Seems kinda nice."

Mikey pushed her hair back. "That's just it. He's so damned nice." She fell back against her chair and crossed her arms. "He opens doors for me. Brings me food. Buys me stuff." She lifted her bag.

"Is that bad?"

"No, it's not bad. It's just...just...a bit much." She eyed the counter where Kyle ordered the coffees and joked with the barista. "He's almost too perfect."

"You don't like perfect?"

She straightened. "I'm certainly not perfect."

"What are you saying? You don't deserve him? You're not worth his time and attention?"

"I don't know what I am."

"Just because he's nice doesn't mean he's perfect. He has flaws. You just haven't seen them yet because you won't let him get close enough." Mikey didn't answer but started to type. "Have you gone on any more dates since he started helping us out?"

She stopped typing. "I did what you suggested and told him we needed to just focus on work right now. With Margaret and Mason's issues and trying to keep SCOPE afloat, it's just too much to deal with."

Trick noticed she hadn't mentioned Remalla. "What did Kyle say?"

"What do you think he said?" She chuckled softly. "That he completely understood. To take all the time I needed. That he was there for me and happy to help with anything. But when the time was right, he looked forward to resuming our relationship."

"Wow," said Trick, looking back at Kyle. "He's good. Maybe he could give me a few tips."

"He no doubt would."

Trick picked up his coffee. His stomach rumbled, and he debated getting a piece of coffee cake. "Seems to me we did the right thing by bringing him in, regardless of your reluctance."

"Oh, we did the right thing." She swiped a finger across the mousepad. "I got a message from Mrs. Hanover, who called us in to investigate that haunting in her rental house. She loved Kyle and said he handled it with ease. She's had no issues since Kyle left."

Trick nodded. "I heard the same from Dixie Patterson. Said Kyle was amazing. She found her late husband's watch and her missing wedding ring."

Mikey frowned. "Didn't Kyle go there because she said she had a poltergeist?"

"He did. Turns out the poltergeist was her husband. Kyle communicated with him, and they apparently had a lively conversation. The husband said he was just trying to get his wife's attention."

"I guess I shouldn't be surprised." Mikey eyed her laptop. "He also got glowing reviews from the couple buying their first house. It's a historical landmark, and they wanted someone to check it to be sure it wasn't haunted. Kyle assured them they were safe, and they're moving forward with the sale."

Trick pointed. "That's an untapped market. We should pursue more home-buyers. With Kyle's abilities, we'd rake in the money."

Mikey glared at him. "I think you like him more than me." She paused. "You realize this is just temporary. When Mason returns, we won't need Kyle anymore."

"Of course, I know that. No one can replace Red." Trick shook his head. "Hell. I'm more worried you'll replace me."

"Never say never."

Trick glared back at her.

"Kidding," said Mikey. "No one's replacing anybody."

"Better not," said Trick. "Or else how will you two resume your relationship?"

Mikey huffed.

"Here you go." Kyle returned to the table. "A caramel latte." He set a cup down in front of Mikey. "And a piece of coffee cake." He slid a plate and fork over to Trick.

Trick dropped his jaw. "How did you—?"

"Intuition." Kyle held his own coffee cup and sat beside Trick. "What are we discussing?"

Trick put his cup down and picked up his fork. He spotted the woman across the shop with the dark, sexy hair, who still sat with the man with equally sexy hair watching them. "We were talking about how perfect you are."

Mikey kicked him under the table, and he bit back a grunt.

"Perfect?" asked Kyle. He smiled at Mikey.

"Yes," said Trick, scowling at Mikey. "Every client loves you. Not a single complaint. You've been a great addition to SCOPE."

"Thank you," said Kyle. "I'm having fun. I'm glad you asked for my help. But not everybody loves me. Not yet, at least." He shot a look at Mikey and sipped his drink.

Mikey went back to studying her laptop screen.

Trick looked between the two of them. "We have any more clients?" he asked, trying to change the subject. He noted that the woman was still looking over at them, her eyes narrowed.

"Yes, actually," said Mikey. "A Milam Broadstreet. Swears he's got an evil spirit lurking in his house."

Trick moaned, recalling Mr. Dark. "Not another one of those."

"It's not a problem. I can check it out," said Kyle.

"Just be careful," said Mikey. "We've already met our annual allotment of negative attachments."

"I hear you," said Kyle. He leaned in. "But personally, I like the challenge."

"Okay," said Mikey, typing. "I'll send you the details." She picked up her pen and wrote something on her notepad. "And Trick. I talked to someone who's looking for a parent who gave them up for adoption. I told them it was a long shot, but they still wanted us to try."

"I can take that. Just send it my way." Trick eyed the woman as she rose from her seat and headed toward their table. "Either of you two know this lady or am I about to get lucky?" He sat up.

Mikey turned, and Kyle looked over.

"Never seen her before," said Kyle.

The woman stopped at their table, her mouth open.

"Can we help you?" asked Trick.

"Mikey?" asked the woman. "Mikey Redstone?"

Mikey stared wide-eyed. "Oh, my God. Gina?"

Chapter Five

MIKEY DID A DOUBLE take, unsure if she was seeing right. "Gina Rodriguez?"

Gina nodded. "Yes."

Mikey stood, a swirl of emotions running through her. "My, God. How long has it been?"

Gina walked closer. "Too long." They hugged tightly.

Mikey pulled back. "I thought you got married and moved away."

"I did." She paused. "But then I divorced and came home. It didn't work out the way I expected."

"Does it ever?" asked Trick.

Kyle smiled. "Things work out for me pretty often. Guess I'm lucky."

Trick raised his brow at him.

Gina glanced at Kyle and Trick.

"I'm sorry," said Mikey. "Trick, Kyle. This is Gina Rodriguez." She pointed. "Gina. This is Trick Monroe and Kyle Willow. We...uh...well, we work together."

"Nice to meet you," said Trick and Kyle. "How do you two know each other?" asked Trick.

Mikey and Gina made eye contact. "We go back a few years," said Gina.

"We had mutual friends," said Mikey, uncertain of how much to say. "We used to hang out a lot." Her mind flashed back to memories of her and Gina at one of Victor D'Mato's many parties. She recalled the drugs and the booze and, blinking, came back to the present. "But those days are over. We've both moved on."

Trick eyed her curiously. "It sounds like you two had fun."

"That's one way of putting it," said Gina. She took Mikey's hand and squeezed it. "But Mikey's right. We both survived to see better days."

Mikey squeezed Gina's fingers in return, happy to see her friend, but also uncomfortable with the unexpected memories. "We did." She let go of Gina's hand. "How long have you been back in town?"

"Not long. Just a few months. My brother..." she gestured behind her, and Mikey spotted a man sitting at a table across the shop. "...he's been helping me get back on my feet. Coming back is sort of like starting all over again."

"I know the feeling," said Mikey, recalling leaving Victor's cult with Mason's help and trying to find her footing in a world she barely recognized.

"It's an adjustment," said Gina, "but I'm getting there."

"I'm sorry about the divorce," said Mikey.

Gina scoffed. "Believe me. It was for the best. After David and I married, I saw life with new eyes, and I knew our time was short. He came and went for a reason. I'm thankful for that."

Kyle stood. "Would you like to sit?" He offered her his chair.

"Oh, no. Thank you," said Gina. "You're very sweet, but I didn't mean to interrupt your meeting." She pulled out her cell. "We should exchange numbers and catch up sometime soon."

"That would be great," said Mikey. "I'd like that."

They exchanged contact information, and Gina put her phone away. "How's your brother?" asked Gina. "Is he still in the Rangers?"

Mikey eyed Trick. "No, he isn't," said Mikey. "He's moved here now and opened his own P.I. firm. I help manage it, and Trick's his partner. Kyle's assisting us temporarily."

"It's called SCOPE," said Kyle. "The Study of Cryptids or Paranormal Entities. It's a cool gig." He returned to his seat and smiled.

"You're private investigators?" asked Gina. "Seriously?" She glanced back at her brother.

"Yes," said Mikey. "I think I told you about Mason's abilities? Well, he decided to put them to good use."

Gina nibbled her lip. "You guys just do paranormal stuff, or do you take on other, not-so-paranormal, stuff?"

Trick pulled his coffee cake closer and held his fork. "Why do you ask?"

Gina put her hand on the back of a chair. "Because I may need some help."

"What kind of help?" asked Mikey.

Gina paused. "My younger sister, Lenora. Did you ever meet her?"

Mikey thought back, but so many memories of her friendship with Gina were a haze. "Not that I recall."

"She's one reason I came home. Ronald, my brother," Gina nodded toward the man at the table, "he told me she was mixed up with someone, but she would never tell him who." Her grip on the chair tightened. "She got caught up in the wrong crowd. Booze, drugs and sex." Mikey half expected Gina to finish her sentence with 'you know how that goes,' but thankfully, she didn't.

"Where is she now?" asked Mikey. "Is she okay?"

"No," said Gina. "She's dead."

Mikey dropped her jaw.

"I'm sorry," said Kyle, his face falling.

"What happened?" asked Trick.

Gina blinked watery eyes. "They said she overdosed, either accidentally or intentionally. But I don't believe that for a second. I think she was murdered."

Chapter Six

MASON SET HIS NAPKIN on the table and pushed his plate back. After eating a bland strawberry salad with chicken and drinking some water, he leaned back in his seat and eyed his surroundings. The dining area sported four large round tables with tablecloths and fresh flower arrangements. Diners could come and go as they wished during designated hours and were offered a choice of three dishes and a beverage. You could eat in the dining room or request a to-go box and eat outside on the grounds.

After his breakfast and a meditation circle that morning, he'd had a rousing group therapy session where he'd kept to himself yet again but had gained new insights into his fellow patients. A woman named Sadie had been introduced to meth by her boyfriend at the age of eighteen, and by the age of twenty, she'd been living on the streets and stealing from her family to survive. Another patient, Barry, had been drinking every day since the age of twelve and had been told by his doctor if he didn't stop, he'd be dead by the age of fifty. Barry had ignored him and after suffering a heart attack and almost dying at the age of forty-nine, he'd checked himself into rehab, determined to kick his drinking habit.

While Mason listened, he'd watched as an older female spirit appeared behind Barry. He'd felt certain it was Barry's mother, and she stood for a while, listening, and then she'd smiled at Mason and faded away. Mason debated whether to tell Barry that his mother was watching out for him and had forgiven him for his transgressions, but after the meeting, Barry had taken off to an art class, so Mason had held off.

After group, he'd taken a walk on the grounds, and then had visited the stables. He'd never been much of a rider, but after watching a man during a horseback-riding lesson, he'd been intrigued. A man named Kessler, who'd taught the lesson, had introduced himself and had encouraged Mason to meet the horses.

After talking to Kessler and visiting the stalls, he'd agreed to a lesson. He figured if it was free, he might as well give it a try. It seemed fitting that a former Texas Ranger should know how to ride a horse. He could only imagine what Trick would think.

Once he'd left the stables, he'd gone to the dining area to get an early lunch and, after ordering and eating the strawberry chicken salad, he made a mental note to find his liaison, Candace, and let her know what he thought about the food.

Spotting a table with coffee and tea, he stood and walked over to it. Flipping through the tea bags, he didn't see what he wanted. A female staff member with brown hair pulled back in a bun and wearing no makeup, stopped at the table to clean it. He asked her if they had Earl Grey, and she'd nodded and told him to wait. She'd gone to the back, and after a minute, had returned. Smiling, she handed Mason a tea bag and added several others to a bin on the table.

"Thank you," he'd said, pleased she'd been able to help. Opening the tea bag, he debated stopping at the library to find a book to read when he noticed a woman watching him. Holding his tea, he glanced at her, but she looked away. A memory flashed, and he recognized her. It was the young woman with the dark hair who'd walked by the window while he'd had his last meeting with Hamlish. He debated saying hello, but someone sat beside her at the table and started speaking to her. Mason turned, dunking his tea bag, and added a dash of cream to his tea. When his tea was the desired strength, he disposed of the tea bag and turned. Looking toward the dining tables, he saw that the woman was gone. Deciding to finish his drink before heading to the library, he sat on the couch in the sitting area in front of a fireplace and set his cup down on the coffee table. He leaned against the cushions, thinking of Mikey and Trick, wondering what they were doing and how things were going at SCOPE.

"You really should put that on a coaster."

Mason glanced up to see the woman who'd been sitting at the dining table standing beside him. Her hair trailed down her back, and she wore a white t-shirt with jeans. She waved a napkin at him.

"Excuse me?" he asked.

"Your drink." She stepped over to the table and put the napkin under his cup. "It will leave a ring."

"Oh," he said. "I figured in a place like this, they'd just buy a new table."

She sat in a chair beside the couch. "They might, but what really chaps my ass is why they don't just buy damn coasters."

"Seems like a simple solution."

"In a place that should be full of them."

Mason smiled. "Nothing's ever simple though, is it?"

"Not when it comes to life choices, but a coaster seems pretty mind-numbingly easy."

"Maybe it's part of their evil plan," said Mason. "No coasters, rings on tables and lack of simple solutions."

"It's shit like that that makes me want to drink," she said, sweeping her hair off her shoulder. "Granted, I'm a little OCD, but it seems counterproductive if you ask me."

"I guess if you can manage your coasterless world here, you'll be better prepared for it out there."

"I call bullshit," she said, "but what do I know? I'm not a doctor."

"Neither am I," said Mason. "Guess we're screwed."

"That's why we're here, right?" She smiled and held out a hand. "Carla Wilcox. I drink too much vodka and tequila."

Mason shook her hand. "Mason Redstone. I love pain pills."

"There's a lot of that going around."

He let go of her hand. "So I hear."

She studied him. "You a first timer?"

He raised an eyebrow at her.

"This is your first time here?" she clarified.

Mason nodded. "And hopefully the last."

"Good luck with that," she said. "This is my third go 'round. Hopefully, it's the charm."

"Really?" asked Mason.

"I guess Windhaven's world-class behavioral therapy isn't a hundred percent. Apparently, I'm an anomaly. But they keep taking me back, so I guess they're determined."

"Despite what our therapists may say, relapse is not that uncommon."

Her expression softened. "The outside world...it's tough."

Mason thought back. "It's my first time in Windhaven, but not my first rodeo. I've relapsed myself, so no judgement from me." He couldn't help but wonder about returning to his old life. Would he be able to stay off the pills?

"Life sucks and then you die, right?" she asked.

Mason thought of Detective Remalla, who'd spoken the same phrase a time or two. "That it does."

"At least they're not charging me."

"Me either," said Mason. "Guess we're two of the lucky ones."

"I suppose." She pointed. "I like your boots."

Mason raised a booted foot. "Thanks."

"You from around these parts?" she asked. "You don't see many men with handlebar mustaches wearing boots." She studied him. "You're very Sam Elliott, only younger."

He had no idea who she was talking about. "I'm from Texas. Used to be a Ranger."

Her eyes widened. "No shit? What the hell are you doing out here? You get lost?"

Mason chuckled. "No. I guess I needed a change of scenery. My brother lives out here, and I wanted to open my own P.I. firm, so I took the leap."

"Last I heard, you can open P.I. firms in Texas."

"I specialize in the paranormal side of things. My friend at the time convinced me California was the place to be, and at least back then, I trusted him." Victor D'Mato's face flashed in his mind, and Mason almost grimaced.

She swiveled in her chair. "Paranormal? Like ghosts and shit?"

He nodded. "Yes, like ghosts and shit, as well as other things."

"Do you talk to ghosts?"

"I do."

"Anybody cool?"

He frowned at her. "Cool?"

"You know. Like celebrities?" She leaned closer and lowered her voice. "They tell you any secrets? Like who shot Kennedy or murdered Marilyn Monroe?"

Mason shook his head. "No. They haven't. But to be honest, I'm not that familiar with many celebrities, so I probably wouldn't know one if I saw one."

Her mouth fell open. "You're sitting at the Windhaven Behavioral Treatment Center where all the cool kids come for rehab, and you don't know your celebrities?"

"I'm afraid I don't."

A group of people walked into the dining area and studied the menu. Carla turned to look and then stood and sat next to Mason on the sofa. "Consider yourself lucky you met me. I am a celebrity aficionado, and you're about to get up to speed on your fellow patients."

"You really don't have—"

She pointed but kept her hand low to prevent it from looking obvious. "You see him? The guy with the bald head and shades?"

Mason looked over. The man she described walked up to the counter and ordered. "Yes."

"That's Thomas Brennam. A soap opera star. Thinks he's cool as shit, but he's an ass."

"Good to know."

"The woman standing behind him is Felicia Avermore. She's graced more fashion magazines than Cindy Crawford. She got hooked on cocaine trying to stay skinny."

Mason didn't recognize either of them. "I'll take your word for it."

"And the guy chatting up that pretty lady by the entrance? That's Sam Bartholomew, the singer. Won some Grammys, but it's been a while. Hasn't had a hit in years, which is probably why he keeps drinking."

"It must suck to not keep winning Grammys."

She poked him in the arm. "You honestly don't know these people?"

Mason pursed his lips. "Nope. I've never been—"

Her gaze darted back to the entrance. She opened her mouth and smacked him on the shoulder. "Oh my God. Oh my God."

Mason followed her gaze and saw an older man with olive skin, thick, jaw-length, dark hair slicked back against his scalp, flashing a wide grin with super white teeth enter the dining area. "What?" he asked.

"He's here," she said. "He's actually here."

"Who?" He watched the man greet a woman who was wiping down one of the tables. It was the same staff member who had brought Mason his tea.

"That's Ruben Montes. I know you've heard of him."

The name seemed familiar, but Mason couldn't place it. "Not sure."

She rolled her eyes. "He reminds me of Antonio Banderas, don't you think?"

Ruben eyed the menu and put in his order to the man behind the kitchen counter. His grin never wavered. "Anthony who?" asked Mason.

Carla huffed. "I can see I've got my work cut out for me." She patted him on the knee. "You're my new project. You're about to get a quick class on who's who in Windhaven."

"Seriously, that's not nece—"

"Ruben Montes is a billionaire. His family got rich in pharmaceuticals. They basically made a killing in the opioid crisis." She paused. "Sorry. Bad choice of words."

"How ironic. Is Ruben a victim of that crisis?"

"You could say that." Carla moved closer. "He's the black sheep of the Montes family. He grew up in the business, but when he realized the damage it was doing, he broke ties and started his philanthropic pursuits. He's donated money here to build a separate wing at Windhaven. Apparently, it's super-secret and where the uber celebrities go to maintain their privacy. It's where Ruben stays, but I heard he visits over here on occasion, and this is the first time I've seen him."

"He stays at a treatment center?"

"Well, not stays as in lives, but in his younger years, he was a party boy, and he still has his vices. Word is, when he needs a refresher or just needs to clear his head, he'll come here."

"That sounds crazy. Why stay in a rehab center?"

"When you're as famous as he is, it kind of makes sense. It's private."

"Why is he so famous? Just because his family is in pharmaceuticals?"

She rolled her eyes again. "No. He was accused of murder. His trial was front-page news."

Mason studied Ruben Montes again. Ruben had found a magazine and had sat to read and wait for his lunch. "When was that?"

"It's been several years, but I'll never forget it. It was riveting. I watched the whole thing. Of course, I was drinking my vodka and tequila at the time, so that didn't help." She pulled her feet up and tucked them under her legs. "Ruben was married to a wealthy and gorgeous woman named Christine McGarren. She was an international attorney who fought for human rights and all that shit. Rescued dogs, too. Very impressive. Looked like Jessica Rabbit brought to life. In front of the cameras, she and Ruben were madly in love, and their pictures were splashed all over the tabloids. Christine's law partner was Ben Montclair, an Idris Elba lookalike. Hot and smart. The rumors, at least according to the gossip mags, were that Christine and Ben were having an affair and her marriage to Ruben was on rocky ground." She paused and watched Ruben read. "I can't believe he's sitting over there."

"I suspect he eats just like the rest of us."

Carla looked back. "Anyway, Christine wasn't the only one sleeping around. Ruben was rumored to be seeing Fay Hamptis, the wealthy fashionista who opened the *Foxy Woman* stores and had her own line of clothing. Looked like Kim Kardashian. Her stores were about to go international when she died."

"Died?" asked Mason. "What happened to her?"

"Not just her. Christine, too. Ruben supposedly came home after a trip and found Christine dead in the kitchen. She had multiple stab wounds. If you believe the internet, she'd been stabbed ninety-nine times. Not long after that, Fay was found at the bottom of an oceanside cliff, impaled on the rocks."

"Did Ruben kill them?" Mason eyed the handsome and friendly-looking man reading the magazine across the room.

"He went to trial for Christine's murder, but Fay's death was ruled a suicide. Most think Ruben pushed Fay because she was about to come forward with some damaging testimony to be used against Ruben at trial, but nobody could prove it."

"What happened at the trial?"

"It was all over the news for a year, but he ended up acquitted. His attorney did a fantastic job of making it look like Ben, Christine's partner, could have been the one to kill her. His defense offered plenty of reasons for a jury to consider reasonable doubt."

"He must have had a hell of an attorney."

"He did. Her name is Robin Everton. Reminds me of Scarlett Johansson. Famed defense attorney to the stars. She's a former downhill skier who won a gold medal and hiked Everest in record time. Word is she was faster than the Sherpas. She blew out her knee, though, and ended up going to law school."

Mason widened his eyes. "Wow."

"Crazy, right?"

Mason eyed the mild-mannered man still reading his magazine. "What happened after he was acquitted?"

"That's when Ruben supposedly turned his life around. He left the family business, started traveling and donating to worthy causes all over the world. Then he met his second wife. Floyce Hormellas. If you believe the internet, she's a descendant of African royalty. She's very Viola Davis. Outspoken and opinionated with causes she believes in. She's also a food critic and sommelier. One word from her can make you or break you in the restaurant business."

"Impressive. Why'd Floyce marry Ruben?"

"That's a great question. Was it for love or money? Nobody knows. It didn't last, though. They divorced after a couple of years."

"At least she's not dead," said Mason.

Carla nodded. "That's a plus."

"So now Ruben bides his time, spending his money where he deems fit and comes here and hangs out in his private wing when he needs a break?" Mason recalled walking around the property. "Where is this elusive wing?"

"I heard there's a private tunnel that connects this section with the secluded one, but no one really knows. I guess that's the whole point of keeping it private."

"Then what's he doing over here with the commoners?"

"I don't know. Maybe he likes to mingle with the little people." She leaned in. "I did read that there's speculation that Judith Bisham is residing in the private wing. She's kicking booze and a serious sugar addiction."

"Sugar? In the private wing? Who's Judith Bisham?"

"Bestselling novelist. Her books sell faster than illicit drugs at Windhaven. She wrote the bestseller *A Murder in Crested Butte*. They made it into a movie, and it won all the awards. And if you're paying what she probably is to stay in the Montes wing, I bet they cater to any addiction requested." She whispered again. "My guess, though, is she's not there to kick anything. She's getting the scoop from Ruben about his trial and writing her next book. It'll make millions, so her stay is essentially paid for."

A server in a uniform brought a plate to Ruben, who smiled and put his magazine down. He thanked the server, picked up his napkin and set it in his lap, just as he glanced toward Mason and Carla.

Carla ducked back. "Oh, my God. He's looking over here." She swiped at something on her pants.

Mason smiled and raised a hand. Ruben held his gaze, waved back and returned to eating.

"What's he doing?" asked Carla.

"He's having lunch," said Mason.

"Did he see us staring?"

"I think so, but I'm sure he's used to it."

"I wish I had a camera. Do you know how much a picture of him from inside here would be worth?"

Mason scowled. "I think that's the whole point of him being here, don't you think? To get away from all that?"

She shrugged. "Doesn't mean I can't dream." She checked her watch. "Ah, shit. I'm late for group. I've got to go." She stood. "Care to hang out at dinner? I'm free. I suspect you are, too."

"Uh...sure. Why not?"

"Great." She patted him on the knee again. "I'll see you at six. I'll tell you about more celebrities."

"Can't wait."

She stared at Ruben Montes, who chewed a bite of his sandwich. "If he does anything cool, let me know."

"If he eats his chips weird, you'll get the scoop."

"Awesome."

"Hey, Carla."

Carla stopped. "Yeah."

Mason eyed Ruben, who continued to eat. "You think he did it?"

"You mean kill his wife and mistress?" Carla hesitated and peered at Ruben. "I don't know. It's hard to say."

"What does your gut tell you?"

"Honestly?" Carla stilled. "Montes is guilty as hell."

Mason set his jaw, and Carla turned, making side glances at Ruben, and strode out of the dining area.

Chapter Seven

MIKEY SAT AT HER desk, studying the screen, but not paying much attention to what she was reading. She kept thinking back on her history with Gina, and despite the years that had passed, it was as if it had all happened yesterday.

She sipped her coffee, recalling meeting Gina at one of Victor D'Mato's parties. By then, Mikey had been fully entrenched in Victor's group of followers and had lost herself in his world. She'd fully believed that she and Victor were destined for each other and that all the crap he'd been spewing about Mason and other outsiders was true. Her sister Margaret hadn't helped. It was as if seducing Mikey to the dark side was one big middle finger to the rest of the family, and whenever Mikey had shown an inkling of logical thought that perhaps Victor was a sadistic psychopath, Margaret would be the first to tamp it down. The booze and drugs made it worse, and before she'd realized it, Mikey was caught up in a world she couldn't escape. Victor had targeted her because of his falling out with Mason, but she'd been too flattered by Victor's attention to see it, and had ultimately been claimed by him, becoming his lover.

The stark reality had hit her though when she realized Victor had many mistresses, and when she'd objected, Victor had told her that she was the only one he loved. She'd known in her gut he was lying, but Victor's rise to power and his control over the group and those he'd converted had become dangerous. Most of his followers had some unique ability that Victor had found useful and used to his advantage. Mikey understood that his attraction to her was also her protection. She'd seen how other women had been used to satisfy Victor's cohorts, who could be just as scary as Victor. Margaret had been one of them, but while some women cowered to Victor and his friends, Margaret never did. She wanted to collaborate with Victor, but also with other powerful men and women, and if sleeping with them meant access to their knowledge, she welcomed it.

Gina had arrived not long after Victor had taken Mikey as his own, and Mikey had been existing in a haze of sex, drugs and alcohol. Gina had her own gifts, and Victor had groomed and invited her in. Gina could sense things in a similar way to Mikey, and was highly intuitive, but she also had the added gift of psychokinesis, or PK, where she could move things mentally, although she had little control over it. The only time she could use it was when she got angry. Mikey once saw Gina get pissed at a man who'd slapped her. It had been during a late-night party at Victor's beach house. The campfire blazing, Gina and Mikey had been talking and laughing until Victor had called Mikey over and she'd gone to sit with him. Another man had sat beside Gina, and Mikey had realized that Victor had sent him. Gina had complied at first, but then the man had spoken in Gina's ear, and Gina had shoved him. The man had grabbed her arm, and Gina had tried to pull away, and the man backhanded her. Mikey had wanted to stop it, but Victor had held her back, and with an ugly grin, he'd told her to watch.

Uncomfortable, Mikey had stayed put and watched as Gina tried to get free and as the man raised his hand again to hit her, Gina's face changed. Mikey could describe it only as pure rage. The man had frozen, his hand still, and then he'd flown backwards, straight into the campfire. His butt hit the flames, everyone at the party shrieked, and Victor had laughed. With Mikey staring in shock, the man had screamed, jumped off the embers, and, his pants burning, had rushed to the beach and dove into the waves.

People had stared for a second and then resumed the party, returning to their drinking and drugs, and Gina had disappeared. After the party and leaving Victor's room, Mikey had sought her out to ensure she was okay. She'd found Gina on the beach, staring out at the waves, and they'd talked for the rest of the night. They'd remained friends until Gina had met David and left the cult around the same time that Mason had found Mikey and was attempting to get her away from Victor. Mikey felt certain that it was Gina's encouragement that had helped her to see Victor and Margaret for who they were and accept Mason's help.

Sitting back in her seat, Mikey sighed. She rarely thought of the past if she could help it but seeing Gina again had brought it all back. Not even recognizing her old self anymore, she wondered how she'd ever been the sort of woman to have been lured in by a man like Victor.

The front door opened and closed, and she eyed the cameras. Trick walked into the inner office holding a bag and two drinks in disposable cups. "Hey," he said. "I brought lunch."

"Thanks." Mikey shook off her reverie and closed her laptop. "How'd the meeting go?"

Trick sat on the couch and put the bag and drinks on the coffee table. "It went well. I like Ronald. Based on what little I know about Gina, he and his sister are a lot alike."

Mikey stood and went to the couch. "I'd never met him before the coffee shop."

"You should have come with me."

Mikey shook her head. "No. It was better for you two to talk alone. Besides, I wanted to do some internet searching on Lenora. See what I could learn about her." She recalled their conversation with Gina in the coffee shop. They'd set a meeting to talk later that day at SCOPE about Lenora. Ronald had returned to work but had set up a time to meet with Trick later.

During the meeting with Gina, Mikey and Trick had learned that Lenora had been a bright and beautiful student at a local college where she'd been studying to get a business degree. Ronald had been closest to Lenora since Gina had moved away, but Gina had told them how, according to Ronald, Lenora had become distant. The more he'd tried to inquire about what was wrong, the more he suspected she was seeing someone, but Lenora wouldn't tell him who. As time progressed, Lenora continued to decline. Her grades fell, she stopped going to school and then dropped out. Despite that, she'd moved to a nicer apartment and was wearing expensive clothes. Not long after moving, she'd been arrested for possession of a narcotic and public intoxication. She'd received probation and had been sent to a thirty-day program at a local rehabilitation center to get clean.

Ronald had said that after completing the therapy, she'd seemed to improve. Lenora had re-enrolled at school, moved out of the fancy apartment, and had found a job. Ronald had told Gina that Lenora seemed happy and excited about the future. She'd started dating and had even introduced Ronald to a new boyfriend named Frank. Ronald felt confident that Lenora was on her way back until the day he'd received a phone call from Lenora. She'd been crying and was slurring and almost incoherent. Ronald had tried to talk to her to find out what was wrong, but she'd hung up on him. He'd rushed to her apartment and had found her unconscious. He'd called nine-one-one, but she'd died en route to the hospital from a drug overdose. The police had found drugs in her apartment, and they'd ruled it accidental, but both Ronald and Gina had disagreed. They'd believed there had been foul play, and that whoever had messed Lenora up to begin with, had returned and had messed her up again.

Trick pulled a wrapped sandwich out of the bag and handed it to Mikey. "Tuna salad on wheat."

"Thanks." Mikey took the sandwich and a napkin.

Trick took his own sandwich and unwrapped it. "You find anything on the web?"

"Nothing earth-shattering." Mikey stood, went to the desk and grabbed her coffee mug and sat again on the couch. "It's like Gina said. Lenora was a bright student with everything going for her until it wasn't. From what I can tell, Lenora had friends, active social media accounts, and worked at a retail store. And then she fell off the radar. I found her mugshot online. She looked terrible. The only other thing I could find was a picture of her and her boyfriend Frank about a week before she died. She looked a million times better than her mug shot, so Gina was right. Lenora was better. The question is what happened after the picture was posted." She held her sandwich. "What did Ronald have to say?" She took a bite.

Trick finished chewing and sipped from his cup. "Pretty much the same as Gina. Lenora's initial decline couldn't be explained. Ronald could never figure out who Lenora had been seeing, but whoever it was had money. He'd obviously been paying for Lenora's apartment and clothes."

"And drugs." Mikey took a drink from her coffee mug. "So we need to figure out who this mystery man or woman is."

"Ronald gave me the address to the fancy apartment she'd been living in," said Trick. "I can make a visit out there. See if I can talk to the manager or maybe a few neighbors. Maybe they remember something."

"I can go to the apartment she'd moved back to. Lenora had a roommate. Angela something. I can try to talk to her."

"That's a good idea." Trick wiped his mouth with a napkin. "Did you call Rem? Was there an autopsy report?"

Mikey nodded. "There was. Lenora died of an overdose of heroin laced with fentanyl. There were no other drugs or alcohol in her system."

Trick lowered his cup. "Heroin? Was that her drug of choice?"

"I don't know. I'm not sure Gina or Ronald does either."

"That's pretty heavy stuff." Trick stared off. "I wonder if we can get her records from her stay at rehab. That might enlighten us as to exactly what Lenora was dealing with."

Mikey sighed. "We have to consider that this was actually accidental, despite what Gina and Ronald think. After a relapse, people can die because they take the same drugs as before, but their bodies can't tolerate it, and they inadvertently overdose."

"I agree, but let's try to find our mystery man first. If he's the one who got Lenora hooked and then he showed up with the same goods and enticed her to use again, at least we'll have an explanation."

"That's the likely scenario," said Mikey. "Gina and Ron haven't provided any reason as to why anyone would want to murder Lenora, and I haven't found anything suspicious." She wiped her fingers on her napkin. "Unless we can prove that someone forced drugs on her, then we're stuck with the police theory. She relapsed and died."

"It's a tough case, but if it will offer Ron and Gina some peace of mind, then it's worth pursuing." He took another bite of his food.

Mikey chewed and stared off, thinking again about Gina.

"Where's Kyle?" asked Trick.

"He's investigating the evil spirit."

"Any word on how it's going?"

"None. I'm going to assume no news is good news."

Trick studied her. "You doing okay with all of this?"

"I told you. Kyle and I are just friends for the moment."

Trick set his food down. "I'm talking about Gina." He picked up his cup. "You seemed unsettled when you bumped into her at the coffee shop." He sat back. "Can I take a wild guess and say your mutual friend is Victor D'Mato?"

Mikey eyed Trick. "Is it that obvious?"

"Mason told me a little about what happened when he pulled you out of Victor's cult. I don't mean to pry, but seeing Gina must have brought up some hard memories."

Mikey debated how much to say. "I guess it was inevitable that one day I'd reconnect with a friend from my past."

"Were you two close?"

A memory surfaced in Mikey's mind. It hadn't been long after Gina had joined the cult and she and Mikey had gotten to know each other. Victor had sent Mikey on an errand to buy more alcohol, and when she'd returned, she'd seen Victor's closed bedroom door. Her heart fell when a fellow member had told her Victor had company and not to disturb him. She'd hidden on the stairwell and waited and eventually had seen Gina slip out of Victor's room, her hair disheveled and holding her shoes. She didn't see Mikey and had left the house. Minutes later,

Victor had stepped out and spotted Mikey on the steps. Despite her obvious distress, he'd grinned at her as if he'd won a chess match. Mikey hadn't said a word but had gone to an upstairs bedroom to sleep.

Her appetite waning as the memories swirled, she set her sandwich down. "We shared more than I care to admit." She held her head. "Those were times I'd rather forget. I'm sure she feels the same way."

"You sure about that?"

Mikey looked up. "What do you mean?"

Trick shrugged. "I realize that with my law enforcement history, I tend to think the worst because, well, it usually turns out that way. But I find it odd that she just happened to be in the coffee shop when you came in."

Mikey narrowed her eyes. "She didn't know I would be there. Hell, we haven't been to that coffee shop since..." She tried to think.

"Since before Margaret got loose." He swiped a crumb off his pant leg. "I realize we've been staying close to home recently for obvious reasons, but prior to that, we frequented that coffee shop more than once."

Mikey dropped her jaw. "Are you saying Gina's been waiting for me to show so she could bump into me and hire me to find out who killed her sister? That's a bit of a reach, don't you think?"

"As I said, I tend to think most people are dangerous and deadly until they prove otherwise." He rubbed his stomach and grimaced. "Too bad I didn't pay attention to that advice on our last case." He paused. "I'm just saying to be careful. In all likelihood, this is legitimate, but you have to consider the fact that Margaret is out there, and now you happen to meet an old crony of Victor's—"

"You think Margaret and Gina are working together?"

"I'm just saying..."

Mikey started to chuckle. "I appreciate your concern, but I doubt it. Gina and Marge hated each other." The thought of the two women in cahoots was almost funny. "Gina slammed Marge into a wall once and put a hole in the drywall. Marge retaliated by poisoning Gina's drink. She was sick for days."

Trick blanched. "Remind me not to make either of them angry."

"I wouldn't recommend it. Gina's PK comes out when she's pissed. And Marge, well, she's pissed all the time and knows a million ways to screw with you."

"PK?" asked Trick.

"Psychokinesis," said Mikey. She explained Gina's unique abilities to Trick.

"All the more reason to be concerned." Trick groaned. "I'm glad we're bunking at Mason's for the next couple of months. I may consider staying there after Mason comes home."

"Between the three of us, it will be a slumber party."

Trick raised the side of his lip. "I love a good pillow fight."

"I bet you do."

"Back to the point, though," he said. "Even if Gina and Margaret hated each other, you don't know anything about Gina's life since you last saw her other than what she's told you."

"She married and moved away, got divorced and came home."

Trick hesitated. "Mikey, just be smart. I know you two share a difficult history, and your initial reaction is to help your friend whose sister died under strange circumstances. And based on what we've learned, that's all accurate. Gina is probably telling the truth and just needs our help, but if she isn't..."

Mikey slumped in her seat. "Gina is not out to get me, Trick. She and I relied on each other through some shitty times. If it hadn't been for her, I might still be under that cult's influence and maybe Marge's, too. I owe her."

"Doesn't she owe you, too? It sounds like you helped her as much as she helped you."

"Maybe." Mikey considered another alternative. "But if you want to switch this around, that could be why she's here. She heard about Marge's escape and wants to ensure I'm okay. Have you considered that?"

"I'd love to, but sadly, the good-guy scenario is rare."

"I suppose, but I'm not buying the bad guy scenario either. Gina needs help, and we bumped into each other at the right time. She isn't evil, nor does she have any reason to be." She paused. "I'd stake my life on it."

Trick stared, and Mikey picked up her sandwich to take another bite.

"Let's hope it doesn't come to that," said Trick with a sigh. "Because if it does, Mason's gonna be pissed."

"Eat your lunch," said Mikey, "and stop worrying."

Shaking his head, Trick sat forward and picked up his sandwich.

Chapter Eight

MASON SAT IN HIS chair during his group therapy session, listening. Sadie, a middle-aged woman with thin graying hair and a sad face, had spoken about her reluctance to speak with her family when they came for their first visit, and Barry had discussed how his drinking had been a crutch for him since his teens, and he worried it might continue after he left therapy. Another patient, Charlie, whose paunchy belly barely fit beneath t-shirts that had to be two sizes too small, reluctantly discussed his wife and her own addictions and how they'd self-sabotaged each other. A newer patient named Amanda, whose petite frame was swallowed by an oversized sweatshirt and pants, sat beside Mason and didn't speak either.

As Charlie finished, Dr. Hamlish eyed Mason. "Is there anything you'd like to contribute, Mason?" he asked.

Mason squirmed. "Not at the moment."

Hamlish propped an ankle on his knee. "You've been quiet. Do you have any reactions to what the others have talked about today?"

Mason scratched at his pant leg. "Uh...well..."

"You're safe here, dude," said Thomas, who appeared to be in his twenties and was into his last thirty days of therapy. "All of our shit stinks. You might as well jump in and get flushed with the rest of us."

The others in the group chuckled.

"I appreciate the metaphor, Thomas," said Hamlish.

"I aim to please, Doc," said Thomas with a smile.

Mason looked around, seeing all eyes on him. He knew he'd have to speak eventually, and apparently his stalling was over. "I can relate to all of you." He thought of Mikey and Trick. "While I look forward to seeing my family soon, I'm nervous about it. I wonder what they'll think and what I'll say." He glanced at Barry. "And taking pills was a big crutch for me, and I wonder if that will continue, too. I relapsed once, and I don't want to do it again." He spoke to Charlie. "I'm not married, though, so I don't have to worry about a self-sabotaging spouse, so I guess that's a plus."

"Is there anything in particular you'd like to discuss with the group?" asked Hamlish. "About any of the above, or something different?"

Mason thought of Carla, who he'd befriended and shared his last few dinners with. "I've learned a lot since arriving. I had no idea I was surrounded by so many celebrities. If you happen to be one, I apologize if I don't recognize you."

"Nah, man. Don't worry about that," said Thomas. "This is a sponsored, non-celeb group. Just regular Joes here. We don't warrant the fancy treatment."

"That's an inaccurate statement, Thomas," said Hamlish. "Everyone is treated the same at Windhaven."

"Not from what I've heard," said Barry. "Isn't there a private wing that only the super-rich have access to?"

"I heard that, too." Sadie leaned in with a frown. "And I saw Ruben Montes the other day. You all know who *he* is. You can't tell me he's not getting special treatment. He paid for that secret wing and offers it to his wealthy friends."

Hamlish raised his hand. "Actually—"

"He's a murderer," said Amanda, who finally spoke although she remained slumped in her chair as if embarrassed. "That man killed his wife and mistress. How come everybody treats him like royalty?"

"'Cause the dude's got more money than most countries," said Thomas, rolling his eyes. "Duh." He lowered his voice. "I heard all the rumors about his wife and mistress, though. They sounded like they might have had it coming." He scrunched his face and laughed.

Sadie sat up. "Had it coming? What kind a stupid comment is that?"

"You're repulsive," said Amanda, suddenly animated. "No one deserves to be murdered."

Thomas put his hands up. "I'm just joking, ladies. Keep your shorts on. Shit."

"You're an idiot," said Charlie. "Read the room."

"Okay, everyone," said Hamlish, jumping in. "Let's keep it together and not attack each other. We're here for support, even if we don't agree with someone."

"That's bullshit," said Sadie. "He keeps spewing crap like that, and he's gonna get my support right up his ass." She glared at Thomas.

"Any time you're ready," said Thomas with a grin.

"That's enough," said Hamlish. "Everyone calm down."

The animosity rising, the group went quiet.

"Sorry," said Mason. "I didn't mean to stir the waters. I thought my comment was an innocent one."

"Your comment stirred up some interesting reactions," said Hamlish, "which isn't inherently bad. It will offer more for us to discuss..." He gazed at the group. "...in a mature manner." He settled back in his seat. "But let me clarify a few things that perhaps I should have addressed earlier. I realize that as a patient at a renowned and expensive treatment center, you will all see people and hear things that might surprise you." He paused. "Yes. We treat the wealthy, which includes celebrities, but no, we do not have a super-secret wing where only the ultra-rich reside. Ruben Montes, who's no stranger to the limelight, did donate to Windhaven to create his own wing, but you're currently sitting in it. He comes here when he needs to and doesn't get special attention, but due to his unique set of circumstances, it is sometimes more appropriate for him to keep to himself. He can be a trigger for some patients, as we've already proven."

"He murdered two women," said Amanda, softly.

"He went to trial and was acquitted, and now requires help just like the rest of us," said Hamlish. "You can use that to stoke your anger, or you can focus on your own issues and let him deal with his. I think we can all agree that life isn't fair, and whether you believe he's guilty or innocent, none of it should affect you negatively, unless you choose to allow it to. Which is why we're all here." He intertwined his fingers. "Once you leave Windhaven, you will have to face your own Ruben Monteses to some degree. The question is how do you cope? How do you handle it without reverting to your pills, or booze or hard-core drugs? That's the question worth discussing. It's why we meet."

The group went silent again. Sadie crossed her arms, and Mason heard Amanda sigh.

Thomas blew out a breath. "I apologize if I upset anyone," he said, eyeing the ground. "That's sort of my thing. I trigger people, which diverts attention away from me." He paused. "I've gotten good at it, which is probably why most people hate me."

"Thank you for the apology, Thomas," said Hamlish. "And nobody hates you." He looked at the others. "Would anyone like to respond to Thomas' apology?"

"It's all good with me," said Charlie. "No hard feelings."

Sadie stared off, and Amanda hesitated. "Apology accepted," said Amanda, picking lint off her shirt.

Sadie didn't answer, but everyone continued to wait. She narrowed her eyes at Thomas. "I'm still pissed, but I appreciate your effort. If you say something stupid like that again, though, I will kick your ass."

Thomas nodded. "I hear you."

"Thank you, everyone," said Hamlish, "for your honest and open conversation." He hooked his hands around his knee. "Is there anything else anyone would like to say?"

Barry cleared his throat. "I have a question."

"Yes?" asked Hamlish.

Barry pointed at Mason. "I hear you do paranormal shit. Do you really talk to the dead?"

"Him?" Thomas' eyes widened, and he gestured at Mason. "No shit? Seriously?"

Mason sat still, although everyone stared at him.

"Would you like to address that, Mason?" asked Hamlish. "Since we appear to be clarifying some truths today?"

Mason shrugged. "I'm a medium and paranormal researcher and investigator. So, yes, Barry. I talk to the dead."

"I'll be damned," said Thomas. "You talking to anybody dead right now?"

Mason almost chuckled. "Seeing as how all of you are alive, no."

"But have you?" asked Amanda. "Since you've been here?"

Mason recalled the woman from his room and the man he'd seen in Hamlish's office. "I've seen a few things."

"Like what?" asked Charlie.

Hamlish raised his hands. "Okay, everybody. Now is not the time to drill Mason over his experiences with…with…"

"The devil?" asked Sadie. She eyed Mason. "You should be careful about what you're doing. You may think you're talking to the dead, but the devil can trick you. You should stop before you end up under his influence."

Mason almost groaned. "It's not the devil."

"You don't know that," said Sadie.

"I think I do," said Mason. Sadie wasn't the first who'd believed his abilities were evil, and she wouldn't be the last.

"Have you seen anyone connected to us?" asked Barry, his eyebrows raising.

"Listen, everyone—" Hamlish spoke.

"I saw your mother, Barry," said Mason. "She was standing behind you at our last meeting."

Barry's mouth fell open.

"No shit," said Charlie.

"Cool," said Thomas.

"Wha...what did she say?" asked Barry.

"Hold up," said Sadie. "He says it was your mother. What if it wasn't?"

"What did she look like?" asked Amanda.

Mason recalled the woman behind Barry's chair. "I'd put her around sixty. Salt and pepper hair. Wearing a skirt and blouse." He tried to think of something more detailed. "She wore a long necklace with a gold V, and she kept holding it."

Barry's eyes rounded, and he sucked in a breath. "I gave her that necklace. Her name was Vicky." He swallowed. "Did she say anything?"

Sadie grunted, and everyone else leaned in. Even Hamlish looked interested. Mason didn't see any harm in sharing the message. "She's proud of you for getting help. She wants you to know she loves you and she's watching over you."

Tears sprouted in Barry's eyes. "She's not mad at me?"

"No," said Mason. "She forgives you for everything."

Barry's eyes filled, and tears spilled over his lashes.

"Oh, for hell's sake, Barry," said Sadie. "How much more general can you get? He could have said that to anyone, and it would have made sense."

Barry swiped at his cheeks. "He knew about the necklace. Mom always liked to touch it. No one could have told him that."

Mason nodded. "Take it or leave it. It's up to you."

Sadie glared, and Amanda stared as if Mason were one of the celebrities at the facility. Everyone started to speak at once, either inquiring about whether Mason could communicate with their loved ones, or just generally expressing their amazement.

Hamlish put his fingers in his mouth and whistled. "Everybody settle down."

The group went quiet again.

"Listen," said Hamlish. "Mason is not here to do readings. He's here for help, just like you. Please offer him a safe space to do that, okay?"

Barry sniffed, and Amanda scoffed.

"No more reading requests or ghostly visitations, all right?" He eyed Mason.

"It doesn't exactly work like that, but I'll see what I can do," said Mason.

"Like we say at the end of our sessions, just do your best," said Hamlish. "That's all we ask at Windhaven."

Tingles ran up and down Mason's arm, and the hair on his neck raised. He tensed and watched as an apparition appeared behind Hamlish. It was the same man who had appeared in Hamlish's office. His hair was still frizzy, and he wore the same hospital gown. The blood from his ear ran down his neck and dribbled down his front, creating ugly red splotches. He stared at Mason, and blood trickled from his nose.

Mason didn't move and did his best not to react.

"If you see an older woman with smooth silver hair, flashy jewelry and big blue eyes, tell her I said hi," said Thomas. His shoulders rounded and his face fell. "And that I miss her."

"Let me guess," said Sadie. "Is that your mom, too?"

"No," said Charlie. "That's Amelia. She was a patient here. She died a few weeks ago." He paused. "Just before you and Mason arrived."

"She was a nice lady," said Barry. His tears had slowed, but his cheeks were wet.

"She was in this group, and she was a friend," said Thomas. He slumped lower and crossed his arms. "They say she got a hold of some drugs and killed herself, but I don't believe it."

"We've talked about this, Thomas," said Hamlish. "I know it's hard to believe that someone we care about could take extreme measures, but we don't always know what someone's thinking. Amelia struggled with many issues, and much of her outer persona was a mask that hid a lot of turmoil."

The spirit behind Hamlish remained quiet. Keeping an eye on him, Mason sensed Thomas' distress, and his curiosity grew. "Why don't you believe it was suicide?"

Thomas raised his head. "I think Amelia knew something."

Mason frowned. "Like what?"

"I think that's enough for today," said Hamlish. "We all need a break and some time to cool down. It's been an intense but productive session." He stood. "If anyone has anything they'd like to discuss privately about what we've covered," he glanced at Thomas, "you know my door is always open." He clasped his hands together. "Do your best, everyone."

The spirit behind Hamlish lifted his arm and pointed at Mason. Hamlish left the room as the others stood and began to leave as well.

Do your best. Mason heard the man say in his head. *Do your best.*

Chapter Nine

THE ELEVATOR DINGED, AND Trick stepped off and eyed the numbers on the wall. Finding the one he wanted, he walked past a few doors and stopped in front of what had been Lenora Rodriguez's apartment. He took a second to study his surroundings, seeing the thick carpet, wood-paneled walls, wide-framed beveled mirrors and elegant flower arrangements placed on narrow glass tables located between each apartment. He wondered how Lenora had ended up here since the building looked like it would appeal to an older crowd, not a young partygoer.

He knocked and waited, wondering who would answer and hoping they would know something about Lenora. Several seconds passed, and he knocked again, but with no response. He eyed the door to his right, walked over to it, and knocked on that one. Another few seconds passed, and he heard a female voice speak from inside.

"Coming."

The doorknob turned, and a woman with silver-gray hair pulled up in a bun, wearing a flowery blouse and jeans, opened the door. Seeing him, her eyes widened, and she looked him up and down. "Please tell me you're the plumber."

He removed his cowboy hat and smiled. "No, ma'am. I'm not the plumber."

She rested a hand against the frame. "What a shame."

Her appraisal of him almost made him blush. "I...uh...I'd hoped to talk to your neighbor next door." He gestured to his left. "But he's not answering."

"Norman?" She made a snort. "Good luck. He's either still asleep or doesn't have his hearing aids in." She leaned against the door and raised the side of her lip. "Can I help you with anything?"

Although tempted to flirt back since that was his style, he stayed in business mode. "Maybe you can." Trick pulled out and showed his P.I. badge. "My name is Trick Monroe. I'm a private investigator looking into the death of Lenora

Rodriguez. She lived next door for a while, and I'm hoping to talk to anyone who met her. Did you know her?"

The woman's smile fell, and her relaxed demeanor evaporated. "I did." She crossed her arms. "Such a shame what happened to her."

"You heard?"

"Through the grapevine, and then I saw her obituary in the paper."

Trick nodded. "You mind if I come in?"

She hesitated and then looked down the hall. "You know how to fix a broken toilet?"

"No, ma'am, but I can make a great taco with homemade salsa."

Her smile returned. "My name's Joanna, and I don't joke when it comes to food. I may put your cooking skills to the test."

"I don't joke around either when it comes to tacos and salsa."

She stepped back. "Come in."

"Thank you, Joanna." Trick stepped into a large living room with pretty furniture that didn't match the exterior hallway in the slightest. Everything here was pastel, and contemporary artwork decorated the walls. Bright light shone in through a large window, and there were plants everywhere.

"Have a seat," she said. "Can I get you something to drink?"

Trick sat on the sofa. "Some water would be great. Thank you."

"Be right back."

She disappeared into the kitchen, and Trick put his identification away and set his hat on the glass coffee table. A few seconds later, she reappeared with two glasses of ice water. "Here you go."

Trick took his glass and sipped from it. "I appreciate it."

Joanna sat beside him. "How can I help?"

"How well did you know Lenora?"

She stared off. "Not well. She didn't live next door for very long. Maybe six months?" She looked back. "I hate to say it, but I wasn't very nice to her."

"Why is that?"

She shrugged. "She didn't seem to be in the right place. This residence is mainly for retirees and people with old money. Most are in bed by ten and up by seven, and that's being generous. Lenora was awake at all hours, and slept through the afternoon, and when I did see her, she wore dark sunglasses, probably to hide the bags under her eyes. She was too skinny, didn't shower regularly, and was never completely coherent. It wasn't a huge stretch to assume she was either drunk or high." She drank from her water glass and held it. "I'm ashamed to admit I didn't think much of her and when she moved out, I was relieved."

Trick set his glass down and took out a notepad and pen from his pocket. "Did you ever see anyone with her?" He scribbled a few notes.

Her grip on the glass tightened. "I'm not sure if I should say."

Trick caught the look in her eyes and recognized fear. "Why do you say that?"

She studied her glass but didn't answer.

"Joanna, Lenora is dead. She can't hurt you."

She shook her head. "No. It's not her. It was him."

Trick closed the notepad. "Who's him?"

She inhaled a deep breath and let it out.

"Did he hurt you?"

"No," she paused. "He threatened me."

Trick swiveled toward her. "Whatever you tell me is confidential. And now that Lenora is gone, I suspect this mystery man is no longer a danger to you."

"You're probably right, but still..." She set her glass down and interlaced her fingers. "I can still see his face." She closed her eyes for a moment and then opened them.

Trick felt a flicker of hope that Joanna might know the person responsible for Lenora's death. "Can you tell me what happened?"

She took another breath and seemed to steady herself. "It wasn't long after Lenora moved in. I'd said hi to her once or twice, but she never really engaged with me. I figured she was just young and stuck-up. Probably fell into money and didn't know what to do with it. Then the parties started. People would come and go at all hours. The music was so loud my windows shook. I called the cops and complained. They'd show up, and then it would go quiet until the next party, and it would happen all over again. Her guests would get so messed up they would try to get into my apartment instead of hers. I even found someone passed out in the hall one morning." She shook her head. "I'd call the cops each time, and they would come, and everything would quiet."

"How long did that go on?" asked Trick.

"After the first month, I'd called the police six times, and complained to the resident manager and the Board. But nobody seemed to want to do anything. I couldn't understand why until...well...until I met him."

Trick rested his elbows on his thighs. "Met who?"

She bounced a leg. "At the start of the second month, I heard the usual music start up and I knew what to expect. I figured I'd be calling the cops again when someone knocked on the door. I figured it was another lost partygoer. I looked through the peephole and, sure enough, I saw a younger man, with long hair, stubble on his jaw, and a face tattoo staring back at me. I'd had enough by then, and I opened the door. I told him Lenora was next door and suggested they put up a sign to indicate to their wasted friends who can't read numbers where the party was, and to do all the residents a favor and keep the noise level down."

Trick waited, but Joanna had gone quiet. "What did he say?"

"It's not so much what he said, but what he did." She paused and ran her palms over her knees. "He stared for a second, then smiled, and walked right up to me. I sort of froze. I didn't want to back up into the apartment, and I didn't want to show fear. He stood there, just looking at me, and I knew he wanted to intimidate me. And he did. My heart started to race, and I realized he could have easily pushed me inside and shut the door. I cursed myself for answering."

Trick's heart thumped, too. He wondered what kind of man would threaten an older woman? "What happened then?"

"He was inches from me, just staring down at me. He asked if I was the one calling the cops." She reached for her glass and took a sip. Trick could see her fingers tremble. "I didn't lie because I figured he already knew the truth. So I said yes." She paused. "He just stood there, breathing on me, and he said, 'Don't do it again.'" Her grip tightened again on the glass. "Then he reached into his pocket and pulled out a wad of cash. He counted out five hundred-dollar bills and handed them to me." She lowered the glass and rubbed her forehead.

Trick furrowed his brow. "Five hundred dollars?"

"I didn't understand, and I hesitated. He took my wrist and put the money in my palm. I tried to pull away, but he wouldn't let go. He closed my fingers over the money and told me he'd pay me each time there was a party next door." Her face pale, she stared off. "I told him I didn't care about or need the money. I just wanted some peace and quiet." She dropped her head. "That's when he squeezed my fingers to the point where it hurt. I winced and tried to get away, but he just squeezed harder. He told me to accept the money with gratitude, and if I called the cops again, the next time he visited, he'd break my fingers instead." She bit her bottom lip.

Trick's anger grew. "I thought you said he didn't hurt you."

"He let me go then and stepped back. Told me to have a nice night and then disappeared into Lenora's apartment." She sighed. "I never called the cops again, and he slipped five hundred dollars beneath my door every time the music started up after that. It lasted until the month Lenora was arrested. And then the movers showed up, and I heard she was moving out. I didn't see her or that man again."

Trick almost asked Joanna if she needed something stronger to drink. "How much money did he end up paying you?"

"Almost ten thousand dollars."

Trick dropped his jaw.

"I donated it all. I couldn't stomach using it for myself. I figured it was better to give that money to someone who needed it, because God knows what it might have been used for instead."

Trick picked up his notepad. "Did you ever get his name?"

"No."

"What about the other neighbors? Did he interact with them? Any of them go to the parties?"

"Not that I know of. I think they were scared of him, too."

"Can you describe him?"

Her story finished, she seemed to relax. "Tall. Maybe six-two. Very handsome. Dark hair that went to his chin. The tattoo on his temple was a snake with a forked tongue. He was probably around thirty. Lean, but muscled. Snappy dresser with an expensive watch on his wrist and polished shoes on his feet. I get the sense he is used to getting his way."

Impressed with her description, Trick made some notes. "I can see why." He looked up. "If you saw him again, would you recognize him?"

"In a heartbeat, but I hope I don't." Her face fell. "He terrified me."

"It sounds like he's terrified a lot of people."

"Be careful if you find him. He's not someone you'd want as an enemy." She clutched her chest. "That poor girl. I don't know what Lenora got herself into, but if she was involved with that man, then God help her soul."

Mikey knocked on the apartment door. She noted the quiet courtyard and parking lot she'd just left. It looked like any other apartment building where two roommates would live during and after college, who were beginning their adult lives.

The door opened, and a pretty girl with round blue eyes and dark blonde short hair that flattered her features answered.

"Angela?" asked Mikey.

The woman nodded. "Yes. You're Mikey?"

"Yes. I called earlier about Lenora."

Her expression softened, and Mikey sensed her sadness. Angela opened the door wider. "You can come in."

"Thank you." Mikey walked inside to a small living area with a worn leather sofa and a nicked coffee table. A sliding glass door revealed a small patch of grass outside. "I promise I won't take too much of your time."

"Have a seat." Angela gestured toward the couch. "I just made some iced tea. You want some?"

"I'd love some. Thanks." Mikey sat and put her purse on the floor. She spotted a photo on the wall and recognized Angela and Lenora, smiling at the camera with their arms around each other's shoulders.

Angela returned with two tall glasses of iced tea. She set them on the table and sat. "What did you want to ask about?"

Mikey opened her purse and took out her notepad and pen. "First of all, thanks for meeting with me. I know this must be hard for you."

Angela sighed and pushed the long sleeves of her shirt up to her elbows. "I don't know that I'll be much help. Lenora never told me much about her private life despite what others may think, and I was out of town the weekend she died."

"It's okay. But any small thing may be important. Just talking about it may spark a memory."

She hesitated, but then nodded. "Okay. I'll try."

"I appreciate it." Mikey attempted to put up a mental wall to prevent Angela's heavy emotions from sidetracking her. Sometimes, her own empathic abilities made her job hard. "When did you two become roommates?"

"Our last year of college. Neither of us had a lot of money, and we were working near each other, so it made sense."

"Was she a good roommate?"

"She was great. We kept similar hours and had the same work ethic. She cleaned, and I cooked. We shared the bills. We never had any issues." She paused. "We were friends."

"When did that start to change?"

Angela shifted on the couch and put her arm over the back of it. "We went to a party thrown by some corporate big shot. I think she knew him from work, and he'd invited her. We met some people, and Lenora and I ended up going to another party across town. It got late, and I wanted to go home. Lenora wanted to stay, though. She'd started hanging on some guy, and she told me to leave. Said she'd be fine and would find her way home. I didn't like it. The whole thing seemed weird. There were drugs going around, and we didn't usually mess with that scene."

"Did you leave?" asked Mikey.

"No, I didn't. I stayed. I asked for some water and told Lenora I would wait because I didn't feel comfortable leaving her there. I drank the water, and the next thing I remember I was waking up in my bed."

Mikey straightened. "Here? In your place?"

"I had no recollection of how I got here. It's a complete blank. It scared me because I worried that maybe I'd been assaulted, although I didn't show any signs of it. I got up and looked for Lenora, but she wasn't here. I found a note on the dresser, though. It was from her. She said I'd fallen asleep at the party and her friend had put me in a car and ensured I got home safely. She said she'd be hanging out with this friend and would be back later."

"Did you believe that?"

"About me falling asleep? Hell, no. I'm sure I was drugged. I was so freaked out that I went to the doctor. They couldn't find any indication of sexual assault, and my blood results showed nothing unusual." She rested her head in her palm. "I didn't know what to think."

Mikey agreed it was odd. "When did Lenora come home?"

"That night, like she said. But she wouldn't tell me anything about where she'd spent the night or who she'd been with. And she insisted no one had hurt me. She had been promised that I would be returned home safely." Angela shook her head. "I saw her eyes though, and they didn't look right. I'd asked if she'd taken anything, and she said she hadn't, but I didn't believe her. After that, she started going out more and more. And the drugs took over. She'd disappear for days at a time, stumble home out of nowhere and pass out. She stopped going to school and work, but she always had money. She kept paying the bills, and then she started showing up in new clothes and expensive jewelry."

Mikey wrote in her notepad. "She never told you anything? About the man or where she was getting the money?"

Angela reached for her iced tea, took a sip and set the glass down. "Nothing. We argued about it. The worse she got, the more our friendship crumbled. She was falling down a deep well, and I was powerless to stop it. Her brother tried, too, but she wouldn't talk to him either." She returned her arm to the back of the sofa. "And then she left."

Feeling her anxiety, Mikey debated how much to push. "Why did she leave? Did something cause it?"

Angela swallowed. "We...we...I don't know." She sighed. "That last night is hard to talk about."

Her distress wafted through Mikey, and Mikey tensed against it. "Anything you can recall might help."

Angela stared off. "Lenora was getting dressed to go out again, but she was drunk and in no shape to go anywhere. I told her to stay home and sober up." She shifted again on the couch and sat back against the cushions. "For the first time in a while, she looked at me with understanding, as if she knew she was messed up and needed help. She started to cry, so I got her into bed and told her to sleep. I'd hoped that was a turning point, and she'd come around. I took her phone and put it out here so it wouldn't wake her. About an hour later, it rang. It was a number I didn't recognize. It kept ringing on and off for the next two hours. I never answered, figuring whoever it was would get the message that Lenora wasn't going out that night. It finally stopped, and I planned to go to bed myself when someone knocked on the door."

Mikey looked up from her notepad. Angela's face was pale, and her eyes wide. "Angela? You okay?"

Angela rubbed her head. "I...I did something stupid."

Mikey set her notepad down beside her. "What?"

Angela's face tightened. "I kept what happened next to myself. Something I should have mentioned to the police after Lenora died, but I was too scared." She hugged herself. "I'm still scared."

"What is it? What did you keep to yourself?"

Angela sniffed. "I...I...told everyone that Lenora had left in the middle of the night, but..." She stammered and squeezed her temples. "...but that's not the whole truth." She put her face in her hands. "Oh, God. I should have said something."

Mikey reached over and put her hand on Angela's wrist. "It's okay. It happens. If you were traumatized, it's understandable you'd protect yourself." She recalled some of her responses to fear during her days with Victor. She wasn't proud of them, either. "Don't be so hard on yourself."

"I said I'd gone to bed, but I didn't." Angela clenched her eyes shut. "I opened the door."

Mikey took a centering breath, doing her best to stay unaffected by Angela's swirling emotions. "Who was there?"

Angela opened her eyes. "It was a man." She went rigid and held her elbows. "He asked for Lenora. I told him she was sleeping, and she couldn't be disturbed." She dropped her head and bit her lip.

"Angela," said Mikey. "Stay with me." She took Angela's hand. "What happened next?"

"He...he threw me across the room. Only...not with his hands." She looked up at Mikey. "He never touched me."

Mikey's skin broke out in chills.

"I swear I'm telling the truth." She gripped Mikey's fingers. "I remember it so clearly, but I knew no one would believe me."

Mikey held her gaze. "I believe you."

Angela stammered. "I couldn't understand it. I thought I'd missed something. That he must have shoved me. I stood, but then I flew up and over the couch. I hit the floor hard." Tears sprang to her eyes. "He came in and shut the door. He told me to stop interfering with Lenora or he would make sure I'd end up just like her, drunk and drugged, and they'd find my dead bloated body down by the river, and everyone would think I'd overdosed."

Shivers ran down Mikey's back. "What did he look like? Did you get his name?"

Shaking, Angela nodded. "He was tall and lean, but you could tell he was strong. He had dark hair and a tattoo on his face. I think it was a snake. And he was wearing a suit. It was the same man Lenora had been hanging on at that party where I'd been drugged." She stared at Mikey with haunted eyes. "I swear he wanted to kill me."

"Stay calm. You're safe."

Her tears spilled over her lashes. "I told him to leave Lenora alone, and he came toward me, and I braced, expecting to be thrown again, but then Lenora walked into the room." She swiped at her cheeks and nose. "She was all dressed and her hair done, and she smiled at him." Angela paused. "She called him Rain."

Mikey reached for her notepad. "Rain? Like in rainstorm?"

"Yes." She sniffed. "When he saw her, he left me alone. He went over to her, and hugged her, and she apologized for falling asleep, but I saw her eyes. She was scared, but she went with him anyway." Her eyes filled again. "Hell. She was protecting me, and I couldn't, and didn't, do anything."

"You did the best you could at the time. What happened when they left?" Mikey spotted some tissues on an end table and grabbed some. She handed one to Angela.

Angela took it and blotted her face. "He...he sneered at me and took her by the elbow, but she came over and helped me up. She told me to leave it alone. That it was none of my business, and then he...he told me to keep my mouth shut about what had happened. I huddled on the couch until the morning. I was terrified he'd come back." Her breath caught. "Lenora moved out the next day." She started to cry more.

Mikey gave her another tissue. "It's okay. Take it slow."

"What if he's the guy who killed her?" She dabbed her eyes with the tissue. "And he got away because I didn't say anything?"

Mikey hesitated. "Do you think she was killed?"

Fresh tears spilled down her cheeks. "Something's wrong with him. If she resisted, he may have retaliated."

"Didn't she get better after she was arrested and went to rehab? Was he still around after she moved back here?"

Angela composed herself and blew her nose. "After rehab, she seemed like her old self. It was like she'd never changed and had never done drugs. It was crazy how she turned it all around so fast. I just figured it was Lenora, you know? Once she set her mind to something, she usually did it."

"Was there any indication that she'd seen Rain after rehab?"

"No. She told me she was done with him. I worried he might come back, but she told me it was over. Lenora was happy after that. She started seeing Frank, who was really nice, and then I went away that weekend, and...and...I never saw her again." She turned toward Mikey, her eyes wide and watery. "He killed her, didn't he? That man, Rain. He came back and killed her." Her face crumpled, and she burst into tears.

Chapter Ten

MASON CHEWED A PIECE of his pork chop and grunted.

Carla, who sat beside him at the dining table, looked over. "Something wrong?" She took a bite of her chicken.

Mason took a drink of water and swallowed. "Don't you find the food here to be shockingly bad?" He wiped his face with his napkin and set it back in his lap.

She made a face at him. "Are you serious?" She cut into her meat. "I think it's delicious. I don't eat like this outside of here, so I appreciate it while it lasts."

"This is the blandest food I've ever tasted." He looked around and noted how others at the tables appeared to be enjoying their dinner. "I don't know how anybody else likes it." He spotted Amanda, the quietest new member of his therapy group. She sat at another table and seemed to be the only one picking at her food. Her expression suggested she wasn't any happier with her meal than Mason. He made a mental note to ask her about it.

"I think it's a latent desire to gain control over something tangible. You don't have control over anything else, so you complain about the food." Carla smiled at him and took a bite of mashed potatoes.

"What? Are you Hamlish now? Diagnosing my taste buds?"

She shrugged. "I've been here enough times that I probably could diagnose people." She sipped her iced tea. "Maybe I've missed my calling."

Mason stabbed another piece of meat with his fork and sniffed it. "Yeah, well, don't quit your day job." He put the fork down without eating the bite.

"That would be good advice if I had a day job."

He shot a sideways glance at her. "I'm going to talk to—"

"Mason Redstone?"

He startled and looked up to see a woman standing and grinning beside him. She had blonde hair, lots of white teeth, and her perky nature sparked a memory. "Yes?" he asked.

She held out a hand. "I'm Candace. Your patient liaison."

He recalled her introducing herself on his first day at Windhaven. "That's right. I believe I met you when I arrived." He shook her hand.

Her smile widened. "You remember? I'm flattered." She released his hand and sat beside him. "I have to apologize for not speaking with you sooner, but it's been a crazy few weeks. Lots of people to talk to and lots of needs to meet."

"I bet," said Mason.

She eyed Carla. "Hi, Carla. How are you? Did you get the pens you requested? And the notebook?"

"Hi, Candace," said Carla. "I'm great. And yes. I got the pens and notebook. Thank you."

"You're very welcome. Maybe one day your writing will be on the bestseller rack. It's very exciting." She bunched her shoulders, and Mason half expected her to squeal.

"Writing?" asked Mason.

Candace put her hand over her mouth. "Oh, no. Did I let the cat out of the bag?"

Carla set her napkin on the table. "It's fine, Candace. It's no big deal. It's just scribbles on a page, anyway."

Candace widened her eyes. "Don't say that. I know you must write more than scribbles. You have an amazing life to draw from. Maybe you should let Mason read something. You might be surprised."

Mason studied Carla. "What do you write?"

"Nothing," said Carla. "It's no big deal."

"Something to think about at least," said Candace. She put a hand on Mason's forearm. "The reason I'm here is you, though. A little birdie told me you're unhappy with the food?"

Mason pushed his plate back. "I'm not usually one to complain, but I haven't had a decent meal since I arrived. I can appreciate the amount of money you put into this place, so it amazes me the food doesn't taste better."

She patted his arm. "Don't you worry about a thing. I want our residents to let me know when they're unhappy about something. I'll talk to Tracy and Manolo about your feedback. We'll make sure you get something tasty from now on." She pulled out her phone and started punching buttons.

"Tracy and Manolo?" asked Mason.

She lowered her phone. "Tracy is our nurse practitioner and licensed nutritionist. You'll see her on occasion in the kitchen with Manolo or in the clinic. She prepares the menus and ensures everyone gets a wide array of delicious but healthy options. Manolo is our five-star chef. He'll occasionally come out and make the rounds, but only when I pressure him. He tends to get moody sometimes, so he sticks to the kitchen."

Mason deflated. "I'm complaining about a five-star chef?" He looked around and saw everyone eating. "I'm obviously the odd man out."

Carla grinned. "It's that whole control thing." She pulled a plate with a piece of chocolate pie closer to her. "You want a bite, or are you going to bitch about the desserts, too?"

Mason shot a glare at her.

"Would you like to meet Manolo?" asked Candace. She pointed toward the kitchen. "I can bring you back. You can tell him you don't like his food."

Mason dropped his jaw.

Candace broke into laughter and smacked his shoulder. "I'm just kidding." She held her stomach and giggled. "You should have seen your face."

Mason sighed. "I didn't know what to say. I was picturing Manolo spitting in my chicken salad."

Candace laughed some more and dabbed at her eye with her fingertip. "Oh, my. I crack myself up."

Mason glanced at Carla, who looked like she was holding back a smile, and took a bite of her pie. He looked back at Candace. "That was a good one." He paused. "Are you going to tell Manolo it was me, though? I don't want to piss off a moody chef."

Candace patted his shoulder again. "Don't worry about it. I've been doing this job long enough to know how to approach testy chefs. I'll talk to Tracy, and we'll get this sorted out." She leaned in and spoke to Carla. "How's the pie?"

Carla moaned. "Delicious. My compliments to Manolo."

Mason glared at her again.

Still holding her phone, Candace clapped her hands together. "That's excellent. I love to hear a good review." Her eyes widened, and she snapped her fingers. "Oh, and I heard you wanted a haircut?"

Mason touched his hair. "I'd love one. Plus a shave."

"You got it. I'll talk to Tammy and arrange it. I'll get you in this week."

"Thanks," said Mason.

Candace's phone beeped, and she tapped on it, read it, typed again and then slid it back into her pocket. "I trust that the next time I speak with you, Mason, I'll be hearing good reviews from you, too, about the food and your hair." She crossed her fingers.

"Let's hope." Mason put his napkin on the table. "I appreciate you checking in on me, Candace. I have to say that despite the food, this place provides amazing amenities and service." He shifted in his seat, feeling the tightness in his muscles, and almost groaned.

Candace's face fell. "Are you okay?"

Carla spoke between bites of pie. "He had his first horseback-riding lesson today. His ass hurts."

Candace's expression softened. "I see you've met Kessler. He's an excellent equestrian."

Mason rubbed his outer thigh. "He knows his stuff, although I think I amused him when I kept yelling 'Whoa, Doggie' at my horse."

"Were you riding Storm or Thunder?" asked Candace.

Mason slumped in his seat. "Neither. Try Tinkerbell."

Candace clapped again. "Tinkerbell? I love Tinkerbell. She's our gentlest horse. Kessler only lets the...the...well, other gentle souls ride her."

Carla put her fork down. "You mean the delicate, slow learners who should stick to cars?"

Mason set his jaw. "Maybe you should go sit somewhere else."

Carla chuckled. "Easy, Cowboy. Or should I say, jogger? I think you do better on two legs."

Candace's phone beeped again. She sighed. "Duty calls. I'll leave you two to finish your meal. You need anything else, you let me know. I'll be around." She stood. "And I'll check in soon to see if the food's improved and let you know about the hair appointment." She paused and patted his wrist. "And I'll have some Epsom salts delivered to your room." She smiled, waved and stepped back. "Have a good evening."

"Thanks, Candace," said Mason. He moved and winced.

"Just wait till tomorrow," said Carla. "You're going to hurt like hell."

A familiar pang hit him, and Mason wished he could take a pill. "It will be a good test of my resilience."

She offered him a knowing glance. "It won't be the first or the last test."

The pang lingered, and Mason started to sweat.

"You okay?" asked Carla.

Mason dabbed at his forehead with his napkin. "It will pass."

"Amazing how the body remembers. It gets easier though." She slid her plate over. "You sure you don't want some pie? It might take the edge off."

Mason breathed in and out slowly. "I'm good. Thanks." He tried to think of something else. "Tell me about your writing. How come you never mentioned it before?"

She sat back. "I don't know. It's not that big of a deal." She fiddled with her napkin. "It's just about stuff I see around here. Reflections on life. Things I remember that I don't want to forget. That sort of thing."

"It must be a lot if you have to order pens and paper."

"Sometimes it is."

Mason caught the odd tone in her voice. "What exactly do you see around here that you want to write about? What don't you want to forget?"

She fidgeted. "Just stuff. I notice things."

"What do you notice?"

Carla looked around as if expecting someone to be listening. "I just...I'm observant. It's my third stay here and, well, I've made some observations."

Sensing her uncertainty, Mason swiveled toward her. "Why are you deflecting?"

"I'm not deflecting."

Mason raised an eyebrow. "Don't tell me. Tracy's having an affair with Manolo, who's secretly in love with Candace, and Hamlish shoplifts from the commissary."

"We don't have a commissary."

"We should."

"Tell Candace. She might create one." She grinned. "I think she likes you."

"Now you're changing the subject."

"I'm not changing anything."

A female server came by and picked up their plates. Mason recognized her as the woman who'd brought him his Earl Gray tea bags. He read her name tag. "Thanks, Serena."

She smiled. "You're welcome. You two have a nice dinner?"

"Delicious, as usual," said Carla.

"It was fine." Mason tapped on the tablecloth and leaned toward Carla. "What aren't you telling me?"

Carla frowned. "You want some coffee?"

"Hell. You're worse than my sister, Mikey, when I'm trying to pry something out of her. Hopefully, you'll talk as much as she does when she finally opens up."

Carla stood. "I'm going to get some." She went to the table with a large coffee dispenser. She grabbed a mug and began to fill it.

Mason got up from the table and joined her. "What's up with you?"

She found some sugar and added it to her mug. "Just get some coffee and come sit with me." She poured some cream, stirred her drink and walked away.

Mason wondered about the cloak and dagger routine. He picked up a cup, added some coffee and followed Carla to the small sitting area where he'd first met her. He sat beside her on the couch. "Okay. I'm sitting."

"Drink your coffee."

Mason stared for a second and then looked around. Nobody seemed to care about the two of them sipping coffee and talking. "Who are you? Columbo?" asked Mason.

"I thought you didn't watch T.V."

"It was one of my mom's favorites."

She drank from her mug. "I'm just being careful."

"About what?"

Carla's gaze darted around. "This place."

"What about it?"

"Things happen here."

Mason relaxed against the cushions. "I would hope so, or it would get really boring. I can only stare at the walls for so long."

She nudged him, and he almost spilled his coffee. "I'm talking about bad things."

"What bad things?" Studying the surrounding people, his investigative instincts kicked in and his heart rate increased. "What do you know?"

Carla nibbled her lip and held her coffee. "I can't say for sure, but I have my suspicions about Windhaven."

"Is it something illegal?" His adrenaline levels rose, and he shivered. It was his first awareness in years of feeling excited and intrigued about a case without drugs in his system. He hadn't realized how much the pills had dulled his senses until now. "Do you have proof?"

She glanced over at him. "Listen, Mason. The only reason I'm telling you this is that you're a private investigator and a former Ranger. If anyone can relate, it will be you."

"Relate to what? You still haven't told me anything."

She sipped from her mug and laughed as if he'd told her a joke. He played along and smiled back at her, and she poked his shoulder. "You're crazy," she said.

"That's what they all say," said Mason.

She whispered. "People have died here."

Mason thought of Amelia, Thomas' friend. "You mean not from natural causes?"

"Nope. Although that's what they want you to think."

"Who died?" asked Mason.

"The last one was Amelia Iverhart. They claim she got hold of drugs and overdosed. They found her in her room."

"I heard about that. She used to be a member of Hamlish's group." He drank from his cup and smiled at a patient who walked by. "Are you saying her death is suspicious?"

"She was sixty-two years old and doing well with the treatment. She was getting ready to be released and excited to go home. Then she winds up dead."

Mason spoke softly. "Just because she acted happy doesn't mean she was. She could have been planning to kill herself and was just waiting for the chance to do it. In my experience, if you want to do drugs, they're not hard to find. Even in a place like this." He pointed. "In fact, it's probably even easier in Windhaven. People are eager to cater to rich people and celebs."

"Amelia wasn't rich or famous, and she was a drinker. Not a drug user. Plus, she had a granddaughter who'd been born while she was here. She couldn't wait to get out to meet her."

"Why would anyone want to kill a sixty-year-old grandmother?"

Carla crossed one leg over the other. "That's the million-dollar question." She sipped more coffee. "She wanted to talk to me before she died. We were in a painting class together, and she implied that Windhaven's therapy may not be as healthy as they suggest it is." She waved at someone across the room. "We were going to meet and take a walk around the grounds, but she never showed and then I heard about the overdose."

Mason shifted his position on the sofa and winced when his muscles protested. "In and of itself, that means nothing. Maybe she had dementia. Maybe she was going to tell you she saw Hamlish hide the bloody knife in the beauty parlor after making out with Candace."

"I'll admit. She also told me she thought the staff was watching her, and that someone was stealing her lipstick. Maybe she was just paranoid, or maybe she knew something someone didn't want her to share, and they killed her before she could tell me."

"That's a big assumption." Mason set his coffee down and leaned back against the sofa. "What else have you got?"

A woman walked by and smiled at Carla.

"Hey, Suzanne," said Carla. "How was dinner?"

Suzanne stopped. "I had the pork chops, and they were delicious."

Carla offered Mason a sidelong glance. "I heard." She sat up. "Have you tried the pie?"

"I'm heading that way now."

"Don't miss it. You won't be disappointed."

Suzanne sighed. "It doesn't replace a shot of whiskey, but it's better than nothing." She started to walk away. "See you in group tomorrow."

"See you," said Carla. She spoke to Mason. "That's Suzanne. She and I reminisce about our good ole' drinking days."

"Sounds nice." He rubbed his sore legs and looked forward to using the Epsom salts.

Carla spoke quietly again. "The other patient of interest is August Delroy. I met him during my second stay here. Nice man. Eager to get clean and start a new life. Had a wife and kids. Was doing the program and seemed fine, but then he started to act weird."

"How so?"

"He got paranoid, like Amelia, but worse. Thought people were lying to him. He threw his food at the wall one day, and they had to subdue him when he fought the orderlies. It was scary. They took him to the clinic and kept him there for a day."

"They didn't take him to the hospital?"

"No. I saw him, though, after they released him from the clinic. He acted fine, but he wasn't himself. Seemed detached. The day after that, he was gone."

"Gone?" asked Mason. He reached for his coffee with a groan. "Gone where?"

"They said he'd checked out and left treatment early. I found it very strange because he didn't have much longer to go." She waved and said hello to someone else who walked by. "I went to find him after I was discharged. I wanted to see if he was okay."

"Was he?"

"He was dead. His poor wife was distraught. Said not long after August returned, he'd relapsed. The police found him in an alley, unconscious. They'd taken him to the hospital, but he'd lapsed into a coma and died a couple of days later. His wife said after he'd returned from therapy, he wasn't the same man as before."

"He'd been an addict who'd gone through recovery. It's not surprising that he might be different."

"It was his wife of over thirty years. I think she knew him better than anyone. She said none of it made sense. She had no inkling of why he'd gone back to the drugs so quickly. It was as if all the work he'd done to get better had vanished, like it had never happened."

"That's still not enough to warrant wrongdoing on Windhaven's part."

"Maybe not on its own, but combine it with Amelia, and something starts to stink."

Mason wasn't convinced. "Anybody else on your radar besides Amelia and August?"

She nodded. "Chauncey Pendleton. I met him during my first stay here. We came in at around the same time. He was a hardcore drug user. He did it all. Heroin. Meth. Cocaine. Alcohol. Partied hard, rarely slept, and his family broke ties with him. He was a total mess who was lucky to be alive. We bonded when I met him." She sighed. "I'm kind of a sucker for lost causes."

Mason scowled. "What does that say about me?"

She patted his knee. "That was back then. I have made some progress."

"That gives me some comfort."

"Anyway, Chauncey went through rough withdrawal, but once he got past it, he dove into his therapy. He did everything and seemed to flourish. He gained weight, started to sleep regularly, got through his family visits with reluctance but determination, and made friends with me and others."

"This doesn't ring any alarm bells," said Mason.

"His last week here, he was so excited and ready to turn over a new leaf. He seemed jittery, but I attributed that to his nervousness about going home. The jitteriness got worse though, and he got feverish, then he collapsed outside the stables. They called an ambulance, and I saw him when they loaded him up and took him away." Carla's cheeks lost some of their color. "He was bleeding from his nose and ears."

Mason went still, recalling his visions of the man in the hospital gown behind Hamlish and the woman in his room.

"He died en route to the hospital. They said he had a seizure and his heart stopped. They couldn't get him back."

"Maybe he had a heart condition."

"I think it was more than that."

"How can you be sure?"

She went quiet and studied her mug. "Mason, there's something going on here, and I'm on the verge of proving it."

Mason sat up. "Proving what?"

"Proving what happened to Amelia, August and Chauncey, and probably others I'm not aware of. It wasn't accidental, and I'm not the only one who agrees."

"What are you saying? Are you talking to somebody about this?" He held his breath and eyed the various staff wandering the dining area. "Do you have an informant?" he whispered.

"I've probably said too much." She started to stand.

Mason grabbed her hand. "Wait. Is that it?"

"I have to be careful. Knowing all of this puts you at risk."

"That means you're at risk, too."

"I can take care of myself." She tried again to leave.

"Carla, wait."

She sat again with a groan. "We'll talk again tomorrow. We don't want to stir up any extra attention by hanging around each other for too long."

"Before you go, tell me one thing." He debated minding his own business, but figured he'd heard too much to stop now. "What did August Delroy look like?"

Carla furrowed her brow. "August? He was a Black man in his fifties, with graying hair and a paunchy belly. People always gave him shit about his frizzy hair and asked him if he'd stuck his finger in a light socket. Why?"

A shiver ran up Mason's spine. She'd perfectly described the apparition he'd been seeing. "No reason. Just curious."

"I should go."

Mason stood with her and put his coffee cup down. She set her mug next to his. "Carla, listen. If there is a connection between these people and they did die for some sinister reason, you might make yourself a target."

"We've talked enough for tonight. We can discuss more tomorrow."

"Who's your source? How are you getting this proof?"

"Mason, I can't—"

A loud alarm started to whir, and a swirling light came on in the room.

Mason jumped. "What the hell?"

"It's an alert," said Carla. "It usually means someone triggered a proximity alarm on the property. It's usually nothing."

Mason watched as the residents stood and milled around as if waiting for something. "Does it happen often?"

"Depends," said Carla. "It's usually a nosy paparazzi trying to access the grounds and get the money shot of some celebrity at Windhaven. You'd be amazed how often it happens."

"What do we do?"

"They usually tell us to go to our rooms until the offender is located and the police or security escort him off the grounds."

A man in uniform appeared at the entrance to the dining area. He raised his arms and spoke loudly. "Everyone? I need your attention. As a security measure, I need to ask you to please go to your rooms until otherwise notified."

"See," said Carla.

People started to walk out, and Carla left the sitting area.

"I'm sure it's nothing serious," said the man, "but we need to account for everyone and make sure no one is on the property that shouldn't be. Thank you for your understanding."

The dining room began to clear, and Mason followed Carla out into the hall.

"I'll see you tomorrow," said Carla. "Want to do lunch?" Her serious demeanor from earlier was gone, and her jovial manner had returned.

"Carla," Mason couldn't detach as easily and, thinking of August, his concern remained. "If something happens…"

She put a hand on his shoulder. "I'm fine. Besides, I'm not stupid. I've got a few tricks up my sleeve." She leaned close. "I'm not as lost as you may think."

Mason didn't know what she meant, and he watched her walk away.

Chapter Eleven

Detective Aaron Remalla studied himself in the bathroom mirror. He noted his reflection, seeing his slender frame, slight shadows beneath his eyes and long dark hair hanging to his shoulders. Although he'd gained some weight back since returning from visiting his aunt in Merrimac, he still hadn't completely shaken the haunted look. Knowing Margaret Redstone, a sociopath with dangerous abilities and an even more dangerous attraction to him, was still on the loose hadn't helped, but a month had passed with no incidents, and he'd finally started to sleep again. Even the nightmares had lessened. His appetite had improved, too, and he'd done his best to eat in front of his partner, who seemed to carry a perpetual look of worry.

After recovering from the shock of Margaret's escape, he'd done his best to improve his mood and demeanor around Daniels to ease his partner's mind. And concerned about Mikey's safety, he'd refrained from spending too much time with her. He didn't need to give Margaret any more reasons to come after either one of them, and as much as he wanted to see Mikey, he couldn't risk it. He missed her company, though, and their separation weighed on him.

Despite his attempts to appear unaffected by the situation, the more time passed, the harder it became to keep up the persona. On top of that, Allison Albright's trial was five months away, and that scared him, too. Allison had been a disciple of Victor's and had drugged and assaulted Rem, conspired to kidnap him with Victor's help, betrayed and killed Victor, and had almost sacrificed Rem to her followers. Rem didn't relish reliving all of that at trial. And Allison hadn't stopped there. She'd since claimed to be carrying Rem's child and expected him to help her raise it. He still hadn't come to terms with that revelation and wondered if he ever would. Until he could verify the child was his, though, there was little he could do. He did his best not to dwell on it, although sometimes the dark thoughts reared their ugly heads and he'd fall apart. He kept that to himself, too.

Running his hands through his hair and tying it back in a ponytail, he leaned over the restroom sink and splashed cold water on his face, then dried it with a few paper towels. He hadn't slept well the previous night. A raccoon had gotten into his garage and knocked over a stored end table, creating a loud clatter. Hearing it from inside his house, Rem had half-expected Margaret to stomp in with her loud cackle and blazing blue eyes, but his alarm system had not been triggered and the police in the patrol car parked on the street hadn't moved. Telling himself he was a cop and could investigate a strange noise, he'd deactivated the alarm, pulled out his gun and entered the garage. The raccoon had scampered off beneath the partially opened garage door that had never shut properly, and startled, Rem had almost shot it.

Frustrated, he'd told himself it was time to fix the stupid garage door and had gone back inside, downed a shot of vodka, reset the alarm and had tried to get some sleep. Tried being the operative word.

Staring at himself in the mirror, he decided that his pallor was the best it was going to get, and he smoothed his t-shirt, tossed the towels, and left the bathroom. He walked down the hall and back into the squad room. As the doors swung shut behind him, he spotted a large disposable cup and a bag of popcorn on his desk. Daniels was sitting at his own desk, across from Rem's, studying a file and popping popcorn in his mouth.

"Is that for me?" asked Rem, approaching his desk.

"It is," said Daniels. "They've got a popcorn machine in the cafeteria today. I figured you wouldn't complain if I got you some. I tossed in a large cup of coffee because I like you."

"How nice," said Rem. "At least the Remalla charm works on someone." He sat and ate a piece of popcorn. "It's good." He sipped the coffee and sighed. "It's perfect. You even added the extra sugar."

"I didn't have much choice. You caught me when I tried the sweetener, and you won't touch it if it's unsweet."

"I've finally trained you." Rem smiled. "It took years, but it was worth the wait." He took another sip.

Daniels rolled his eyes. "I haven't given up. One of these days, I'm going to wean you off sugar. Or at least the extra sugar."

"That'll be the day I get you to add sugar to yours."

"Never gonna happen."

"Exactly." Rem sat back with his coffee and eyed Lozano's office. His captain's blinds were open, and Rem saw Kate Schultz, the prosecuting attorney on the Allison Albright case, sitting across from Lozano. He frowned. "When did Kate get here?" He sat back up. "Were we supposed to meet?"

"She came in while you were in the restroom. Said she wanted to talk to Lozano."

Rem watched his captain and Kate talk. "She say what it was about?" Lozano wore his usual long-sleeved shirt with the cuffs rolled up, and when he leaned back in his chair, the shirt pulled across his belly.

Daniels shook his head. "Nope. I figured we'll know soon enough if it's important."

Rem saw Lozano nod, his expression serious, and then he looked through the glass, and seeing Rem, he waved. "I think that's our cue," said Rem, standing and holding his coffee.

Daniels stood too. He picked up his bottled water. "Maybe it's good news."

Rem scoffed. "When's the last time we heard that?" He headed toward Lozano's office.

"That's my point," said Daniels. "We're way overdue."

He followed Rem to the door, and Rem opened it. "Hey, Cap."

"Come on in," said Lozano. "Take a seat. Kate's got some updates."

Rem walked in and sat beside Kate, and Daniels grabbed a fold-out chair leaning against the wall, opened it and sat beside Rem. "What's up, Kate?" asked Daniels.

"Is this about Allison?" asked Rem. He held his coffee and told himself to relax.

"It is," said Kate, wearing a navy suit with a white blouse. She crossed her legs and sat back in her chair. "I was telling Lozano that we may have some issues with Penny Bartolo and Dexter Fallon."

"The two followers who agreed to testify against Allison?" asked Daniels. "What's the issue?"

"Fallon is hesitating," said Kate. "He got an anonymous phone call yesterday, telling him to be careful. Whoever it was hung up, but it freaked Fallon out. He thinks Allison's followers are targeting him. I talked to him this morning and managed to pull him off the ledge, but I don't know how long that will last. Especially if he gets more phone calls."

The familiar knot in Rem's stomach grew. "What about Penny Bartolo?"

"She got the same phone call, but is less bothered by it," said Kate. "She told me they'd have to do a lot better than that to get her to back off."

Daniels scowled. "What does this mean for the case if we lose one or both of them?"

"It's not good," said Kate. "Their corroboration of your accounts is important."

"You think Measy has something to do with this?" asked Rem.

Kate shrugged. "I don't know. Allison's attorney is known for his dirty tactics, so it's possible, but there's no way to prove it." She interlaced her fingers. "But it's also possible Allison's groupies are intimidating the witnesses."

Daniels cursed. "So how do we keep them on board? Can we protect them?"

Lozano grunted. "Short of putting them in safe houses, which we can't do based on a phone call, no, we can't. We could bug their phones, but I doubt that will do much."

Rem held the bridge of his nose. "It won't matter. Allison's followers know exactly what they're doing." He looked up. "They'll keep the pressure on, and it won't require much. A quick phone call, the brief bump-into on the street, a nasty note in the mail. It will be little things, but they will add up."

Kate sat forward. "How's the investigation going with Margaret Redstone? Any progress?"

Rem lowered his hand. "None."

"There's no indication of where she is," said Daniels. "I'd love to think she left the country and is sunning herself on some island somewhere, but I doubt it."

"She's waiting us out. She wants us to get comfortable and relax," said Rem, sighing. He wondered if he would ever relax again.

"We're still looking though," said Lozano. "I've notified everyone in the state and beyond to be on the lookout. If she so much as sneezes funny, we'll get her."

Kate nodded. "You think she might interfere with the upcoming trial? Could she have something to do with the phone calls?"

"I doubt it," said Rem. "Allison and Margaret were rivals from what I could tell. They didn't like each other. If anyone would love to see Allison rot in prison, it would be Margaret. I suspect she'd scoop up the remnants of Allison's followers in a heartbeat."

Lozano crossed his arms. "Maybe that's a way to track her. Keep an eye on the followers and see if Margaret makes contact."

"If you can find them," said Daniels. "They scattered when Allison was arrested."

"That was almost four months ago," said Lozano. "Margaret's probably hoping once enough time has passed, that they'll relax, too, and start to come out into the open." He put his elbows on his desk. "That may be our lucky break."

"It's something to consider," said Rem, scratching at a stain on his jeans. "Mel and Garcia said when they went out to Victor's old beach house, where he was murdered, they saw signs of activity."

"We checked it out, though, remember?" said Daniels. "Somebody else rented it. The new tenant didn't have any red flags."

"Doesn't mean they don't have a connection to Margaret or Allison," said Rem. "Maybe it's worth swinging by again."

Daniels nodded. "I'm up for it if you are." He sipped from his water.

"There's something else regarding Allison," said Kate. She eyed Remalla. "Something I want you to think about."

Rem tensed in his seat. "What's that?"

Kate eyed Lozano, who raised a brow. "A plea bargain," she said.

"A what?" asked Daniels, narrowing his eyes.

Rem slumped. "Why would I want to consider that?"

"Just hear me out," said Kate. "Okay?"

"This better be good, Kate," said Daniels.

Kate stood and began to pace. "I'm going to give it to you straight, Rem, or else I wouldn't be doing my job."

Rem rested his coffee cup on his knee. "I wouldn't expect any less."

She stopped pacing. "If we lose Penny and Dexter, then this case becomes more difficult, and Measy knows it." She paused. "Right now, what we've got is your testimony that Allison drugged and sexually assaulted you."

The memories swirling, Rem shifted in his seat. "She did."

"I know," said Kate, "but you didn't report it, or get a drug test. It's your word against hers. She's saying it was consensual."

Rem swallowed. "I know." He caught Daniels bouncing his knee.

She leaned against Lozano's file cabinet. "Then we have your abduction, where Victor picks you up and takes you to the warehouse. But your neighbor says she saw you get in the car willingly."

Rem stilled. "You know why."

Kate nodded. "Because Victor had threatened Daniels and his family, and Mikey. But again, no one else can testify to that."

His face furrowed, Daniels pointed. "Dexter said he saw them arrive at the warehouse, and Rem had a hood over his head."

"Let's assume we no longer have Dexter's testimony," said Kate.

Daniels cursed under his breath.

Kate gestured toward Rem. "They put you in a dark room—"

"Pitch black with rats," said Rem, almost shivering at the memory.

"Yes," she said, "A pitch black room with rats, for twenty-four hours, before you were drugged again and brought to the warehouse where Allison confronts you and you were tied down on the slab." She put her hands in her pockets. "Both Dexter and Penny can testify to that, but again, let's assume we don't have them."

Rem could see where Kate was going, and he groaned.

"But," said Kate, "after Daniels found you, you didn't go to the hospital or get a drug test."

"Wait a minute," said Daniels, his posture rigid. "You're skipping an important part. Mason Redstone and I found him in that warehouse. We ran in and saw Allison with the damn knife at his throat. We can both testify to that, and to Rem being drugged."

"And Measy will say you're his partner, and that you'll do whatever's necessary to protect him, and Redstone is currently in a drug treatment center for a pain pill addiction. You know how that will play with a jury once Measy is done with Mason?" She eyed Rem. "And when you take the stand, he'll suggest that you and Allison were lovers and planned the whole thing as a display of her power. He'll suggest she never planned to kill you. When your tryst with her was discovered, you lied to cover it up and send Allison to prison."

Daniels stood, his face red. "This is ridiculous. That's all bullshit. And you didn't even mention how Allison killed Victor."

"Says who?" asked Kate. "Dexter and Penny?" She pushed off the file cabinet.

"Allison told me she killed him," said Rem.

"But you said you were under the influence of drugs. Measy will use that to say your testimony can't be trusted." She paused. "And even if our followers testify, they have a history of drug use, both during the time of Rem's captivity and before. They are by no means a slam dunk."

Daniels kicked his chair, and it skittered into Lozano's desk. "What are you saying, Kate? That we don't have a case?"

"Just chill out, Daniels," said Lozano. "Nobody's saying anything."

"That's not what it sounds like to me," shouted Daniels. He shot a hand out at Rem. "She slid a damn knife down his chest. You want him to show his scar to the jury?"

"That's enough," said Lozano.

"Are you calling him a liar?" asked Daniels.

"It's okay, Captain," said Kate. "He has a right to be frustrated. It's a frustrating case."

"That's an understatement," said Rem under his breath. His stomach was in knots, and he couldn't drink his coffee.

Kate walked up to him. "Listen, I'm not saying we can't win. We have damaging evidence against Allison, but I intentionally made it sound horrible because I want you to get a feel for what Measy is going to try to do. You need to be prepared."

Rem looked up. "You think we're going to lose?"

She shook her head. "No. Not at all. Despite all of that, we have your testimony. And Daniels. Both of you are respected and decorated officers. That will be a big factor with the jury. Measy will try to discredit both of you, but I think a jury will see through that."

"What about the video of me wandering the precinct, high as a kite after Ginger dosed me in the cafeteria?" asked Rem. "What if they play it?"

"It's risky if they do," said Kate. "Measy will have to explain where he got it, who took the video and why he has it. It could easily backfire on him, which is why I think he won't use it." She paused. "My thought is that was a scare tactic to get you to back off, and to influence you to visit Allison in jail."

Rem couldn't decide whether to be relieved or disgusted.

"And there's Allison's pregnancy to deal with," said Kate. "Measy will no doubt try to sneak it in during the trial that her child may be yours. Especially if he puts her on the stand."

"You think he will?" asked Rem.

She held his gaze. "If I were him, I would. The question is, what will she say?"

"It sure as hell won't be the truth," said Daniels, doing his own pacing.

"Exactly," said Kate. "Which is why I brought up the plea bargain. I talked to the D.A. about it, and he's leaving it up to me, so I'm leaving it up to you."

Rem set his cup on Lozano's desk. "What would you offer?"

Daniels stopped and put his hands on his hips.

Kate looked between the two of them. "Voluntary manslaughter for Victor, and false imprisonment and aggravated assault with a deadly weapon for you. Twenty years, but she could be paroled in fifteen."

Daniels set his jaw, and Rem just stared, his mind whirling.

"Fifteen years?" yelled Daniels. "That's it? For everything she's done?"

"Settle down, Daniels," said Lozano. "Nothing's decided yet. Kate's just doing her job. Remalla doesn't have to do anything."

Kate settled her gaze on Rem.

"And if I say no?" asked Rem.

"Then we go to trial, and I'll do everything I can to put her away for life, which is where we roll the dice. If the jury believes you, she'll never see a patch of green grass again. But if they believe her..." She hesitated. "She may be acquitted."

"Shit," said Daniels, pacing again.

"But on the bright side," said Kate, "if they take the plea bargain, then that's it. No trial and no testimony from you or Daniels. You're done, and she's in prison."

"Until fifteen years later, when she's out," said Rem.

"And she'll be almost fifty years old," said Kate. "Starting all over again."

"With a fifteen-year-old kid that I might be raising," added Rem. He studied his hands.

"There's a lot to think about," said Kate. "So take your time. You don't have to decide today. And keep in mind that Measy may not go for it. He may roll his own dice and take it to trial."

"That wouldn't surprise me," said Rem.

She checked her watch. "Sorry to leave abruptly, but I've got a meeting." She turned and picked up her briefcase from the floor. "Just consider it, and if you have any questions, you know where to reach me."

"Thanks, Kate," said Lozano, standing. "We appreciate it."

She went to the door and opened it. "You got it. Talk soon." With a last look, she walked out and closed the door.

Lozano sat and eyed Rem. "Well? What do you think?"

Daniels erupted. "What does he think? What the hell kind of question is that? She basically told us we don't have a case."

Lozano glared. "That's not what she said. She just said that this isn't a slam dunk. It's not like you didn't understand that. You both knew there would be challenges along the way."

"Challenges?" yelled Daniels. "Fifteen years for murder, attempted murder, abduction and assault? It's disgusting."

"You know the job," Lozano yelled back. "This is the way it works sometimes. If she can't guarantee that our two followers will testify, then this becomes more difficult. Rem needs to know that."

"Right now, they're still on board," said Daniels. "She doesn't know they won't testify. So why the plea bargain?"

"Let's just say the writing is on the wall." Rem sighed and stared at the ceiling. "God, this sucks."

Daniels deflated, pulled his chair back and sat with his head in his hands. "I'm sorry, partner. I'd hoped it would be good news."

"Maybe one day," said Rem.

"Would you two listen to yourselves?" asked Lozano. "You act like Allison's already won." He picked up a pen and pointed with it. "Kate didn't say to go one way or another. She gave you a choice and told you the difficulties you're going to face. That doesn't mean she wants you to offer the deal. It means you have options."

Rem straightened, although he felt like curling up on the floor. "It doesn't matter either way. There's no way Measy's taking that deal. His ego is too big."

"You don't know that," said Lozano. "And it's not up to him. It's up to Allison."

Rem blew out a breath. "So I either avoid trial and Allison gets out in fifteen to twenty, or I testify and Measy tries to prove I'm a liar and a jury decides whether Allison goes free." He slapped his knee. "Sounds pretty clear-cut to me."

"What do you want to do?" asked Daniels.

"I have absolutely no idea." Conflicted, Rem picked up his coffee. "What would you do?"

His eyes weary, Daniels sighed. "I don't know."

"While you two are thinking about it," said Lozano, "I have something else for you to ponder."

"Wait. Don't tell me," said Rem. "More good news?"

Lozano rocked in his chair. "The chief didn't approve the extension of the police protection for you and Mikey Redstone. After this week, it ends."

"Are you kidding?" asked Daniels.

Rem chuckled. "Of course it does."

"It's been a month since Margaret escaped with no incidents," said Lozano. "The chief doesn't think that warrants more protection. The department is short-staffed, and we need the officers."

"And when Rem and Mikey turn up dead, then what's he going to say?" asked Daniels.

Rem recalled his shrink's advice but struggled to stay positive. "He'll cry at our funerals, toss a flower at our caskets and blame Lozano."

Lozano snorted. "Don't think I don't know it."

"Any other wonderful info you want to throw our way, Cap?" asked Daniels. "You planning on firing Rem anytime soon?"

"That might be the good news I'm waiting for," said Rem.

"Maybe he'll fire both of us," said Daniels.

"Nobody's going anywhere," said Lozano. "Not if I can help it."

"Too bad," said Rem. "But if you ever need someone for traffic duty, I'm your guy."

"I'll keep that in mind," said Lozano. "But how about we focus on finding Margaret Redstone first. Then you won't have to worry about police protection."

Relaxing a little, Rem shrugged. "To be honest, Cap, I doubt that any police presence will stop Margaret. It helped a little with my sanity those first couple of weeks, but now, I kind of feel for whoever gets stuck sitting outside my door, twiddling their thumbs for the night."

"You know this is exactly what Margaret wants, right?" asked Daniels. "For us to let our guard down."

"You got any better ideas of what to do, you let me know," said Lozano. "For now, though, we're stuck with what we got." He raised a brow at Rem. "Unless you want to go back to the safe house."

Rem grimaced. "I'd rather live with my mother."

"That's an option," said Daniels. "She's the only person who might be capable of scaring Margaret away."

"You may have a point," said Rem.

"You want me to call Mikey and let her know?" asked Lozano.

Rem hated the thought of telling Mikey her protection was ending. "No. I'll do it." He stood. "Anything else?"

"I'd say that's enough, wouldn't you?" asked Lozano. He waved a finger. "Go on. Make yourselves useful."

Daniels stood and followed Rem to the door. "We'll do our best," said Daniels.

"Thanks, Cap." Rem opened the door and walked out. He headed for his desk, sat and finally took a sip of his coffee. His stomach curdled, though, and he set the cup down.

Daniels sighed and sat across from him. "I'm sorry I lost my temper in there. If anyone should be upset, it's you."

"No need to apologize. I was upset, but acting like it doesn't seem to help."

Daniels picked up a pencil and fiddled with it. "You know whatever you decide with the plea bargain is fine with me. I don't want to give the impression that I expect you to do something."

"No. I know." Tired, Rem leaned back and eyed the ceiling, wishing he could go home, crawl into bed, and sleep for the next year.

"You going to call Mikey?"

Rem looked up and eyed the phone. "I am."

"Good." Daniels rested his elbows on his desk. "While you're at it, maybe you should tell her about Allison and the baby."

Rem closed his eyes and groaned.

"You said you were going to talk to her. You promised."

"That was before I knew Margaret was loose."

Daniels wouldn't give up. "Maybe you should stop trying so hard to protect her and tell her how you feel."

Frustration with the case and everything else bubbled up. "So I can fall for her and then grieve when Margaret kills her, too?" Frazzled, Rem stood and dumped his coffee in the trash. "I can only take so much."

"Rem, I'm only—"

"Well, stop, okay. I just..." He stammered, not knowing what to say. "Of course I want to tell her how I feel. Of course, I've thought about it. But I hate worrying that her connection to me might get her killed, and I can't do that again. I just can't."

"You don't know that," argued Daniels. "She's Margaret's sister, remember? Maybe your connection to her is what protects her. Hell, you're apart right now, and I don't see either of you feeling very safe. I don't think Margaret's going to back down either way." He sat forward. "But Mikey should at least know about Allison. The longer you wait to tell her, the harder it will be."

Rem held his temples. "I don't want to talk about this right now." His head swam, and all he wanted to do was disappear. "I'm so sick of thinking, I want to scream." He paused and dropped his hand. "I just need some time."

Daniels watched him with the familiar look of worry. "Then take it. Get out of here for a while. Just let me know where you are."

"Kind of hard not to. I've got a patrol car following me, at least for the rest of the week." He reached for his jacket.

"Just be careful, okay?"

Rem almost laughed. It felt to him like he'd been trying to be careful for a lifetime. And where had it gotten him? "Yeah, sure." He slid on his jacket, grabbed his keys, and headed for the door.

Chapter Twelve

"How do you want to handle this?" asked Trick. He sat at his desk at SCOPE and watched Mikey pace.

"I'm thinking," she said. She sat on the back of the couch.

"Well, think fast, because Gina will be here soon." He propped a booted foot on the edge of his desk. "Where's Kyle?"

"He's following up on that house clearing he did. He wants to be sure he hit all the nooks and crannies. He'll swing by when he's done and make his notes in the file."

"He's thorough. That's for sure."

"I think he likes the scary stuff. He says it's fun to kick some ass."

"Good for him, as long as nothing follows him home," said Trick, recalling Mason's encounter with Mr. Dark with a shiver. He paused and thought about Gina. "I say we confront Gina with what we know."

Mikey swiveled her head. "Confront her?" She stood. "You want to dump all of this on her at once? That her sister Lenora was seeing some bad dude with a snake tattoo who threatened Lenora's neighbors and roommate, threw cash around like candy and could toss someone across a room with no visible means? Is that what you want to do?"

"Sometimes the surprise tactic works wonders. They don't see it coming, and you can widen some cracks and spill some secrets."

"You act like Gina has those secrets, but what if she doesn't?"

Trick dropped his foot to the ground. "Come on, Mikey. This man, Rain, can move things with his mind like Gina, and you don't think Gina knows something? That coincidence is not passing the smell test."

"Just because Rain has some PK abilities doesn't mean Gina is a friend of his. There isn't some PK meet-up group where they all hang out."

"You sure about that?" asked Trick. "How many people do you know that have PK? I'd say the fact that you're aware of two beats huge odds. And they both have a connection to Lenora Rodriguez." He paused, and Mikey paced again. "Think about it. What if Rain has a connection to Victor? What if he and Gina met through one of Victor's parties? Maybe Gina didn't realize it, but she ended up with a stalker who targeted her sister. Or maybe Gina is still caught up in the party and drug scene, which is how Lenora met Rain."

Mikey rubbed her head. "I don't believe that. You forget. I was at those parties, too. I never met anyone who matches Rain's description. And Gina never mentioned any man like that."

"It doesn't mean he didn't exist, Mikey. I doubt you met all of Victor's cronies. Maybe Rain got past your radar."

"Whether Gina knew him or not, she certainly wouldn't be complicit in Lenora's death."

Trick raised a brow. "How do you know?"

The buzzer rang, and Mikey eyed the cameras. "It's her." She reached down and hit a button. "Come on in."

"I'm just saying, Mikey," said Trick, lowering his voice. "You haven't seen her in years."

The front door opened and closed, and Gina poked her head inside the interior office of SCOPE. "Hey."

Mikey turned. "Hey, Gina. Glad you could stop by. Have a seat." She gestured toward the sofa.

Gina walked in, looking stylish in pressed brown pants and a black-collared shirt with silver jewelry. Her long dark hair ran down her back. "Thanks." She went to the couch and sat, her face pensive. "When I heard you had some updates, I came as fast as I could." She eyed Trick. "Hey, Trick."

"Gina," said Trick.

Mikey walked to the chair and sat across from her. "Trick and I wanted to ask you some questions about Lenora."

Gina rubbed her legs. "Okay. I'll do my best to answer."

Mikey fiddled with the ring on her finger. "Lenora never mentioned anything to you about who she was seeing?"

Gina shook her head. "No. Not at all. I told you that. Ronald didn't know either."

"Did you or Ronald ever go see her? Either at her old apartment or her new one?"

"I saw her at her old place, and I met her roommate. Nice girl. But that was before Lenora started to fall apart. Ronald visited her once at the new place. Said it was a wreck. Lots of empty bottles of booze, and it needed to be cleaned. Lenora wouldn't listen to him, though, about getting out of there, and she asked him to leave."

"Do you know whether Ronald saw anyone else around at the time?" asked Trick.

Gina pursed her lips. "No, not that he mentioned. And I never saw anyone odd at her old place." She narrowed her eyes. "What's this all about?"

Mikey leaned in. "Does a man named Rain with a snake tattoo on his temple ring a bell?"

"A man with a snake tattoo?" asked Gina. She stared off. "No. Not at all."

Trick studied her but didn't catch any of the usual signs of deception. "He's tall, with dark hair. Good-looking, wears expensive clothes, and he flashes his cash." He hesitated. "And he likes to intimidate."

"Is he the man Lenora was seeing?" asked Gina. "Did you find him?"

"No. We didn't find him," said Mikey. "All we know so far is that he goes by Rain, which may be short for something, but we're not sure. But he knew Lenora, and we suspect he's the one who was paying her bills."

"And provided the drugs and alcohol, too," added Trick. "He definitely didn't do Lenora any favors."

"Is he the man responsible for her death?" Gina gripped her knees.

"It's possible, but we can't be sure," said Mikey. "If we could locate him, or get his last name, that would help."

Gina held her head and closed her eyes. "Oh, Lenora. What were you doing?" She sighed. "Why were you mixed up with this guy?"

"Gina," said Mikey, eyeing Trick. "There's something else."

Gina looked up. "What is it?" Her face fell. "Is it bad?"

"It's about Rain," said Mikey. "When I talked to Angela, Lenora's roommate, she told me something important. Something she'd kept to herself until I questioned her."

"Wh...what's that?" asked Gina.

"Just before Lenora moved out of their apartment, Angela encountered Rain." She paused. "She told me he got angry with her for trying to prevent Lenora from going out that night. He, uh...well, he threw her across the room and over the couch."

"He what?" asked Gina. "He's violent, too?" She put her hand over her mouth. "Did he hurt Lenora when they were together?"

"No," said Mikey, raising her hand. "Not that we're aware of. But it's the way he threw Angela that's important."

"I don't understand," said Gina.

"He used PK," said Mikey.

Gina frowned. "He what?"

"He threw her mentally, not physically," said Trick. "Which is something Mikey says you are familiar with."

Gina dropped her jaw. "You told him?" she asked Mikey.

"Trick's aware of my past," said Mikey. "He knows the people I've been around and what I've experienced. Plus, he's partnered with Mason and me, so stuff like this comes with the territory. He's also on this case, so he needs to know everything."

"I'll keep your secrets," said Trick. "But I have to admit I find it odd that the man we're looking for shares the same abilities as you."

Gina shot a hard gaze at Trick. "Are you saying I should know Rain?"

"Did you ever meet someone matching his description at any of Victor's parties?" asked Mikey. "Did Victor ever introduce you to someone like that?"

Gina furrowed her brow. "No. Not that I recall." She crossed her arms and hugged herself. "Are you saying this has something to do with me? That Lenora was targeted?"

"I'm not saying anything," said Mikey. "But it is strange that this man Rain has similar abilities."

"Is it possible you knew him, but don't remember?" asked Trick.

Gina's mouth fell open. "Why am I getting the impression you two think I know more than I'm saying?" She straightened. "Do you think I'm lying?"

"No. I don't think you're lying, Gina," said Mikey.

"Mikey backs you up a hundred percent," said Trick. "I am a little more dubious."

"Trick...," said Mikey.

Gina stood. "You think I know the person who is responsible for Lenora's death, and for some reason, I hired you to investigate? Why would I do that?"

Trick shrugged. "Maybe you have a history with this Rain. And whatever that may be, it didn't end well. He went after Lenora next, only it went too far, and Lenora died. Now you want us to find him so you can avenge your sister. Or if we want to go darker, you know him and you still know him, but you're protecting him. Did Lenora get caught up in her big sister's mess? Were you and your sister at odds so Lenora went after your old lover? After you learned what happened, you wanted to be sure your friend Rain couldn't be implicated. So you hired us to find out how exposed your boyfriend is."

Gina's eyes flashed. "You son of a bitch."

"Trick. Stop it." Mikey stood too. "Gina, listen. He's just trying to—"

Gina whirled on Mikey. "After all we've been through, you're going to listen to him? Do you really think I could do something like that?"

Trick laid a hand on his desk and stayed calm. "Gina, as I said, Mikey didn't—"

Gina whirled toward him next. "You shut up. You don't know me. You don't know anything about me. And you have the audacity to imply that I might have had something to do with my sister's death? That I know the man that killed her and I'm protecting him?"

"Or you want to kill him," said Trick. "I suggested that, too."

"Trick. Stop talking," said Mikey. "Gina—"

"How dare you?" said Gina to Mikey. "I asked for your help, and this is what I get? What am I paying for?" She stepped closer to Mikey. "I thought we were friends."

Mikey stiffened. "Friends?" Her own eyes narrowed. "I can appreciate that. And yes, you and I have been through a lot, but you left, and I haven't seen you in years."

"I left?" asked Gina, pointing at herself. "You're damn right I left. You were so hung up on Victor that you'd sacrifice anyone, no matter how low they were on the totem pole, to keep him. You let monsters mess with the weakest of us just to protect yourself."

Mikey froze but then scowled. "Protect myself? If anyone knew how to protect themselves, it was you. I saw how you were with Victor. You think I didn't know what you were doing behind my back? How you lied to me to get what you wanted?"

Trick stood, his heart thudding. "Ladies, maybe we should table this and talk about Lenora?"

Gina laughed. "I lied? I lied?" She scoffed. "That's rich. You lied all the time. About me. About other followers. You fed us to the wolves, Mikey. And you know it."

"Hey," said Trick. "Maybe we should take it easy."

Mikey stepped closer to Gina. "The only one feeding anyone to the wolves was Victor. And if I had to protect myself by sticking to his side, then I did. But that didn't stop you from trying to claw your way in. Don't act like you wouldn't have done the same, and you sure as hell tried. I don't doubt that if you could have fed me to the wolves, you would have."

Gina's eyes rounded. "You think you're so damn smart. You're just as smug now as you were then. And you know what?" She jabbed a finger toward Mikey. "You're right. I did want you out because I was sick of the damn servitude. I played Victor's games, and you know what I got for it? Nothing. But you? You acted like royalty. You were enjoying the spoils while the rest of us paid the price. And then, when I met David, I thought I'd won. I'd beaten you. I met someone who cared enough about me to rescue me and put me first, and then your brother showed up. Mr. High-and-Mighty Texas Ranger. It made me sick, and I let Victor know as much. I told him about Mason and his attempts to save you, and I'd hoped Victor would find a way to keep you close, and he almost did, but that stupid sister of yours interfered. She told Victor to let you go."

Mikey sucked in a breath. "Margaret? She did what?"

Caught up in the conversation, Trick wasn't sure what to do or say.

"I hated her," said Gina. "I should have known you would be just like her. Using people to satisfy yourself. I should have suspected Margaret didn't like you any closer to Victor than she was, so she wanted you gone. I was stupid when it came to both of you, so I left, and didn't plan to see you again. But when I came back after my divorce, I heard about Allison's arrest. I got curious and asked around. I learned you were working here, and I figured you'd eventually show at that coffee shop."

Trick cocked his head. "So that wasn't an accident."

Gina ignored him and sneered at Mikey. "I wanted to see you. I wanted to know about you. What your life was like after Victor. I thought I'd say hi and that would be it. But then we talked, and it stirred up all those old memories, and I sensed how Kyle liked you. And how you'd landed on your feet and seemed to be doing well. So, I told you about Lenora. Everything I've said about her is true. I don't know why I told you, but I did. Maybe I'd hoped you'd changed, but I think in some small way I wanted to see you fail. It's something I'd wanted with Victor, and I still want it. The anger. The resentment. It's like it never went away, and now you have the nerve to accuse me of hurting my own flesh and blood." Her face red, she glared. "It's my own damn fault, though. You always found a way to blame everyone else, and now you're doing it again, but I did nothing to hurt Lenora." She paused to catch her breath. "But you, Mikey? You, I'd happily strangle."

Mikey stared in shock, and Trick took a step. "That's enough."

Gina turned and pointed a finger at Trick. "I said shut up."

Something hot hit Trick in the chest, and his feet left the floor. He barely had a second to acknowledge that he'd left the ground before his back hit the wall and the air left his lungs in a whoosh. He hung there for a second before he slid down, and his butt hit the floor with a thud.

"Trick!" yelled Mikey, running over to him.

Trick doubled over, clutching his chest and trying to catch his breath. "I'm okay," he wheezed.

Mikey squatted beside him but shouted at Gina, who still stood near the couch. "He's just out of the hospital," she yelled. "What's the matter with you?"

Gina lifted the side of her lip. "There's a lot wrong with me. Just like there's a lot wrong with you. Nobody who stayed with Victor for long left without damage. Is that fair to either of us? No, it isn't. But I can't do anything about it, and neither can you. What's done is done."

"Get out," said Mikey.

"With pleasure." Gina headed to the door but turned before leaving. "And I heard about Margaret's escape. I know she's free and I know what she's up to, and all I can say, Mikey, is good luck." She offered an ugly smile, shoved the door open and stomped out.

Chapter Thirteen

MIKEY STARED AT THE empty doorway in complete disbelief, unsure she'd heard Gina right. Trick moaned as he uncurled, and Mikey grabbed his arm. "Take it easy."

Trick put a hand on the edge of his desk. "I'm okay. Just got the wind knocked out of me." He pulled up and grimaced.

"Here. Wait." Mikey stood and offered him her hand. He took it and managed to get to his feet with Mikey's help. He wobbled for a second and held his stomach. "You were right. Gina packs a punch when she's angry."

Mikey swung his chair over. "Sit."

Trick sat with a grunt. "I'm fine. Don't worry."

Mikey studied his face. "How's your side? You feel any pain?"

"I told you I'm okay." He looked up at her. "You, however, are a little pale. Maybe you should sit, too."

"Did you hear her?" asked Mikey. "Did you hear what she said? About Margaret?"

"I heard it all."

Mikey hurried over, shut the door and locked it. Worried Gina might return, she went to the computer and set the alarm system.

"Does that make you feel better?" Trick rubbed his stomach and took a breath.

"It does." Trying to process everything that had just happened, Mikey went to the couch and sat. "You were the one who was right, though. I never expected Gina to react like that." She held her head. "I thought we were friends."

Trick sighed. "It's not your fault, Mikey. You and Gina just handled Victor's manipulation differently. She blamed you for her problems, and you blamed Victor."

"She thinks I hurt others to protect myself. That I used my connection to Victor as a shield." Reflecting on her past, she took a slow breath, and the memories rushed at her. "She's not wrong. There are things I did I'm not proud of."

"You did what you had to do during a horrible situation to survive. As you said, Gina would have done the same thing, and it sounds like she did. She tried to prevent you from leaving when Mason found you."

"And Margaret told Victor to let me go." She shook her head. "I don't know what to think about that."

Trick stood slowly. "Margaret didn't like your closeness to Victor any more than Gina did."

Mikey tried to think, but her thoughts swirled after Gina's accusations. "Victor listened to Margaret, Trick. There are a million things she could have done to keep me away from him but still under his influence. I didn't threaten her. She had way more sway with Victor. Gina knew that." She bit her lip, coming to the hard-to-believe conclusion. "Which is probably why it pissed Gina off." She eyed Trick, who walked to the sofa. "Margaret saved me. Maybe as much as Mason did."

Trick sat beside her. "Maybe she did. Maybe she had a moment of sanity, realized the damage she'd done, and took care of you."

"It didn't last, though. She tried to kill me after what happened with Rem. Whatever slivers of sanity she may have had have long since been severed."

"She doesn't like your connection to Remalla. She may have put up with you and Victor because she believed she still pulled the strings, but it's different with Rem."

Mikey leaned back into the cushions. "Well, she's getting what she wants. Rem is staying away."

"That won't last forever."

"Won't it?" She glanced at him. "Rem's already had his heart broken once. He's protecting himself as much as I am."

Trick turned his head toward her. "Are we finally admitting you two have feelings for each other?"

Mikey picked up a throw pillow and held it. "Maybe. I'd be lying if I said I didn't miss him. More than I thought I would."

"And Kyle?"

"I like him, too. Just differently."

"But if Rem were to walk in that door right now, professing his love to you?"

Mikey swallowed, and her skin prickled. She shook her head. "Maybe we should talk about something else. This is not the time for me to start anything, much less a love affair. Gina just left, admitting she hates me. Lenora's death is still a mystery, Margaret's out there and apparently Gina's aware of whatever she's up to, and we're due to hear from the treatment center about visiting Mason." She rested her head in her palm. "What the hell are we going to tell him?"

"We're not going to tell him anything. As far as Red is concerned, everything is smooth as glass at SCOPE. Kyle is helping us out, business is booming, and all is well in the world."

"You can lie to him like that?"

"If we don't, he'll check himself out. You and I know he won't stay if he learns of Margaret's escape. We're not lying for our sake, but for his. He needs this time, Mikey, to figure out his demons. I don't want to take that from him." He paused. "He'll be pissed when he finds out later, but I can deal with an angry, sober Red. It's the addicted one that scares me."

Mikey had to admit Trick was right. Mason had always looked out for others but never himself, and if lying meant it would give her brother the time and treatment he needed, then she'd do it. "Okay. I hear you. SCOPE is the Candyland of P.I. agencies right now, and Glinda the Good Witch is our right-hand woman."

He chuckled. "Don't go too crazy. We'll have a few troubles, or else he'll see right through it. I don't see the harm in telling him about Gina and Lenora."

"I guess. With a few redacted details."

Trick grunted. "I'm going to assume Gina won't be paying us."

"I think you'd be accurate." She hugged the pillow. "What do we do about Lenora, though? Should we still investigate? That guy Rain is still out there, and he may have had something to do with her death."

"I say we move on. To be honest, I don't know what else we can do. We'd have to locate Rain, and unless you want to spend a lot of time and resources to do that with no compensation, then we look for the next case." He ran his hand over his stomach gingerly. "And I doubt Gina would be open to our continuing the investigation, or even talking to us again."

"It sounds like Lenora got mixed up with the wrong guy and paid the price. It's tragic, but I don't know if it's criminal."

"And even if it's criminal, I don't know how we prove it."

Mikey set the pillow aside. "So we move on."

"Agreed."

Mikey nodded. "You think Gina's really been in touch with Margaret?"

"No. I don't. I think she's lying. If she still runs in similar circles as Margaret, it wouldn't be hard for her to learn about Margaret's escape. I think she threw that out there to mess with your head."

"Probably, but maybe I should tell Rem. If Gina knows where Margaret is, the police can pursue that. Maybe Gina could lead them right to her."

"Unlikely, but I see your point. I doubt Margaret would be that stupid, but if it's a potential lead, it should be followed." He nudged her. "Plus, it would give you a reason to call him."

"Don't start."

He smiled. "Just making an observation."

"I'm sorry I said anything."

"It's not like you revealed anything surprising. Everybody else can see you two like each other. Why you two don't see it for yourselves is the mystery."

"It's not like there hasn't been a lot to deal with lately. It's been a little stressful."

Trick straightened. "There's always going to be something, Mikey. At some point, you have to take a shit or flush."

Mikey frowned. "What does that even mean?"

"I'm not sure, but it sounded good. Red would have appreciated it."

Mikey raised her brow at him. "I think you need to get some more rest."

Trick stood slowly. "I may take you up on that."

A buzzer sounded, and Mikey's heart thumped. Trick glanced at her, walked to the desk and eyed the cameras.

"Is it Gina?" asked Mikey.

Trick smiled. "Well, well, well. Look who's here." He turned off the alarm and hit the button. "Come on in."

Mikey stood. "Who is it?"

Trick grabbed his hat from the coat rack. "I'm going to step out for a bit. I'll be back later."

"Trick, what is going—"

Trick unlocked and opened the door. "Hello, Detective."

"Hi, Trick," said a familiar voice, and Mikey stared as Remalla walked in.

Chapter Fourteen

"Rem?" Mikey asked.

"Hey, Mikey." Remalla entered the office and stopped in front of the couch. He wore his usual jeans and t-shirt with a jacket to cover his holster. His dark hair was tied back in a short ponytail. "Sorry for dropping by unannounced." He paused. "You...uh...have a minute to talk?"

"The timing's perfect, Detective," said Trick. "I was just stepping out for...a rest." He put his hat on and winked at Mikey. "You two enjoy your visit."

"Thanks, Trick," said Rem. "See you."

"See you," said Trick. He left and shut the door.

Mikey heard the lock engage, and she waited for him to leave through the outer door before reengaging the alarm.

"I'm glad you're being careful," said Rem.

Mikey thought of Gina. "I am. What about you? Any updates on Margaret?"

"I wish." He slid his jacket off and tossed it onto the couch. "Have you had any issues?"

"Not with Margaret, but I may have a lead for you to follow."

"Really? What is it?"

"A woman named Gina Rodriguez. She told me she knows what Margaret is up to. I don't know if she's actually seen her, but it may be worth following up on."

"Who's Gina Rodriguez?"

Mikey sighed. "A woman from my past." She paused. "With Victor."

Rem paused. "I see. You think Margaret's been in touch with her?"

"I doubt it, but Gina said it like a threat, so who knows?"

Rem frowned. "A threat? Who is this woman? Is she dangerous?"

Mikey bit back a groan. She had no idea if Gina was a threat or not, but the thought that she could be had to be considered. She hated telling Rem, though, that there could be another unstable person on the loose. Didn't they already have enough to deal with? "Have a seat, and I'll fill you in. You want a coffee?"

"You know the answer to that." Rem walked around the sofa and sat.

Mikey walked to the coffee machine and picked up the container of grounds. "How's Daniels?" She added a filter, then scooped some grounds into it.

"He's okay. He's back at the station."

"You take the afternoon off?" She put the grounds away and grabbed the pot.

"Not exactly." He hesitated. "I just needed some fresh air."

On her way to the closet where they kept the water cooler, she noted how he hunched over and studied his hands. "Bad afternoon?"

He looked up. "I've had worse, but I've also had better."

Mikey could still hear Gina yelling at her. "Me too." She went to the closet and filled the pot with water.

"You tell me yours, and I'll tell you mine."

She stuck her head around the doorway. "Deal."

"Let's get the coffee going first."

"Good idea." She finished filling the pot and brought it over to the coffeemaker, where she filled it, slid the pot back and flipped it on. She walked over and sat next to Rem. "You want to go first?"

"Why don't you go?" he said. "I need to gather my thoughts, and I want to hear about this Gina person."

"Okay." Mikey told him about meeting Gina and her history with her, and her and Trick's subsequent investigation into Lenora Rodriguez and her association with the man named Rain with the snake tattoo.

"You think this Rain hurt Lenora?" he asked.

"Well, he certainly wasn't a good influence, and he's likely the reason she got hooked on drugs. Whether he's the reason she overdosed is uncertain, but it wouldn't surprise me if he was involved."

"And why did Gina threaten you? If she and Margaret hated each other, why would Gina know anything?"

Mikey grabbed the throw pillow, sat back and held it in her lap. "Gina got angry when Trick pushed her buttons."

"What buttons did he push?"

"Pretty much all of them. He accused her of knowing Rain."

"Why would she know Rain?"

Mikey debated whether to tell him about the psychokinetics. Before she'd known Rem, he'd had a run-in with another man with PK abilities that hadn't ended well. Rem didn't like to talk about it. She took a breath. "Gina and Rain both have psychokinetic gifts. They can move things with their minds."

Rem paled and went still.

She reached over and took his wrist. "I know you have some ugly history with that, and I hope I'm not upsetting you. Gina can only use it when she's mad, and Rain—well, he tossed Lenora's roommate across a room, so he's obviously dangerous."

Rem took a second and nodded. "It's fine. You just took me by surprise." He shook his head as if to clear it. "So, Gina took offense at the suggestion she knew Rain, stormed out and threatened you regarding Margaret."

"Pretty much," said Mikey, leaning back again. "And that was my afternoon."

"Never a dull day, is there?" He reached to grab his jacket and slid it over.

"No, never."

He pulled a small notepad out of his pocket along with a pencil. "It's Gina Rodriguez?"

"It is. You're going to check her out?"

"I am. I want to know exactly what she's up to, and if she's really in touch with Margaret."

"Personally, I think it's an empty threat. She was mad and knew where to aim."

"You think she'll come back?"

"I doubt it. She vented and left. I've never known her to be violent."

He scribbled on the pad. "She threw Trick against the wall."

"You know Trick. Does that surprise you?"

He smirked. "Not really. Trick could aggravate a light pole."

"He's unique that way." She put the pillow down and stood. "So, how was your afternoon?"

"Not any better than yours. We had a visit from Kate Schultz today in Lozano's office." He returned the pencil and notepad to his pocket.

She grabbed two mugs and set them beside the coffeemaker. She added creamer and sugar to both. "About Allison's case?"

"Yes."

He went quiet, and she added coffee to the mugs, stirred the contents and brought the mugs over. She handed one to Rem. "Here. This will help."

"Thanks." He took the mug and sipped it. "It's good."

Mikey sat, sipped her own and set the mug on the table. "Spill it. What'd she say?"

Rem stared at his mug. "She wants me to consider offering a plea bargain to Allison."

Surprised, Mikey shifted to face him. "What for?"

Rem explained the potential loss of the testimony of the two followers and how it would affect the case, how Measy would twist his testimony, and how Allison might be acquitted. He told her that Kate had suggested the plea bargain and what she would offer.

Mikey's stomach turned. "That's it? Fifteen years?"

"Maybe twenty, if we're lucky."

Mikey stammered. "I don't believe it. After everything she's done, and what she did to you?"

"Peachy, isn't it? On the plus side, though, I wouldn't have to testify."

Mikey did her best to control her anger. She knew Rem had a lot on his mind and had some big decisions to make. "Do you not want to testify?"

"I'm certainly not looking forward to it. Measy will do his best to make me look like a drug user and liar who was in cahoots with Allison."

"But you aren't, and you weren't. A jury will see that."

He looked over at her, his eyes weary. "You sure about that?" He set his coffee cup down on the table.

Mikey reached over and took his hand. "Absolutely, I am, Rem. You can't let all of this stop you from believing in yourself. The truth is all you need to say. The jury will know the difference between that and Measy's lies."

He squeezed her fingers. "Maybe."

"If you want Kate to offer the deal to Allison in order to move on and get your life back, I understand. No one will judge you for that. But if you want the chance to say your piece and tell the world exactly what that woman did to you, then don't be afraid to get up there on that stand and tell them everything. It might be cathartic." She paused. "And if Allison takes the stand and lies, then the jury will know that, too. Your story is far more believable than hers could ever be. And if she goes free, then at least you know you did your best, but I don't think she's going anywhere but straight back to prison, where she belongs."

He seemed to relax and glanced at her. "Thank you. That helps."

"I'm glad." His hand felt warm in hers, and she continued to hold it. "We haven't had many talks lately. I've missed them."

"I've missed them, too, but you know why I've been distant."

"Yeah. I know. But it stinks."

He smiled softly. "Maybe I can sneak out my window and meet you under the bleachers at the park."

"Margaret will never know." She smiled back. "We can hang out, talk, drink something tasty, and watch the stars." Her mind drifted to other things they might do, and her body warmed.

"That would be nice." He held her gaze, and she wondered if he was thinking the same thing.

They stared for a second before Rem, his cheeks pink, cleared his throat and looked away. "How's Mason? You heard from him?" He let go of her hand and reached for his coffee.

Mikey suspected she was a little flushed as well. What was the matter with her? She and Rem had had numerous conversations without getting uncomfortable. "We're waiting to hear from the facility. After this week, we're allowed to visit. I can't wait to see him."

"I bet. I'm sure he's eager to see you, too." He sipped his coffee. "He still doesn't know about Margaret?"

"Nothing. Which is for the best. I just hope you guys find her before Mason leaves rehab. Or he'll set out on a mission to hunt her down himself."

"You think that's what Margaret's waiting for? For Mason to get out?"

Mikey slumped. "I've thought about that. It wouldn't surprise me. It's enough time for her to reconnect with people, get settled somewhere, allow us to ease up, and wait for Mason."

"What do you think she's planning?"

Mikey shook her head. "I don't know. She's always harbored a grudge against Mason, and she hates me for no longer being under her thumb and making a life for myself, and also, well, for liking you."

"And she wants me because I'm the light." He cursed. "You think she really believes the crap Allison was spewing?"

"I have no idea what she believes anymore. At this point, she's so far down the rabbit hole, she can't see anything at the end of the tunnel. I think she's evil because she likes it. Victor had some sway over her, though, so maybe she buys all that light and dark stuff."

"Or she just uses it to scare people, especially me."

"Margaret could talk about snowbells and sleigh bells, and schnitzel with noodles and still be scary."

"And brown paper packages tied up with string," added Rem. "We should watch that movie. It might make us feel better."

"I'm game if you are."

He smiled. "How's it going with you and Trick staying at Mason's?"

"He's not a bad roommate, actually. We get along well and, thankfully, keep the same hours. And he's not a total slob, like some people I know."

Rem chuckled. "I've gotten better. It's amazing what a little cleaning will do to take your mind off things." He paused. "I'm glad he's nearby, though, because there's another thing I need to tell you."

"Oh, boy," said Mikey. "Do I need to brace myself?"

Rem eyed her, his expression somber. "Our police protection ends after this week. The Chief didn't see the need to continue it since nothing's happened."

Mikey reached for her coffee. "I'd be lying if I said I'm surprised. To be honest, I didn't think we'd keep it as long as we did." She drank from her cup.

"I'm sorry. I hate being the bearer of bad news."

"It's not your fault."

"It just sucks that Margaret has to hurt someone before we get any more help."

"It's kind of the way it works, unfortunately. Tell the truth, though. You think that squad car out there is going to stop her?"

He sighed. "No. I know it won't. But at least it offers some measure of comfort that someone's got your back."

"Daniels has your back, and so do I. Not that I can do much."

"You can do a lot," he said. "Just talking helps." He paused. "And I have your back, too. You and I are really the only two people who understand what the other is going through, and I appreciate that I can discuss it with you."

Hearing a tone in his voice, she narrowed her eyes. "You and Daniels doing okay? Obviously, you can talk to him, too."

"I try not to worry him. He's been through a lot with me, and I try to assure him I'm fine, but I know he can see through me."

"Fine? There's a madwoman running loose who may come after you, a trial looming that's going to dredge up a lot of hard memories, and you're still dealing with the trauma of what happened to you." She scoffed. "I can't imagine what's bothering you."

He set his elbows on his knees and stared off. "Yeah."

She put a hand on his wrist. "Daniels knows you're doing your best, but he also wants to be there for you. Don't be afraid to let him know if you're struggling. He'll be pissed at you if you don't."

"I know." He looked down and studied his shoes. "Listen, there's something else..."

"What is it?"

He blew out an uneven breath. "It's...it's..." He interlaced his fingers. "It's about Allison."

"What about her?"

"She...uh..." He set his jaw. "You know when I went to Merrimac?"

Mikey nodded. "To visit your aunt? Yes."

"I...um...I went there to get away."

"I don't blame you. You needed it."

"I did. I was having a hard time." He smoothed a wrinkle in his jeans.

She sensed his difficulty with what he was about to say. "You all right?"

Rem stood and shook out his hands. "God. I don't know why this is so hard."

Mikey put her coffee mug down. "What's the matter?"

Rem turned and stared down at her, his face tense. "I went to see Allison. In jail. Before I went to see my aunt."

Mikey took a second. "You went to see Allison?"

He ran a hand over his head. "Allison wanted to talk to me, and she found a way to get me there."

"Way? What way?"

"That's not important. What matters is what she told me."

Mikey stood. "What happened? What did she say?"

Rem put his hands on his hips. "She...uh...she told me..." He bit his lip. "Hell. She told me she—"

Mikey heard a door open, and the alarm beeped. "Shit. Hold on." She ran over to the computer, saw Kyle enter SCOPE on the monitor, and hit a few buttons. "Sorry."

"It's okay."

Knowing Kyle was about to walk in, Mikey raced to the door. "Hold that thought."

The inner door unlocked, and Mikey stopped as Kyle entered. "Hey, Mikey," he said.

She put a hand on his shoulder. "Hey, Kyle, listen. Can you—"

Kyle caught sight of Rem. "Oh, sorry. Am I interrupting? I finished up with the house clearing, and I was going to update the report, but I can come back later."

Mikey pushed on his shoulder. "That's probably a—"

"You're Kyle?" asked Rem. He stepped closer.

Mikey's heart thudded. This was not how she envisioned them meeting. And if she were honest, she'd hoped they'd never meet at all. "Rem..."

Rem held out a hand. "I'm Aaron Remalla. Mikey told me you were helping out at SCOPE. Nice to meet you."

Kyle's eyes widened. "You're the detective? Mikey told me about you, too. It's great to finally meet you." He shook Rem's hand warmly.

"It's kind of you to pick up the slack while Mason's away," said Rem. "I know Mikey appreciates it." He eyed Mikey.

"I do," said Mikey. Her mind raced with what to say. "Kyle's been a big help."

"It's been a blast," said Kyle. "I'm going to miss it when Mason returns. But at least once he's back, maybe Mikey and I can start getting coffee again." He smiled at her.

Rem nodded. "Mikey's an easy person to talk to. She's a good friend." He paused. "I should go."

Mikey raised a hand. "No, wait." She spoke to Kyle. "Can you give us a few minutes? Rem and I..."

Rem turned and grabbed his jacket from the couch. "It's okay. It's no big deal. I've got to get back to the station. Daniels will be wondering where I am."

Mikey struggled with what to say. "Rem—"

"Thanks for the coffee," said Rem.

"What about Allison?" asked Mikey. Rem was going to tell her something important, and now he was dodging it. "What did she tell you?"

Rem shrugged. "She told me she'd see me at trial, but she'd pull out all the stops to discredit me. You know the drill. Nothing I can't handle."

He shifted away from her and avoided eye contact, and she knew he was lying.

"It was nice to meet you, Kyle," said Rem, heading for the door.

"Nice to meet you, too," said Kyle. "Maybe one day we can all go out and you can tell me what it's like to be a detective."

Rem smiled, but it didn't reach his eyes. "Can't wait."

"I'll walk you out," said Mikey. She followed him into the outer office. "Rem, listen..."

Rem went to the outer door and opened it. "It's fine, Mikey. You and Kyle have work to do." Holding his jacket, he started to leave.

"Would you stop?" He hesitated at the door, and she held his arm. "I know you're not telling me everything. I can see it in your eyes and feel it coming from you. What is it?"

He stared for a second, and then his face relaxed. "It's nothing. I'm making a big deal out of it. I'm just sorting some things out, but it's all good." He eyed the interior. "Kyle seems nice."

"Damn it, Rem."

"I'll call you." He paused. "And be careful. Stick close to Trick and don't go anywhere on your own. You got it?"

"When will I see you again?"

He shrugged. "Time will tell. Take care."

Her heart dropped as he headed down the stairs.

Chapter Fifteen

MASON SAT IN GROUP as Amanda talked, but his mind wandered. It had been two days since talking to Carla about her suspicions regarding Windhaven, and he hadn't seen her since. The day after the proximity alarm had gone off, he'd waited for her at lunch, and then dinner, but never saw her. Worried, he'd asked a few people if they'd seen her, but no one seemed to know anything. He'd located her room and had knocked, but after not getting an answer, he'd opened the door. The room was empty except for a made bed, a desk with a lamp, and a side table. The bathroom was clean, but empty, too, and there were no clothes in the closet.

A member of the housekeeping staff had passed by, and he'd stopped and asked her about Carla. She'd smiled and told him that Carla had voluntarily checked out, and her room had been cleaned. Mason had asked for an explanation, but the woman didn't have one. She'd left, and he'd sat on the bed, wondering what to do next. Carla hadn't been due to leave for a few weeks, and she'd had no plans to stop therapy early. What had happened? Had someone found out about her prying into Windhaven and the strange deaths? Had Carla gotten too close for someone's comfort?

Mason had recalled Carla's writing. He'd searched the room but found no paper or notebooks. It was as if she'd never been there. Concerned, but determined to get answers, he'd left to search for someone who could tell him something. He'd eventually tracked down Candace, who was chattering to someone in the cafeteria. She'd confirmed the housekeeper's account and told him that Carla had exited abruptly and that she was just as disappointed about it as Mason. She'd placated him by telling him that some patients assumed they were well enough to go home despite their doctor's advice. She'd smiled then and reminded him of his upcoming appointment for a haircut and a shave.

Frustrated, Mason had spent the rest of the afternoon looking for and talking to anybody friendly with Carla, and asking what they knew about her departure, but none of them were any help.

"Mason?" asked Hamlish. "What do you think about Amanda's revelation? Can you relate?"

Mason blinked and looked around the room. All eyes were on him as Hamlish waited for a response. "Mason?" he asked. "You listening?"

Mason shifted in his chair. "I apologize, Amanda. My mind wandered, and I didn't hear what you said." He rubbed his scruffy jaw. "Can you repeat it?"

"Are you seeing another ghost?" asked Barry, leaning forward. "Is it my mom?"

Sadie snorted. "Oh, please."

"No," said Mason. "It's not a ghost." He paused. "I'm just a little distracted."

Amanda, who was wearing another set of baggy sweats, played with a strand of her hair. "I was saying I was nervous about coming here and revealing myself to others. I've never been comfortable with it. I prefer to stick to the shadows rather than come out into the light. I think it's because I don't think people will like me."

Hamlish waited, and Mason responded to Amanda. "I don't see anything strange about that. I think most of us here prefer the shadows. And we've hidden behind drugs and alcohol to protect ourselves. And I think we all fear not being liked."

Amanda nodded. "I guess."

Hamlish grasped his knee with his hands. "You're due for your first family visit soon, Mason. How are you feeling about it?"

He thought of Trick, Mikey, his girlfriend Valerie, and his brother Max. "I can't wait. I've missed them."

"Have you decided what you want to talk about?" asked Hamlish.

"Talk about?" asked Mason.

"You know," said Thomas with a grin. He wore a short-sleeved shirt, and tattoos ran up and down his forearms. "The doc wants to probe all the deep stuff." He rolled his eyes. "They love to make you cry around here. My first family visit? I bawled on my mom's shoulder for an hour."

"Mason doesn't have to discuss anything he doesn't want to," said Hamlish. He pointed toward Mason. "Although I encourage you to use this time wisely. If you have something you want to bring up, now's the time to do it."

"Like what?" asked Mason.

"Any deep, dark family secrets?" asked Charlie. "Any physical or sexual abuse, abandonment, or depression. Did your parents use drugs?"

Mason shook his head. "No. None of that."

Sadie rolled her eyes. "Now who's stuck in the shadows?"

Mason tried to think of what issues he might have. "I mean, my dad and I weren't close, but my mom and I were. My brother Max and I have had our problems, but we're working on them. And my sister Mikey and I have always shared a tight bond, and Margaret..." He gripped his armrest.

"Bingo," said Thomas. "Here come the true ghosts."

"Margaret?" asked Hamlish. "Your other sister?"

Mason had no doubt that Hamlish knew all about Margaret. "She's unstable and currently residing in a psychiatric facility. But that's nothing new to anyone. She's never been right in the head."

"How did it feel growing up with a sister like that?" asked Hamlish.

"How did it feel?" asked Mason. "It sucked."

Charlie chuckled. "I hate my sister, too. She's not in a psycho ward, but she ought to be."

"I didn't say I hated her," said Mason. "But Margaret has never had empathy for anyone, so I've never liked her." He picked at the seam in his pants. "She liked people's suffering back then. Still does."

"What'd she do?" asked Barry.

"What hasn't she done?" asked Mason. "She picked on all of us when we were little, especially me and Mikey because we were the youngest. She played mean tricks, made us look like idiots at school, bullied us and other kids. By the time we were teenagers, we barely talked to her, and then she left home right after high school graduation. She'd visit on occasion, but usually only when she wanted something. We all kept our distance though, except for Mom." He paused, thinking of his mother. "She always held out hope for Margaret until the end."

"Why is she in a psychiatric facility?" asked Sadie.

Mason crossed his arms. "She tried to slice my sister's throat and came close to causing the death of one detective and helped assault and almost murder another."

"Shit," said Thomas, his eyes wide. "I wouldn't want to meet her in a dark alley."

"No, you wouldn't," said Mason. "Neither would I."

"How do you feel about the havoc she's caused and the danger she presents?" asked Hamlish. "It can't be easy for a former Texas Ranger to deal with a mentally ill sister who commits terrible crimes."

Thomas furrowed his brow. "You're a paranormal investigator *and* a former Texas Ranger?"

Mason nodded. "I am."

"Damn. It's like we're in group therapy with Superman or something." Thomas slapped his knee.

Sadie grunted. "Please. It's not that big of a deal."

"I think it's cool," said Amanda.

"My cousin was a cop," said Charlie. "But he sucked at it." He raised his eyebrow. "Did you ride a horse?"

"Have you killed anyone?" asked Barry.

Hamlish raised his hands. "Okay, everybody. I realize it's exciting to meet a Texas Ranger, but let's allow Mason his time. You can ask him about his Ranger escapades outside of group."

Mason squirmed under the attention. "I've fired my weapon, Barry, but never killed anyone. Unfortunately, though, my partner has." He eyed Charlie. "And no, Charlie. I suck at riding horses. Much like your cousin does as a cop." He spoke to Hamlish. "And as far as dealing with an insane sister while being a Ranger, it didn't really matter. The only person who knew about her was my partner, and I didn't have much to do with Margaret by then, anyway."

Hamlish studied him, and Mason felt exposed, as if Hamlish knew more than Mason realized. "When did you start using drugs?" asked Hamlish.

Mason's heart rate picked up. "When I was a Ranger."

"You want to talk about that?" asked Hamlish.

"It's a little uncomfortable," said Mason. "It's not something I'm proud of."

"There's no judgement here," said Hamlish.

Mason picked at his pant seam some more but felt the eyes of the group on him. "I...uh...was struggling with my abilities at the time. I could see and hear things that others couldn't, like the dead victims of grieving family members. I didn't have good boundaries back then, and it all sort of came at me at once. Then I injured myself, and a doctor prescribed some pills."

"Famous last words," said Thomas. "Let me guess. You liked them."

Mason rested his ankle on his knee and fiddled with his pant leg. "They helped with my anxiety and seemed to slow down the visions, but after a while, I needed more to get the same effect, and I found more doctors who prescribed more pills." He paused. "And then I almost shot someone." He shook his head at the memory, realizing how close he'd come to losing everything. "Long story short. My partner figured out I was using, and I was so mortified by what I'd done and who I'd become that I stopped cold turkey. I didn't use again until..." He set his jaw and looked away.

"Until when?" asked Hamlish.

The group waited for Mason to answer, but he couldn't bring himself to speak. "Mason?" asked Hamlish.

Mason cleared his throat. "Maybe we save that for another meeting."

Hamlish paused. "We still have a few minutes."

"So talk to Sadie," said Mason. "She looks bored."

Sadie looked up from studying her nails. "What?" She straightened. "I'm listening."

Hamlish nodded at Mason, who looked away. "Okay. We'll pick up there when we meet next time."

"Mason looks thrilled," said Thomas. He checked his watch. "But now I have time to go hit the ice cream bar." He stood. "Anybody want to join me?"

"I will," said Amanda.

"Pass," said Sadie, standing.

"Do they have hot fudge?" asked Barry.

"I don't know," said Thomas. "Let's find out."

"Dairy doesn't agree with me," said Charlie. "But I love vanilla ice cream."

"You can come as long as you sit away from us," said Thomas. "Mason? You want any?"

Lost in his thoughts, Mason shook his head. "No thanks, Thomas. You guys enjoy some for me."

"Cool. I'll eat your scoop. See ya later." Thomas and the others left the room as Mason stood.

"You okay, Mason?" asked Hamlish as he began to gather and fold the chairs. "You were distant today."

Mason hesitated and debated whether to mention Carla. "Yeah. I guess I was."

"I heard you were looking for Carla Wilcox."

Mason stiffened. "I was told she left Windhaven early."

"It happens." He folded a chair. "Carla had some suppressed emotions. She'd gotten better at handling them, but sometimes they reared up on her."

"I talked to her the day before she left. She seemed fine. There was no indication that she was considering leaving."

"Just because she didn't mention it doesn't mean it wasn't on her mind. She may not have wanted to tell you."

"Carla was an open book."

Hamlish folded a chair. "Not about everything."

Mason sighed in frustration. "Is there any way I can get a hold of her? Can I call her to be sure she's okay?"

"We can't give out a patient's personal information. But if you want me to call her, I'd be happy to do it."

Mason nodded. "I'd appreciate it. I'd just like to know she's all right."

"Of course." Hamlish folded another chair. "You two were becoming good friends, weren't you?"

"I guess so. She was easy to talk to."

"Carla was friendly with most. She'd been here a few times and had gotten to know the staff. They liked her, too." He set the chairs against the wall. "She was assigned to me during her second stay. I always found her to be open and honest." He paused. "It's a shame she struggled as much as she did. She was a bright woman."

Mason frowned. "Why do you keep referring to her in the past tense?"

Hamlish stilled. "Only because she left and isn't here anymore. No other reason." He tilted his head. "Why are you so worried about her?"

Mason considered his answer. "She confided some things to me the night before she left, and I thought..."

Hamlish waited. "You thought what?"

Mason shook his head. "Nothing. It's nothing. I was just surprised."

"We were too. Let's just hope she lands on her feet and doesn't have to return here again."

"I agree."

Hamlish grabbed the last chair and set it to the side. "Did she tell you she was a writer?"

"Uh, yes, she did. That took me by surprise, too."

"She wrote a lot, apparently. About many things." Finished with the chairs, Hamlish faced Mason. "Did you ever read anything she wrote?"

An icy trickle of worry raced up Mason's spine. "No. I didn't."

"Too bad." Hamlish paused for a second before heading to the door. "I heard it was interesting stuff."

"I heard the same," said Mason.

"Guess we'll never know." Hamlish opened the door and looked back. "You have a nice evening, Mason. Maybe go get some of that ice cream with the others. Make some new friends."

Mason debated joining the group for a snack. "Yeah, maybe."

"Good." Hamlish smiled. "See you tomorrow."

Chapter Sixteen

MASON TOSSED AND TURNED in his bed, still thinking about Carla. Flipping onto his back, he stared at the ceiling and again thought back on his last conversation with her. She'd mentioned three people who'd died under strange circumstances. Amelia Iverhart, August Delroy, and Chauncey Pendleton.

Fluffing his pillow, Mason wondered about Carla's writing. Based on what she'd implied, she'd had a source at Windhaven who'd confirmed her theories and suspicions. But who was it? And what had Carla planned to do with her information? Was she writing a book? Was she going to the authorities? Had someone stopped her before she could reveal her findings?

Groaning, Mason rubbed his temples. Was he overthinking it all? Carla was on her third stint of rehab, and Mason hadn't known her that well. Had she just been looking for something to occupy her time? Was she delusional? Was she taking the explainable deaths of drug addicts and alcoholics and turning them into murders?

Mason closed his eyes and went quiet. It's what Mikey had suggested when he got into overdrive mode. He took long, deep breaths, relaxed his muscles and silenced his mind. It took a few minutes, but he eventually achieved a sense of peace and calm just as tingles ran up his arms and a chill ran through him.

Recognizing the signals, he opened his eyes to his dark room and slowly raised his head. The woman he'd seen during his detox stood in the corner as before, her nose bleeding and wearing the same black dress. Her dark hair fell over her shoulders, and she stared at Mason but didn't move.

Mason sat up slowly, not wanting to scare her away. He sensed an apprehension in her energy, and he could see it in her eyes. "Hello," he whispered.

She didn't react.

"I'm Mason," he said. "I remember you."

She blinked at him.

"You told me I should have listened."

Nothing.

"What should I have listened to?" He waited, but she didn't respond.

Her nose began to bleed from both nostrils. "What happened to you?" he asked. "Did someone hurt you?"

She squirmed as if she didn't like the question.

"Who hurt you?"

The woman spoke in a whisper. "She's dead."

Mason's chills turned ice cold, and he shivered. "Who's dead?"

"You should have listened." She took a step toward him.

Mason's heart raced. "Listened to who?"

"She knows." The woman took another step.

Mason didn't understand. "Who knows? Are you talking about Carla?"

The woman moved closer, and more bloody dribbles ran from her nose and dripped onto her dress. More coherent than before, Mason stayed put and tried to stay calm. "Were you a patient here?"

She spoke louder. "You should have listened."

Mason gripped the sheets as she encroached. "I don't understand."

The woman strode to the side of the bed, and Mason forced himself not to pull back. She was obviously trying to tell him something, and he had to figure it out.

Leaning over him, her dark eyes glittered, and a drop of blood fell from her nose. "She told me."

"Told you what?" Mason's heart slammed against his chest. "Who is she?"

"You know."

He shook his head. "But I don't."

She studied him and blinked again. "Find the notebook."

Mason swallowed. "What notebook?" A drop of blood dripped onto his sheets, and startled, he swiped at it. The blood evaporated, though, and when he looked up, the woman was gone.

❧

The next morning, he ordered his breakfast and, weary after a lousy night's sleep, he got himself some hot tea, still thinking about his encounter with the woman with the bloody nose. Who was she, he wondered? It wasn't Amelia

Iverhart, since Amelia had to be a good thirty years older. Sipping his tea, he considered where to sit in the dining room when he saw a familiar face. He recognized Susanna, the woman Carla had spoken to the night before the alarms had gone off. Hoping she might know something, Mason approached and sat beside her.

"Hello," he said. "Susanna, right?"

Slathering jam on a piece of toast, she widened her eyes. "Yes."

"We haven't formally met." He set his mug of tea on the table. "I'm Mason."

She set her toast down and wiped her hands on a napkin. "How are you?"

"I'm fine." He eyed her food. "I see you got the pancakes. How are they?"

"Delicious. But most everything here is, isn't it?"

Mason nodded. He had to admit that, since speaking to Candace, his food had improved dramatically. "I agree. My ahi tuna last night was some of the best I've ever had."

"I had that too." She smiled and held her chest. "And that chocolate cake. To die for."

"I bet Carla would have liked it."

Her expression fell, and she picked up her fork. "Probably."

Mason unfolded a napkin and set it on his lap. "I was surprised when I heard she'd left. She didn't strike me as someone who would stop treatment early. She seemed to be doing well."

Susanna picked up her glass of juice. "Surprised me, too."

"Did she mention anything to you about leaving?"

Susanna sipped her drink and set it down. "No, she didn't."

"How well did you know her?"

She cleared her throat. "Not very well. She was in my group though, and we were friendly."

Mason sensed her reluctance to talk to him. He softened his tone and leaned in. "Listen. I'm sorry if I'm making you uncomfortable. I'm just concerned. Carla and I had become friends, and she confided some things to me. I just want to be sure she's okay."

Susanna glanced at him. "I'm sure she's fine. Carla's a smart woman. She knows how to land on her feet."

"So you must have known her well."

She poked at her pancakes with her fork. "Carla...she's observant."

Mason perked up. "What did she observe?"

"I don't know. But I think it was touchy stuff."

"Why do you say that?"

She set her fork down. "Listen. I don't know you. And I don't think we should be talking."

"Why not?"

Susanna looked around the room. "Because someone knew what Carla was writing about. They watch us around here."

Mason lowered his voice. "Do you know what she was writing about?"

"She didn't tell me. But she considered it important enough to hide it."

"She hid her stuff?" He eyed the area, but no one seemed to be paying attention to them. "Where?"

Susanna huffed. "How should I know?" She stabbed at a piece of pancake. "I just know Carla was excited about something, and whatever it was, it was coming up fast. And then she was gone."

Mason tried to look casual and sipped his drink. "You don't have any idea what she was writing about?"

Susanna shook her head as she chewed. "By the way she talked about it, it was big. But I think she got caught before she could reveal what she'd found."

"Have you mentioned this to anyone other than me?"

"Hell, no. Carla told me that if something happened to her, not to say a word to anyone, unless it was someone I trusted who wasn't connected to Windhaven."

Mason leaned closer. "She thought something might happen to her?" He cursed, realizing now that Carla had indeed been onto something and wishing she'd told him more. "Isn't there someone you can trust who might help?"

Susanna raised an eyebrow at him. "No."

"What about calling the police?" he asked.

"Would you shut up?" She set her fork down with a clatter. "I've got two weeks left, and I intend to leave here upright, you get it?"

Mason held his breath. "You think Carla didn't?"

"I don't know, but whatever happened, it has something to do with this place. Besides, what would I tell them? I'm an addict, and so is Carla. Who's going to believe either of us, or you for that matter?" She wiped her mouth with her napkin. "My advice? Keep your head down, finish your therapy, and get out." She pushed her plate away and shoved her seat back. "What you do after that is completely up to you. But be careful because I think Windhaven's reach is farther than most think."

"Susanna—"

Susanna looked behind him and smiled. "Hey, Tracy. Good morning."

Mason went quiet.

"Good morning, Susanna," said a woman who walked up beside Mason's chair. She had stick-straight black hair that fell to her chin and framed her round cheeks. "How was breakfast?"

"Fantastic," said Susanna, "as usual."

"I'm glad," said Tracy. "You leaving?"

"Just finished." Susanna grabbed her juice glass and napkin. "I've got a painting class to get to." She stood.

"Mind if I sit?" Tracy asked Mason.

Susanna eyed Mason. "Have a good day," she said.

"You too," said Mason as Susanna walked away. He looked at Tracy. "Do I know you?"

She sat and held out a hand. "My name's Tracy. I'm Windhaven's nurse and nutritionist."

Mason shook her hand. "That's right. Candace mentioned you."

"How's your stay so far? Everything going well at Windhaven?"

Mason caught a few curious diners glancing toward them. "I can't complain. The therapy is challenging but helpful, and all the staff are pleasant."

"That's great to hear. Candace told me about your concerns with the food, and I wanted to check in and see if things had improved." She set her elbow on the table. "I talked to Manolo, and he had some wonderful suggestions."

"Well, whatever they were, they were great. Everything's been delicious since I spoke to Candace. Please convey my appreciation to Manolo."

"I will. He'll enjoy hearing you're happy. And I suspect because of you, the food will be better for everyone. Which is why we encourage our diners to speak up if they're unhappy. So, thank you."

Tracy seemed like another happy staff member eager to please, much like Candace, and Mason had to wonder if Carla had been barking up the wrong tree. "You're welcome. I'm not usually one to complain, but I'm glad I mentioned it." He paused. "You mind if I ask you something?"

"I'm happy to answer any questions. Shoot."

"You're a nurse?"

"I am. I work in the clinic. I help the new patients going through their detoxification and am available to assist with any minor injuries or illnesses. Plus, I keep track of patients' medications and prescriptions while they're here."

He nodded. "That makes sense. Did you know Carla Wilcox?"

She nodded. "I did. Nice lady."

"She left treatment early."

"I heard. It's disappointing, and it doesn't happen often, but we can't force someone to stay."

"I'd gotten to know her, and I found it odd she'd leave so abruptly. I was just wondering if she'd been to the clinic. Had she had any issues that might explain her disappearance?"

"Well, I can't discuss her ailments, but she stopped by once or twice. She could be a little accident-prone, but it was nothing serious."

"Accident prone?" He wondered what that meant.

"Yes." Tracy didn't elaborate.

A server came by and set Mason's plate of eggs and bacon in front of him. "Thank you," said Mason to the server.

"I'll let you eat," said Tracy, standing, "but if you have any other issues or concerns, please let me or Candace know." She smiled. "Enjoy your breakfast."

"I'm sure I will." Mason picked up his fork. "Thanks, Tracy."

She bobbed her head at him and walked away.

Watching her go, Mason decided then that he would keep digging. If something bad had happened to Carla, then he needed to know. And if she'd uncovered a terrible secret at Windhaven, then he'd do his damnedest to uncover it, too.

Chapter Seventeen

MASON SAT OUTSIDE THE small one-room salon where a woman named Tammy cut hair. After breakfast, he'd had a difficult individual session with Hamlish where Hamlish had attempted to get Mason to talk about his relationship with his mother. Thankfully, Hamlish had needed to head out early for a patient's scheduled family visit, and Mason had left, glad to be out of there. Killing time before his hair appointment, he'd headed to the library and perused the books and had asked the librarian about Carla, but she hadn't known her.

His appointment time nearing, he'd headed toward the hair salon and had passed a room where he'd been told family visits took place. The door was closed, and the small light above it was on, indicating that a session was in progress. Mason moved on, found the salon down the hall, and sat outside on a bench while Tammy finished with another patron.

While he waited, he considered what to do next about Carla. He'd asked Hamlish about whether he'd called her, and Hamlish had confirmed he had tried, but she hadn't answered, and he would try again later. Mason found it difficult to read Hamlish. The doctor was obviously well-versed in disguising any indication of what he was feeling or thinking. Not wanting to seem dubious, Mason hadn't pushed further, and they'd continued with the session.

Resting a booted foot on his knee, Mason recalled again what Susanna had said. Had Carla known that someone was on to her? Had she realized she was in danger and left? And the female spirit with the bleeding nose who'd told him to find the notebook, was she referring to Carla's writing? Had Carla hidden a notebook somewhere on the grounds? And if she had, could he find it?

"Mason?"

Startled out of his thoughts, Mason looked to see Candace walking toward him, her smile as wide as her eyes. "Hi, Candace."

She stopped beside him. "I've been looking for you." She put a hand on his shoulder. "I have great news. I just spoke to your sister, Mikey."

Hearing his sister's name, Mason sat up. "You did? How is she?"

"Delightful woman. I set up your first family visit for tomorrow at two. She'll be here with your girlfriend, Valerie, and your partner. Trick, is it?"

"Yes." Mason's heart thudded. He couldn't wait to see them.

She frowned. "Unfortunately, your brother Max is in Peru, so he won't be able to make it. But hopefully next time."

"That's Max. Duty calls, but that's okay."

She smiled again. "I'm glad. I can see you're excited. Sometimes our patients dread their family visits, but obviously that's not the case with you."

"I'm looking forward to it. This is the longest I've ever gone without seeing my sister since..." Mason recalled Mikey's time with Victor. "Well, in a while."

She patted his shoulder again. "Your sister said the same thing. I hope I'm around tomorrow and get the chance to meet them."

"I'm sure they'd like that."

She sat beside him. "Just so you know how it works, they'll come in and sign some paperwork. They can't bring you food or drinks, but I told your sister if they want to bring you any clothes or something from home, that's fine, although it is subject to inspection." She lowered her voice. "You'd be surprised how some will try to smuggle drugs to their loved ones."

"Hard to believe."

"And your family will have to leave their cell phones at the front."

"Understandable."

"Your visit will be for one hour in a designated family room with Dr. Hamlish leading it, and if you'd like, you can have fifteen minutes to show your family your room and visit in the lobby before they leave. That's usually only permitted, though on the first visit. After that, it's on an as-needed basis."

"Okay."

"We try to keep visits very structured so everyone knows what to expect and there are no misunderstandings. Seeing as we are an exclusive facility with some well-known patients, it's best to keep any moving around to a minimum." She leaned in. "Some people get a little star-struck, not to mention it violates other people's privacy."

"I get it. Not a problem."

"Wonderful." She stood. "After they arrive, we'll show them to the family room, which will be the one down the hall." She pointed to the door with the light on above it. "Be there at five till two and we'll show them in."

Mason sighed in anticipation. "I will. Thanks."

She clapped her hands. "And you'll have a fresh haircut and shave, too. What perfect timing."

"I can't wait." He touched his hair.

"Tammy's amazing. I think you'll be pleased. She's been here for years, and the patients love her."

"I bet." He immediately thought of Carla. Would Tammy know anything about her exploits? His hopes rose. Hair stylists typically knew a lot about their clients' secrets, and he hoped Tammy would be no exception. "I've been looking forward to it."

"I'm sure she'll be done soon. She's usually right on sched—"

The door down the hall flew open and banged against the wall. Mason heard shouting. "You don't understand. You never did." Barry stepped out of the family room, his face red and angry. "I hate you," he yelled.

Hamlish's voice traveled. "Barry. Please don't leave. Your father is trying—"

"I don't give a shit. I don't want to talk anymore," yelled Barry. "To any of you."

"Oh, dear," said Candace.

Barry turned and stomped down the hall toward Mason and Candace, swiping at his face. He passed them without a glance and disappeared around a corner. Hamlish appeared at the door. "Barry...wait," he said.

When Barry didn't return, Hamlish eyed the interior of the room, shook his head, then went back inside and closed the door.

"I guess that didn't go too well," said Mason.

Candace sighed. "Now you see why some don't look forward to their visits."

Mason couldn't imagine arguing like that with Mikey, Trick or Valerie. "Does it happen often?"

"Not usually. Dr. Hamlish handles it well, though. He'll give the patient time to cool off while he talks to the family for the remaining time. Sometimes it helps to speak with them without the patient in the room."

Mason hoped Barry was okay. "It's not easy, is it?" asked Mason. "For anyone."

She eyed him somberly, which he suspected was rare for her. "It never is."

The door to the salon opened, and a young woman with soft blonde highlights and smooth, flowing hair emerged. "Everything okay out here?" she asked.

An older woman with short layered white-gray hair and fine lines around her eyes and mouth popped her head out and looked down the hall. "We heard yelling."

"It's fine, Tammy. No need to worry," said Candace. "Justina, your hair looks amazing. I love it."

Justina touched her hair and grinned. "Tammy works wonders."

"That she does," said Candace.

The older woman eyed Mason. "You Mason?" she asked.

"It is," said Candace. "He's your ten o'clock."

"Great," said Tammy with a smile. "Come on in."

Justina and Candace said their goodbyes as Mason entered the salon and sat in the chair.

Tammy threw a cape around him and secured it behind his neck. "You're here for a shave and cut, right?" she asked.

"I am," said Mason. "But you can leave the mustache. Just trim it up."

"I haven't seen a handlebar mustache in years. Tom would be envious." She went to the sink and turned on the water.

"Tom?" he asked.

"Tom Philips. He's an actor who does Westerns. Finished treatment about a week ago. Said he'd admired cowboys from back in the day who'd had a handlebar mustache. He'd always wanted one, but his agent advised against it." The water began to steam, and she tossed a towel under the spray. "Too bad he didn't listen when it came to the drugs and booze." She laughed.

Mason's hope that Tammy was a talker bloomed. "I bet you've met all sorts of people doing this job. How long have you worked at Windhaven?"

"Almost eight years, and you bet I've met some people. I've done more celebs and rich people than Heidi Fleiss." She laughed again and squeezed out the towel.

Although Mason didn't know who she meant, he laughed, too, and kept up the conversation while Tammy steamed his jaw, applied shaving cream, and gave him a shave. Mason found her to be funny, personable and good at her job. She didn't nick him once. After the shave, she trimmed his mustache, sat him up and began to cut his hair. "I've been meaning to ask you something," she said, snipping with the scissors. "The administration here frowns on my getting too personal, but you don't strike me as someone who'd mind."

"Feel free," said Mason.

She stopped cutting. "Do you really talk to ghosts?"

He chuckled. "I do."

Her eyes widened. "I'd heard about people who could do that, but I've never met any before. Isn't it scary?"

"It can be, but I've gotten used to it over the years, and I'm usually good at keeping the bad ones at a distance." He thought of Mr. Dark, and a shiver ran through him.

"I find that absolutely fascinating." She went back to cutting his hair. "Have you always been able to do it?"

"Since I was a kid. I thought I was hallucinating at first, but my mom taught me how to handle it."

She stared at him in the reflection in the mirror. "Your mom could do it, too?"

"Not as well as I did, but she knew enough."

"Well, I'll be damned." She paused in her cutting and sighed, then shook her head and started to cut again. "Do you just get a feeling when they come around, or do you summon them?"

"Both, depending on the circumstances."

She snipped around his ears. "I don't suppose you're picking up on anything around me?"

Mason had half expected the question. When she'd started to cut his hair, a man had materialized behind her and had been watching and listening with a half-smile on his face.

"I am, in fact. There's a man standing behind you. He's enjoying our conversation."

She stopped and dropped her jaw. "What?"

Mason focused on the male spirit. "He's a little taller than you. With brown eyes and a warm smile. He's wearing a Grateful Dead t-shirt."

Her eyes filled. "Are you pulling my chain?"

"No. Not at all." Mason closed his eyes and listened. "He says he visits you often. He likes the changes you made to the house." He opened his eyes and watched tears spill down Tammy's lashes.

"Oh, my God," she said.

Mason picked up on something else. "He says he's glad you keep the letter by your bedside."

Tammy put a hand over her mouth. "He knows I read it?"

"He does." Mason paused. "He's not mad."

Tammy held the scissors and sat on the chair with the attached hair dryer. "Oh, my word. You have no idea the relief I feel."

Mason felt the warmth of love flow through him. "He says he cherished being your husband, and not to miss him too much, because he's there whenever you need him."

Tammy sniffed and grabbed a tissue from the counter. "I can't help it. I wish he were here every day."

"He is."

Tammy's husband slowly faded from view, happy his message had been conveyed.

"You okay?" asked Mason.

Tammy composed herself. "Is he gone?"

"For now."

She blew her nose. "I better pull it together or I'm going to run late." Wiping her eyes, she stood and dabbed at her face. "Thank you so much. I'd been carrying that worry around for a while now."

"Most of us carry around a lot of things we don't need to."

She tossed her tissue in the trash and blew out a breath. "I sure appreciate it. You ever need anything from me, you let me know." She grabbed the comb. "When you're out of here, you get free haircuts for life. I sometimes take clients at my home, and you'd be one of them."

Mason decided it was a good time to bring up Carla. "That would be great, but I'm actually curious about someone who was a patient here until recently."

She eyed his reflection. "Really? Who?"

"Carla Wilcox."

She nodded. "I know Carla. She's been in this chair a few times. I heard she left early. Damn shame. I hope she doesn't relapse again."

"You have any idea why she left?"

"No. Not really. She didn't talk about deep stuff like that with me."

"What did she talk about?"

"It's not so much talk as ask. She had a lot of questions." After combing his hair, she started cutting again.

"What kind of questions?"

"Usually about the staff. She was curious about a lot of them." She shrugged. "Not that I could tell her much. They don't confide in me like most."

"Anyone in particular she seemed to have more interest in?"

"Hmm. Let me think." She sighed and stared off. "She asked about Candace, Dr. Hamlish, Windhaven's nurse, Tracy, and even Manolo, the chef. Oh, and that horse fella, Kessler."

"Kessler?" asked Mason. "She asked about him?"

"She did. Carla liked to visit the stables and ride Storm. It may have had to do with her falling off Thunder and banging her head. She didn't usually ride him, but she did once or twice. And not long after that, she cut her hand. Tracy had to bandage her up."

Mason narrowed his eyes. Carla had never mentioned riding horses or even visiting the stables. "Are you sure?"

Tammy nodded. "I remember. She came in here with a bandage on her thumb. Said she'd been clumsy and sliced it in Storm's stall."

"When was this?"

"On her previous visit." Tammy stopped cutting and lowered the scissors. "Can I tell you something, just between you and me?"

Mason's heart rate picked up. "Of course."

"I wondered if she might have done it on purpose."

"You mean cutting her thumb? Why?"

Tammy eyed the door as if someone could be outside. "I think she wanted a reason to talk to Tracy, and maybe check out the clinic."

"Why do you say that?"

"Just a hunch. I think she had some suspicions about this place." She shook her head and resumed cutting.

"Suspicions? Like what?"

"I don't know, and I didn't ask. All I do is cut hair and leave it at that. I don't stick my nose where it doesn't belong."

Mason wondered why Carla would be interested in the clinic.

"And you know who else she asked about?" asked Tammy, her eyes wide. "Ruben Montes." She made a tsk-tsk sound with her tongue. "I told her to keep her distance from that man."

"Why? Have you cut his hair, too?"

"Oh, Lord, no. He's got his own people for that. But that man has a vibe I don't like. I almost bumped into him a year ago just walking down the hall. He smiled and said, excuse me, but I veered away. You may be able to pick up on ghosts, but I pick up on what I call the bad willies, and that man's got some." She leaned close. "You heard what he did?"

"I heard what he was accused of, but he was acquitted."

"Acquittal doesn't mean innocent in my book." She patted his shoulder. "I'll give you the same advice. Steer clear."

"What could he possibly do? Isn't he here for help like the rest of us?"

Tammy glanced at him in the mirror. "That man's here for a lot of different reasons, I suspect. And it may be for an addiction or maybe it's something else. I can't say for sure."

"But you suspect it's something not good?" He paused. "You think Carla was thinking the same thing?"

Tammy set the scissors down and picked up the clippers. "I see that look in your eye. It's the same look Carla had." She flicked on the clippers and shaved the hair at Mason's neck. "I'll tell you the same thing. Be careful. Some things are meant to stay secret."

"You think these secrets have anything to do with why Carla left early?"

Tammy paused mid-shave. "I mentioned how she fell off Thunder?"

"You did."

"Carla wasn't sure if that was an accident. She'd wondered if the horse had been deliberately spooked." She whispered in his ear. "And if she left Windhaven voluntarily, I'll shave my own head."

Chapter Eighteen

MIKEY SIGNED IN AT the front desk along with Trick and Valerie. The receptionist took their phones and asked them to sign some paperwork regarding the rules of the facility and patients' privacy. Eager to see Mason, she signed it and slid it back. Trick and Valerie did the same.

"This place reminds me of my second stepdad's house," said Trick. "I could never get in and out of there without an interrogation."

"I guess they have to be careful," said Valerie, "considering their clientele. They probably have paparazzi snooping around."

The receptionist checked their paperwork and asked to see Mikey's bag.

"It's just a blanket." Mikey handed it over the counter.

The woman dug through it and handed it back. "Just wait in the lobby. Someone will be out in a minute to show you back. You can pick up your phones on the way out."

Trick nodded and thanked her, and they went to the couch and sat.

Mikey admired the ornate lobby with large landscape art and big potted plants. Wide windows provided ample light. "Some place, huh?"

"Red definitely lucked out in the fancy department." Trick looked around. "I wonder if they really teach art classes here. You think Red's learned how to paint?"

Mikey and Valerie frowned at him. "I doubt it," said Valerie.

"Me too," said Mikey. She eyed the bag with the blanket and pulled it closer. The blanket had belonged to their mom, and Mason kept it at the foot of his bed. Mom had always wrapped it around her shoulders when she'd been cold, and Mason had requested it after she'd died. Mikey figured it would be a little taste of home while Mason was here.

A minute passed, and Mikey heard the click of heels against the tiled floor and a woman's voice. "Mikey Redstone?"

Mikey turned to see a pretty lady with bouncing blonde hair and bright blue eyes approach. She held out a hand and smiled, and her teeth were blazing white. "I'm Candace. I spoke to you on the phone. I'm so excited to meet you."

Mikey stood along with Trick and Valerie. "Hi, Candace." She shook hands with her and introduced Trick and Valerie.

"Dr. Hamlish would normally greet you, but he's slightly delayed, so he asked me to show you back." She clapped her hands together. "Mason is so eager to see you."

Mikey couldn't help but return the smile. "We feel the same."

"How is he?" asked Trick.

"He is fantastic," said Candace, waving a hand. "Follow me and see for yourself."

"I don't know why I'm so nervous," said Valerie.

"It's perfectly normal," said Candace, heading down a long hallway. "It's a big day." Candace turned and headed down another hall, and they stopped just before a door. "Your session will be in here, and it will last about an hour. Dr. Hamlish will be in soon. In the meantime, go say hi to Mason." She beamed another smile at them, walked to the door and opened it.

Mikey entered and saw Mason standing beside a big window with a willowy tree and a manicured lawn outside. He turned and before he could say a word, Mikey darted in, dropped the bag and ran into his arms, giving him a big hug. Tears sprang into her eyes, and she felt him hug her back.

"Hey, sis. How are you?" he said.

"I've missed you." She sniffed and pulled back. "It's so good to see you."

Mason's own eyes watered, and he smiled. "I've missed you, too."

"Damn, Red," said Trick. "Look at you. It's like you just stepped out of Ranger training."

Mikey stepped back, and Mason shook Trick's hand and pulled him in for a warm hug. "Thanks to you," said Mason, "I wouldn't be here otherwise."

They patted each other's backs, and Trick cleared his throat. "You're a sight for sore eyes, partner," said Trick. His voice thick, he pulled away. "Valerie's waiting."

Mason sniffed and wiped at his eye. "Hey, Val."

Valerie stepped close. "Hey, handsome." He gave her a quick kiss, and they hugged warmly.

"God, it's good to see you," said Mason. He loosened his hold and looked down at her. "You been okay?"

She slid her hand into his. "We've been okay. But I hate not seeing you every day." Her gaze traveled over him. "Trick's right, though, you look good. You've lost weight."

"Not much," said Mason.

"And you've got a twinkle in your eye," said Mikey. "I haven't seen that since before Mom died." She picked up the bag. "I brought you something."

Mason took the bag and opened it. He stared and then pulled out the blanket. "Mikey, you brought me the blanket?" He held it.

"I did. I thought you might like to have it while you're here."

Mason nodded, and his eyes watered some more. "Thank you. That means a lot."

"You're welcome," said Mikey. "I think it will be a good reminder that Mom's with you, too."

"I'm sure she is," said Mason. He set the bag down and put the blanket back in it.

Composing themselves, the siblings sniffed and wiped their eyes.

"Look at us," said Trick. "It's like we haven't seen you in years." He grabbed a tissue box from the end table beside the couch and offered it to Mikey and Valerie. They each took one and dabbed their eyes. Mason took one too, and Trick pulled one out and set the box down.

"Why don't we sit?" said Mason, wiping his nose. "We might as well catch up before Hamlish comes in and gets all serious."

Mason took a seat beside Valerie on the couch, and Mikey sat with Trick on another couch facing them. An empty chair had been placed between the sofas.

"How's SCOPE?" asked Mason. "It still up and running?"

"It is," said Mikey. "It was rough at first, but things are smoothing out."

"Mikey's been doing a fantastic job keeping everything afloat," said Trick. "You'd be proud."

"I'm always proud," said Mason. He eyed Mikey. "You've always been the one to right the ship, and it doesn't surprise me you did it again." He paused. "How have you handled the paranormal cases?"

"Kyle Willow," said Mikey, trying not to show any reaction. "He's been helping us."

"Really?" asked Mason, raising a brow. He paused. "You two seeing each other?"

Mikey shook her head. "No. Gosh. Not right now. It's a professional arrangement. We're just friends."

Mason held her gaze. "Good. I'm glad it's working out."

"He's been a huge help, Red," said Trick. "Guy knows his stuff. And the clients like him."

"Valerie's helped with a few cases, too," said Mikey, eager to change the subject.

Mason took Valerie's hand. "You have?"

Valerie shrugged. "Nothing big. Just whatever I can do to help."

"How's your brother?" asked Mason.

Valerie nodded. "He's doing okay. He's got a birthday coming up, so I'm flying out to Texas this evening to see him."

"That's great. I'm sure he'll be happy to see you," said Mason. He squeezed her hand and looked at Trick. "And you look like you're recovering well."

Trick patted his stomach. "Almost good as new. Mikey won't let me miss any physical therapy sessions."

"And I make sure he gets a decent breakfast," said Mikey.

Mason frowned. "Breakfast?"

Mikey inwardly cursed. She forgot Mason didn't know that she and Trick were staying at his house because of Margaret.

"Oh...uh, yeah," said Mikey, glancing at Trick. "We're, uh, staying at your place." She couldn't bring herself to lie.

"My place?" asked Mason.

"Mikey insisted, Red," said Trick. "After you came here and I got out of the hospital and recuperated, she wouldn't let me back at SCOPE until I agreed to come stay with her at your house so she could keep an eye on me." He shot a knowing look at Mikey. "You know how your sister can be."

Mason looked between them. "Don't I ever. It's a good idea, though. You suck at watching out for yourself." He spoke to Mikey. "Thanks for taking care of him."

"It was for my benefit as much as his," said Mikey. "I didn't need him collapsing on me in the middle of a case. I need his warm, upright body in a chair to help with the non-paranormal stuff."

Mason nodded. "I'm glad you two are taking care of each other. Have you had any interesting cases?"

Mikey thought of Gina Rodriguez. "You could say that."

"Nothing we can't handle," said Trick.

Mason nodded. "Good. How's Rem and Daniels?"

"Fine," said Mikey. "Just fine." She hadn't talked to Rem since he'd left SCOPE a couple of days before.

"The drama continues," said Trick.

"No, it doesn't." Mikey glared at him.

"Something tells me it does," said Mason.

Mikey crossed her arms. "We're here for you. Not me."

"Oh, I don't know," said Mason, with a gleam in his eye. "Maybe Dr. Hamlish can fit you in for a few minutes."

Mikey dropped her jaw. "Don't you dare."

"Did I hear someone say my name?" A middle-aged man walked in with a beard and graying hair. He stopped and smiled. "I see Candace got you and your family together."

"She did," said Mason.

"Sorry to be late," said Hamlish, closing the door.

"It's okay," said Mason. "We were catching up."

"I can see that." Hamlish walked around, introducing himself and shaking hands. Mikey found him to be warm and friendly.

Hamlish sat in the chair. "I just want to thank all of you for coming. I know things like this can be stressful, but I know how much you all mean to Mason, and it's wonderful you showed up for him today."

"We wouldn't be anywhere else," said Valerie.

Mikey nodded and situated herself on the couch, facing Hamlish. "How's everything been going with his treatment? He hasn't been difficult, has he?"

Hamlish regarded Mason. "Would you like to answer that?"

Mason sighed. "I've had my days. Detoxing was rough. It took longer than I thought, and then when that was done, I had to get used to the talking part. That hasn't been easy for me. But I've met some good people here. The staff is excellent, and I'm getting better with the group therapy. And I even rode a horse."

Trick snorted. "You're kidding."

"Nope," said Mason. "I was sore for days though, but I'm due for another lesson tomorrow, so we'll see how it goes."

"Now I know this place works miracles," said Mikey.

"Can you turn water into wine?" Trick asked Hamlish.

"Not yet," said Hamlish, "but we're working on it." He crossed his legs. "So, I usually like to keep family visits informal, especially the first one. They're once a week, but if additional visits are needed, they can certainly be arranged. While some patients are allowed a phone call every seven days, I ask that you refrain from that for the next month until we have a few of these visits and establish a comfortable dynamic."

"No phone calls?" asked Mason.

"Just at first," said Hamlish. "I don't see it being an issue, but I've had patients who've had initial friendly visits only to get in touch by phone and have a huge fight. Then, the visits become more difficult, if they happen at all. Let's see how it goes after we meet a few times, okay?"

Mikey detected an edge of concern in Mason's tone, but then he relaxed.

"Okay," said Mason.

"Great," said Hamlish, relaxing back in his seat. "Then let's get started. We'll keep it simple. Anyone have any questions for Mason or me?"

The next fifty minutes were filled with Mason and Dr. Hamlish filling all of them in on Mason's treatment, struggles and successes, and what was expected next. They had a good conversation, and before Mikey knew it, the hour was over, and knowing they would have to leave, an unexpected sadness fell over her.

Hamlish smiled. "This has been a good first session. Next week, though, it's your turn to talk about your experience with Mason's addiction, so bring to the table whatever's been on your mind. No question is off-limits. And we'll go for ninety minutes, so Mason will have plenty of time in the hot seat."

"Lucky me," said Mason. He squeezed Valerie's fingers. "I just want to thank you all for coming. I know I still have a long road ahead of me, but this makes it easier, knowing you've all got my back."

"A hundred percent, Red," said Trick.

"Whatever you need," said Valerie.

"I know you said you're proud of me," said Mikey, "but it goes both ways. What you're doing here takes a lot of courage, and I'm super proud of you, Mason."

"Thanks, Mikey," he said, his voice soft.

Hamlish stood. "Then we'll end it here. Mason, if you'd like to show them back to your room and drop off the blanket, that's fine, and then you can have a few minutes to walk them to the lobby and say goodbye." He checked his watch. "Same time next week?" he asked.

Everyone nodded.

"Great." Hamlish walked to the door while everyone stood. "I'll head to our group meeting, Mason. You can join us after you see them out. It was nice meeting everyone."

Mikey, Trick and Valerie said goodbye, Hamlish left, and they followed Mason out of the room and down the hall.

Trick looked around. "Any celeb sightings, Red?"

"Yes," said Mason, "but not that I would know it."

Mikey didn't see anyone else. "It's so quiet."

Mason turned a corner. "They ask patients not to hang out in their rooms during the day. Being by yourself invites depression, and they provide plenty of activities to keep people occupied."

"You take any art classes yet?" asked Trick.

"Not yet, but I don't think painting's my strong suit," said Mason. Holding Valerie's hand, he stopped at a door and opened it. "It's nothing fancy, but it's home for the next couple of months."

Mikey walked in to see a sparse room with a bed, end table and lamp, along with a desk, bureau and private bathroom. One window looked out onto the grounds. "I can see why you wouldn't stay in your room." She pulled the blanket from the bag and laid it on Mason's bed. "That's nice. It warms the place up a bit."

Mason smiled. "Thanks. It feels better in here already."

"Do you get lonely?" asked Valerie. "Being around strangers and away from home?"

"I was at first," said Mason. "But then I started to meet people, and I've made some friends."

"Anybody famous?" asked Trick.

"Not famous, but definitely interesting." Mason walked to his desk and opened a drawer. He pulled out a piece of paper with writing on it and found a pen. He wrote something else, then folded it and put it in his pocket. "Let's head back to the lobby before Candace tracks us down and chatters on about my excellent progress and fantastic haircut."

"She is a happy gal, isn't she?" asked Trick.

"Your hair does look good," said Valerie.

"Thanks," said Mason, touching his hair. "Candace is the patient liaison." He walked out the door. "I guess it's her job to be happy."

They followed him out, and Mason shut the door behind him.

"Patient liaison?" asked Mikey. "That sounds fancy." They walked down the hall toward the front of the facility.

"Can she get you chocolate and a massage?" asked Valerie.

"Maybe," said Mason. "I haven't asked." He pointed. "Go to the end and turn right."

"Maybe you should," said Trick. He narrowed his eyes. "And what's up with the horseback riding?" he asked. They turned the corner, and Mikey saw the lobby.

"Figured now's as good a time as any," said Mason. "Plus, I think the stables might hold something interesting."

"Like hay and horseshit?" asked Trick.

They entered the lobby and approached the front desk. "Something like that," said Mason.

Sad that they were leaving, Mikey took her cell phone from the receptionist, as did Trick and Valerie.

"You mind if I walk them out, Gloria?" Mason asked. "I swear I won't make a run for it." He grinned at her.

Mikey recognized that look. Mason flashed that grin whenever he was turning on the charm and wanted something.

Gloria seemed to hesitate, eyed all of them, but then relaxed. "Sure." She hit a button, the door buzzed, and Mason followed them outside. "Back in a sec," he said to Gloria.

Gloria nodded and went back to studying something on the desk.

They stopped on the front steps. "I'm going to miss you, but I'll see you next week," said Mikey. She hugged him hard.

"It'll be here before you know it," said Mason. He gave Valerie a kiss and a hug. "Say 'hi' to your brother."

"I will," said Valerie.

"See you next week, Red," said Trick. He shook Mason's hand, and he and Mason hugged warmly.

Mason pulled back and glanced behind him. "Before you go, I need a favor." He pulled the paper out of his pocket.

"Favor?" asked Mikey. She eyed the paper as he handed it to her. "What's this?"

"Don't open it right now," said Mason. "Take it to the car."

"Everything okay?" asked Valerie.

"What are you up to, Red?" asked Trick.

"It's probably nothing," said Mason, "but I need some information. And you'll need to get it for me."

Mikey slid the paper into her pocket. "Is it serious?"

"I hope not." Mason rubbed his jaw. "But if it is, I need to do something about it."

"You're in treatment," said Valerie.

"And I intend to stay in treatment," said Mason. "This shouldn't interfere with that. But someone could be in trouble, and waiting could be detrimental for her and maybe the rest of us. But I won't know until I get more information."

Trick dropped his jaw. "Are you working a case? Inside Windhaven?"

"Are you in danger?" asked Mikey. She wanted to read the paper but forced herself to wait.

Mason shook his head. "No. I'm not. But somebody else might be." He glanced back inside again. "I need to get back. Just read the paper and see what you can find out."

"Do I need to cancel my trip?" asked Valerie.

"On the contrary," said Mason. "Don't cancel anything. Stick to your routines, and we'll figure out the next steps when you return."

"How will we communicate?" asked Trick.

Mason held Trick's look. "Just read my notes. And I'm sorry about the secrecy stuff. I just have to be careful."

Mikey didn't like what he was implying. "Mason...," she said.

"Don't worry." He took her hand and held it. "Trust me." He let her go. "I've got to get to group. I love you guys. See you next week."

He turned and knocked. The buzzer sounded, and he walked back into Windhaven.

Chapter Nineteen

THEY RETURNED TO TRICK'S truck and got in. Mikey pulled the paper from her pocket and held it out. She recognized Mason's familiar scrawl. Trick leaned to look, and Valerie slid forward from the back seat to read it.

Check out Carla Wilcox. She's had three stints in WH and left abruptly a few days ago without warning before her ninety days were up. Is she okay?

She'd been investigating three suspicious deaths of former patients. Check out –

Amelia Iverhart

August Delroy

Chauncey Pendleton

I need to know what happened to all of them. Thanks.

And added below it...

Trick – I'll need your help. We need to pull a Jack Del Rio next week.

Trick took the paper from Mikey.

"What is he up to?" asked Mikey.

"Who is Carla Wilcox?" asked Valerie.

"I think we're about to find out," said Trick. He lowered the paper.

"Suspicious deaths?" asked Mikey. "What is he talking about?"

"It sounds like Mason's worried that Carla discovered something about these three people and it wasn't good," said Trick.

"And he's trying to find out what she knew?" asked Valerie. "What the hell is he thinking? He's in the middle of therapy."

"That's Red," said Trick. "Always helping the underdog."

Mikey eyed Trick. "And what does he mean by pulling a Jack Del Rio?"

Trick smirked. "Just something from our Ranger days." He paused and folded the letter. "It means be careful. He knows how I like to run my mouth, and usually at the wrong time."

"You think I should stay here?" asked Valerie. "I don't want to leave if he's in danger."

Trick glanced back at her. "My advice is to do as Mason said. Stick to our routines. I'm sure if he was concerned, he'd have us contact Rem and Daniels. You go to Texas, and Mikey and I will check out the names and see what we find. Hopefully, it's nothing like Mason says."

"You'll let me know if it's more than that?" asked Valerie.

Mikey nodded. "Of course. Go see your brother and I'll keep you posted." She raised a brow at Trick, sensing that the Jack Del Rio reference had nothing to do with being careful. "And we'll meet up again next week." She paused. "But how are we going to tell Mason what we've learned if he wants to keep this secret?"

Trick handed the paper back to Mikey. "You let me worry about that." He started his truck, backed up and drove down the driveway.

Mason approached the stables. Not seeing Kessler, he entered and wandered through the stalls. Thunder quietly ate some hay, and Mason passed him and went to Storm's enclosure. Seeing him, Storm stuck her head out, and Mason patted her neck and rubbed her nose. "Hey, girl," he said. "I hear you know my friend, Carla."

Storm bobbed her head, and Mason looked around her and into the stall. He saw hay and dirt, and that was it. The horse nickered, and Mason ran a hand down her face. "She tell you anything important?" he asked. "Because I could use the help."

Storm bobbed her head some more but offered no information.

"Hi, Mason."

Mason turned to see Kessler enter the barn aisle. Carla had mentioned he had a Jimmy Stewart look about him, and since Mason knew who that was, he had to agree Carla was right. Kessler had a long and lanky frame and a face that invited conversation and trust. Holding a saddle, he wore battered jeans and boots and a black leather vest over a dusty long-sleeved blue shirt.

Mason patted Storm's neck again. "How are you?"

Kessler eyed Storm and then Mason. "You're early."

"I had a few minutes, so I thought I'd say hello to Storm and Thunder."

"Don't forget Tinkerbell. You'll hurt her feelings."

Mason regarded the horse in the stall next to Storm's. "Tink and I will no doubt have plenty of time for conversation today."

Kessler smiled. "I expect so." He set the saddle on the ground and pulled off his gloves. "How's it going?"

"Pretty well. I've settled in. Saw my family yesterday."

"That's terrific. Good for you."

Mason recalled his day after leaving Mikey, Trick and Val. He'd attended group therapy; everyone was there except Barry. Hamlish had encouraged Mason to discuss his visit and had tried again to lead him toward the subject of his mother. Mason had once more avoided the topic, and after therapy ended, had spent the rest of the day conversing with others, hoping to learn more about Carla. He'd discovered that she was an accomplished rider with an affinity for Storm, but she'd revealed none of that to Mason, and he wanted to know why.

Kessler walked up to the stall. "You thinking about graduating up to Storm?" He patted the animal's mane.

Mason chuckled. "Not yet. A few more sessions with Tinkerbell would be safer." He paused. "I heard Storm's a great horse, though. Didn't Carla like to ride her?"

Kessler's hand stopped, and he stared for a second. "You know Carla?"

"I was getting to know her. She introduced herself and we hit it off, but then she up and left out of nowhere."

"I heard."

"Did she mention anything to you about leaving?"

Kessler dropped his hand from Storm's neck. "I tend the horses, Mason, not the patients." He turned. "I'll get Tink saddled up."

Mason followed. "How well did you know her?"

"I know Tink pretty well."

Mason smirked. "I mean Carla."

Kessler picked up the saddle. "We were friendly." He walked to Tinkerbell's stall. "She'd been in Windhaven more than once."

"Did you teach her to ride?"

Kessler stopped and faced Mason. "You're asking a lot of questions about a woman you were just getting to know."

Mason joined him outside Tinkerbell's stall. "I knew her well enough to consider her a friend, and when she left without notice, I was concerned."

"Concerned about what?"

Standing there, Mason summed up that Kessler was a cool customer. Unlike Tammy, he was not an open book, but was it because he was protecting Carla, or protecting himself? "She told me a few things about Windhaven."

Kessler furrowed his brow. "Like what?"

Mason paused, debating how much to say. "A few suspicious deaths."

Kessler set the saddle down. "It's a drug treatment center. It helps most, but not all. What's strange about that?"

"Carla thought how they died didn't make sense."

"Carla thought a lot of things." Kessler pulled out his gloves and put them back on. "I wouldn't put too much stock in Carla's theories."

"Why do you say that?"

Kessler opened Tinkerbell's stall. "She thought the moon landing was faked, that the Mob killed Kennedy, that aliens exist and walk among us, and she even went to a flat-earther meeting once. Thank God she didn't go back."

"Other than the flat-earther thing, most people agree with her. That doesn't make her questions about Windhaven any less important."

Kessler studied him. "Why are you here, Mason?"

"To get a riding lesson."

"No. Why are you at Windhaven?"

Mason hesitated. "To treat an addiction to painkillers."

"My advice?" said Kessler. "Focus on you right now. Whatever Carla was or wasn't into, isn't your business."

Mason set his jaw. He didn't know whether Kessler meant to help or harm, but until he pushed some buttons, he'd never know. "Do you know what she was investigating? Is that why Carla visited the stables?"

Kessler raised the side of his lip and rested his forearms on the edge of the stall door. "I heard you're a former Texas Ranger."

"I am."

Kessler nodded. "I can appreciate that. I can imagine the things you've seen and done and the perpetrators you've caught, but this is not Texas, Mason, and you are no longer a Ranger. You're a man getting treated for an addiction."

Mason narrowed his eyes, uncertain what to think.

"I'll tell you what I would tell anyone else. Stick to the program, finish your treatment, and get out of here." He straightened. "And don't relapse." He turned toward Tinkerbell and patted her neck. "I'll get Tink saddled, and we'll start your lesson."

Frustrated, Mikey closed her laptop.

Trick looked up from his desk. "Problems?"

"I can't find anything about Carla Wilcox. At least not one who's been in Windhaven three different times."

Trick leaned back in his seat. "Nothing on social media?"

"Nothing. You'd think she'd at least have a mug shot or something."

"Maybe she's never been arrested."

"I just figured she might have had some problems with the law considering her history." She scratched her head. "The problem is, I don't have much to go on. I don't have an address or next of kin. Mason didn't give us much information. I even tried calling Windhaven."

Trick held a pen and chewed on the end of it. "How'd that go?"

"It didn't. I told them I was Carla's sister and was looking for her, but they wouldn't tell me squat."

"Not surprising. They probably have gossip mags trying to get personal stuff on their clientele all the time. Unless you've got a court order, they won't say a word."

"So, I'm stalled. How about you?"

"I found the other names Red listed. Amelia, August and Chauncey. Amelia and August died of drug overdoses. Amelia died at Windhaven after supposedly getting hold of drugs from an unknown source, and August after leaving treatment early. Both families believe something was amiss. Amelia's daughter had spoken to her mom the day before her departure, and her mother was excited to come home and meet her grandchild. Amelia was also an alcoholic, not a drug user, so the fact that she took pills didn't make sense. August's wife said when he came home, he'd initially been fine. It had been explained to her that he'd been released early due to a chronic illness. They'd gone to the doctor, but August had seemed okay, although mentally, he'd been detached. Not long after, he'd left to get some groceries and hadn't returned. They'd found him in the alley after overdosing, and he died at the hospital. His wife still doesn't understand it."

Mikey tapped on her desk. "Both of those deaths are suspicious."

"They may be, but there's nothing to prove they're criminal. We both know that addicts can act one way and then do something completely the opposite. They're good at hiding things, especially when it comes to using. They may have been suicidal."

"So if Windhaven has something to do with these deaths, the odds of proving it are slim to none." Mikey shook her head. "What about Chauncey Pendleton?"

Trick read from his notes. "Collapsed and died at Windhaven, but not from an overdose. Family was told it was a heart condition caused by all the damage from his drug abuse." He lowered his notes. "Apparently, he was a hardcore user. He was lucky to be alive at all."

Mikey eyed the ceiling. "That's not going to help us either."

"No. It isn't."

"You think we're chasing windmills?" asked Mikey. "Is Carla barking up the wrong tree?"

"If we could find her, we could ask her."

Mikey groaned. "I could call Rem." She fiddled with the pencil on her desk.

"You could. I'm surprised you haven't already."

Mikey stood and walked to the coffee machine. "I guess I've been hoping he'd call me, considering how he left the other day." She pulled a mug off the shelf.

"You think meeting Kyle bothered him?"

"It didn't thrill him, that's for sure. And the timing was horrible." Remembering the encounter, she inwardly cringed. "He was about to tell me something." She pulled out the coffeepot and filled her mug.

"I'm sure if it's important enough, he'll tell you eventually."

"I suppose." Mikey put the pot back and added creamer and sugar. "I just felt terrible." She stirred the brew and took a sip.

"Terrible about what? You didn't do anything."

She turned toward him. "I never expected Kyle and Rem to meet. And then when it happened, it felt like this odd betrayal."

Trick put his pen down. "Mikey, you're not with either of them." He pointed. "And maybe this is a good thing. They each know their competition now."

"Competition?" Mikey frowned. "I'm not a prized cow."

"No, you're not. But you're a woman, and you've got two men who like you. We already know where Kyle stands, and Remalla's only shortcoming is that he's plagued by his trauma and is hesitant to act. Which is understandable, considering. The question really falls to you, Mikey." Trick rested his elbows on the desk. "If both of them were outside the door right now, vying for your affection, who would you choose?"

Mikey sipped her coffee, but her stomach churned. "You're loving this, aren't you?"

Trick grinned. "It's like our mini version of *The Bachelorette*."

Mikey glared. "Can we get back to business, please?"

"Suit yourself." He closed his laptop. "You going to call Rem?"

Mikey slumped. "I can't win, can I?"

"That's what's so interesting about this," said Trick. "You actually can. Both men would actually suit you well. They're smart, handsome and would treat you like a queen. You really can't go wrong."

"Except telling one of them that they're not the one."

Trick shrugged. "There is that."

Mikey closed her eyes and sighed. Thinking of another issue, she opened her eyes. "What does it matter, anyway? Even if Rem could dig up some information on Carla, how are we going to tell Mason any of it? We can't exactly discuss it during our session with Dr. Hamlish."

"We don't have to worry about that."

"What do you mean we don't have to worry about it?" She noted Trick's expression. "What do you know that I don't?" She raised her eyebrows. "Does this have something to do with that Jack Del Rio reference?"

He smirked. "Maybe."

Mikey walked closer to his desk. "Don't give me that maybe crap. What do you know?"

Trick stared off, before crossing his arms. "I didn't want to mention it with Valerie around because Miss Vain would not have approved." Trick eyed Mikey. "But I'll need your help."

Mikey scowled at him. "How nice of you to include me. What the hell is going on?"

Trick swiveled toward her in his seat. "When Red and I were Rangers, we had a suspect in a murder investigation named Jack Del Rio. Real squeamish guy.

Paranoid as hell. We suspected he'd killed his mother because he was under some delusion that she'd formed a group composed of people who wanted to kill him."

"Was he on drugs?"

"Not that we could tell. He was bipolar and likely had a personality disorder. He somehow got it in his head that the people close to him wanted him dead. His mother had been shot while leaving a convenience store, and everyone we spoke to claimed Jack had to be the killer. The problem was we couldn't prove it."

Holding her coffee, Mikey leaned against the back of the couch. "Jack doesn't strike me as a guy who would be good at covering his tracks."

"Surprisingly, he was. His paranoia took care of that. We knew he had a secret hideaway where he kept weapons, computers and his plans for who he would kill next."

"Next? Who else would he kill?"

"I told you how he thought his loved ones were after him. His brother was terrified he was next, and Del Rio's ex-girlfriend wouldn't leave her house."

"He had an ex?"

"He did, and she was surprisingly normal." Trick shook his head. "Anyway, Red and I decided we had to use this guy's paranoia to our advantage." He picked up a pencil and twirled it between his fingers. "Jack was deathly afraid of electronics that weren't his own. The only way Red and I could interrogate him was to keep him isolated and to leave our phones in another room. He seemed to think he could be tracked in some way."

"He did have some issues, didn't he?"

"He was spooked, especially when it came to his mother."

"His mother? But she was dead."

"He kept saying he could see her. I asked Red about it, but he wasn't picking up on any ghosts. We didn't know if Del Rio was trying to prep for an insanity defense or if he was actually seeing his mom. So, we tried an experiment."

Intrigued, Mikey tilted her head. "What did you do?"

"We took Del Rio's mother's cell phone and snuck it into the interrogation room. Del Rio liked to pace during questioning, which we allowed because it helped him talk. When the moment presented itself, Red created a crazy diversion, saying he could see Del Rio's mom, and I slipped the phone into Del Rio's pocket. Then we had our sergeant call it."

Mikey stared. "What happened?"

"Del Rio heard it ring and didn't know what to do. His face went white, and he pulled it out of his pocket. It kept ringing, and he started to cry. He was convinced his mother had sent the phone and was trying to communicate. Riddled with guilt, he confessed to everything."

Mikey narrowed her eyes. "That is the strangest thing I've ever heard. Is that actually true?"

"You can ask Red. It was his idea to plant the phone. He had a hunch, and I trusted those hunches."

"He's always been pretty intuitive." Mikey chuckled and lifted her mug to take another sip when the reason for the story hit her. She widened her eyes at Trick. "Is that what Mason wants you to do? Slip him a phone the next time we go to Windhaven?" She lowered her mug. "Is he crazy?'

Trick smiled. "I'll just need you to create the diversion."

Standing in shock, Mikey cursed.

Chapter Twenty

REM FOLLOWED DANIELS TO the door of the apartment. It was open, and a police officer stood outside of it.

"Hey, Charlie," said Daniels.

"Hey, Daniels. Rem," said Charlie. He was taller than Rem, thin and had a baby face. "The body's inside on the couch. Ibrahim's here and is checking it out, but it looks like another overdose if you ask me."

"They seem to be adding up," said Daniels.

"Thanks, Charlie," said Rem. They walked inside, and Rem saw Ibrahim leaning over a female body. She was fully clothed, wearing jeans and a t-shirt, and a trickle of blood ran down her nose to her upper lip. A bottle of bourbon sat on a table beside her along with a bottle of pills.

Ibrahim straightened. "Hey, Detectives."

"Hey, Doc. What do we have?" asked Daniels. "Another overdose?"

"Probably." Ibrahim gestured toward the table. "Looks like booze mixed with drugs."

"How long's she been dead?" asked Rem.

"I'd say three to four days." Ibrahim pulled off his gloves.

"Any sign of foul play?" asked Daniels.

"Not that I can tell," said Ibrahim, "but I'll know more after the exam."

Rem eyed the door and apartment. There were various piles of paper on the dining table, dishes in the sink, and some folded clothes in a side chair, but nothing seemed out of place. "I don't see any signs of forced entry or a violent altercation."

"Probably an accidental overdose," said Ibrahim, "but if Lozano sent you, he must be concerned."

"Drug overdoses are up almost twenty percent the last six months," said Daniels. "He's wondering why."

Ibrahim nodded. "If I could connect them, it would help, but they're all varied. Some fentanyl, some heroin, some a combination with drugs and alcohol, others not. So, it's hard to say if it's one person or thing."

"It's still strange," said Rem. He eyed the body. "You got an I.D. on her?"

"Yeah. Her purse is over on the table." Ibrahim pointed. "The license says Laura Dunn."

Rem wandered around the apartment and studied a diploma on the wall. "She's got a degree in journalism from UCLA." Next to the degree was an award. "And she won an award for excellence in journalism last year." He turned. "She's obviously accomplished."

"We'll look into it," said Daniels, "but something tells me this will go into the sad, but not much we can do about it, category." He walked to the table. "We'll have to find and notify her family."

"We can talk to the neighbors," said Rem. "Ask if they've seen or heard anything. But if we don't find a red flag, Daniels is right. This will get tucked away into the overdose pile, which is getting pretty high." He thought of Mikey's latest case, Lenora Rodriguez, who'd fallen into the same pile. "Maybe it's just a bad time of year."

"That's usually during the holidays," said Ibrahim. "And if it's this bad now, I don't want to see what happens then." Walking toward the door, he tucked his gloves away and grabbed a leather bag. "I'll leave the rest to you. I'll send you my report when I have it."

"Thanks," said Daniels.

Ibrahim left, and Rem stepped into the bedroom. He saw an unmade bed and an open suitcase partially unpacked. "Looks like she'd been traveling."

"Maybe her credit cards and phone records will tell us something," said Daniels. He poked his head into the bedroom. "You see a laptop or computer?"

Rem shook his head. "No."

"What kind of journalist doesn't have a laptop?"

"Maybe she was with someone, and they helped themselves when she didn't wake up."

Daniels entered the bedroom. "Could be."

Stifling a yawn, Rem looked forward to going home, popping a beer, and crashing in front of the TV. Ever since meeting Kyle at SCOPE, his lack of sleep had worsened. Between the potential plea bargain, trying to tell Mikey about Allison, and meeting her potential new suitor, he hadn't gotten much rest.

Daniels pulled out a pair of gloves and slid them on. "I'll check the drawers and closet."

Rem nodded. He was about to put on his own gloves when his cell rang. He pulled it out and groaned.

"Problem?" asked Daniels, looking up from a drawer.

"It's Mikey," said Rem.

Daniels closed the drawer and opened the next one. "You're going to have to talk to her eventually."

Rem debated whether to answer.

"You keep avoiding her, you know—"

"All right. All right." Rem hit the button. "Hey," he answered, walking back into the front room.

"Hey," she said. "You got a second?"

Rem eyed the couch. "I'm staring at a dead body, but sure."

There was a pause. "You didn't kill Daniels, did you?"

Daniels left the bedroom and mouthed *tell her* at Rem before walking to the dining table.

Rem rolled his eyes. "No. Not yet, anyway. But the day's not over."

"I'm glad to hear you're holding off."

"What can I do for you?" He didn't bring up Kyle and hoped she wouldn't either.

"I'll talk fast since I know you're busy. I saw Mason yesterday."

"That's great. How is he?"

"He's doing really well. I couldn't believe how good he looked. It's like he's ten years younger."

"I'm glad. I know how worried you've been."

"It was a huge relief to see him, but when we left, he asked me and Trick to investigate some names from the facility he's in, Windhaven."

Rem frowned. "Mason asked you to investigate some names? What names?" Daniels looked up from searching through Laura's purse and Rem shrugged at him.

"There have been some suspicious deaths, and apparently Mason's checking into it."

"During his therapy?" asked Rem. "Seriously?"

Daniels began to go through the papers on the table.

"Seriously. He met a patient there who was doing some digging, but then she disappeared. They said she left treatment early, and Mason wants us to find her, but I've hit a wall. There's literally nothing out there on her."

"What's her name?"

"Carla Wilcox. She's done three stints at Windhaven."

Rem sighed. "Three stints? That doesn't bode well."

"I know. But Mason had us check out three of the deaths, and they are suspicious, but there's nothing to connect them other than they were patients at Windhaven. If I can find Carla, maybe she'll have some answers."

Rem watched Daniels pull out a paper and read it. "Okay," said Rem. "Check out a Carla Wilcox from Windhaven. You have anything else on her?"

"Unfortunately, no."

Daniels' face froze, and he looked up from the paper. He stared at Rem, and Rem noted his expression. "Give me a second." He lowered the phone and held it against his shoulder. "Something wrong?"

"Did you say Carla Wilcox?"

"I did," said Rem. "Mikey says Mason wanted her to check out the name. She may be wise to some suspicious deaths at Windhaven, where Mason's being treated."

Daniels stilled. He read the paper again and held it out.

Rem knitted his brow. "What is it?" He studied the paper.

"A copy of admittance paperwork to Windhaven...signed by a Carla Wilcox. There's more than one."

Rem dropped his jaw.

Daniels gestured toward the couch, where two crime scene techs were prepping the body for removal. "If I were to guess, our journalist, Laura Dunn, may be Carla Wilcox."

Shocked, Rem darted his gaze between the body and Daniels. "Are you kidding me?"

"I think we have our red flag, partner," said Daniels.

"Rem," said Mikey from the phone. "You there?"

Rem put the phone to his ear. "You owe me a beer."

"Why?"

"Because I think I've got something for you."

Mason knocked on Hamlish's office door. He heard a soft "come in" and he entered. Since their individual and group sessions took place in designated rooms with cozy furniture and picturesque window views, Mason had not been in Hamlish's private office before. It was sparse, with a desk, chair and file cabinet, some artwork on the walls, another door which was likely a closet, and one window with a view of the rear of the property.

Hamlish sat at his desk with an open laptop. "Have a seat, Mason. I'll be right with you."

Mason sat across from him, wondering what this was about. He and Hamlish had already had their individual session that morning, and group therapy was in fifteen minutes. Resting his elbows on the armrests, he watched Hamlish type quickly, then close the laptop. He scribbled something on a piece of paper, stood and walked to the file cabinet. He opened it, filed the paper and closed the drawer.

"You still keep paper files?" asked Mason. "I thought everything was digital nowadays."

Hamlish returned to his seat. "I'm old school. I transcribe my notes to the laptop, but I keep my handwritten notes for a year in case I need to refer back to them."

"Makes sense." Mason straightened. "Did you forget to ask me something I didn't want to answer this morning?"

Hamlish smiled. "No. This isn't about your therapy. I spoke to Candace earlier. Apparently, you've been asking a lot of questions about Carla."

"I suppose I have. I guess I was just wondering if she'd talked to anyone about leaving."

Hamlish interlaced his fingers. "I can appreciate that, but Candace has detected some pushback from the other residents. Some of them are wondering why you're so interested."

"It wasn't my intention to cause any discord."

"I'm sure it wasn't, but Candace asked if you would refrain from any more scrutiny regarding Carla. I know you're concerned, and I'll continue to try and reach out to her, but I'd prefer that you keep the other residents out of it."

Mason nodded but kept his feelers up for any signs of dishonesty from Hamlish. "Okay."

"I appreciate it, and so will Candace. She's already had a couple questions about Carla's departure. Her job is hard enough as it is, so we don't want to make it harder."

"I was only hoping to understand why Carla had left so abruptly."

Hamlish tapped two fingers together. "I'm going to tell you something that I think will help, but I ask that this stay between you and me."

Curious, Mason raised a brow. "What is it?"

"Carla didn't leave on her own. She was discharged for breaking the rules. Twice. We gave her leeway the first time around, but after the second offense, she could no longer stay."

Mason frowned. "What did she do?"

"That is confidential, but the rules exist for a reason, Mason, and if we don't adhere to them, there have to be consequences. That goes for everyone at Windhaven."

Mason had the uncomfortable feeling that Hamlish was referring to him, but he attributed that to his own paranoia about asking Trick for a phone. "Understood. I won't make any more waves."

Hamlish relaxed. "Thank you." He paused and held out a finger. "I also wanted to let you know that I've asked to move your next family visit to tomorrow. I've accepted a speaking engagement for a colleague who had to back out, so I needed to do some rescheduling. Candace checked in with your family, and they're fine with it. That okay with you?"

Mason's heart thudded. It was more than okay with him since he'd get his phone sooner and would learn more about Trick and Mikey's search for Carla. "Not a problem."

"Great. Tomorrow it is." Hamlish stood and smoothed his shirt. "You ready to head to group?"

ell

Thirty minutes later, Mason wished he could leave Windhaven like Carla had. He'd been talking more about his relationships and how the drugs had affected them, but the conversation had once again returned to his mother.

Thomas snickered. "You know you do this every time? You avoid your mom. C'mon already. Everybody hates their mom. Just admit it already."

"I don't hate my mom," said Mason.

"I do," said Sadie.

"I don't particularly like mine either," said Charlie.

Barry hung his head. He'd returned to group but had been somber and belligerent since his painful family visit, where Mason had seen him storm out. "My mother's the only good thing I had in my life, but I lost her, too," he said, picking at a stain on his jeans.

"My mom died when I was six," said Amanda, "so I wouldn't know."

Hamlish raised his hands. "Let's allow Mason to talk." He put his palms on his thighs. "Why do you resist discussing your mother, Mason?"

Mason crossed his arms. "It's not an easy subject."

"Jeez," said Thomas. "You had an easy family visit, and you can't mention your mom? Did she do something to you?"

"No," said Mason. "I was close to my mother."

Barry snorted and stared at the floor.

Hamlish shot a glance at Barry and looked back at Mason. "Can you elaborate?"

Mason wanted to groan but sighed instead. "She always supported me. I could tell her about anything, including my unusual gifts, and she understood."

Barry snorted again. "Lucky you."

Mason could see a sheen of sweat on Barry's forehead. It had become obvious that whatever had been said during Barry's visit with his loved ones hadn't been helpful.

"You okay, Barry?" asked Hamlish.

Still staring at the floor, Barry gave an uncomfortable smile. "Just great."

Hamlish stared for a second but then returned his attention to Mason. "We know your mother died, Mason. How did that affect you?"

"Did she die before or after the drugs?" asked Sadie. "Did she know you were an addict?"

Mason wanted to shrink and disappear. He hated thinking about what his mom would have thought of him if she'd known. "No. She never knew."

"Did you steal pills from her?" asked Thomas.

Mason's cheeks heated. "Can we talk about something else?"

"That's a yes," said Sadie. "Join the club. I took drugs from my old man. Who cares?"

"Why does this bother you so much?" asked Hamlish.

"Because she never knew you stole from her, did she?" asked Amanda, who hadn't said much. "And you're ashamed."

Mason blew out a ragged breath, recalling his mother's funeral. "It's not my proudest moment."

"What do you think she would have said?" asked Hamlish.

"Uh..." Mason wondered about that. "Sadly, she would have been...I don't know...concerned. She would have wanted to help me, and I think that's what so hard about all this." He cleared his throat. "I let her down. She deserved better from me."

Barry chuckled.

Hamlish eyed him. "You have something you want to say, Barry?"

Barry chuckled some more. A drip of sweat ran down his forehead, and he swiped it away. "It's all bullshit."

"What's all bullshit?" asked Hamlish.

"Him." Barry waved a hand at Mason. "You. This whole damn group."

"Why do you say that?" asked Hamlish.

Barry looked up with a sneer. "You're such a fool." He pointed at Mason. "He gets away with anything. He talks when he wants, about whatever he wants, and nobody cares. But me? I don't answer one simple question and it's 'you're an idiot,' or 'Barry's insane.'"

Mason sensed Barry's anger stemmed from more than his family session.

"Nobody said anything like that," said Hamlish. "Nobody thinks you're insane."

Agitated, Barry bounced his knee. "Everybody bows down at his feet. Why? Because he can see ghosts? He's a damn Ranger? Who gives a shit?"

Mason wondered why Barry's antagonism was directed toward him. "I don't think I'm getting any special treatment."

Barry glared. "Aren't you? How many times have you directed the conversation away from your mother?" His voice raised. "How many?"

"Hell. That's nothing new. We all avoid shit." Thomas' eyes widened. "What's up with you?"

Hamlish spoke calmly. "If you think we have different expectations of Mason, that's incorrect. We are all expected to talk about things that are uncomfortable, but for some of us, it takes a little longer."

Barry grinned, and Mason's alarm bells blared. Something was definitely off.

"You're so full of shit. You coddle him. All of you do." Barry stood, and his chair fell backward. "None of you want to push his buttons, but you all want to push mine."

"Barry," said Sadie. "Chill out."

"Chill out?" yelled Barry. "Chill out?" He shot her a stony stare. "Go fuck yourself."

Hamlish stood slowly. "Why don't we take a second? If this is getting to be too—"

Barry whirled on him. "Shut up. I don't want to talk anymore. About anything. I'm sick of the whole fucking thing." He reached into his pocket and pulled out a knife.

Amanda sucked in a breath, and Charlie stood and stepped back.

"Whoa," said Thomas, holding out his hands. "Easy, dude."

Barry put the knife to his own neck. "I can't do this anymore."

Mason jumped out of his seat, and Hamlish held out his hand. "Barry. Don't."

"Barry," said Mason, trying not to sound scared. "Stop."

Sadie stood and took several steps away.

"I'm going to do it," said Barry. His voice and fingers shook.

"Barry. Listen to me." Hamlish softened his voice.

"I don't want to listen to you," screamed Barry. "Not anymore." He pressed the knife harder against his skin.

Mason took a step closer. His heart racing, he tried to think. "Barry? You want to know about my mom?"

Barry darted his gaze back and forth between Hamlish and Mason. Sweat dripped down his face.

"You want me to tell you? About what I did?" asked Mason. He took a step closer.

"Stay back," yelled Barry, still holding the blade to his throat.

"Barry. Please," said Sadie.

"Take it easy," said Hamlish.

Mason took a slow breath, determined to project calm. "I killed her. I killed my mother."

Barry hesitated, and Hamlish glanced at Mason. Nobody else moved, but everyone stared at Barry.

"That's right," said Mason. "You think I'm some cool guy because I've seen a few ghosts and caught a few criminals? You're wrong." He shook his head. "I'm not."

Barry sneered again. "You're a liar. You're just trying to stop me."

"I'm not lying," said Mason. "I didn't shoot or stab her, but it's still my fault."

Barry breathed fast and blinked but continued to press the knife against his skin.

Mason took another step, and Barry watched him. "You know how I told you I came out here after leaving the Rangers?" asked Mason. "Well, I didn't come alone. I came with my best friend, Victor. Or at least I thought he was my friend."

Barry swallowed, and his knuckles turned white as his grip on the knife tightened.

"After we arrived, and I opened my P.I. business, Victor changed. He became power hungry. He wanted me to use my gifts in ways that gathered and controlled others, but I refused. We went our separate ways, and Victor dove into the dark arts and cultivated a group of followers with unique abilities who cowered to him. He was charismatic and conniving, and before I realized it, he'd created a cult." Mason paused. "One that both my sisters had joined."

Hamlish took a step back while Mason spoke to Barry.

Mason took another steady breath. "I was a fool. Margaret didn't surprise me. She'd always been enamored of Victor. But my younger sister, Mikey, shocked me. I didn't realize what was happening with her and Victor until it was too late. Victor had manipulated her and his followers with drugs, sex and booze, and as much as I tried to get her out, I couldn't. I thought I'd lost her." Mason hated recalling those days. "I...I failed Mikey. I should have been there for her." Trembling, he took another step.

Barry moaned but stayed put. More sweat glistened and streaked down his temple.

Mason kept talking. "And what's even worse is that I didn't realize the depths that Victor would go to target me in revenge. After luring Mikey in, he went after my cousin and killed him."

Barry blinked through drops of sweat, but his gaze remained on Mason. Hamlish took another step back, now out of Barry's line of sight, and slowly removed his phone from his pocket. Nobody else said a word.

"They found his body on the docks," said Mason. "They didn't know who'd killed him, but I did. It was Victor or his groupies. I told the cops but they couldn't prove anything." His skin prickled at the memory. "It was around that time my mother fell ill, but I was so caught up trying to stop Victor and save Mikey that I delayed my trip to go see her." He set his jaw. "That was a mistake."

Barry made a quiet keening noise, and his hand shook. "You're lying," he whispered.

"I'm not," said Mason. He kept Barry's attention on him while Hamlish texted on his phone.

"But when I was told how much she'd declined, I went to see her, and the minute I walked into her room, I knew it was bad." He whispered. "With Margaret's help, Victor had done what I had never expected."

Listening, everyone stared at Mason.

"What'd he do?" asked Thomas.

Barry blinked again, and a tear escaped and slipped down his cheek.

"He'd sent a box," said Mason. "I told you he manipulated people with abilities. The box was cursed. I felt it the moment I entered my mother's room. Victor had sent it to her, she'd opened it, and it made her sick."

"That...that's not possible," whispered Barry.

"It is," said Mason. "That box contained a dark energy designed to attach, weaken and break a person down. It would have wreaked havoc on a strong and healthy person, but my mother's health was already poor, and that box stole her final years away from us." Mason's voice quivered. "I took the box and cleaned it and the energy from it, but it was too late for my mom. She died not long after."

The room was silent, and Mason took another careful step.

Barry's hand shook, and more tears fell and slipped down his face.

"After that, I contacted the authorities, called in all my favors, and got Victor arrested and sent to jail. That's when I finally got through to Mikey. She was starting to see the light before then, but with Victor out of the way, it got easier. Margaret disappeared, but there was nothing I could do about her." He paused, trying to keep his emotions at bay, but the memories made it difficult. "I got Mikey to come to Mom's funeral, and it was afterward, at Mom's house, where I stole my mother's pills from her medicine cabinet," said Mason, "and I started using again." He hated saying that, but he had to keep Barry's focus on him. "And that's the kind of son I am." His own eyes welled with tears of regret.

Barry moaned but maintained his grip on the knife.

"So, if you're thinking I'm some sort of big shot who gets special treatment," said Mason, "you're wrong. I'm a coward and a fool. My mother died because of my neglect and stupidity, and then I let her down further when I used her death as an excuse to use again. I will never forgive myself for that." He slowly reached out to Barry. "So please don't hurt yourself over me. I'm not worth it." His fingers shook.

The doors pushed open behind Barry, and Mason saw two burly orderlies quietly walk in, one holding a syringe. Hamlish stopped them and shook his head, and they waited.

Barry started to sob. "I can't think anymore. Nothing makes sense."

"Join the club," said Thomas.

Mason eyed Hamlish, who indicated to keep Barry talking. "I get it," said Mason. "It's really hard. This whole process is really, really hard."

Barry's grip on the knife loosened. "I see things."

"What do you see?" asked Mason.

"Monsters." Barry gulped in air. "They're going to take me when I die."

"There are no monsters, Barry. I promise," said Mason.

"Don't lie to me," yelled Barry. His expression hardened, and a trickle of blood ran from his nose. "You know better than anyone about the monsters. You see them, don't you? But you don't tell us."

The trickle of blood dripped down his mouth and chin, and Mason was reminded of the female spirit in his room. "I don't see monsters, but if I did, I promise I'd tell you." Barry's arm drooped, and Mason hoped Barry was tiring.

"I can't stop them," said Barry. "They're coming." His face fell, his nose bled, and he shed more tears. "They're coming for all of us."

"It's not your job to save us, Barry." Mason took another careful step and was almost within arm's reach. "We have to save ourselves."

His eyes glittering with tears, Barry whispered. "Nobody can save us." He swallowed and blinked. "It's too late." He paused. "The monsters are coming."

Sensing an opening, the orderlies slowly walked closer to Barry.

Mason kept an eye on the knife, but Barry's white-knuckled grip had eased. "That's the thing about monsters," said Mason. "They want you to think they're big and scary when they're actually tiny and weak. You're stronger than they are."

The blood running down his jaw and neck, Barry didn't move, but he started to laugh. Another tear slid down his cheek. "You'll find out soon enough." His gaze darted around the room. "You all will." His body drooped, he weaved as if drunk, and then his knees buckled, his eyes rolled back, and he collapsed. Sadie screamed, and the orderlies were on Barry in a second, although it didn't matter anymore. Barry had lost consciousness.

Chapter Twenty-One

MIKEY SAT ON A chair next to the couch, where Trick sat next to Mason. Hamlish took notes in a chair across from Mikey. They were nearing the end of their second family session and, after listening to Mason and his revelations, Mikey swiped a tear from her eye. "I can't believe you blame yourself for what happened to me," said Mikey. "It's my own damn fault that I got caught up with Victor. Not yours."

"I should have seen the signs," said Mason, his face pale. "I knew Margaret was involved with him, but I didn't do anything about it, and then you visited, and you were trying to mend fences with Margaret. I should have warned you."

"You did warn me, and I ignored you. I did everything to prove I could take care of myself, and I didn't need you," said Mikey. "I was the idiot." She shook her head. "When are you going to get it through your thick skull that I'm responsible for my mistakes? I made the choices I made. You didn't hurt me; Victor did. You saved me."

Mason dropped his head. "I don't see it that way."

"Take some credit, Mikey," said Trick. "You saved yourself, with Mason's help." Trick glanced at Mason. "But she's right. You can't take on the world's problems, Red. Those burdens get too heavy to carry, and then you need a pill to cope."

"I let you down, too," said Mason.

"We've already talked about that," said Trick. "I don't carry a single grudge or regret, and neither should you. God knows I've made my share of mistakes and let you down." He shifted to face Mason. "The point is, everybody wishes they could do things differently. You're not alone in that. You just need to ease off the gas in the guilt department. You didn't kill your mom, and you're not responsible for Victor's evil. And if you don't find a way to deal with that, you'll always be looking for an escape." He paused. "And if Miss Vain were here, you know she'd tell you the same thing. She's seen the real Red, and she still sticks with you. That should tell you something."

Doubtful, Mason rubbed his neck. "I think it's going to take some time."

"Which is why we're here," said Hamlish. "To finally take the time." He set his notepad on a side table. "We have a couple more minutes. Is there anything else you'd like to say to Mason?"

Mikey dabbed at her eyes with a tissue. "Just that I'm so glad we're talking about this. You've always avoided the subject."

Mason cleared his throat. "I was ashamed."

Mikey scoffed. "Well, stop it. If I'd known what you'd been carrying, I'd have sat you down a long time ago and set you straight. I don't blame you for anything and never did. And I certainly never blamed you for Victor or what happened to Mom. I love you, you big oaf. I need you to get that through your thick head."

Mason smiled softly. "I love you, too. But the rest of it..."

"We'll work through it," said Trick. "The good news is that we've at least started."

"And when Max finally gets back in town, he'll tell you the same," said Mikey with a sniff. "He might say a lot of things, but in his heart, you know he loves you, too, and doesn't blame you."

"I'm not too sure about that," said Mason.

Hamlish straightened and set his palms on his knees. "That will be a good place to start next week." He spoke to Mason. "Anything you'd like to say before we adjourn?"

Mikey's heart raced. Now that the session was ending, it would be time to sneak Mason the phone.

Mason looked between her and Trick. "Just that I'm glad you're here and that we can talk. It helps. And I love you both." He chuckled. "Kind of reminds me of the time we interviewed Jack del Rio when we were Rangers. Remember, Trick?"

Trick smiled and patted Mason on the elbow. "He did open up, didn't he? I thought he was going to cry on my shoulder during the entire interrogation."

"I guess this could be worse," said Mason. "Your shoulder is still dry."

Hamlish stood. "I'm sure you two have some interesting stories to tell."

"That we do," said Trick, standing. "That we do." He eyed Mikey.

Mikey's heart raced faster.

Mason stood and nodded. He wore a light jacket, and he put his hands in the big pockets. "It was good to see you guys. I'm sad Valerie couldn't make it. Tell her I'm thinking of her and hope her brother is okay."

"They're doing tests," said Trick, "but hopefully it's nothing serious and she'll be home soon. Thankfully, his health took a turn after his birthday, but while Val was there to help." He raised an eyebrow at Mikey.

Mikey took a breath. *It's now or never.* She picked up her water glass and stood. Holding the glass, she took a step toward Hamlish. "I just want to thank you so much for all you're doing, Doctor." She hesitated, then crumpled her face. "You have no idea how much it means to me to have Mason back." She walked over and fell into Hamlish's arms, who stumbled back a few steps, and grabbed her shoulders.

"Oh, my, well, yes." Hamlish patted her shoulder. "That's my job."

"You...you...you're so smart." She made a sobbing sound and gripped him with her free hand while he tried to pull away. "Mason's in good hands."

"Thanks," said Hamlish. "I appreciate that."

Hoping she'd given Trick and Mason enough time, she stepped back, but then worried it wasn't enough and she let the water glass slip from her fingers. It dropped at Hamlish's feet, and water sprayed up over his pant legs. She gasped and put a hand over her mouth. "Oh, no. I'm so sorry."

Hamlish swiped at his pant legs. "It's fine. It's just water. No harm done."

"I'm so clumsy. Do you have a towel?" Mikey tried to smack at his legs, but Hamlish backed away.

"It's okay," said Hamlish. "It will dry."

Trick grabbed some tissues from the table. "Use these." He handed them to Hamlish, who dabbed at the wet fabric.

"You okay, Mikey?" asked Mason.

Seeing Trick and Mason standing beside the couch, looking pretty satisfied with themselves, she smiled. "I'm feeling much better." She fanned her face. "I don't know what came over me. I guess I just got a little overwhelmed by it all."

Hamlish tossed the tissues into a trash basket. "Not a problem. It happens." He walked to the door. "You ready? Same time next week?"

Mason stopped. "Actually, do you mind if we do it earlier? Maybe twice this week? I think we made some breakthroughs today, don't you? And I'd like to keep that going without a long break in between."

Hamlish pursed his lips and regarded Trick and Mikey. "I'm fine with that? How about you two?"

Trick nodded. "I'm game."

"Me too," said Mikey, wondering what Mason was up to.

"Great," said Hamlish. "We'll set it up." He opened the door and stepped out. "I'll let Mason walk you two to the front." He shook his foot. "I'm going to go change my shoes."

Mikey held her chest. "I'm so sorry."

"It's fine," said Hamlish. "My tennis shoes are more comfortable, anyway. See you soon."

Mikey nodded, and Hamlish turned, walked down the hall and disappeared around the corner.

"Let's head out," said Mason. "I'll walk you to the lobby."

"That's great," said Trick, not mentioning the phone. "You mentioned you had a difficult group therapy session yesterday. Everything okay?"

Mason shrugged. "One of the patients had a meltdown. He's okay, but they had to take him to a psychiatric unit."

"That's too bad. Hope he recovers," said Trick.

Mikey was about to yank on Mason to ensure the phone exchange had occurred but realized he and Trick were intentionally acting as if nothing had happened. She looked around. Were there cameras? Were they being watched? She didn't see anything but couldn't be sure.

Nearing the lobby, Mason glanced at her. "How's the cohabitation going at my place? You two still getting along?"

"We're doing fine," said Mikey.

"Trick still burning the midnight oil? He keeping you awake?" asked Mason.

Mikey wondered why Mason cared about what time they went to sleep. "No. It's been good," she said.

"I may stay up occasionally to watch a game, Red, but I still tire easily after my surgery," said Trick. "I'm not up that late."

"Glad it's working out," said Mason. They entered the lobby. The receptionist looked up but then returned her attention to reading something at her desk. Mason stopped at the door. "I actually get to bed at a decent time around here. In my room by nine, then lights out at ten. Gives me time to relax, though, before getting some shut-eye."

Trick nodded. "Glad you're getting your rest. You need it."

"See you in a few days," said Mason.

"Take care," said Trick.

Mason hugged Mikey, and she held his gaze. "You be careful," she said softly. He smiled. "Always am. Talk soon and don't worry."

He stepped back, waved, and walked away.

Anxious, Mikey followed Trick out of the building and to his parked truck. She slid into the seat as Trick got in and started the engine.

"Well?" asked Mikey, her voice rising. "What the hell happened? Did you give him the phone?" She smacked him on the arm. "Did it work?"

Trick chuckled. "You were brilliant, Mikey. Just the right touch. Red has the phone and the portable charger I got him."

Mikey exhaled. "That scared me to death."

"You did great. You're a natural."

She leaned back against the seat. "So what now? Just because he has a phone doesn't mean he can use it. He's not supposed to hang out in his room. And what if it's searched?"

"I'm sure Mason has that all figured out. And he'll call us between nine and ten tonight."

Mikey recalled the conversation in the lobby. "That's what he was talking about? I was wondering why he cared about how late we stayed up."

"Red's got something on his mind. I could see the look in his eyes. I'll be curious to hear what's going on." He backed out and drove down the driveway.

"I hate to tell him Carla is dead. I hope he doesn't blame himself for that, too."

"My worry is he'll get pissed. If someone killed her, he'll want to know who, and if it's someone from Windhaven..."

Mikey rested her head back against the headrest. "I hope we did the right thing. He gets caught with that phone, or if someone gets wind of what he's up to, he could put himself in somebody's crosshairs." She glanced at Trick. "And he's all alone in there."

Trick gripped the steering wheel. "Which is why it will be up to us to stop whatever's going on before Red does." He raised his finger. "But make no mistake. If we get wind Red's in trouble, we go in and get him out. Treatment be damned." He paused. "You okay with that?"

Mikey nodded. "Of course. There are other centers where he can finish therapy." She watched the traffic as Trick stopped at a stop sign. "But what if the bad guy, if there is one, finds Mason first?"

Turning down the street, Trick sighed, but didn't answer.

Mason spent the afternoon trying to keep busy. They'd had another group therapy session with Barry absent and Hamlish attempting to get everyone to discuss the events from the previous day. The group seemed okay but displayed the expected concerns and worries. They briefly discussed Mason's revelations, but Hamlish allowed Mason a reprieve and kept the questions to a minimum.

After group, Mason took another riding lesson. He didn't talk to Kessler about Carla, and their conversation remained casual. Kessler remarked on Mason's improvement and suggested Mason ride Storm at the next lesson. Uncertain but eager, Mason had agreed. He knew Carla had ridden Storm frequently, and he felt there was some connection between Carla and the stables, but Mason didn't know what. He hoped Mikey and Trick could shed some light when he talked to them that evening.

After their visit, he'd hidden the phone and charger in his clothes bureau. Based on what he could tell, no one had been in his room other than the housekeeping staff, but nothing personal had ever been disturbed, so he had to trust that wouldn't change, as long as he didn't give them reason to look. He figured with the type of clientele at Windhaven, the personal stuff was strictly protected, and he assumed that extended to him.

After the lesson, he had an hour before dinner, so he cleaned up and stopped at the library. After finding a book, he settled in to read, hoping it would help pass the time. But when he found himself rereading the same page several times, he closed and tossed the book onto the coffee table. Eyeing the clock, he saw he had twenty minutes until dinner. The day was moving as slowly as Mikey did in the morning before her first cup of coffee.

A male voice broke the silence. "Can't find anything of interest?"

Mason startled and turned. Sitting behind him on another couch, looking casual in pressed pants and a silk shirt, and holding a magazine, was Ruben Montes.

Chapter Twenty-Two

Surprised that Windhaven's most elusive patient had spoken to him, Mason answered. "I guess not. Too many things on my mind, I suppose."

Ruben closed his magazine. "Funny. We come here to quiet our minds, and we can't stop thinking." His slight accent reminded Mason of one of Margaret's old boyfriends, whose family had originated from Brazil.

"I missed the last two meditation circles," said Mason. "Maybe I should go back."

Ruben tossed the magazine onto the couch and stood. "I've never been one for meditation." He walked over to the sofa where Mason sat. "I find it to be...repetitive. There are more productive ways to use one's mind. Don't you think?" He gestured toward the couch. "You mind?"

Mason scooted to the side. "Not at all."

Ruben took a seat and faced Mason. "Thank you." He leaned back against the cushions.

"I think it depends on what you dwell on," said Mason. "If your mind is your enemy, then the meditation should help, but if you have no inner demons, it's probably unnecessary."

"Do you have inner demons, Mason?" asked Ruben.

Mason stilled, surprised Ruben knew his name. "I've been known to have a few, Ruben." Ruben grinned. "You?" asked Mason.

Ruben paused. "My conscience is clear."

Mason sensed Ruben had plenty of demons. "You're one of the lucky few." He held Ruben's gaze. "Or you're a sociopath." He smiled.

Ruben chuckled. "I've been called worse." He ran a hand down the front of his silky shirt. "I realize I've done things I'm not proud of. I just don't waste time thinking about regrets I can do nothing about." He put an arm on the back of the couch. "Water under the bridge, right?"

"Right." Mason sensed Ruben's curiosity. "I'm surprised you know my name. I'm small potatoes in a place like this."

Ruben widened his eyes. "Small potatoes? You're a medium, paranormal researcher and investigator who's also a former Texas Ranger. Your reputation precedes you. Almost more than mine."

"Really?" Mason wondered why Ruben cared.

"It's rare that I meet someone who fascinates the inmates more than me."

"Inmates?" asked Mason. "Interesting term."

Ruben shrugged. "It fits most of the people who are here. They're basically under a court order after partying too hard or driving drunk one too many times. Their reputation has taken a hit, and in the court of public opinion and the world of celebrity, they have to show remorse and a willingness to get better. So, they pull out the big money, find the most expensive treatment they can, and hope it lands well with the fans once they find out, which they always do. One can only hope it helps the inmate in the long term."

"I'm a sponsored resident. Does that make me an inmate?"

"On the contrary. You are an exception. You wanted help, came willingly and were lucky to have received the scholarship. I donate money to this place specifically to help people like you."

"And to get your name on the building."

"That too." Ruben grinned. "But it's only one wing."

Mason debated how far to go with his questions. He didn't want to scare Ruben back into his secret lair, but something told him Ruben didn't scare easily. "Your description of the others here...the inmates. Doesn't that describe you, too?"

Ruben tipped his head. "It does, or at least it did. I'll admit. I was the typical rich kid with rich kid problems. I drank too much, partied too hard, wrecked expensive cars and enjoyed beautiful women. It was fun for a time, but then I got bored. That sort of life, while fun, produced nothing of any consequence. How many gorgeous people can you sleep with before they all morph into one?" He rolled his eyes. "And then came the extortion attempts and bribes. Scam artists who thought by threatening to ruin my reputation, I'd pay them money." He shook his head. "I never understood how they didn't realize that I didn't have a reputation. My family was on the verge of disowning me." He pointed. "There was one benefit to it, though. I learned who my friends were. Who was loyal, and who wasn't."

Mason half-expected Ruben to pull a cigarette from his pocket, light it and take a puff. "Were there many who were loyal?" he asked.

"Fewer than I expected. It was enlightening." Ruben traced a seam on a couch cushion. "I realized then what true power was, and it had nothing to do with sex, drugs, guns, or money." He narrowed his gaze at Mason. "But it had everything to do with respect."

"The money didn't hurt, though."

Ruben smoothed his hair with his fingers. "No. It didn't, but even if I hadn't been wealthy, the same rules applied." He gestured toward Mason. "You're an example. You're a smart man. Wise. Compassionate. Always helping the underdog. You're not rich, but yet you command respect. It's an admirable trait."

"Money would be nice."

"Money only allows me to give at a higher level. I can donate to places like this, help the hungry, sick, and homeless, and donate to research labs to find cures for illnesses neglected by other big-name charities." He leaned in. "That's the beauty of wealth, Mason. Using it to change people's lives."

Mason listened but questioned Ruben's honesty. He suspected Ruben still demanded respect, but with more than money. "If that's true, then why are you here? Shouldn't you be traveling the world, helping those in need?"

Ruben crossed his legs. "I usually am, but everyone needs a little R&R once in a while."

"And you come here?"

"It affords me the privacy I require. Staying in a private villa or an ornate mansion doesn't exactly invite alone time. I have people who make demands of me. The phone rings, the meetings add up, the assistant expects decisions, and the donation requests never stop. I find without the occasional escape, the inner demons are tempted to return."

Mason relaxed against the couch. "Is it true there's a secret wing where the uber rich and super celebrities mingle with you, out of sight of the inmates and paparazzi?"

Ruben laughed. "That is a popular rumor, isn't it?"

"Is it true?"

Ruben hesitated. "If I told you, I'd have to kill you."

Mason squinted. "Might hurt the reputation."

"Depends on how it's done."

Mason held eye contact with Ruben, sensing this was somehow a test. Of what, he didn't know, but he wanted to pass it. "I'll take my chances. Big money and the people who have it don't scare me."

"When's the last time you encountered it?"

"Your kind of money?" asked Mason. "Never."

"Then how do you know?"

"Because I've encountered ghosts, demons and even a few cryptids in my life, Ruben. Once you see a monster, or feel the breath of evil on your neck, or speak to a dead person with their head blown off, the definition of fear changes."

Ruben stared. "I've never thought of it that way."

"Life is scary, but the afterlife...," Mason spoke low, "...that'll scare the shit out of you. It's one of the reasons I started taking pills." He sighed but aimed a hard look at Ruben. "Be glad you made some changes. Let's hope they do as much good as you say." Mason didn't necessarily believe in hell, but something told him Ruben did.

Mason detected the slightest tick in Ruben's cheek before Ruben relaxed, and the moment was broken. "I like you, Mason." He put a hand on the back of the couch. "Few surprise me."

"When it comes to the living, I'm sure you've seen a lot more than I have."

"I have my share of experience with death, too."

Mason thought of Ruben's wife and girlfriend, both deceased. "I've heard."

Ruben waved a hand. "Who hasn't? It seems that no matter what I do to improve the plight of others, interest in that nasty business of my personal life never wanes. I suppose it will haunt me until my death claims me."

"I hope you're not haunted in other ways."

Ruben scratched his jaw. "No ghosts that I'm aware of."

"Count yourself lucky." He set his elbow on the armrest. "You ever want a reading, though, you let me know."

"I think I'll pass. I've spoken enough about those days to fill a hundred books. I, as I said, have no regrets."

"I guess that means you're not harboring a famous novelist in your lair to tell your life story."

Ruben groaned. "Yet another painful rumor." He sat up. "Maybe one of these days, though, when your therapy has ended and you're right with the world, I'll invite you to my secret space. I sense my privacy is secure with you."

"I wouldn't tell a soul."

"I hear you're also becoming a skilled rider. Perhaps you and I could take out Storm and Thunder one day. Explore the grounds of Windhaven."

"You've obviously heard false rumors about my riding skills. I'm more likely to fall off Storm before I reach the back gate of the stables."

"A few more lessons from Kessler, and I suspect you'll be more ready than you think." He leaned close. "Never underestimate yourself is my motto. You'd be surprised what can be done with a little time, hard work and practice." His eyes glimmered in the lamplight. "Especially when it comes to something important."

Curious, Mason tipped his head. "Are we still talking about horseback riding?"

Ruben raised the side of his lip. "What else would we be talking about?"

Uncertain, Mason wondered about the strange deaths Carla had been investigating and her words of warning about Ruben Montes. Did he have something to do with what was happening at Windhaven?

Neither said a word until Mason heard someone clear their throat. He turned and saw Candace at the library door, her usual exuberant mood dampened.

"I'm so sorry to interrupt," she said. "I was asked to remind you, Mr. Montes, of your appointment."

Ruben offered her an energetic smile. "Candace. How are you?"

"I'm well," she said, flashing her pearly white teeth. "Thank you."

"How's Tracy?" asked Ruben. "And Manolo?"

"They're well, also," she said. "Manolo's cooking you a lovely redfish tonight."

"That's wonderful," said Ruben. He eyed Mason. "You enjoying the food here, Mason? It's exceptional." He stood.

"I am now, but it was a rough start." Mason stood, too. "I guess I should head to dinner."

"Manolo's doing Italian for the residents this evening," said Candace. "I think you'll be pleased."

"I'm sure I will," said Mason.

"Residents," said Ruben. "Such a pleasant word." He made a slight bow toward Mason. "It was my privilege to talk with you, Mason. I hope we get the chance to do it again before you leave."

"Maybe," said Mason.

Ruben headed toward the door. "And if you change your mind about the horseback riding, let me know."

"How do I get in touch with you?"

Ruben stopped before leaving. "Just let any of the staff know. They can find me if I'm on the grounds. Right, Candace?"

Candace smiled again, but Mason caught Candace's stiff body language. "Of course," she said. "Anyone would be happy to help." She waved. "We've been trying to get Mr. Montes out of his room more often."

"You know me, Candace. I like my solitude." Ruben lightly touched her elbow, and Candace stiffened more.

She eyed her watch. "You don't want to be late."

"Ah, yes. You're always looking out for me." Ruben waved at Mason. "Until we meet again, Mason."

"Can't wait," said Mason, feeling a sense of dread he hadn't felt before.

Ruben winked, smiled at Candace, and left.

Chapter Twenty-Three

MIKEY CHEWED A NAIL and paced while Trick sat on the sofa, watching her. After visiting Mason, Mikey had done her best to stay busy until it was time for Mason to call. She'd talked to Kyle about an upcoming case, and Rem had contacted her, reminding her that her police protection would end that day. He'd asked her to stick close to Trick and do her best not to go anywhere alone.

He'd also told her he'd checked out Gina Rodriguez and had found no serious red flags, but they were surveilling her house for any signs of Margaret. Nothing unusual had happened yet, but he'd said he'd keep Mikey up to speed if that changed. Mikey had inquired about the Carla Wilcox/Laura Dunn investigation and Rem conveyed it was still early, but they were digging deeper into it and were not convinced it was an accidental overdose.

She'd tried to bring up the subject regarding whatever he'd been trying to tell her, but he'd told her he was going into a meeting with his captain and had to go. Whether that was true, Mikey didn't know.

After the workday ended, she and Trick had returned to Mason's house, eaten some dinner, and waited to hear from Mason.

Seeing it was nine thirty, Mikey continued to pace. "Why hasn't he called?"

"He still has thirty minutes." Trick munched on a cookie and sipped some coffee. "These cookies are delicious."

Mikey wrung her hands. "I bake when I'm nervous."

"I'll remember that. I love chocolate cake, by the way."

Mikey eyed the clock again. "You think he's okay? What if he got caught?"

"He didn't get caught. His jacket had big pockets, and unless they searched him, which I doubt, he successfully hid the phone."

"Don't forget the charger. He had two things to hide, remember?"

"I had to include the charger. It's hard to talk if the phone is dead."

"He'll have to charge both."

"I told you. The charger has a solar panel. If Red can get it in the sun, it will be fine."

Worried, Mikey huffed. "You can't exactly stick something in the window when you're trying to hide it."

"It's charged now, which should get him through the rest of his time at Windhaven," said Trick. "Hopefully, we'll have solved this thing long before then and it won't be an issue."

"I hope you're right."

Trick followed her progress while she paced. "You should relax."

"I can't. Not until he calls, and I know he's okay. This cloak and dagger stuff scares me."

"You're worrying too much. Red knows what he's doing."

"Maybe, but he has a reckless side, especially when he's in protective mode." She stopped. "He'll put others' safety before his own."

"When we know more about what's going on, then I'll worry. But for right now, there isn't much to go on other than a few suspicious deaths."

"What if—" Trick's phone on the coffee table rang, and Mikey jumped. She ran over to the couch and sat beside Trick when he leaned over and hit the speaker button.

"Hello?" asked Trick.

"Trick?" asked Mason.

"Red? It's me and Mikey. You're on speaker."

"Mason?" asked Mikey. "Are you all right?"

"I'm fine," said Mason. "I'm sitting on the edge of the bathtub before lights out, trying to talk softly. I would have called sooner, but I got caught up in a card game after dinner."

"Sounds like they're keeping you entertained," said Trick.

"I was trying to pass the time before this call," said Mason. "This day slowed to a crawl after you left."

"You're not kidding," said Mikey. "I've been a nervous wreck. Are you able to hide the phone?"

"Yes. It shouldn't be an issue, as long as I don't arouse suspicion," said Mason. "And thanks for adding the charger."

"It's got a solar panel if you need to charge it, but hopefully you won't need it," said Trick.

"That should work fine. Thanks," said Mason. "Did you look into Carla?"

Trick glanced at Mikey. "We did." He paused. "It's not good."

"What is it?" asked Mason.

"I couldn't find anything on a Carla Wilcox who'd been in Windhaven," said Mikey, "and thought I'd hit a dead end, but then we learned that Carla is an alias. Her real name is Laura Dunn, and she's an investigative journalist."

"You're kidding," said Mason.

"Rem and Daniels were called to a crime scene," said Trick. "A woman had overdosed, and it turned out to be Laura. They found paperwork leading back to Windhaven and three sponsorships under Carla's name." He leaned in. "She wasn't at Windhaven by accident. She was investigating something and, I suspect, planning to publish whatever she'd discovered."

Mason didn't speak for a moment. "She's dead?"

"I'm sorry, Red," said Trick.

"Damn it." Mason sighed. "Did it look staged?"

"Hard to say," said Trick. "From what Rem and Daniels have told us, there were no signs of forced entry, but booze and pills were near the body. We're still waiting on a toxicology report."

"Nobody heard or saw anything?" asked Mason.

"They're still checking," said Mikey. "Apparently, there's been an uptick in drug-related overdoses, and Lozano wants them to dig deeper. They're not convinced it was accidental."

"What about a laptop, or any notebooks?" asked Mason. "If she was writing something, it had to be there, or she gave it to someone."

"No laptop at the scene, which is why it's suspicious," said Trick. "No notebooks, either. She was freelance, and we haven't found anyone she may have planned to publish with who might have a copy of whatever she was working on."

"What about at Windhaven?" asked Mikey. "Could she have left something there?"

"I don't know," said Mason. "I know she was writing something, and I'm trying to find out what, but haven't had much luck. What about the other names I gave you?"

Mikey told him what they'd learned about Amelia, August and Chauncey. "It's all suspicious, but nothing overt enough to open an investigation. They were all drug users at or near the end of their treatment. The cops think they just relapsed."

"I figured," said Mason.

"What do you think is going on, Red?" asked Trick. "What was Laura onto?"

"I don't know," said Mason. "But I keep seeing a female spirit at the end of my bed at night. Her nose is bleeding, and she keeps telling me I should have listened. Then I saw the spirit of August Delroy. He was bleeding from his ear. Chauncey died bleeding from both his ears and nose, and then there's Barry."

"Who's Barry?" asked Mikey.

"The guy in group therapy who lost it yesterday," answered Mason. "Threatened to slit his throat right before his nose started bleeding and he collapsed."

"Interesting coincidence," said Trick.

"Too many if you ask me. And now Carla...or Laura." Mason paused. "She knew something."

"Without more to go on, we're stuck," said Trick. "You have any ideas?"

"I do," said Mason. "I talked to the hairstylist here. Carla was asking her questions about some of the staff. The problem is, I don't know their last names."

Mikey found a piece of paper and a pen. "Who are they?"

"Candace," said Mason. "You met her."

Mikey scribbled on the paper. "And?"

"Tracy. She's the nurse and nutritionist. And Manolo, the chef. And Kessler. He runs the stables and is the riding instructor. Oh, and Dr. Hamlish. I know his first name, though. It's Marcus. Check him out, too."

Mikey jotted down the names. "I have an idea how to find out more about them. I'll see what I can do. Any idea how they fit into Laura's investigation?"

"No. Not yet," said Mason. "There's another name, too. Ruben Montes."

Mikey sat up. The name was familiar. "Ruben Montes?"

Trick narrowed his gaze. "Isn't he the rich guy who killed his wife and lover but got away with it?"

Mikey stared at the phone. "That guy? He's at Windhaven?"

"He is," said Mason. "I talked to him tonight. He's as slick as a snail. Apparently, he's donated enough money to have a wing named after him and provide my sponsorship along with several others."

"His family is loaded," said Trick.

"Why do you think he's involved?" asked Mikey.

"Call it a hunch," said Mason. "He keeps to himself around here, but the staff caters to him. I get the feeling he may get more than therapy."

Mikey wrote Ruben's name. "Are you sure? Maybe he is just there for treatment."

"I heard he used to throw lavish parties. The drugs and booze were highlights," said Trick. "Not to mention the destruction. More than a few venues were wrecked. The Montes family paid a fortune in damages alone."

Mason grunted. "Montes says he's reformed and now lives to help the disadvantaged. Maybe he is just a sleazeball who still requires the occasional psychiatric visit, but I need him to be ruled out. Carla...or Laura...warned me about him, and I want to know why."

"Okay," said Mikey. "I'll see what I can find out."

"Anything else?" asked Trick.

"There is, and you might not like it. There's a reason I asked to have another family visit this week."

Mikey set the pen down. "What are you up to?"

Mason hesitated. "I need another performance."

Trick frowned. "What kind of performance?"

"I need to get into Hamlish's office. And the only way to do it is for you two to divert Hamlish."

Mikey dropped her jaw. "That's insane. He's your doctor. If you get caught, they'll kick you out."

"I have to take the chance. Hamlish keeps his personal notes in a file cabinet. Carla had been his patient on her previous visit. I want to read those notes."

"How exactly do you plan on us diverting Hamlish?" asked Trick.

"An argument," said Mason. "At our next meeting. It needs to be just you and Mikey. Not Max or Val."

"I think this is a bad idea," said Mikey. "What if there are cameras?"

"I've checked. Most cameras are on the grounds or common areas. Hamlish's office is towards the rear of the facility, near the resident's rooms. There are almost no cameras there. I'll be careful, but I think I can get in and out without being seen."

Shaking her head, Mikey didn't know what to say. She knew how stubborn her brother could be when he'd made up his mind about something.

"What kind of argument should we have?" asked Trick.

"Something traumatic enough for me to stomp out during the meeting. Hamlish will stay with you two until the end of the session. That will give me time to get to his office, find the notes and then get out of there."

"I don't like this," said Mikey.

"I'm questioning this, too," said Trick. "You sure you want to take this risk?"

"If Laura was murdered," said Mason, "then it had something to do with Windhaven. People around here are too evasive when I bring her up, and after what happened to Barry and the other patients, I have to do something. Besides, the worst that can happen is they'll kick me out."

"But then you'll lose your connection to the facility," said Trick. "And you'll need to go somewhere else, because you have to continue treatment, Red."

"All the more reason to be careful and not get caught," said Mason.

"You two seem to have forgotten something important," said Mikey, bouncing her knee. "Except for Barry, these people are dead, and Ruben Montes could be a murderer."

Mason sighed into the phone. "I know."

Anxious, Mikey leaned toward the phone. "The worst that can happen isn't you getting kicked out. It's you getting dead, too." She glanced at Trick. "And you're in there all alone. There's nobody to back you up."

Mason didn't respond.

"If they target you," said Trick, "they'll make it look like an overdose. Like the others. They'll say you relapsed."

"Let's not think the worst," said Mason. "I hear you, though, and understand the danger. But if the people in here are at risk, then somebody's got to help them."

"And if you become another victim?" asked Trick.

"Then it'll be up to you two to figure it out," said Mason, "because either way, I'm going to find out who murdered Carla."

Chapter Twenty-Four

MIKEY FLIPPED THROUGH THE printed papers, reading the information. She heard the outer door open and peered at the cameras. It was Trick entering SCOPE, holding two coffees and a bag.

The inner door opened, and Trick walked in, set the coffees and bag on the coffee table, and tossed his hat in the chair. "I grabbed some donuts. I figured we deserved them."

Studying the paperwork, Mikey nodded. "Great."

There was a pause. "I also spotted Margaret out on the sidewalk, wearing shades and a long trench coat," said Trick. "I cuffed her and called Daniels and Rem. They're on their way."

"Nice," said Mikey, still reading.

Trick sat beside her. "Obviously, what you've got there is way more interesting than me." He picked up a coffee and held it out. "Is this the elusive info you've been waiting for?"

Mikey took the coffee. "It is."

"Well. Don't keep me in suspense." Trick picked up his own cup and took a sip.

Mikey held up the papers. "I got the scoop on the staff."

Trick widened his eyes. "What do you mean? How'd you do that?"

"I can't tell you," said Mikey.

"Or you'd have to kill me?" he asked.

"Something like that."

"Does this have something to do with Rem?"

She shook her head. "No. He'd kill me too if he knew. Then you and I would both be dead."

Trick frowned. "What're you up to?"

"Let's just say I hired someone to do some digging into Windhaven. Someone with technology skills way beyond mine. They pulled the staff files and researched the names that matched the ones Mason gave us."

Trick stilled. "Did you hire a hacker?"

Mikey slumped. "I had to. We can't afford to wait for information. I'd rather ask someone sketchy to do a little digging if it means protecting Mason."

"Mikey, if your hacker gets caught, it will lead straight back to you."

"That's the least of my worries. And he's not going to get caught. He's got great credentials. Nobody is going to find out."

"You're as crazy as your brother."

"It runs in the Redstone family," she said, reaching for the bag of donuts. "Did you get chocolate?"

"What am I? A sadist? Of course, I did."

Mikey pulled out a donut and handed Trick the papers. "Check out what he discovered."

Trick set his coffee down, took the papers, and started reading. His eyes tracked across the page. "Whoever he is, he's good."

"He is." She took a bite of her donut.

He read aloud. "Tracy is Tracy Pham. A nurse practitioner and certified nutritionist. Started working at Windhaven two years ago." He paused. "Huh. She's also got a degree in biology, specializing in epidemiology."

"It's the study of disease in groups of people and the factors that cause, prevent and control it. I googled it," said Mikey.

He looked up. "That's pretty advanced for a nurse working in a drug treatment center."

"I agree. Doesn't necessarily mean anything bad, though."

Trick kept reading. "Candace is Candace Whistler." He paused. "Nothing sticks out about her. Degree in Communications. Moved from L.A. Divorced with an eight-year-old son. Been working at Windhaven for eighteen months." He narrowed his eyes. "She had a brother in rehab?"

"At Windhaven," said Mikey. "He did his three months and was discharged right before Candace was hired. And he's still alive."

"That's always a plus. Looks like he's married with a kid now. So his rehab stuck."

"He's one of the success stories, it appears." Mikey sipped her coffee. "Kessler is next."

"Phillip Kessler," said Trick. "Age fifty-two. Been at Windhaven for ten years. Did a stint in the military and after he got out, became an accomplished equestrian until he was injured in a riding accident during a competition."

"It was bad," said Mikey. "He almost didn't walk again."

Trick nodded. "He's lucky. Broke his back and recovered, but never competed again." He flipped through to the next sheet. "He did a stint in rehab?"

"He did, but not at Windhaven," said Mikey. "It was after leaving the military. It's been several years, so I guess he's another success story."

"Good for him." Trick read down the page. "Manolo Breznaro. Immigrated to the United States from Argentina. Father opened a restaurant serving authentic South American food and did well. Manolo is the eighth of eight siblings and went to culinary school, where he graduated at the top of his class. Worked at several well-known restaurants before he opened his own in San Diego." Trick stopped.

"You obviously got to the good part."

Trick lowered the papers. "Ruben Montes invested in Manolo's restaurant?"

"He did. Ruben and Manolo's father are apparently buddies. Ruben visited Manolo's father's restaurant frequently."

Trick frowned and read some more. "Manolo's dad would bring Ruben food while Ruben was awaiting trial?"

"The families must be close."

"This hacker guy got some good stuff. How did he get this level of detail?"

Mikey shrugged. "I don't ask questions."

"I'm afraid to ask what you paid for this," said Trick.

"It's out of my own pocket, not SCOPE's, and it's well worth it."

Trick flipped to the last page. "Dr. Marcus Hamlish. Graduated from Harvard with a specialty in addiction psychiatry. Had a thriving practice in the northeast but closed it and came out here. Been at Windhaven six years. Married with two kids and a dog. Nothing too exciting about that." He got to the end. "Where's the goods on Ruben?"

"I'm still waiting. I told my guy to send me what he initially had. I suspect Ruben's results will be as long as this." She pointed at the papers.

"Well, we already know something about Ruben just from public knowledge." Trick set the papers down. "He was accused of murder but was acquitted, but everyone still thinks he did it."

Mikey sipped some more coffee. "He married and divorced again after the trial. Does he have kids?"

"Not by his wives, he doesn't. It's possible he's got illegitimate ones, which wouldn't shock me." Trick reached for the bag of donuts and pulled one out.

"His family made their money in pharmaceuticals," said Mikey.

"Still do." Trick took a bite of his donut.

"From what I heard, he left the business after the trial and now devotes himself to philanthropy. I wonder if he's still close with his family."

"Maybe your hacker can find out."

"I'm sure he will." Mikey set her coffee down. "What do you think about what we have so far?"

Trick chewed. "Hard to say. Nobody's an obvious ax murderer, which is unfortunate because that would have helped."

"Except for Ruben."

Trick smirked. "There is that." He swallowed and sat back. "Let's say he did it. That means killing someone wouldn't shock him. You think he's got something to do with the suspicious deaths?"

Mikey shrugged. "He's got to be mixed up in this. If Laura was onto him, then that would explain the danger. If Ruben suspected she was getting close to discovering Windhaven's secrets, maybe he had her killed, too."

"The question is, what did she know and how did she know it? Laura had to have had a source."

Mikey considered that. "Someone at Windhaven?"

"Probably one of the people in that report."

"If that's true, then that person could be in just as much danger."

"Probably. Whoever they are, they better be careful."

"You think Laura revealed her source to whoever killed her?"

"Don't know, but no one else has died, so that's a good sign."

Mikey nodded. "I bet if there is a source, they're freaking out."

"Which brings us to Laura's notes," said Trick. "The source is likely mentioned in them. But where are they?"

"Her laptop was taken, so that's of no use."

"Mason said she was writing at Windhaven, so there's something hand-written somewhere."

"You think she hid it at Windhaven?"

"Probably. Something like that wouldn't be safe in her room. And if she left or was forced out abruptly, she may not have been able to retrieve it."

Mikey groaned. "This is such a mess."

"Maybe Mason can shed more light on this once he gets into Hamlish's office."

"The deeper we get, the more I think he should back off," said Mikey. "If Ruben Montes is waist deep in this, Mason could be walking into the middle of a firing range."

"I admit. It's risky."

"We could back out. Not create the diversion."

"It's too late. We already agreed. Mason's expecting it tomorrow."

"We can tell him tonight, when he calls."

"He won't call tonight unless he's got something new, which is unlikely. He's at a dead end until he can read Hamlish's notes."

"We could still back out."

Trick finished his donut, sipped his coffee and sat up. "I know you don't like it, but we have to trust Mason. He's been in difficult situations before, and he's managed to find his way. If he wants to do this, then as his partner, I'll back him up."

"What if it gets him killed?"

"You can't think like that. If we had as Rangers, we would have never completed an investigation. Mason may have left the job, but the job hasn't left him. If someone at Windhaven is killing people, and Carla, or rather Laura, found out and died because of it, then it has to be exposed. Mason has the unique advantage of being in there. Without him, a killer will keep killing."

"Hell." Mikey expelled a deep breath. "Why couldn't Mason have been an accountant?"

"Because he sucks at numbers."

Mikey dropped her head.

"Maybe once we get the report on Ruben, this will come together."

"I hope so. I don't think my heart can take it."

Trick set his cup down. "I should tell you. Rem called me while I was out."

Mikey looked up. "He did? Why?"

"He reminded me about your protection ending. Wants me to be aware and keep an eye out."

Mikey rolled her eyes. "I talked to him earlier about the same thing. He's freaking out."

"He has good reason. He's worried." He found a napkin and wiped his fingers. "Did you tell him about our talk with Mason?"

"I did. They should know that Mason is doing his own digging into Carla's death."

"You tell them everything?"

Mikey nibbled her lip. "I mentioned how we gave Mason a phone. He didn't seem too thrilled, but he understood. And I told him about the missing notebook and how it might be at Windhaven."

Trick nodded. "But you kept the hacker to yourself and the staff info? And Mason's plan for tomorrow?"

"Hell, yes. I'm not stupid. If you think I'm hesitant about all of this, Rem would be even worse. I figured if we'd found a smoking gun among the staff, then I'd say something, but we haven't. Besides, all I had at the time were first names. Not much they could have done with that."

"We've got more than first names now. That excuse won't hold up."

Mikey held up a hand. "Let's just deal with one thing at a time, okay? Between Mason and Margaret, I'm getting a headache."

Trick tossed the napkin on the table. "How worried are you about Margaret, because you've seemed pretty calm."

Thinking about that, Mikey swirled the coffee in her cup. "I don't think Margaret's going to do a damn thing. Not yet, at least."

"Why's that?"

"Because," she met Trick's gaze, "I think she's waiting for Mason to leave rehab. He's as much a target as me and Rem."

Trick rested his elbows on his knees. "That's interesting." He rubbed his neck. "Doesn't that scare you?"

"It does, but I've still got time to figure out what the hell to do about it."

"You have any ideas, you let me know." He straightened. "In the meantime, we need to catch a killer and keep Red alive. Then, once he's out of Windhaven, we can tell him Margaret's free and he's still in danger." Trick sighed. "That ought to be a fun day."

"Let's just get him out of there first, then we'll deal with Margaret." Her cell rang, and she picked it up. "It's Rem again. He's definitely worried." She answered. "Rem? What's up?" Rem spoke quickly and listening, Mikey's stomach flipped. "Are you serious?" She listened some more. "Are they sure?" She set her drink down.

His face furrowed, Trick sat up.

"I don't believe it," said Mikey. "No, I haven't spoken to Gina since we argued." She nodded. "Okay. I will. Thanks." She hung up.

"What is it?" asked Trick. "Did they find Margaret?"

Mikey stared in shock. "No. It's not that. It's Laura."

"What about her?"

Mikey set her phone down. "Rem and Daniels talked to the neighbors at Laura's apartment building. They found someone who told them they had seen Laura the morning of her death in the parking lot. She was talking to a man."

"A man? Did they find out who he was?"

"No, they didn't, but the neighbor was adamant about the description. He was tall and slim, with dark hair and well dressed...," she swallowed. "...and he had a snake tattoo on his temple."

Chapter Twenty-Five

MASON SET HIS JAW. "I don't think I was that bad."

Trick scoffed. "You sure about that?"

Mason eyed Mikey, who couldn't sit still. He could tell she didn't like this. They'd been talking with Hamlish for twenty minutes, and Mason figured it had been long enough to establish a groove and start the argument. "What do you think? Do you agree with Trick?" he asked her.

Mikey didn't answer but stared at her fingers.

Hamlish leaned in. "It's okay to tell him how you feel. It's a safe space here."

Mikey nibbled her lip.

Trick raised his hand. "Come on, Mikey. Tell him what you told me. It's not all lollipops and ice cream. It's been a rocky road."

Mason studied her, almost willing her to engage. He decided to give her some help. "You two haven't exactly been easy either, you know. You aren't a shining example of moral perfection, Trick, and you constantly being on my ass, Mikey, is why I took a few of those pills." Her demeanor shifted, and he almost smiled.

Trick snorted. "So the ugly side of Mason finally emerges."

Hamlish waved his pen. "Okay. So we've hit a few nerves here, which, to be honest, I expected. There's usually some emotion below the surface that eventually comes out."

Mikey sat up. "I can't believe you just said that, you idiot. How dare you lay that crap at my feet? The only one to blame for your pill addiction is you. And there's a reason I get on your ass. Because if I don't, it doesn't get done. The whole reason you have a successful business at all is because of me."

Mason sneered but was secretly proud. "Oh, please. You constantly bring that up. The high and mighty Mikey, who can do no wrong."

"Stop it," said Trick. "She's your sister."

"And don't even get me started on you, partner." Mason sneered. "You think your shit sparkles. But you stink just as much as I do. You just hide it better."

Hamlish shook his head. "Let's keep this amicable. It's okay to express frustration, but in a positive way."

"Tell him that," said Mikey, pointing toward Mason. She glared. "This is what always pisses me off. You're so sweet and nice one minute, and a complete jerk the next. You blame Trick for thinking he's smart? Maybe you should take a look in the mirror. You've always thought you were so much better than everyone."

"That's because I am," said Mason.

"Mason," said Hamlish, "try to be—"

"You're a real son of a bitch," said Trick. "I should have requested a new partner years ago, but instead I stuck with you. I guess that does make me an idiot."

"If the shoe fits," said Mason.

Hamlish tried again. "Mason, don't—"

"Mom would be horrified to see what you've become," said Mikey. "Don't you have any empathy for what you've done to us, or to her?"

Her words struck Mason, and he wondered if she was still pretending. "Don't bring Mom into this."

"Why not?" Mikey straightened. "She's what this is really about, isn't it? You blame yourself for her death. And you take it out on me and Trick. Max, too."

Mason raised his voice. "I don't want to talk about Mom."

"Maybe it's time you should," Mikey argued back. "If you really want to get better, then get a spine and face the music. Be honest with yourself."

Trick looked between them, and Mason gripped his armrest. "Be honest about what? How I did my damnedest to take care of her? How I failed?" Mason pointed, too. "And while we're being honest, how about you do the same? I'm not the only one who left her. So don't lay all that shit at my feet."

"Listen—" said Hamlish.

"Calm down, Red," said Trick.

Mikey's eyes widened. "You're going to blame me for Mom? How dare you!" She stood. "I did everything I could for her."

"Like what?" asked Mason, his voice rising. "Call her on the weekends and send her gift packages in the mail?"

Her mouth fell open. "Compared to you, that was a windfall."

Mason patted his chest and stood too. "You don't know a damn thing about what I did for Mom."

"Yes, I do. She got the box, didn't she?" Mikey yelled.

Mason's heart thumped. "The only reason she got the box was because I was trying to save you from Victor."

Mikey's eyes flared. "And you failed at that, too, didn't you?"

Trick stood, too. "Maybe we should—"

"Shut up, Trick," said Mason, breathing hard.

"Let's take a break," said Hamlish.

"And I didn't fail at that. I got you out," said Mason.

"You didn't do anything." Mikey shot a thumb at herself. "I got myself out. I take credit for that. You don't get to. Not anymore."

Mason stared, knowing this was planned, but certain Mikey had stopped acting. He wanted to say something useful but had to keep up the charade. "I don't have to listen to any of this. I'm sick of the treatment, and I'm sick of both of you. This is a waste of time. I'm out of here." He strode toward the door.

"Mason, wait." Hamlish stood.

Mason hated looking at Mikey's stricken face. "You sit and talk with my so-called family. You're better at wasting time than I am." He opened the door and stomped out.

Trying but failing to forget Mikey's words, he headed down the hall, turned the corner and stopped. He waited to see if Hamlish would follow or return to the room. A few seconds passed, he heard a door close, and he peeked around the corner to see an empty hallway. The plan had worked. Hamlish had stayed with Mikey and Trick.

Pleased, but ruffled by the argument, he told himself to focus on the job at hand, and taking a breath to calm himself, he headed down the hall toward Hamlish's office.

Mikey sniffed, holding back tears. The fake argument had escalated into unpleasant territory, and she felt horrible.

Hamlish closed the door and returned to his seat. "You two okay?"

Trick sighed and sat. "That didn't go well."

"It happens. It's difficult to hear the truth. Most need some time to absorb it. Mason will be fine. He'll come around." Hamlish eyed Mikey. "You all right?"

Mikey swiped at her eye and also sat. "I've been better."

Hamlish nodded. "I know it's hard, but you are making progress." He paused. "If you two would like to end early, I understand. We can pick this up next time after everyone's had time to cool off." He stood. "Can we schedule the same time next week?"

Trick straightened, his face tense. "Absolutely not. We need to talk about this."

Mikey looked between the two of them and burst into sobs.

Mason stopped at the end of the hall toward the rear of the facility. He looked around the corner and saw the door to Hamlish's office. Scanning the area again, he didn't see any cameras, and certain no was around, he tiptoed down the hall and approached the door. The only thing he couldn't be sure of is whether Hamlish locked his office during the day. If he did, this jaunt would be over sooner than expected. He reached for the knob, turned it, and breathed a sigh of relief when the door opened. Mason quickly stepped inside.

Daniels opened the door to the Windhaven Treatment Center and held it for Rem. "Age before beauty."

Rem smirked. "Or brains before bananas." He walked in.

Daniels rolled his eyes and followed Rem inside. "That's the best you could come up with?"

"You caught me on a bad day." Rem stopped and looked around. "Wow. This is quite the place."

Daniels noted the opulent surroundings. "Mason didn't do too badly, did he?"

"He got a helluva scholarship," said Rem. "No wonder the rich and famous come here."

A door opened behind a counter in the reception area, and a woman walked in carrying a mug. "Can I help you?" She sat at the front desk and set her mug down.

Daniels walked over and pulled out his badge. "I hope so. I'm Detective Daniels, and this is my partner, Detective Remalla."

Rem held out his badge. "How are you?"

"I'm fine. What's this about?" she asked.

Daniels read her nametag. "Well, Gloria. It's about one of your former patients. A Carla Wilcox."

Gloria looked appropriately concerned. "What about her?"

Rem eyed Daniels. "We'd like to talk to Dr. Hamlish about that. Is he available?"

Gloria hesitated. "I don't know. I'd have to check."

"Would you mind?" asked Daniels. "It's important."

She stared for a second, but then reached for the phone. "Sure. Give me a moment."

"Thank you," said Rem. "We'll wait over here." He gestured toward the sofa.

She nodded, and Daniels followed Rem to the couch, where they took a seat.

"You want to make a bet about whether he talks to us?" asked Daniels.

"He will."

"He could be busy. We could have called ahead."

"We could have, but it's better to catch him by surprise." Rem rested an elbow on the back of a cushion. "If Gloria comes back with a no, you want to be the bad guy?"

Daniels touched the leaf of a shiny plant beside him on a side table. "I think it's your turn. Besides, you're better at it."

Rem frowned. "Since when?"

"Since I'm feeling lazy today. J.P.'s got a cold. He kept me and Marjorie up a good part of the night."

"Fatigue can be helpful. Makes you crankier. I should know."

Daniels rested back against the cushions. "You didn't sleep either?"

Rem shrugged. "I got a few hours in. Can't complain."

Daniels studied his partner, wondering how much Rem was hiding from him. He'd noted how little Rem had said recently about the upcoming trial, and

Allison, to keep him from worrying. "Well, you're better at cranky than me, so I'll leave it to you."

"I don't know if that's a compliment or an insult."

"Neither do I."

Rem shook his head.

A minute passed, and Daniels was about to ask Gloria what was up when he heard heels clicking on the white-tiled floor and a woman with bouncing blonde hair and brilliant white teeth approached. "Detectives?" she asked.

Rem and Daniels stood.

"I'm Candace." She held out her hand, and Rem and Daniels each shook it. "I hear you're looking for Dr. Hamlish?"

"We are," said Daniels. "We'd like to discuss a former patient of his. A Carla Wilcox."

"Does he have a few minutes?" asked Rem.

"He's actually in a family session," said Candace. "May I ask what this is about? Is Carla okay?"

"No, actually. She isn't." Daniels put his hands on his hips. "Do you know when Dr. Hamlish will be available?"

Candace hesitated and checked her watch. "Not for a while. Can we set up an appointment in the next day or two? That might work better. He's very busy."

Rem glanced at Daniels. "What do you think, partner?" asked Daniels.

"What do I think?" asked Rem. "I'll tell you what I think. I think we sit our butts down on this lovely sofa until Dr. Hamlish is free. You have anything to do today?"

"Nothing critical," replied Daniels.

"Good. Neither do I." Rem sat. "I don't mind waiting."

Candace's face fell. "Well...uh...it could be a while." She glanced at Gloria, who was observing the discussion.

"You got any vending machines around here?" asked Daniels, looking around. "I could use a snack."

"Good idea." Rem nodded. "And I could use a coffee. You got a coffee machine?" He pointed at Gloria, who held her mug. "She's got some." He stood. "We'll help ourselves. I'm sure a place as nice as this has something for us to eat and drink."

A man and a woman walked into the building and entered the reception area. They approached Gloria, who welcomed them and held out a sign-in sheet.

Rem watched and spoke with a raised voice. "I mean, we are two detectives wanting to talk to a doctor about a patient and how she was treated in this facility. If abuse is an issue here, we need to get to the bottom of it. And not tomorrow. Today. Unless he's avoiding us."

The couple looked over at them.

Candace shook her head. "Abuse? What abuse?"

"That's what we're here to discuss," said Daniels.

"And the sooner, the better. Before somebody else gets hurt." Rem scratched his jaw.

"What's going on?" asked the woman at the front desk. "Is everything okay?"

"It's fine," said Gloria. "Just have a seat. Someone will be with you in a second."

"Come join us on the couch," said Rem, patting the sofa. "Me and my partner here can tell you all about Windhaven." He offered Candace a half-smile. "We've heard some interesting rumors."

Candace paled and glanced at the couple. "Don't worry. It's all fine." She waved Rem and Daniels toward the hall. "Why don't you two come with me?"

Daniels almost chuckled. His partner did cranky well. "Thank you, Candace. We appreciate it."

"Right this way." Candace headed toward a hallway.

Rem passed the couple. "You two have a pleasant visit and keep an eye out while you're here. You can never be too careful." He eyed Gloria as he followed Candace. "Maybe Gloria here can get you some coffee. I bet it's delicious."

Daniels bit back a grin as they left the reception area.

Mason flipped through the files in the cabinet, listening for any sounds of someone outside the office, and tracking the time. He couldn't assume that Hamlish would keep Mikey and Trick talking for the rest of the appointment, so he moved fast. Seeing a folder marked *Wilcox, Carla*, his heart thumped, and he pulled the folder out. He sat it on Hamlish's desk and opened it. Moving his finger down the paper, he wished he had a camera to take a picture. He quickly scanned the notes.

Possible depression and suicidal tendencies. Alcohol dependency, but drugs also an issue? Hasn't admitted drug usage, despite questions. Avoidance of something bigger? Family issues? Dig deeper for cause. Shame?

Mason read further past the clinical issues and stopped at another note that caught his eye.

Early indications suggest trial is effective. This is her second admit. Negative effects negligible. Consider stopping or reducing dosage?

Mason frowned. Was Carla, or Laura, on some sort of trial? She hadn't mentioned it to Mason, but the notes were regarding her second visit. Not her third. He kept reading.

Scale back to study effects? Confirm with Tracy.

Seeing Tracy's name, Mason held his breath. Obviously, whatever trial Carla had been a part of, Tracy was involved. He read the remaining notes, but nothing else stood out, and he closed the folder. Not hearing anyone outside, he prayed for more time. He returned Carla's file but kept looking. He didn't see any folders under August Delroy, Amelia Iverhart, or Chauncey Pendleton. Frustrated, he began to close the drawer when he spotted another folder marked *Other Patients*.

Moving fast, he pulled it out, set it down, and opened it. It was a list of several names. He scanned it quickly, seeing Carla, August, Amelia and Chauncey listed among several others. Beside each name was either a check mark or an X. August, Amelia and Chauncey all had an X, but Carla had a checkmark that had been scratched through, and an X had been added. What did the X mean? Did it mean relapse? Or something more sinister?

Wondering about the list, Mason almost closed the file when he spotted a name and broke out in a cold sweat. *Mason Redstone* had been added to the end of the list with a small check mark beside it.

Mikey blew her nose into a tissue.

"You okay?" asked Trick. "You need more time?"

Mikey dabbed her eyes. "I'm so sorry. I just had a meltdown, I guess."

"It happens," said Hamlish. "Once you open the doors on unaddressed emotion, it can all spill out at once."

"I didn't realize I was so angry," said Mikey. "Why is that, Doctor?" She couldn't care less about the answer, but she had to keep Hamlish in his seat.

"I'm curious myself," said Trick. "This repressed emotion is fascinating."

Hamlish hesitated, and Mikey caught his glance at his watch. She admired his ability to hide his impatience and could imagine what he was thinking. She and Trick were asking the dullest questions.

"It's a broad subject," said Hamlish. "But it's common, so don't be alarmed."

Mikey held her chest. "I'm just so bothered by it. How will I ever get over this? Will I be angry forever? Is there a cure?"

Trick patted her hand. "You're being too critical. I'm surprised myself over my own hostility, but surely Dr. Hamlish can explain how best to handle it." He glanced at Hamlish. "Right?"

"There are a number of ways," said Hamlish.

"What are they?" asked Trick.

"Let's go over them," said Mikey. "In detail."

Hamlish stared for a second, but then nodded. "Maybe we should—"

There was a knock on the door, and Mikey gripped the tissue she was holding. Had Mason been caught? She eyed Trick, who eyed her back.

Hamlish stood, and Mikey sensed his relief at the break in conversation. "Sorry for the interruption," he said. "Give me one second." He walked to the door and opened it.

Mikey saw Candace in the hallway. Seeing Mikey and Trick, she leaned in. "I'm so sorry. I just need to talk to Dr. Hamlish for a moment."

"What is it?" Hamlish leaned close as Candace whispered something in his ear. Hamlish's eyes widened, and he paused. "I, um..." He glanced back at Mikey and Trick. "I apologize. I have to cut this session short. Something's come up."

Mikey stood, terrified it was about Mason. "Is something wrong?"

Trick stood, too. "What about our repressed hostility? I really think we should talk about it."

Hamlish's usual seamless composure slipped, and his brow furrowed. "We'll bring it up next time. Candace, can you show them out? I'll talk with our guests in my office."

"Of course," said Candace.

"No, wait," said Mikey, shaking with nerves. "I'm really feeling off." She held her head and sat.

"She has these spells occasionally," said Trick, sitting next to Mikey. "Can you help her, Doctor? I'm worried she'll faint."

"Oh, dear," said Candace, stepping into the room. "Can I get you a wet towel?"

"Candace will take care of you," said Hamlish. "She's handled worse. I'm sorry to leave so abruptly, but I'll see you next week. Candace will set something up." He walked out.

Mikey jumped up, determined to keep him from his office. "But I'm worried about Mason."

Candace put a hand on Mikey's elbow. "Maybe you should sit. If you faint, you could hit your head."

Mikey darted out of the room, and Trick followed. "I think she's better now," he said.

Turning, Mikey saw Hamlish approach the end of the hall. "But what about—" She froze when she saw Rem and Daniels at the opposite end of the corridor.

Trick stopped beside her. "Oh, hell."

Rem did a double-take, and Daniels straightened, but neither said a word. Hamlish reached them and shook their hands. Then he gestured down the opposite hall, and they turned and left. Rem eyed them as they walked away.

"Are you sure you don't want to sit for a second?" asked Candace from the door. "You look pale."

Mikey waved her off. "No. I'm fine." She grabbed Trick's elbow. "Let's go."

Candace sputtered. "But you said—"

"I'm feeling much better. Thanks, Candace." She strode down the hall, walking fast, with Trick beside her. "We have to hurry," she whispered and pulled out her phone.

"I thought you said you left your phone in the car."

"I lied when I signed in, in case we needed it." She started typing.

"Smart. But why are we hurrying?" asked Trick. "We can't follow Hamlish to his office. And we don't want Hamlish to realize we know Rem and Daniels. They must be here to ask about Carla."

"No. We can't follow." Mikey took a turn. "But I can text Rem and tell him what's going on."

"You think there's enough time?"

"Mason better pray there is." Walking into the reception area, she finished and sent the message.

Mason stared at the list. Why the hell was he on it? And what did the checkmark mean? After taking a second to think, he closed the file and returned it to the drawer, then slid his finger down to the R's and stopped at a file marked *Redstone, Mason*. Nervous, he pulled it out, opened the folder, and recognized Hamlish's scrawl on the page.

Opioid addiction paired with fear of failure. Obvious need to please and prove worth. Is paranormal real? Or induced to connect with others and appeal to his sense of duty? Ranger work suggests latter. Tendencies to withdraw when forced to face the reality of his mother's death. Is there more to it? Confront shame.

Mason swallowed. It was hard to see his own doctor's evaluation of him written in words on a page. Was he that messed up? Is that how people saw him? Were his inner demons that obvious?

Feeling sick, he almost closed the file, but a note at the bottom caught his attention and he read it.

Trial begun at initial stage. Monitoring. Increased dosage when showed signs of resistance. No issues. Suitable candidate for phase two.

Mason went still, but his fingers shook. He was part of the trial? But what trial? And what resistance did he show? And what was phase two?

Voices sounded from the hallway, and Mason jolted out of his shock. Someone was coming. He closed his folder, slid it back into place and carefully shut the drawer. The voices neared, and he realized he wouldn't be able to leave. Eyeing the closet, he ran over to it, widened the door and stepped inside. He returned the door to its partially open state and pressed himself against the wall just as he heard someone enter the office.

Walking down the hall, following the doctor, Rem wondered about Trick and Mikey's presence. They must have been here to see Mason, and it was likely the family visit they'd interrupted. He breathed a sigh of relief that they hadn't bumped into each other, because it would have been difficult for him to hide his reaction.

Heading toward his office, Hamlish was rattling on to him and Daniels about the facility when his phone buzzed. Daniels glanced back as Rem reached into his pocket. Seeing it was from Mikey, he read the text message and frowned.

Hamlish rounded a corner, headed toward a door and reached for the knob.

"Uh, um, wait," said Rem, wondering what the hell to say.

Daniels looked back. "Something wrong?"

Rem stammered. "Uh, can we meet somewhere else? It's so claustrophobic around here." He chuckled at Hamlish, who narrowed his eyes at him. "I get a little anxious." He pulled on his shirt as if he were sweaty.

Daniels shot him a what-are-you-up-to look, and Hamlish answered. "My office has a window. I think you'll be fine." He opened the door.

Flustered, Rem reached for his elbow. "Are you sure—" The door swung open, and Rem got a look inside. The room was empty. There was no sign of Mason.

"You okay?" asked Daniels, following Hamlish.

Entering the office and glancing around, Rem nodded. "Great. I feel fine. The doc's right. The window helps." He held out his phone to Daniels. "I got a text, though. You should read it."

Hamlish went to his desk and sat in his chair as Daniels read the text. His eyes widened. "Interesting." His gaze darted around the room.

Rem walked to the window and tucked his phone back in his pocket. "Not much of a view. You think you'd get a better one."

Hamlish tossed a pen into a cup. "I'm not in here much. I spend most of my time in therapy rooms. This is just where I come to get away from everyone and get the admin stuff done. The views are saved for the patients."

Rem nodded and turned. He spotted a closet door partially open. "It is quiet."

"You don't see patients in your office?" asked Daniels.

"No. I don't," answered Hamlish. "You wanted to ask about Carla?"

Rem walked around the desk toward the closet.

"We do," said Daniels, standing beside the desk.

Rem peered inside the closet and froze. He saw a clear outline of a man standing in the darkness of the small space. Swiveling, he walked away and stood on the opposite side of the room near the file cabinet.

"Why don't you two have a seat?" Hamlish waved toward the chairs across from his desk.

"Thanks." Daniels sat.

"I prefer to stand," said Rem, hoping to keep Hamlish from looking toward the closet.

Daniels gave him another funny look.

Needing a distraction, Rem pointed at the floor and gasped. "Is that a roach?"

Hamlish jumped and searched the floor. Rem made eye contact with Daniels, tipped his head, and eyed the closet. Daniels glanced at the closet door.

"Where?" asked Hamlish, raising his feet.

"Sorry," said Rem. "My bad. I think it was just your shoe."

Hamlish looked up. "My shoe?"

Daniels stared at the closet for a second before looking back at Hamlish. "His eyesight's not so good. You really need to get your prescription checked, partner."

"I would," said Rem, "but I hate doctors." He smiled at Hamlish. "No offense."

Hamlish gave him an odd look. "None taken." He checked his watch. "Not to rush you, but I have a group therapy session soon, so..."

"Of course," said Daniels. "This shouldn't take long. We'd like to ask you about Carla and her therapy here. You were her doctor, right?"

Hamlish nodded. "Yes. I was. Not on her latest admittance, but I was on her previous one. Why?"

"She have any issues that stood out?" asked Rem. "Any problems with the patients or staff?"

"No. She got along well with everyone. Other than her addiction, she didn't have any problems." Hamlish sat back in his seat. "I can't really say much more due to patient confidentiality." He paused. "What's this all about? Is Carla okay? Has she relapsed?"

Rem and Daniels made eye contact. "She's dead," said Daniels.

Hamlish's face fell, and the color in his cheeks faded. "She's what?"

"Dead," said Rem. "As in no longer breathing."

Hamlish put a hand on his stomach and sat up. "Wha...what happened?"

"We're trying to figure that out," said Daniels.

Hamlish closed his eyes, and then opened them. "Was it an overdose?"

"What makes you say that?" asked Rem. "Wasn't she an alcoholic?"

Hamlish bit his lip. "She was, but if she was suicidal, that's usually done with pills."

"Who said she was suicidal?" asked Daniels.

"Nobody," said Hamlish. "She was my patient, and, well, I can't go into detail, but it's not uncommon for addicts to have thoughts of suicide. I just assumed." He hesitated. "Was it suicide?"

Daniels rested his ankle on his knee. "It hasn't been ruled out."

"There were drugs and booze at the scene," said Rem.

Hamlish rested his elbows on his desk. "This is just awful. Does her family know?"

Rem leaned against the cabinet. "That all depends."

Hamlish interlaced his fingers. "I don't understand. Depends on what?"

"What family are you referring to?" asked Daniels.

Hamlish shook his head. "I don't know what you're talking about. Carla has family. If I recall, she had a sister."

Rem nodded, remembering the paperwork they'd found in Laura's apartment. She'd listed a sister as a family member, who had yet to be located, so they assumed she was fake. "Did you ever meet her?"

"No," said Hamlish, "despite my efforts. They were estranged."

Rem recalled the rest of the paperwork. Hamlish had been listed as Carla's doctor on all three of her stays at Windhaven. "You say you were her doctor on her second admittance here, but you're her doctor on file for all three visits. Why is that?"

Hamlish took a second. "Probably because I'm the senior medical doctor here. I sign off on all the treatment, and even though I wasn't her primary doctor on her first or third visit, I still met with her once or twice and discussed her treatment with her other doctors." He fiddled with some papers on his desk. "I can put you in touch with her other physicians if you'd like to speak with them."

"You'll do just fine," said Daniels. "For now."

Hamlish narrowed his gaze. "I feel like I'm missing something. Carla was an addict, and we obviously failed at helping her. Sometimes a patient who returns to the outside world will take their life, or accidentally overdose, as sad as that might be."

"We see your point," said Rem.

"Then why are you here?" asked Hamlish.

"Because Carla wasn't Carla," said Daniels, aiming a hard stare at Hamlish. "Her real name was Laura Dunn. And she was an investigative journalist."

Hamlish's face went white. "She was a what?"

Rem leaned in and spoke louder. "An investigative journalist."

Daniels stood, leaned over, and put a hand on Hamlish's desk. "We think she was investigating Windhaven. The question is why."

Rem walked closer. "Her laptop was missing, too. Which is odd for a suicide, don't you think?"

Hamlish's mouth opened and closed, but nothing emerged.

"You have any idea what Laura Dunn was investigating?" asked Daniels. "Or who may have killed her?"

Hamlish blinked. "Killed her? You think she was murdered?"

"It's looking pretty obvious," said Rem. "She was onto something and got too close. Someone didn't like it and took care of the threat. They made it look like suicide and took the evidence with them." He waited for Hamlish to absorb the information coming at him. "The question is, who did it?"

Hamlish cleared his throat. "I...I...don't know. I don't know anything about this."

"You don't know a thing about what Laura was investigating at Windhaven?" asked Daniels.

"No...No...I don't," sputtered Hamlish. "I swear."

Rem chuckled and eyed Daniels. "They always swear, don't they?"

Hamlish smacked a hand on the table. "I don't know what's going on."

Daniels smirked. "Let's hope not."

"We heard that Carla, or Laura, wrote things down in a notebook when she was a patient. Any idea where that notebook is because we found nothing at her apartment." Rem glanced at the closet and then back at Hamlish.

"I know she liked to write. I just assumed she took all of that with her," said Hamlish.

"Could it still be here?" asked Daniels.

"Where?" asked Hamlish.

"At Windhaven," said Rem with an impatient sigh.

"How should I know?" asked Hamlish.

"If it is, and somebody finds it, then let's hope you're not mentioned." Daniels leaned in. "Because that could be bad."

"Maybe not," said Rem. "If Dr. Hamlish were to find that notebook and turn it in, it would certainly be a show of good faith, and we always appreciate a little help from the inside, right?"

"We do. It can go a long way with a judge, too," said Daniels.

"A judge?" asked Hamlish. "What judge?"

Daniels shrugged. "Of course, on the flip side, if somebody else found it and turned it in to us first, well, then, we'd appreciate them more."

"We sure would," said Rem.

"Unless we find the killer first," said Daniels. "Then all deals are off the table. If he, or she, folds and starts naming names, there's nothing we can do at that point."

"It'll be a damn shame," said Rem. He eyed Hamlish. "I'm sure you've worked hard to get where you are. Losing your reputation would be disastrous." He paused. "My guess is you live in a fancy neighborhood. Hard to stay there when the money stops coming in and people look the other way when you walk by."

"I don't know anything," said Hamlish. "You've got this wrong."

"Then you won't have any issues helping us, will you?" asked Daniels. "Especially if other lives could be at risk."

"Someone else dies, you could take the fall," said Rem, making a tsk, tsk sound. "I'd hate to see that."

Hamlish stood. "This is ridiculous. If her laptop was taken, then anything she wrote probably was, too."

"You sure about that?" asked Daniels. He tapped on Hamlish's desk. "According to Carla's paperwork, she was escorted out after being asked to leave treatment early. There was an itemized list of the items she left with. A notebook was not mentioned."

Hamlish dropped his jaw.

"If she didn't take it out of here, then where is it?" asked Rem. "And why did she have to leave treatment early?"

Hamlish shook his head. "I think I've said enough. I still have to consider Carla's, or rather Laura's, privacy. I don't know what she wrote, what she was investigating, or why she died." He crossed his arms. "And I don't like the way this conversation is going."

Rem stared back. "This conversation is easy, Dr. Hamlish. You'll know when it gets harder. It will be crystal clear."

"You think you're flustered now?" asked Daniels. "You haven't seen anything yet."

Hamlish swallowed. "I think you should leave."

"No problem. We'll go." Rem looked toward the closet.

"But we'll be back with more questions. For you and the rest of the Windhaven staff," said Daniels. He pointed. "Someone killed Laura Dunn. And something tells me that doesn't shock you at all."

Hamlish set his shoulders. "You two are wrong about me and Windhaven. This place is a haven for those in need, especially for a lot of powerful people."

Rem smirked at Daniels. "Really?" said Rem. "Thanks for the reminder." He met Hamlish's gaze. "But there's one thing I've learned about powerful people in all my years of law enforcement. When the going gets tough, they turn on each other, and it's usually the person who knows the least that takes the fall. They'll crap all over you, Hamlish, while they scurry out of the light."

"You play your cards right, and you might get out of this without a prison sentence," said Daniels. "Provided you don't wait too long."

Hamlish paled more, and Rem imagined the doctor's mind was whirling. "Despite your flawed assumptions, I can't help you," said Hamlish. "And I've got a therapy session to get to, so if you don't mind..." He gestured toward the door.

Rem lifted a brow. "Suit yourself."

"Maybe you can escort us out like you did Laura?" asked Daniels.

"We'd appreciate it." Rem waved a hand. "These hallways are a maze. We'd probably end up in the cafeteria, which actually might be good. Think of all the people we could talk to."

Hamlish scrutinized them with a look that Rem suspected would have knocked them flat if Hamlish had the mental power to do it. "I'll happily show you out." He stepped around his desk, walked to the door, and opened it. "After you."

Rem followed Daniels as they left. "Thank you," said Daniels.

Hamlish grunted, closed the door behind him, and led them down the hall.

Remaining cautious, Mason waited before moving. After several silent seconds passed, he slowly pushed the door open when tingles raced up his arms and his skin broke out in chill bumps. Rubbing his arms as he stepped out, he saw a woman standing in the corner, wearing a casual top and jeans, her hair falling softly over her shoulders.

He blinked and stared, recognizing the spirit who had materialized. He took another step. "Carla?"

Carla blinked but didn't answer.

Mason didn't know what to say. "You're here."

She blurred in and out of focus, and Mason held up a hand. "Don't leave."

Carla's form became sharper, and he sensed her energy as it filled the room.

"Can you tell me what happened to you?" He waited, but he didn't hear a response vocally or in his head. "Were you murdered?"

She didn't respond.

"Give me something. Please. You must be here for a reason." He glanced toward the office door, hoping Hamlish didn't plan on returning. "I hate to rush you, but I don't have much time."

She stared, her face expressionless.

"Where are your notes?"

No response.

"Who killed you?"

Nothing.

Mason was losing his patience, and worse, he had to get out of there. "Damn it, Carla. Stop being so secretive. You showed yourself for a reason. What is it?"

Raising her arm, she smiled softly, and more chills ran up his spine. She pointed toward the closet.

Mason looked back at his hiding place. "The closet? What about it?"

She continued to point.

"Can't you tell me? I really don't have time for charades."

She glared at him.

"Sorry, but can't you give me a hint?"

A cold gust of air blew across his face. Frustrated, he turned. "Fine." He returned to the closet and peered inside. "What? I don't see any—" A sliver of light caught his eye, and he wondered how he'd missed it. He must have been too distracted listening to the conversation coming from the office. He moved closer and touched the slight crevice in the wall. It was too narrow to see much beyond it, but the light was obvious. There was something on the back side of the closet. Looking for a handhold or something to grasp, he ran his hand along the wall but felt nothing. Expanding his search, he hoped to find anything that might provide entry to the space.

Realizing he couldn't risk staying longer, he turned to leave when he spotted a button along the inside frame of the door just above his head. Glancing back at the sliver of light, he took a breath, said a prayer, and pushed the button. He heard a click, and the sliver of light widened. Mason peered back into the office, but Carla was gone, and he turned back toward the light. He stepped closer, put his hand into the space and slid the panel back. In front of him was a narrow corridor with a concrete floor, metallic walls and the only source of light was a bare lightbulb in the ceiling. The corridor led down a dimly lit hall, which ended in a right turn.

Mason wondered what the hell he'd just found. Where did it lead? What was it used for? Debating his sanity, Mason took a step forward.

Chapter Twenty-Six

TAPPING HER FINGER ON the tabletop, Mikey watched the street while Trick waited at the window for the coffees. After leaving Windhaven, they'd stopped at a nearby parking lot with a food truck. Mikey had texted Rem, asking him and Daniels to meet her and Trick there. The area around them had a few long benches with tables designed to be shared with other patrons. She sat at the end of one of them along with a man eating a salad and two women eating ice cream sandwiches, who sat at the opposite end.

Nervous, she kept an eye out, and stood when she saw Rem and Daniels drive up and park. They got out of the car and, seeing her, they approached her table. The words rushed from her lips. "Is he okay? Did Mason get caught? Did Hamlish see him?" She wrung her hands. "What happened?"

Rem scowled at her. "You want to tell me why Mason is sneaking into Hamlish's office?"

Mikey shook out her hands. "I'll tell you everything, just tell me Mason's okay."

"He's fine," said Daniels. "He was hiding in the closet, but Hamlish didn't see him."

"In the closet?" asked Mikey, putting her hand on her head. "Are you sure Hamlish didn't know?"

"He didn't know," said Rem. "He was so busy trying to fend us off, an elephant could have been in there, and he would have missed it." He pointed. "But I can't wait to hear this explanation." He eyed the menu on the side of the food truck. "You two want a coffee?"

"Trick's getting one for all of us," said Mikey, gesturing toward the truck. "Daniels, I told him to get you water."

"Perfect," said Daniels. "Thanks."

"Thanks." Rem slid onto the bench and sat. "Now start talking."

Mikey sat with them and debated where to begin. "Maybe we should wait for Trick, because I don't want to be the only one you yell at."

"That's not a great way to start," said Rem.

"It's called a delay tactic." Daniels grabbed a napkin from the dispenser and set it in front of him. "Something you know all about."

"How'd it go with Hamlish?" asked Mikey. "Did you get anything out of him?"

"And that," added Daniels, "is a diversion tactic. You've taught her well."

"I didn't teach her anything," said Rem. "If anything, I learned it from her."

Mikey crossed her arms. "Fine. I'll go first."

Trick walked up with a filled drink holder. "Hello, Detectives. You grilling her yet?" He set the holder down and handed out the drinks.

"Just about to start," said Rem, taking his coffee. "Thank you."

Trick set the tray aside and sat beside Mikey. "What'd I miss?"

Mikey held her cup. "You want to tell them why Mason was searching Hamlish's office?"

Trick nodded. "Because Hamlish keeps his written patient notes in a file cabinet. Red wanted to get a look at what Hamlish had on Carla Wilcox. So, we came up with a plan. Have a family argument during a therapy session, Mason storms out, and Hamlish stays with us, giving Mason time to get into the doctor's office."

"Did you know about this plan when we talked?" Rem asked Mikey.

Mikey shrugged. "Maybe."

"What else don't we know?" asked Daniels.

Mikey didn't see the point of hiding anything anymore. "Mason asked us to check into certain staff members, so we did."

"Which staff members?" asked Rem.

Mikey gave him the names.

Daniels drank some water. "Something tells me you did more than a Google search. Dare I ask how you got your information?"

"Mikey hired a hacker off the dark web," said Trick.

Rem glared, and Daniels shrugged. "He probably got better info than we could have," said Daniels.

Rem dropped his jaw. "Are you defending her?"

Mikey glared back. "It was a good idea. Don't tell me you wouldn't have done the same if Daniels' life was on the line."

"She's got you there, partner." Daniels set his water bottle down. "What did you learn?"

Rem scoffed but didn't argue.

Mikey told them about the staff information the hacker had uncovered.

"It's interesting stuff but not earth-shattering," said Daniels. "But the Ruben Montes thing is curious."

"I should get his file today, so I hope that sheds some light," said Mikey. "What did you two learn about Hamlish?"

Rem told Mikey and Trick about how the conversation with Hamlish had gone.

"There was an itemized list from Windhaven in Carla's paperwork?" asked Mikey.

"No. There wasn't," said Daniels. "We made that up."

"We figured Hamlish is too far up the chain to know what's provided to a patient when they leave, so we fibbed a little," said Rem. "We wanted to see his reaction."

"That's smart," said Trick. "What'd he do when you revealed Carla was actually Laura, the journalist?"

"He turned about as pale as the cream in my coffee," said Rem. "Especially when we added in the missing notebook."

Trick grabbed a napkin for himself. "You think it was a good idea to push Hamlish the way you did? What if he's the bad guy?"

Daniels slid his jacket off and laid it across the bench. "It's a risk, but he's the only name we had, at least until today. Regardless, he was Carla's doctor, so even if he's not the killer, he definitely knows something."

"I don't think he killed anyone," added Rem. "He doesn't strike me as the type."

Mikey massaged her shoulders to ease some of her tension. "I hope Mason got a good look at those files. Maybe what he found will help make some sense out of this."

Daniels glanced toward the food truck's window. "I'm going to get an apple." He stood. "You guys want anything?"

Mikey shook her head.

"I'm good. Thanks," said Trick.

Rem eyed the women at the end of the table. "Get me one of those ice cream sandwiches."

Daniels groaned. "How about a banana?"

"How about I don't sneeze in your water?" Rem tipped his head at Daniels' drink.

Daniels narrowed his eyes. "Ice cream sandwich, coming up." He walked away.

Rem looked between Mikey and Trick. "When do you talk to Mason again?"

"Tonight," said Trick. "He'll call between nine and ten. Care to be part of the conversation?"

"Wouldn't miss it," said Rem. "If he risked his butt to read those notes, I want to know what he learned. Right now, we don't have much. Without something concrete, Laura Dunn meeting our tattoo guy in the parking lot doesn't mean squat, even if that same guy is linked to Lenora Rodriguez."

"Tattoo guy, or Rain, isn't just your ordinary guy," said Mikey. "Remember what Lenora's roommate said. He threw her without touching her, so unless she's delusional, he's got some telekinetic ability, which I feared had something to do with Victor because Lenora was Gina's sister." She ran her hand through her hair. "But now Rain's connected to two women who died under suspicious circumstances. Both of whom were dealing with addiction, unless Laura was pretending." A gust of wind blew, and a strand of purple-tipped hair fell in her face. She tucked it behind her ear. "Add to that the deaths of the patients, the likely involvement of the staff and Ruben Montes." She sighed heavily. "It's like some strange conspiracy."

"Conspiracy to do what, though?" asked Rem.

Trick held his coffee and stared off. "I've been thinking since reading about the staff, and I'm pondering a few possibilities. It's just off the cuff, though."

Rem sipped his drink. "Sometimes that works best when you're stuck, which we are."

"Bear with me." Trick squinted. "People in a drug rehabilitation center are dying suspiciously. Some bleeding from their noses and ears." He paused. "That implies they're sick."

"Sick from what?" asked Mikey. "And why are they all suffering from the same thing?"

"Exactly," said Trick, pointing at her.

"You think someone is making them sick?" asked Rem.

Trick rubbed his jaw. "I think it's bigger than that. Carla inquired about several staff members. What if they're all involved?"

"Which is why I said conspiracy," added Mikey. "But I don't get what they'd be trying to accomplish."

Trick leaned in. "I think Ruben Montes is our first clue. He's the only one with enough clout and money to potentially instigate a conspiracy, if that's what this is."

"But why?" asked Mikey. "What for?"

"His family is in the pharmaceutical business," said Trick.

"What do they care about Windhaven?" asked Rem. "An addiction treatment center is small potatoes for them."

"Not necessarily." Trick stared off.

"Oh, man," said Mikey. "He's got that look in his eye. He's either going to tell a lousy joke or come up with a brilliant theory."

"I'll wager you five bucks it's the latter," said Rem.

"I'll take that bet," replied Mikey.

Trick looked back and narrowed an eye at them. "And I'm bothered about Tracy Pham, our registered nurse and nutritionist. She has an advanced degree in biology. Why is she working at Windhaven doling out prescriptions, monitoring patients' health and creating fancy menus?"

"Maybe it pays better," said Rem. He spoke to Mikey. "So far, I'm winning."

"Not yet," said Mikey. "There could be a punchline coming."

Trick paused, still staring off, until he finally spoke. "What if somebody on the inside is using the patients as guinea pigs? Trying out drugs on them as some sort of test."

Mikey sucked in a breath.

"I win. I'll take my five bucks," said Rem.

"How can you not consider that a joke?" asked Mikey. She looked at Trick. "That's insane. How could anybody take that risk and not get caught?"

"I tend to agree with Mikey." Rem wiped a drip of coffee from his shirt. "Wouldn't these drugs show up in an autopsy?"

Trick pursed his lips. "Depends on the drug." He picked up his coffee cup. "Plus, they're addicts. Nobody does much digging if it looks like an overdose."

"But these people are celebrities and wealthy," said Mikey.

"Not all of them," said Trick. "Mason's part of a sponsorship. I found Windhaven through a middleman or woman. Her name was Mallory. She alerted me to the sponsorship and the availability at Windhaven. If she did it for me, she's done it for others. People who get a free ride would be easy targets. They'd fall beneath the radar."

Mikey tensed in shock. "You're right about that. None of the people who've died are rich or famous."

"See? I think I'm onto something," said Trick. He took a sip of his drink.

Rem set his coffee down. "I don't know. It's still a long shot. Isn't Ruben Montes estranged from his family and the family business?"

"That's the rumor," said Trick. "But what if he's more involved than we realize?"

"Even if we buy this wild theory, what would be the purpose?" asked Mikey, trying to make sense of it. "Ruben's already rich. Why would he risk everything to do something like this?"

Rem looked up as Daniels returned. "Maybe we should ask Ruben." He took the ice cream sandwich Daniels offered. "Thanks."

Daniels sat with his apple. "What are we asking Ruben?" He bit into it and chewed.

Mikey snorted at Rem. "Ruben Montes isn't going to say one word to you. He's already gotten away with two murders. You think he's going to be intimidated by two detectives sniffing around?"

"Why are we talking to Ruben Montes?" Daniels repeated and then swallowed and wiped his face with his napkin.

Trick filled him in on his potential theory.

Daniels nodded. "Mikey's right. We talk to Ruben, he'll lawyer up and won't say a word. What we need is evidence."

"What about Mason?" asked Rem. "He told you he talked to Ruben? If they've established a rapport, that might work to our advantage."

Alarmed, Mikey gripped the edge of the table. "Mason is a patient. That makes him vulnerable. He could easily become the next target."

Daniels raised a hand. "Before we get ahead of ourselves here, let's keep in mind that this is still just a theory. If there is a doping mastermind at large inside Windhaven, then how are they distributing these drugs? You can't just ask a person to roll up their sleeve or swallow pills without explaining why."

"Maybe the patient doesn't know," said Trick. "Maybe they're told it's vitamins or supplements."

Rem ripped open the wrapper of his sandwich. "I'm not saying you're wrong, but Daniels is right. We need evidence. If people were dying in droves, we'd have reason to dive deeper. But they're not. Daniels and I did some checking, and most people who leave that facility do so on two feet and live successful, upstanding lives without relapsing, both sponsored and unsponsored. If they're on these drugs, how do you explain that?" He took a bite of his ice cream.

"Whether there's one person involved or several, it would be logical to assume that if drugs are being administered, then they'd have different effects on people," said Trick. "And maybe some don't get drugs at all. Obviously, it wouldn't look too good if a wealthy, famous person died suspiciously after leaving Windhaven. Too much exposure."

Daniels held his apple. "So, if Rain, our tattoo guy, is involved in Laura's death, that would mean he has some connection to Windhaven. How does that fit with Lenora? She was never at Windhaven." He took another bite of his apple.

"She was an addict, though," added Mikey. "Maybe this guy got a hold of whatever drugs that messed up these patients and gave them to Lenora, or maybe she discovered something like Carla did, and got killed because of it." She leaned back and grunted. "And none of this explains his telekinesis."

"We need to find this Rain," said Rem. He licked at the melting ice cream on the edges of his sandwich. "He's the key."

"If any of this is true," said Daniels, "then as their doctor, Hamlish has to be involved. Maybe the threat of Laura's journal being out there will get him talking. He won't want to go down with the ship if he's not the captain."

Rem took a huge bite of his ice cream sandwich. "If he's not the captain," he mumbled around his mouthful, "who is? Ruben?"

"Hard to know," said Daniels. "Like Trick says, he certainly would have the clout."

Trick fiddled with the lid on his coffee cup. "Let's hope Mason got some answers on his hunting expedition. Because if he didn't, as much as I like my theory, we're still grasping at straws."

Slurping at the edges of his treat, Rem nudged Daniels. "Mason's calling Trick and Mikey tonight with an update. Feel like joining the conversation?" An ice cream drip fell on his shirt, and he cursed.

"I told you to get the banana." Daniels spoke to Trick and Mikey. "Absolutely. Wouldn't miss it. Where and when?"

"How about at SCOPE?" asked Mikey. "At nine o'clock."

"Works for me," said Rem. He swiped at his shirt with a napkin, but only smeared the ice cream more.

"The rate you're going, we'll have to stop at your place for another shirt," said Daniels.

Rem popped the last dripping bite of his sandwich into his mouth and quickly chewed and swallowed. "What for? It wouldn't be the first time I had a stain on my clothes."

"That's the truth," said Daniels. "It would be stranger if you didn't have a stain somewhere on you." The two women at the end of the table stood and left. "They look stain-free. Maybe you could ask them for some pointers."

Trick chuckled.

Rem made a face, grabbed Daniels' water and poured it over his hands to clean them. Then he used the water to wet a napkin and dabbed at his shirt. "I'd consider it, but we've got to go."

Checking his watch, Daniels stood. "Yep. We do. Feel free to use my water to clean up." Shaking his head, Daniels sighed as Rem wiped his hands on his t-shirt to dry them. "You guys good for now?" Daniels asked Mikey and Trick. "Any more hidden information you'd like to share?"

"Nothing regarding this case," said Mikey. Rem glanced at her, and Mikey smirked and offered Rem another napkin. "We won't know more until we get the report on Ruben. Hopefully, I'll have that when you come by tonight."

Rem finished with his shirt, stood and tossed his wet napkins into a nearby trash can. "You two be careful. If we have a nut job running around who's willing to kill to hide a secret, whether it's Rain or someone else, then we all need to be aware."

Mikey groaned. "Tell him to join the club. We've already got Marge to worry about."

Rem picked up his coffee cup. "I hear you. Just don't get cocky." He held out Daniels' half-empty water bottle. "You want this?"

"It's all yours." Daniels bit into the remainder of his apple and picked up his jacket.

"I could tell you both the same thing," said Mikey. She spoke to Trick. "We should head out, too."

"I'm ready when you are." Trick stood along with Mikey. "We'll see you two tonight."

"We'll be there," said Daniels, chewing, as they headed toward their car.

ell

Sitting at the opposite end of the bench, eating the last bite of his salad, Kessler watched the group of four leave. He checked the time on his phone, picked up his plate, and stood. Watching the parking lot, he saw the two detectives get in one car and the other two get in a truck. They both pulled out and left. Thinking about what to do next, he tossed his plate and cup in the trash and headed to his own car.

Chapter Twenty-Seven

MIKEY PACED WHILE WAITING for Mason's call. "What time is it?"

"It's a minute after the last time you asked," said Trick from his desk. "Don't worry. He'll call."

Rem leaned back on the couch. "What time did he call before?"

"Nine thirty," said Trick. "Why don't you sit, Mikey? Try and relax."

Daniels sat in the chair beside the couch. "I'm sure he's fine."

Anxious, Mikey walked over and sat beside Rem. "This plan for him to call only when he has information isn't going to work for me. Considering how dangerous this is getting, he's got to check in more often."

"You've got a point," said Daniels.

"Depends," said Rem. "If he struck out, we may have nothing to worry about. We'll be at a dead end."

Mikey held her forehead. "I don't know what to wish for. That he found something incriminating or didn't."

"You get anything on Ruben Montes yet from your hacker?" asked Rem.

"Nothing," said Mikey. "I'd complain, but I don't think you can do that with a hacker."

"You're stuck with his schedule, whether you like it or not," said Daniels.

"Let's hope he didn't disappear with your money, and you never hear from him again," added Rem.

"He'll get in touch." Mikey sighed. "He's probably busy."

Rem smirked. "Hopefully not with cracking the code to some secret department in the Pentagon."

Trick chuckled. "Or the F.A.A."

"Or taking a big corporation hostage with ransomware," said Daniels.

Mikey narrowed her eyes. "Very funny." Trick's phone rang, startling her.

Trick picked it up and answered. "Red? You're on speaker." He stood from his desk and walked to the coffee table, where he put the phone down.

Mason spoke, his voice low. "You two okay?"

Exasperated, but relieved to hear Mason's voice, Mikey huffed. "Us? You're asking about us?"

"We've got Daniels and Rem here, too," said Trick, sitting in the chair next to Daniels. "We all want to know what you discovered."

"Hey, Mason," said Rem. "Glad to see you made it out of the closet."

"You gave us quite a shock," said Daniels.

Mason's quiet voice traveled back over the cell. "Yeah, well, your interrogation of Hamlish made it worth it. You guys had him sweating."

"He didn't crack, though," said Rem.

"Not yet, at least," said Daniels.

"We might change that," said Mason. "I found Carla's file."

Mikey clenched her fingers together. "Anything good?"

"Basic stuff at first," said Mason. "Hamlish suggested she did drugs and booze and thought she might have suicidal tendencies, which doesn't help the case."

"No, it doesn't," said Rem.

"But it's what he wrote next that got me intrigued. She's part of a trial."

Mikey dropped her jaw and eyed Trick. "Trial? What trial?"

"I don't know," said Mason. "Hamlish didn't go into detail. But he made a note to check with Tracy about Carla's dosage. He implied there might be negative effects."

Rem glanced at Trick. "Looks like your theory might hold some weight."

"What theory?" asked Mason.

Trick explained what they'd discussed earlier outside the food truck.

Mason paused. "It's plausible. I also found a sheet of paper with a list of several names with either check marks or X's beside them. It included Amelia, Chauncey, and August. Carla was there, too. She had a check mark that had been crossed out and an X added. Amelia, Chauncey and August all had X's."

"What about Barry?" asked Mikey. "The guy from your therapy group?"

Mason sighed over the phone. "Hell. I didn't notice. I was moving fast, and I'm not sure if he was listed. Plus, I saw another name that distracted me."

"Who?" asked Trick.

"Mine," said Mason. "I was at the bottom of the list with a check mark."

Mikey's blood ran cold. "Are you serious?"

Daniels and Rem tensed, and Trick set his jaw. "What do you think it means, Red?" asked Trick.

"No idea," said Mason. "I checked my own folder. Apparently, I'm also involved in some trial."

Scared, Mikey held her breath. "We have to get you out of there."

"I can't leave, Mikey," said Mason.

"Listen, Mason," said Rem. "Mikey's right. If Trick's theory is accurate and there is some sort of experimental drug treatment going on at Windhaven, it sounds like you're a part of it. It might be wise to check out."

"While you can still do it on your own two feet," added Daniels.

"I don't like this either," said Trick. "You've got no backup in there."

"I don't disagree, but I'm all we've got at the moment." Mason sighed. "I need more time. Whatever it is they're doing here needs to be exposed. I feel fine, so if I am getting something, maybe it's mild and won't have long-term effects."

Mikey did her best to sound calm. "You don't know that." She took a second to collect herself. "I admire you for what you want to do, but it's not worth risking your life over it." She recalled their fight that afternoon. "I said things today I wish I hadn't, and if that ends up being one of the last interactions I have with you, I'll never forgive myself."

"Never apologize for being honest, Mikey," said Mason. "Nothing you said today changes anything between us. True or not, I heard what I needed to hear, and I'm glad you got a chance to say it." He went quiet. "And I still have to stay. I couldn't live with myself if I left these people to fend for themselves. God knows how many are affected."

His face taut, Trick leaned toward the phone. "Then what do you want to do next?"

Mason was silent for a moment. "What did you find out about the staff?"

Trick told him what the hacker had learned.

"That's detailed stuff," said Mason. "You're getting pretty talented on the web, Mikey."

Mikey met the gaze of the men at the table. "It was easier than I thought." She looked back at the phone. "But how does it help?"

"I want to talk to Tracy," said Mason. "See if I can get anything out of her. Maybe look around her clinic. If she's got a strong scientific background, I want to know what she's using it for."

Mikey groaned. "Hell."

"And I want to speak to Manolo," added Mason.

"The chef?" asked Rem.

"Yes," said Mason. "If this is some sort of drug trial, then how are they getting us to ingest the drugs? I haven't been given any pills or shots. The only answer that makes sense is the food."

Trick straightened. "That's why Laura wanted us to check on Manolo." He eyed Mikey. "They're spiking the food."

"That's pretty damn tricky," said Daniels. "How do they keep track of who gets what meal?"

"Windhaven caters to the rich," said Mason. "Everyone gives their order at a counter in the dining room. There's a specific menu each night. If the staff member writes the name of the patient, it would be easy to dose the food."

"That's a hell of an operation then," said Daniels. "And a lot to keep track of."

"I suspect they've been doing this a while," said Mason.

"So, Tracy, Manolo, and Hamlish have to be involved," said Trick.

"They'd have to be in order to observe, study and treat the effects of whatever we're given," said Mason. "I don't know about Candace or Kessler, though."

"What about Ruben?" asked Rem. "Was he mentioned in Hamlish's files?"

"No, he wasn't," said Mason. "But something tells me he's got a finger in the pie. You don't do something like this without serious funding. And his family would be the perfect investors."

Daniels shook his head. "God. Can you imagine if they're involved? Could their pharmaceutical company actually be testing drugs on unsuspecting patients at a drug treatment facility?"

"The scandal would ruin them," said Rem. "That's a lot of money to lose."

"Which is probably why people have died," said Mikey, "to protect the secret." She sucked in a breath. "Maybe that's who Rain works for."

"Rain?" asked Mason. "Who's Rain?"

Mikey explained Rain and his connection to Lenora Rodriguez and Laura Dunn, his tattoo and unique abilities. "Have you seen anyone matching that description?"

"No. I haven't, but I'll definitely keep an eye out," said Mason. "He'd be hard to miss."

An idea occurred to Mikey, and she sat up. "What about a search warrant?" She eyed Rem. "Can you guys go in there based on what Mason saw in the files?"

"I wish," said Rem.

"No," said Daniels. "Mason snuck in and read personal files. A doctor's confidential information is not subject to search unless we have evidence of criminal activity. Right now, our illicit drug trial is still a theory. For all we know, the trial Hamlish mentions in his notes can be easily explained. What we need is to connect someone inside Windhaven to the deaths of the patients or connect this guy Rain to Windhaven. Right now, we can't do either."

"It's a good thought, though," said Trick. He spoke to Mason. "Red. Are you planning on talking to Tracy and Manolo tomorrow?"

"Yes," said Mason. "I've got a riding lesson after lunch, along with my individual and group therapy. I'll fit it in somewhere in between."

"Another riding lesson?" asked Mikey. "Are you starting to like horses?"

Mason gave a small chuckle. "It's an acquired skill. Plus, Kessler is a good instructor, and it gives me a reason to talk to him. He doesn't say much, but maybe I can find out why Laura included him with the other staff members."

"Be careful," said Trick.

"I will."

Worried about her brother, Mikey raised her hand. "Listen. You've got to get in touch with us more often so we know you're safe. This waiting for you to contact us isn't enough."

"Can you reach out more often?" asked Rem.

"I have to be careful not to rouse suspicion," said Mason. "I could call or text you before breakfast, and I can probably swing by the room before lunch, too. I'd have to be quick though. And I'll update you at night."

"I'd rather you call in case we need to pick up and tell you something," said Mikey.

"I won't be able to talk until the evening, so it would have to be for an emergency only," said Mason.

"That's fine," said Mikey. "Plus, it makes me feel better."

"Just a fast ring is all we need. We won't answer unless it's critical," said Trick. "We just want to know you're okay. We don't hear from you, though, then we summon the cavalry."

"I can live with that," said Mason.

"We get the bat signal, and we'll be on our way," said Rem. "Let's hope you find something, though, or we'll catch hell for busting into Windhaven without a warrant."

"I can't foresee a reason why I wouldn't be able to contact you," said Mason, "so feel free to come in guns blazing."

"Candace will love that," said Rem.

"Maybe I'll try to talk to her, too," answered Mason. "Laura included her for a reason."

"What can we do?" asked Mikey. "Besides sitting around and waiting to see if you're still alive."

"Get the information on Ruben," said Mason. "Keep digging into him and try and find this Rain with the tattoo. Maybe between the two, you'll get some answers and then I can get out of here." He paused. "And see if you can check the blueprints on this place. I found a door to a secret hall that led somewhere before I left Hamlish's closet. There was even a hidden button that opened it. I almost had the guts to explore it but backed off."

"A secret room?" asked Daniels. "What would they need a secret room for?"

"Maybe they experiment with more than just drugs," said Rem.

"You had to say that, didn't you?" said Mikey.

Rem made a snort. "Don't tell me you weren't thinking it."

"Rumor has it that Ruben has a wing all to himself," said Mason. "Maybe it's true."

"I doubt it's some bizarre research lab," said Trick. "I don't think Windhaven would go that far." He eyed Mikey. "Let's try not to think the worst, but we'll look for blueprints."

Mikey dropped her head. "I really wish you would reconsider staying, Mason."

His expression guarded, Trick spoke. "You sure you want to do this, Red? The longer you stay, the longer you're exposed to whatever crap they're possibly giving you. We can continue the investigation from out here."

"I understand the danger, but if I leave, you investigate and they get nervous, which they probably already are after Rem and Daniels' visit, they'll pull up stakes and we'll never catch them."

"Mason, it's a huge risk," said Mikey. "You don't know what you've been exposed to or who might be on to you." She tried to think of a way to get Mason to reevaluate his decision. "What if it were me in there? You wouldn't sit by for two seconds before marching in and taking me out."

Mason went quiet. "Okay, Mikey. I hear you. Just give me forty-eight hours. If I don't get something and neither do you, then I'll leave, and hope we can catch them another way."

"You promise?" asked Mikey, feeling more hopeful.

Mason spoke softly. "I promise."

Chapter Twenty-Eight

MASON APPROACHED THE STABLES after a busy morning. After a restless night's sleep, he'd woken early and had attended the meditation circle. He figured that after the anxiety of the previous day and the activity planned over the next forty-eight hours, he could afford to quiet his mind.

After the circle, he'd stopped by his room, called Trick's phone, let it ring a few times, and hung up. Then, after a hearty breakfast where Mason had wondered what could be in his food, he had a session with Hamlish. Hamlish had spent the hour wanting to dive deeper into Mason's outburst with Trick and Mikey. It had been harder to discuss than Mason expected, and he anticipated Hamlish would encourage him to discuss it with the group. Mason hadn't decided yet if he would. It still made him uncomfortable.

Before lunch, he'd seen Candace in the hall. He'd stopped and said hello, but she'd been distracted and not her usual perky self. He'd asked her about it, but she'd told him she'd been under the weather the last few days, and expected after a good night's sleep, she'd be back up to speed. Then she'd claimed to have a meeting and had left.

Mason had wondered if her behavior and mood had more to do with Rem and Daniels' visit. Hamlish had seemed relaxed and had not shown any signs of distress during their session, but Mason suspected his years of experience in hiding emotion had helped.

During lunch, Mason ate quickly and brought his plate to the kitchen. While there, he looked for Manolo, but didn't see anyone. Thinking about how to find and talk to the chef without arousing suspicion, he wondered if he could get an introduction.

He'd left the kitchen, helped himself to a cup of tea and found a spot in the sitting area next to the dining room. Eyeing the time so he wouldn't be late for his riding lesson, he waited. A few minutes passed, and he got lucky when he spotted Tracy walking by. Holding his tea, he stood quickly and walked toward her. "Tracy," he called.

She stopped and swiveled. For a moment, he thought he caught a brief look of anxiety on her face, but then she smiled.

"Mason," she said. "How are you?"

He approached her. "I'm doing well. How are you?"

"Great," she replied. "What can I do for you?"

Mason offered her his most charming grin. "I just can't say enough about Windhaven and the food. I wanted to thank you for checking in with me and following up. I appreciate it."

"I'm so glad. I'm happy I could help."

Mason mentally crossed his fingers. "I was hoping I could meet Manolo. I'd love to thank him in person and meet the man who deserves a lot of praise for the delicious menu."

Her smile froze in place, but then she nodded back. "Uh, sure. I think I can arrange that."

"Is he free now?" Mason checked his watch. "I've got a riding lesson soon, so it would just take a minute."

Tracy hesitated. "I don't see why he wouldn't be available." She glanced toward the kitchen doors. "Let's go check."

"Thank you." He followed her as she walked into the kitchen and stopped at the counter. "Manolo?" She walked behind the counter. "Give me a second. I'll see if he's in the back."

"No problem. I'll wait."

Tracy disappeared behind another door, and he heard her call Manolo's name again. A few quiet seconds passed, and then the door opened. A short, thin man with olive skin and creases around his eyes, wearing black slacks with a white shirt, walked out. "Yes?" he asked.

Tracy appeared at the door and watched them.

"Manolo?" asked Mason. He introduced himself and held out his hand. "I just want to thank you for the wonderful meals. You do a great job feeding everyone here."

Manolo shook his hand. "Thank you."

"It must be hard with so many picky people. Your clientele must be difficult to please. Me included. I know I complained a few times after I arrived."

Manolo dusted what looked like flour from his pants. "You get used to it after a while. It comes with the job."

"How long have you worked here?"

"Four years."

"You must get to know the patients fairly well. I bet you've met plenty of celebrities."

Manolo furrowed his brow. "Not usually. I keep to myself. I prefer to stay in the background."

Mason considered his next question. "I saw Ruben Montes the other day. He must be challenging to cook for." He leaned in. "Is he pretty demanding?"

Manolo squinted, and Mason gauged Manolo had less experience in hiding his thoughts than Hamlish did. "He's a friend, so no, he's not difficult."

"A friend, huh? I've seen him around." Mason sipped his tea. "Does he get to know people, because he seems pretty standoffish."

"I wouldn't know. That's his business."

Mason nodded. Aware of Tracy's gaze on them and his lack of time, he pushed further. "Speaking of business, doesn't his family run a big pharmaceutical company?"

"They do, but Ruben has backed away from all of that."

Mason noted how Manolo had offered information he hadn't asked for. Was Manolo nervous?

"I've heard, but sometimes it's hard to turn your back on family, no matter how hard you might try."

"Maybe. I wouldn't know."

Mason shrugged. "I suppose not. You're too busy dealing with all the food, right?" He chuckled and tipped his head. "To be honest, I'm curious about how you managed me and my complaint so quickly. You literally made my food better overnight. How'd you do it?" He lowered his voice. "Any secret ingredients you want to share?"

Manolo's face fell, and he opened his mouth, but Tracy interrupted. "Manolo," she said from the doorway. "Your phone's ringing."

Mason glanced over at her, and he caught her shift in energy. His question had bothered her. "Sorry. I'm asking too many questions," he said. "I tend to do that." He sighed. "I need to get to a riding lesson, so please feel free to answer your phone."

Manolo paused and studied Mason. "It's no problem. I'm glad you're enjoying the food." He turned but looked back with a grin. "And my secret ingredients? Everybody seems to like them, from what I've seen."

"Manolo, your phone," said Tracy in a sharper tone.

"Nice meeting you," said Mason, as Manolo walked away.

Tracy disappeared into the back of the kitchen with Manolo, and reflecting on his conversation with the chef, Mason had headed to the stables, wondering what Manolo had meant about everyone enjoying his ingredients. Was that confirmation that he was doctoring the food?

Frustrated, Mason rubbed and stretched his neck. It was going to be hard getting anything concrete without coming out and asking if the staff at Windhaven were drugging people without their consent. And worse, he had only another day and a half to find evidence of whatever Carla had discovered. She'd obviously had a source, but he didn't know who. At this rate, Carla's murder would never be solved.

He entered the stable and saw Tinkerbell's head poking out of her stall. He walked over and patted her neck. "Hey, Tink. You ready for a nice slow walk?"

A male voice spoke from behind him. "I told you. You've graduated. You're riding Storm today."

Mason turned to see Kessler walking toward him, holding the reins to Storm, who had been saddled. Storm bobbed her head and nickered. "You sure about that?" asked Mason.

"You can't stick with the easiest horse and expect to improve." Kessler patted Storm's neck. "She's a good horse. She knows what she's doing."

Mason didn't feel as confident. "The question is, do I know what I'm doing?"

"How will you know until you try?" He handed the reins to Mason. "I'll be right beside you with Thunder. You've got nothing to worry about. I told Storm you're a newbie. She'll take that into consideration."

Uncertain, Mason took the reins. "That's good to hear. Let's hope she listened."

"Let me saddle Thunder, and I'll be ready in a second." He walked over to Thunder's stall.

Mason studied Storm, admiring her gray-dappled hair and dark mane. She was a beautiful horse. "Well," he said, "if Carla trusted you, then I'll take that as a good sign."

Kessler spoke from inside Thunder's stall. "Carla loved Storm. I think you know she rode her frequently. Carla visited the stables often."

"She did, huh?" Mason wondered if Kessler knew of Carla's death. He decided to find out. "It's a shame what happened to her."

Kessler didn't answer, but Mason heard shuffling from inside Thunder's stall. It didn't take long before Kessler emerged, holding the reins to a saddled Thunder. "You heard about Carla?"

"I did."

"How?"

"Family visit. I asked my sister to look Carla up since she left so abruptly. I found out yesterday." Mason watched Kessler for any odd reactions. "I can't believe she relapsed."

Kessler didn't say anything, and Mason tried to read him, but found it difficult. Was Kessler angry, grieving or wondering how to kill Mason? Mason couldn't tell.

"Family visit, huh?" Kessler walked Thunder up beside Storm. "Maybe you shouldn't believe everything you hear."

His heart rate picking up, Mason brushed his hand down Thunder's shoulder. "What do you mean?"

"I think you know exactly what I mean." Kessler held Mason's look, and Mason started to respond when another male voice interrupted.

"I see you're riding Storm today."

Mason recognized the accent and spotted Ruben Montes. He'd entered the barn wearing a white, ironed shirt with riding pants and boots. "Care for company, Mason?" asked Ruben.

Kessler stood next to Mason. "He's got a lesson today. It's his first time on Storm, and I was going to join him on Thunder."

"Even better." Ruben approached Thunder and nuzzled his nose. "How about I take you out today, Mason? I believe you promised me a ride."

Mason narrowed his eyes, knowing he'd promised no such thing. "I don't think you'd get much enjoyment out of riding with me. I don't plan to go faster than a disabled turtle."

"All the better," said Ruben. "We'll take our time. Maybe catch up on what you've been up to since we last spoke."

Kessler eyed Ruben and then Mason.

"That sound okay with you, Kessler?" asked Ruben. "I promise I'll go easy on him. No races or jumps." He grinned.

Kessler's expression didn't change. "That's up to Mason. It's his lesson."

Mason's mind whirled. He realized Kessler would be the safer choice, but if he needed information, Ruben was the person to talk to. But if Ruben suspected his motives, Mason could be putting himself in a vulnerable situation. Recalling what Tammy had said about Carla falling off Thunder, he prayed he wasn't being stupid. He petted Storm's nose. "What do you say, Storm? You up for a walk with Thunder and Ruben?"

Storm didn't answer, but Mason caught the slight frown on Kessler's face. "You be careful, Mason," said Kessler. "Take it slow and remember what I taught you. Storm's smart. She'll take care of you."

Mason nodded, and Ruben took Thunder's reins. "Excellent. I've been looking forward to a relaxing ride. And now I get some company." Ruben smoothly hooked his foot in a stirrup and pulled himself up onto Thunder's saddle. "I'm ready when you are."

Mason put his own foot into Storm's stirrup and with a little less grace than Ruben, pulled himself up onto the saddle. Storm bobbed her head as Kessler adjusted the stirrups on both horses and Kessler gently patted Storm's haunches. "You're ready."

Ruben guided Thunder forward, and Mason followed, giving Storm a small nudge of encouragement.

"Go slow," said Kessler from behind him.

"I've got group, so I'll be back soon." Mason moved his body with Storm's as Kessler had taught him. Storm's gait was smooth and unrushed, and she had a soothing energy. Moving slowly, Mason felt comfortable with her. He could see why Carla had liked her.

"How are you doing?" asked Ruben from in front. "Getting the hang of it?"

Mason told himself to relax. "I'm getting there."

"Storm's a good horse. Just wait until you can pick up some speed and gallop. Then you'll understand why riding is so liberating." He slowed and let Mason and Storm come up beside him and Thunder. "When Thunder takes off, there's no stopping him. It's an adrenaline rush."

"I think I'll stick to a slower pace. Besides, by the time I graduate to a gallop, I'll be leaving Windhaven. I suspect my riding lessons will end after that."

Ruben glanced over. "What for?"

"Riding lessons require a disposable income not usually available to a paranormal investigator."

"So consider something different. I'm sure a man of your talents can make a great deal more money working for the right person."

The comment piqued Mason's curiosity. "You offering me a job?"

Ruben smiled. "Surrounding myself with people I can rely on is crucial in my business. When I see a talent I admire and could use, I go after it, especially when that talent is also smart and committed."

"The staff at Windhaven are certainly impressive."

"I can't take credit for that. But they were excellent choices, and they stick around. I myself, prize loyalty above all else."

Mason wondered whether Ruben had more to do with the staff than he chose to admit. He recalled the reactions to Ruben from Candace and Kessler. Did they even like him? He pushed Ruben a little harder. "Do you prize loyalty above the law?"

Ruben sharpened his gaze. "You know something I don't?"

Mason's heart thumped. How far should he go? "No. I doubt much gets past you."

Ruben dipped his head as Thunder passed beneath a low-hanging branch. "If someone under my employment was breaking the rules, the action I took would depend on what rules they're breaking."

"So some actions are justified, despite the consequences?"

Ruben grinned. "Don't tell me you didn't look the other way a time or two as a Ranger. I'm sure you used informants to get important information. And in return, they received lighter sentences or no sentences at all."

"I think you're comparing apples and oranges."

"I'm not sure I am."

Mason relaxed his hold on Storm's reins. He eased into the saddle as Storm strode down the trail. "We could debate that subject for the rest of my stay, but something tells me we still wouldn't agree."

"But you don't even know what I'm referring to."

"You're going to tell me?"

Ruben put his hand on the saddle horn. "I'm not sure you're ready to hear it."

Mason decided to be direct. "Does it involve murder?"

Ruben broke into a laugh. "Murder? How did we get to murder? Is that what you think of me?" He shook his head. "No wonder you don't like me. What exactly have you heard? Other than the obvious, of course. But you don't strike me as a man who makes judgements based on rumor and innuendo."

"Who says I don't like you?"

Ruben flicked a leaf off Thunder's mane. "You're not the only one who senses things, Mason. I think that's why I enjoy talking to you. You're not impressed with me."

"I'm plenty impressed."

"Because you think I'm a murderer?"

Mason scoffed. "I'm not concerned about your past, Ruben. It's your present that worries me." He paused. "And your future."

"You're wasting your precious brainpower on that? There's no need to be concerned about that which you have no control."

Mason thought about Mikey and Trick, and Rem and Daniels, and hoped they were making better progress than him. "I rarely see myself as helpless. That persistence you admire? It usually gets me what I want."

"I feel the same way." Ruben clicked his tongue, and Thunder picked up his pace. "I usually get what I want, too."

Storm matched Thunder's pace, but it was more of a fast walk, and although Mason tensed for a second, he relaxed when he realized he could handle it. "Until you meet your equal, and they want something different."

"Wouldn't that be an enemy?" Ruben glanced over. "I hope I'm not yours."

Mason debated his response. "The greatest threat to me is myself." He reflected on his own past. "Which I suppose is why I'm here."

"Me too." Ruben moved casually in the saddle, and Mason could see he was an accomplished rider. "We obviously have a lot in common," said Ruben.

"About some things."

Ruben smirked. "I sense we've returned to the murder subject." He sighed. "I can assure you, murder is not a solution to anything. Only the depraved use murder to solve a problem that could easily be solved in non-violent ways."

"What ways are those?"

Ruben swiveled and met Mason's gaze. "Why don't you come out and ask me what you want to know? Stop beating around the bush."

Mason stared back.

"Worried I might murder you?" Ruben chuckled and swiveled again to face forward. "So ridiculous. The world's more interesting with you in it."

"Isn't that what Hannibal said to Clarice?" It was one of the few movie references he knew. Mikey had dragged him to see *The Silence of the Lambs* the weekend it was released. She'd gone home and checked every closet and crevice, and Mason had gone to bed and slept like a baby.

"Did he?" asked Ruben. "Smart man." He smiled. "Of course, Clarice was far more attractive than you."

"Says who?" asked Mason. Storm started to trot, and Mason pulled the reins to slow her down. "But if you prefer honesty, then tell me why patients have—"

A piercing shot rang out, and Mason and Storm both startled. Thunder neighed and raised his front legs. "Easy, boy," said Ruben, expertly staying seated.

Mason yanked the reins, but Storm jumped when Thunder did.

"Mason," yelled Ruben, but Mason had no time to respond when Storm shot forward. Unable to hold on, Mason was thrown backwards and landed hard on the rocky ground.

Chapter Twenty-Nine

MIKEY SAT AT HER desk at SCOPE, tapping on her mouse. A notification popped onto the screen, and she sat up and accessed the incoming message. It was the information she'd been waiting for regarding Ruben Montes, along with her additional request.

After the conversation with Mason the previous night, she'd reached out to her hacker, inquiring about Montes' file, and asking for Windhaven's blueprints. It hadn't taken long for him to respond. He'd assured her he could have both by the following morning, with an additional fee for the blueprints.

Mikey had expected that and had made the payment. Worrying about Mason, she'd slept little that night, and she and Trick had arrived at SCOPE early. After getting the morning call from Mason, she and Trick stayed busy with work until they'd received Mason's afternoon call and Trick had left to meet with a potential client. Mikey had stayed behind to meet with Kyle. He'd had a few days off between cases, but two new ones had come in and Mikey needed to review them with him.

Excited to read the information and hopeful it would help Mason, she clicked the print button, and the printer whirred to life and spat out pages.

The outer door to SCOPE opened, and Mikey saw Kyle enter on the camera. Realizing she'd have to wait to read the file on Ruben, she almost groaned in frustration.

Kyle walked through the inner door holding two coffees. "Hey, Mikey."

"Hi, Kyle." Mikey watched another paper feed into the machine. "How were your days off?"

He handed her a coffee. "They were productive. Grandmother and I worked on another banishment."

Mikey took the cup. "You don't always have to buy me coffee."

"I don't mind. I know you like it, and I figure if I'm getting one, I should get you one, too."

Mikey nodded. "Well, thanks. I'll definitely drink it." She sipped it. "How was the banishment? Challenging?"

"Not as evil as Mason's Mr. Dark, but it was persistent. It took almost an entire day." He set his coffee down and slid off his jacket. He wore jeans and a fitted T-shirt, which showed off his muscled arms and shoulders. "How're things at SCOPE? You and Trick keeping busy?"

Mikey hadn't told Kyle everything about the investigation into Windhaven. She figured the fewer that were aware of it, the better. Valerie was due back in two days, and Mikey wondered how she'd handle Mason's role in tracking down Carla's killer. Mason had asked Mikey not to say anything to Val until she returned from Texas, and Mikey suspected Valerie might not be too thrilled.

"You could say that." She gestured at the couch. "Have a seat. This shouldn't take long. Trick's out with a client, but he'll be back soon."

Kyle went to the couch and sat. "How's Mason? How are the family visits going?"

Mikey grabbed her laptop and sat beside him. "He's doing really well and making significant progress. And our sessions with him have been helpful."

"That's good. I'm glad to hear it. I bet you're ready for him to come home."

"I am. I can't wait to see him every day. He'll continue his therapy on an outpatient basis, but at least he'll be back."

"And how's the situation with your sister, Margaret? Any updates?"

"None, I'm afraid." She pulled up the file on their new client. "But maybe no news is good news."

"Sorry to hear it. I hope your detective friends find her soon."

"Me too."

Mikey set the laptop down and told him about their two new customers. The first was a couple who were experiencing strange activity in their home. After doing research on the home's history, they'd learned that someone had died in it and were wondering if that was the reason for the disturbances. The second was a mother whose ten-year-old son was having strange dreams and was claiming to see things in their home. It had frightened her, and she hoped someone could help her figure out what her child was seeing. Although it was not a normal case, Mikey thought Kyle would be the perfect person to meet the boy and see if he could assist. He could talk to the parent as well and help explain things if he confirmed the child had paranormal abilities.

Kyle asked several questions and agreed to handle both. He said he'd follow up with each and would schedule appointments to meet with them, hopefully in the next couple of days.

"Thanks, Kyle," said Mikey, closing her laptop. "I know I'm a broken record, but I appreciate your help. Mason is going to give you a big kiss when he gets back."

Kyle smiled. "Maybe his sister might consider the same."

Mikey blushed. "Be careful what you ask for. Margaret gets attached."

He chuckled. "Maybe the other sister, then."

Mikey studied the floor. "Listen, Kyle. I know this arrangement has been unusual, to say the least."

Kyle relaxed back on the couch. "I didn't say that to make you uncomfortable. And this arrangement has been perfect. It's been nice to get to know you on a business and professional level. I can see why you're such a big help to Mason. You keep his business afloat."

"It's a two-way street. Mason's good at what he does."

Kyle nodded. "I hope when he comes back, that we'll still be able to see each other."

Mikey shifted on the couch. "Of course. We're good friends, Kyle. I hope that doesn't change."

He paused. "You think we might be more than that?"

Mikey stilled, unsure how to answer. That was the thing about Kyle. He didn't dodge touchy subjects. "It's difficult to answer that right now." She thought of Rem. "There's a lot going on, and I don't want to promise something I can't deliver."

"You don't have to promise me anything. I'm just hoping there's a light on somewhere that I might follow." He sat up, and his knee touched hers. "I've never been shy about my feelings for you. I like you. And if there's a chance for us to be more than friends, I'll take it." He paused. "I just want to be sure you feel the same."

She nibbled her bottom lip. "I like you too, Kyle. There's just, I don't know, things I have to consider."

"It's the detective, isn't it? The one I met the other day."

She widened her eyes. "Rem? What makes you say that?"

"The way he looked at you, and the way you look at him. There's an energy between you two."

Mikey sighed. "We have a lot in common. He's been through a lot, and so have I. We've helped each other through some rough spots. I think that's what you're picking up on."

"Probably, but if it's more than that, you owe it to yourself to explore it. If he's someone you want a relationship with, then let me know. But if he isn't, I'd like to know that, too."

Mikey pinched the bridge of her nose in disbelief that she was having this conversation. "God, Kyle. I don't know what to make of you."

"What do you mean?"

She dropped her hand and met his gaze. "You're like this perfect man. Good-looking, kind, talkative, understanding, smart, generous..." She groaned. "You could have anyone you wanted."

"But I don't want just anyone."

"I'm not like you. I'm not perfect. I've got a dangerous, crazy sister who could target you based only on your connection to me, a brother who's in drug rehab, and an ugly history that would scare off a hardened criminal. I don't balance my bank account, I hate to clean, I'm pushy, and ask Mason about my penchant to buy crap I don't need." She snorted. "I'm a mess."

"I love your imperfections, Mikey. They don't scare me."

She huffed. "Maybe you aren't as perfect as I thought."

"I'm not. Nobody is. Although I can be a perfectionist, which drives Mom nuts. I'm pretty sure I have OCD because I'm constantly checking and rechecking things I've done or haven't done, and I'm damn terrified of screwing this job up and making a mistake. The last thing I want is to look like a failure, especially to you."

Mikey dropped her jaw. "You're worried about what I think?"

"Are you kidding? All the time. You're tough, driven and unflappable, and you expect the best from everyone. It's intimidating. Why do you think I always buy you coffee?"

She stared in shock and then smiled. "Seriously?"

He nodded. "Seriously. And I'll tell you another thing. This Margaret problem scares me, too. I hate that you're vulnerable and have to stick next to Trick wherever you go." He shifted to face her. "If you need someone to stay with or watch out for you, I hope you'll feel comfortable coming to me. I've been wanting to tell you that for a while now."

"Why didn't you?"

"Because I was worried it was too much, and you'd say no. I didn't want to crowd you. You seemed pretty overwhelmed."

Mikey dropped her head. "I suppose I have been. It's been a tough couple of months."

"Which is why I've backed off. But Mason will come home soon, and I know my role here will diminish, if not disappear entirely. I'm just hoping I still have a play at the table. If you're betting on someone else, though, I'll honor that. I just need to know."

Mikey wondered how to respond. "Right now, Kyle, my concern is Mason. His well-being is the priority. And with Margaret running around, I don't think it's wise to start anything with anybody. It would be irresponsible." Thinking of Rem, she recalled his saying the same thing to her.

Kyle smiled.

She frowned. "Why are you happy? I just gave you bad news."

His smile grew. "No, you didn't. You gave me honest reasons why we should wait, and you didn't mention Detective Remalla. I'm going to take that to mean I have a shot. That's good news, not bad."

"Kyle—"

He raised a hand. "I'm not saying we're getting married or anything, but as long as there's a chance, I'm going to take it." He leaned close enough for her to feel his breath on her cheek. "Which means I'm going to keep buying you coffee."

His nearness made her skin prickle and her blood warm. "Okay," she whispered.

"Good." He held her gaze, and for a moment, Mikey wondered if he might kiss her, but the front door opened, and Mikey heard Trick yell from the front. "Mikey? It's me."

The moment broken, Kyle smiled again and stood. "I'll let you know how it goes after I contact the clients."

Mikey found it difficult to speak, so she nodded.

Trick walked in holding a handful of mail and stopped. "Oh, hey, Kyle." He eyed Mikey. "Did I interrupt?"

"Nope." Kyle grabbed his jacket. "We're done, and I was heading out. Good to see you, Trick."

"Good to see you, too," said Trick.

Kyle glanced back at Mikey. "I'll be in touch."

"See you," said Mikey.

Kyle left, and Mikey heard the outer door open and close. Groaning, she fell sideways onto the sofa.

Trick tossed his hat onto the chair. "Obviously, I interrupted something."

Mikey grabbed a blanket hanging over the back of the couch and pulled it over herself. "Just let me sleep for the next month or two. Wake me when Mason's home, Margaret's caught, and Kyle starts to lose his hair, his teeth fall out or he gets bad breath, or Rem decides what his next step is."

Trick sat in the chair and sifted through the envelopes. "Will do."

Mikey pulled the blanket over her head and closed her eyes, but then, recalling the printout, she opened them and sat up.

"Feeling better?" asked Trick. "Or do you just want to wish me luck before you hibernate?"

She tossed the blanket aside. "The news about Ruben. I got it." She stood and grabbed the papers from the printer.

Trick set the mail aside. "Why didn't you tell me?"

"Sorry. You might have noticed I had a brief meltdown." She returned to the couch and handed him the blueprints. "See what you can make of that." She started scanning the data on Ruben Montes.

"You got the blueprints, too?" he asked. "I thought we were going to look into that today."

"Why waste time when you have a perfectly good hacker at your disposal? I contacted him last night after we talked to Mason."

Trick studied the document and squinted. "It's not huge, but it's readable." He turned it sideways.

Mikey scanned the high points about Ruben. It covered mostly his younger years, siblings, and education, his parents and the company they'd founded. Then there was a section dedicated to the supposed suicide of his lover, the murder of his first wife and the subsequent trial and his acquittal, plus his second marriage and apparent affairs. The rest was dedicated to his philanthropy work and the various causes he supported.

"I can't make much out of this," said Trick. "How am I supposed to know what's secret and what isn't?"

Mikey lowered the papers. "Check the back of the building. That's where Hamlish's office is. If his closet leads to a secret wing, it would have to be there."

Trick frowned. "Anything interesting on Ruben?"

Mikey felt her frustration rise. "Not much that we don't already know, or that matters. Damn it."

Trick pointed. "Take a look at this." He stood and walked to the couch, where he sat next to Mikey. "What do you think?"

Mikey leaned over to look. She saw a large structure and took a second to figure out what she was looking at. "Is that the entrance?" she asked, spying the parking lot.

"Yes." Trick moved his finger over the paper. "We go in here." He traced a line down a hall. "This must be where we meet for our sessions. And here's a kitchen and dining area and what must be the residences." He paused. "Jeez. The grounds are extensive. They're bigger than I realized."

"I see the stables. That must be where Mason takes his lessons." She wondered where Mason was and what he was doing.

"Then this must be where Hamlish's office is. It looks like a set of offices down that hall."

"I'm sure it's an administrative area. The staff likely all have offices back there."

"There's nothing beyond that, though, except more land," said Trick. "So, if Mason saw a room, it's not on these plans." He lowered the blueprint. "Maybe it is secret, then."

Mikey went back to her papers. "Here. You take some. I've scanned it, but nothing incriminating pops out so far."

Trick took the papers and began to read. Mikey went back over the section on Ruben's family and was shocked to see how much they were worth financially. "These people have more money than some countries. It's crazy."

"Big pharma is known for its ludicrous pricing and its marketing of its products. It's amazing what they get away with."

She turned to another section and read about Ruben's supposed affairs. "No wonder he got away with murder. He probably paid off the whole jury, the judge included." Reading about another woman from Ruben's past, she sucked in a breath and grabbed Trick's elbow. "Trick."

Trick looked over. "You found something?"

Mikey reread the section to ensure she had it right. "Ruben has an illegitimate son. He raised him after an ugly court battle. The mom wanted the child, but also child support. A lot of it. Ruben denied the baby was his at first, but then the mom died in a car accident, and Ruben assumed custody."

"Makes me wonder if the mom's death was accidental."

Mikey eyed Trick. "Guess what the child's name is."

"Give me a hint."

"Rainier Montes."

Trick gripped his papers. "Holy shit."

"We found him," said Mikey. "Rain is Ruben's son."

Chapter Thirty

MASON OPENED HIS EYES, groaned and rubbed his neck.

"How do you feel?"

He blinked and focused in on the woman standing over him and recognized Tracy. "Everything hurts," he said.

"I bet it does."

Mason tried to recall where he was. The walls were white, and he was in a bed, but it wasn't his room. "What happened?"

"You fell off Storm." She leaned over and checked his eyes with a small penlight. "Do you remember?" She clicked the light off and straightened.

Mason blinked again, and the memories rushed back. He'd been riding and talking to Ruben, and then a loud shot had rung out, and Storm had taken off. "I do now." He tried to sit up. "Hell. Did the horse fall on me?"

"Thankfully, no, or you'd be in traction." Tracy sat beside him on the bed. "You hit the ground pretty hard. You probably have a mild concussion. I don't think anything's broken, though. You're pretty lucky."

Mason moved his arms and stretched his neck, happy that he was only sore. His head throbbed, but it was bearable. "Where am I?"

"You're in the clinic. Ruben and Kessler helped you back here and got you into the bed. You were pretty out of it."

Mason had a vague memory of Kessler and Ruben getting him on his feet and walking him back to the facility. He'd been dizzy and disoriented. "How's Storm?"

"Storm's fine. She didn't go far. Kessler retrieved her. She must have spooked and took off on you. Ruben said there was a loud noise like a car backfire."

Mason recalled the loud bang. He'd thought it had sounded like a gunshot, but he couldn't rule out a car, although he didn't think they'd been near the parking lot or a road. "How's Ruben?"

"He's fine. After he helped you here, he stuck around to be sure you were okay. When I told him it didn't look too serious, he left, but asked me to keep him apprised. He was worried about you."

Mason stretched his back. It was stiff but not too painful. "How long have I been here?"

"Not long. Maybe two hours."

Mason raised an eyebrow. "Two hours?"

"You needed to rest, so I let you. I stayed close, though. When they brought you in, you answered questions accurately and weren't delirious, which is a good sign. I was almost ready to call an ambulance when I first saw you."

Mason looked around. He spotted the usual equipment for a clinic. A counter with tissues, cotton balls, tongue depressors, a box of gloves, a blood pressure cuff, and a scale in the corner. Tracy had a stethoscope around her neck. The room was small in scale, but probably the perfect size for Windhaven. A small alcove revealed a clean desk with a chair across from it, a large cabinet, and another door marked private. He spotted a clock on the wall. "I guess I missed group."

"You did. But Hamlish knows what happened, so you're excused."

Mason was glad he'd been able to call Trick before getting thrown off Storm, or the cavalry would have arrived by now. Although his body ached, his fall had provided one small windfall. He'd gotten into the clinic without arousing suspicion. He pushed the covers back.

"Why don't you take it easy?" said Tracy. "Don't rush it. I'm still not sure you shouldn't be in a hospital."

"I'm okay. Just a little sore and embarrassed. I was afraid riding Storm would be too much too soon. I should have listened to my gut." He wondered if his fall had truly been accidental. Had he made someone nervous? Had the loud noise been intentional?

Tracy put a hand on his shoulder. "I'd feel better if you rested a little before getting up."

Mason nodded at her, hoping that if he stayed longer, he'd have time to look around a little. He wondered what was behind the private door.

"Maybe you're right." He rested back against the pillows.

"How's your head?" she asked.

Mason touched the back of his scalp, feeling a lump. "It hurts, but not too bad."

"I want you to stay put for a while. Maybe in an hour, I'll have you get up and walk around. If you get dizzy, I may have you remain here overnight, so I can monitor you."

"I'm sure I'm fine." Mason couldn't sleep there because he had to call Mikey and Trick that evening. He still had one more day at Windhaven, and he needed it to keep digging. "I dealt with worse in my Ranger days."

"Even so, I'll feel more comfortable if you wait a bit. We'll see how you're doing in an hour. But if you show any signs of a serious head injury, I'll call your family and get you to a hospital."

"I'm feeling better," said Mason, "but I'll stay to be sure." He laid his head back and sighed. "I promise I'll take it easy. You don't have to hover over me if you need to go do something."

She eyed him warily. "Okay." She stood. "Close your eyes and try to rest. I'll be nearby if you need something. Just give a shout and I'll hear you. I'll notify Kessler and Ruben that you're doing better."

"Thanks, Tracy."

She nodded, and walking to the door, gave him another glance, and left.

Mason waited a few minutes and listened. He heard muffled voices from the other side of the door, and it went quiet. If Tracy was close enough to hear him call, then he knew she wouldn't go far. He'd have to be quiet, fast and careful.

Moving slowly, he eased the bedcovers back and swung his legs to the side. Stifling another groan when his muscles protested, he carefully put weight on his legs and stood. He wobbled for a moment, but then balanced himself. His head pounded, but his other body parts seemed fine.

Taking a steady breath, but not hearing anything, he moved with cautious steps toward the desk in the alcove. Not seeing anything of interest, he went to the cabinet and tugged on a drawer, but it didn't budge. Disappointed, but not surprised that Tracy was more careful than Hamlish, he headed toward the door marked private.

Reaching it, he listened again for any sounds of anyone approaching, but it remained quiet. He put his hand on the knob, turned it and was relieved when it opened. He peered inside. It was dark, and he stepped into the space. He felt along the wall, found a light switch, and flipped it on. The room illuminated, and Mason found himself in a small laboratory. An impressive-sized microscope, along with Bunsen burners, beakers and pipettes sat atop a wide counter. A refrigerator stood against the far wall, and a sink and another counter with big cabinets above and below it were next to the refrigerator.

Mason stared at the array of equipment, trying to understand why an addiction treatment facility would require a laboratory. He moved farther into the room, opening drawers and cabinets, but only found more supplies, and nothing with any patients' names or papers. He tried another cabinet, but it was locked, and when he opened the refrigerator, he spotted an array of half-filled test tubes, all with numbers on them, plus other beakers with liquid inside them, and a lunch bag and soda can.

"What the hell are you doing?"

Mason jumped. He turned to see Tracy standing at the doorway, her glare aimed at him.

He closed the fridge. "Sorry. I was looking for the bathroom."

She narrowed her eyes. "Does this look like a bathroom to you?"

He chuckled sheepishly. "No. It doesn't. But when I flipped on the lights, I was surprised to see a lab."

"You're not supposed to be in here. That's why it's marked private."

"You're right. I'm sorry." He waved a hand at the lab. "I was just intrigued. I've always been nerdy when it comes to science and experiments. When I saw the microscope, I got curious." He stepped away from the counter and toward her. "What do you do in here? Are you studying something?" He kept his tone light and casual.

She stared for a moment, as if gauging how to respond. "It's not used often. Windhaven used to be a research facility before it was bought and modified to accommodate our behavioral therapy. This lab is the only one that remains." Her tone softened. "I'm nerdy myself when it comes to science, so I use it occasionally."

Mason noticed she didn't offer what she used it for. He met her gaze and surmised Tracy didn't rattle easily.

"You still looking for that bathroom?" She stepped aside.

"Yes, actually."

He walked out, and Tracy closed the door and locked it. "You seem to be up and moving around with no issues. That's good."

He rubbed his neck and shoulder. "I'm a little sore, but I think I'll make it."

"Good. I'll tell Ruben. He'll be glad to hear it. Kessler, too."

She walked to the door of the clinic and opened it. Mason followed and saw a small space with a couch, chair and coffee table. A bottle of water and a magazine were on the table. Beyond that was an exit to a hall that led to the library and the dining area and various therapy rooms.

"Is there a bathroom here?" he asked.

She crossed her arms. "You can use the one outside the dining hall or go to your room."

Seeing her body language, Mason got the message. "I'm guessing my rest is over."

She tilted her head. "I figure if you're well enough to snoop around my office, you're well enough to find your own room and take a nap." She walked into the clinic. "I'll check in on you. If you get dizzy, nauseated, or need an aspirin, you know where to find me."

Mason decided if she could be pissed, so could he. He turned and spoke tautly. "What do you really use that lab for, Tracy? And don't give me the whole 'this used to be a research facility' crap."

She stilled, and her eyes sparkled in the light. "You should be more careful around horses, Mason. Next time, you might not be so lucky." She held his gaze for a second. "I catch you snooping around again, and I'll have your ass kicked out of Windhaven. Just like I did with your friend, Carla." The side of her lip rose, and she turned and shut the door.

That night, Mikey was sitting beside Trick on Mason's sofa when the phone rang, and Trick answered. "Mason?"

"Trick?" asked Mason. "Mikey there, too?"

"I am," said Mikey. "It's just the two of us tonight. How are you?"

Mason made a soft moan. "Sore. And my ego's bruised."

"You okay?" asked Mikey, worried.

"I fell off a damn horse." Mason grunted. "Storm."

"During your lesson?" asked Mikey. "Are you hurt?"

"I'll live. And it was sort of a lesson. I was riding with Ruben. A shot rang out, and Storm took off, only I didn't go with her."

"A shot rang out?" Trick eyed Mikey. "You sure that was an accident?"

"Hard to say. I pushed a little harder around here today, so maybe somebody's warning me off."

Mikey leaned in. "Maybe you should leave sooner. We can pick you up in the morning."

"No. I want my full day. After my encounters with Candace, Tracy, Manolo, and Kessler, I'm sure they know what's going on at Windhaven." Mason told them about his conversations with each of them. "I just have to convince one of them to talk."

"What if you confront Hamlish with what you saw in the files? You think he'd cave?" asked Trick.

"I've considered that, and if I get nowhere tomorrow, that will be my last effort. After that, I might as well check out anyway because Hamlish will have me thrown out."

"There's something else, Mason," said Mikey. "We found Rain." She quickly told him about the data on Ruben and his son, plus the blueprints. "Rem and Daniels are trying to track down Rain but haven't had any luck yet. He's been arrested for drunk and disorderly and a DUI, but neither stuck. His last known address is bogus, but the witness from the parking lot confirmed that Rain Montes was the one talking to Laura the day she died."

"My guess is Ruben's high-powered attorneys took care of the arrests, and Ruben's protecting his son," said Mason. "They're going to have a hard time finding Rain."

"They need to connect him with a patient death from Windhaven. Lenora's not enough. Their next step is to talk to Ruben," said Mikey.

"Good luck with that," said Mason. "He'll just misdirect them. There's no way he'll turn over his son."

"Probably not, but it's worth a try," said Mikey. "Maybe they can instill a little fear into Ruben when he realizes they're zeroing in on his kid."

"I'm not sure Ruben knows what fear is," said Mason.

"The blueprints didn't show any secret room, Red," said Trick. "But if Rem and Daniels ever serve a search warrant on Windhaven, we know where to look."

Mason sighed. "If we can't link the deaths to Windhaven or Rain, then we may never sort this out. Ruben's a powerful guy, and he'll use every means at his disposal to protect himself and Rain."

"Maybe we've gone as far as we can go." Mikey gripped her elbows with nervous anxiety. "Between Ruben and Rain, their money and Rain's abilities, we might not be able to do anything else."

"I'm worried about Rain's connection to Lenora and your ex-friend Gina," said Mason, "who has similar gifts to Rain. It's too big of a coincidence. You think Ruben knew Victor?"

Mikey bounced her knee. "I don't know. Victor dealt with powerful people. It's possible he knew Ruben. I'd ask Gina, but I doubt she'd speak to me."

"Listen, Mason," said Trick. "This is getting dicey. You think they're on to you? Especially after you found the lab?"

"Tracy's suspicious of me. She's way more cautious than anyone else. But I think the worst she could do is get me thrown out."

Mikey snorted. "That's not the worst she could do. If they're drugging the food, they could slip you something you may not recover from. If it happened to Amelia, or even Barry, it could happen to you."

Trick shook his head. "Maybe don't eat tomorrow, Red."

"I still have time," said Mason. "They don't know I plan to leave, so they won't do anything rash. But if I were to stay beyond tomorrow, I'd start fasting. Since it's my last day, though, I intend to rock the boat."

"What's your plan?" asked Trick.

Mason went quiet for a moment. "I'll stick to the same schedule tomorrow. I'll ring you in the morning and at lunch. Then, unless you hear from me or Windhaven after that, pick me up at six o'clock. That's dinner time, and I'll have no plans to eat there, for my own safety."

"What do you think they'll do when you tell them you're checking out?" asked Mikey.

"Nothing. They won't know. I'll grab my blanket and walk out. By the time they realize I'm gone, I'll be on my way home."

"You'll need to find another therapy option," said Trick.

"That's the simple part," said Mason. "If I'm lucky, before I leave, I'll find something incriminating or get someone to talk. Anything that will give Rem and Daniels a reason to investigate Windhaven. Once we have that, I think the floodgates will open."

"I hope you're right," said Mikey. "But something tells me the doors to Windhaven won't unlock too easily."

"No, they won't. But all I have to do is crack them enough to scare somebody. Then the rest will take care of itself."

"It's the unknown that concerns me," said Trick. "We have an idea of what's going on and who the players are, but we may be wrong. Just watch your backside."

"My backside already took the brunt this afternoon," said Mason. "My butt's killing me. I can barely sit on the side of this tub."

Mikey prayed Mason would be safe and sound in twenty-four hours. "You better be sure your backside's still intact after tomorrow. You hear me? And don't ride any more horses."

"My horseback-riding days are over," said Mason.

"Make sure that's all that's over. You got it, Red?" asked Trick.

"I'll have Rem and Daniels on speed dial," said Mikey. "You're late on a phone call, and we're coming. And Candace better not get in my way."

"I'll be careful." Mason paused. "I'll see you two tomorrow."

Feeling emotional, Mikey bit her lip. "I love you, big brother."

Mason spoke softly. "I love you, too, sis."

Chapter Thirty-One

THE NEXT MORNING, MASON attended his last meditation circle at Windhaven. Afterward, he headed to his room, prepared to start his last day with a quick breakfast and a session with Hamlish. He'd decided that if he didn't make any progress that morning, he'd start prodding Hamlish during his group session after lunch. Maybe pushing some buttons in front of others might prove more effective and make Hamlish sweat. After his individual session, he'd planned to find Candace. He suspected she might be the next best person to question. If he probed in the right places, she might cave quickly.

Eyeing the time, he entered his room and closed the door. Needing to make his phone call, he opened the drawer and stopped cold when he saw a folded piece of paper lying on top of his shirts.

Startled, he looked around his room. Someone had obviously entered and left the paper. Had they found his phone?

Mason picked up the paper and dug beneath his clothes. His phone was where he had left it and appeared untouched. He opened the folded paper.

Come to the stables after breakfast.

Mason wondered who could have written it. Was it Kessler? Maybe, but maybe not. He debated what to do. If someone was onto him, was it safer to leave now? He knew he couldn't do that, though. This could be the opening he needed, especially if this note had originated from Carla's source. He doubted whoever had left the note planned any foul play, and if they did, it was a silly way to do it. There were plenty of other options to get to him other than luring him to the stables. Plus, there was the added risk of the note being discovered. He had to stay. Holding his phone, he quickly dialed Trick's number, let it ring a few times, and hung up.

After folding the note and putting it in his back pocket, he returned the phone to his drawer and headed to breakfast.

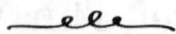

Trick popped the remainder of his biscuit in his mouth and sipped his coffee when his phone rang. He eyed the display and saw it was Mason.

Mikey ran in from the other room. "Is that him?"

"It is," said Trick. The phone rang twice and then stopped.

Mikey sighed. "I wish we could answer it."

"Too risky."

Mikey approached the breakfast table and sat. "This is going to be the longest day of my life."

Feeling the same, Trick swallowed his bite. "He'll be okay."

"Between now and lunch, he's vulnerable." Mikey crossed her arms.

"I don't like it either, but we have to trust him. Give him the time he requested. It's just one day."

"I told Rem to stick by his phone in case I call."

"Hopefully, he and Daniels won't be needed." Trick wiped his mouth with a napkin. "And Mason will be home this evening with or without some evidence of Windhaven peddling drugs to its patients without their knowledge."

"I hope we're wrong." Mikey rested her elbow on the table. "I hate to say it, but I hope Carla died of an overdose. Maybe she was close to something big, but maybe she wasn't. Maybe all those people died of natural causes."

Trick swiped a crumb from his face. "You really believe that?"

Mikey fell back into her seat. "No. I don't. But it helps me to stay calm, because if I think of the alternative, it scares me." She shook her head. "Stuff like this, that involves big corporations, big money and powerful people, means they'll do whatever it takes to protect themselves, and someone usually dies. And it's never one of them."

Trick didn't want to admit that she was right. He checked his watch. "Just give Red ten more hours."

"My gut's telling me that's too long."

"Then give him four. That will at least get us to lunch. And if we can get to lunch, then we can get to six o'clock."

Wishing she'd never agreed to another day, Mikey leaned her head back, and stared at the ceiling.

Mason entered the barn but didn't see anyone. He spotted Thunder in his stall just as Storm stuck her head out of hers. He walked over and patted her neck. "Hey, girl. How are you?" She bobbed her head at him. "Yesterday was a little scary, but no hard feelings, okay?"

She nickered, and he ran his palm down her nose.

"You back for another try?"

Mason turned and saw Kessler approach the stall. Was he the one who'd left the note? "I'll pass, thanks. Just thought I'd check in, though, and make sure Storm and I were still on good terms."

"Don't worry about Storm. She's moved on. Today is a new day." He looked Mason over. "How are you feeling? No lingering effects?"

Mason shrugged. "I'm sore, but I'll survive. I think my ego took the brunt."

Kessler nodded. "You're not sure what the noise was? It's not like Storm to take off like that. It must have been loud."

Mason hesitated. "It was a gunshot."

Kessler tensed and raised a brow. "A gunshot? You sure about that?"

"I was a Ranger. I'm sure." He turned toward Kessler. "The bigger issue is why somebody wanted to frighten Storm and endanger me." He recalled Mikey telling him about Kessler's background in the military. Had he fired the gun? "Any ideas?"

Kessler stared for a moment and ran a hand down Storm's neck. "I like you, Mason, but I get the feeling few others do."

"Carla did," said Mason. "She told me things. About Windhaven."

"Carla did and said a lot of crazy things." Kessler turned and picked up a large, heavily bristled brush. "She used to come to the stables and brush Storm all the time. She called it her 'happy place.'" He held the brush out to Mason. "Maybe you'd like to try it?"

Mason eyed the brush and then Kessler. It was an odd response to his statement. He took the brush. "As long as I don't have to ride."

Kessler smirked. "No riding required." He opened the stall. "Just head on in. Start at her head and work your way back."

Mason studied Storm. "She's not going to jump on me, is she? Stomp on my head?"

Kessler chuckled. "No. Storm loves to be brushed. Carla would sometimes sit in the stall with her when she needed a break. Right in that corner." He pointed. "I figured it couldn't hurt. She kept Storm company and could get some time for herself," he smoothed Storm's mane, "out of sight from others." He held Mason's gaze and stepped back. "Maybe it'll help you, too."

Mason caught the tone in Kessler's voice. "Now I'm curious." He thought of the paper in his pocket.

Kessler narrowed an eye but then waved toward Storm. "Just brush Storm. I'll be cleaning out Tinkerbell's stall."

Kessler walked away, and Mason looked toward Storm, who nibbled on some hay. He entered the stall and closed the door behind him. Holding the brush, he approached Storm and carefully slid the brush down her neck. The horse snorted, but didn't move, and Mason took that as a positive sign. He continued to brush her, wondering about Kessler. If he'd sent Mason the note, he clearly wasn't going to admit it, but no one else had showed. And the way he'd mentioned Carla and how she'd come here to get away—

Mason stopped brushing. He eyed the corner of the stall. Carla would sit there? It didn't look very comfortable. He set the brush down, walked over, and sat in the hay, trying to think like Carla. Why would she have come here? She could have gone for a walk on the grounds or ridden Storm instead.

Mason relaxed against the wooden slats and rested his head back. *What am I missing?* he asked himself. *Time's running short, Carla, so if you've got something for me, I need to know.*

Storm neighed, and Mason pushed back against the wall. The last thing he needed was for the horse to step on him. He put his hand against the wood, prepared to stand, when the wood gave way and buckled. Eyeing the rotten section of slats, Mason leaned close and noticed a small hidden space. Moving the wood aside, he froze when he spotted something red. He reached in and sucked in a breath when he pulled out a spiral notebook.

Mikey sat on the couch at SCOPE, thinking about Mason, but trying not to. It was close to lunch, and he would be calling soon. Trick had stepped out to pick up some sandwiches, and she'd tried to stay busy by talking to Kyle about his progress on his two cases and following up on a few potential new ones.

Her phone rang, and she jumped. Seeing it was Rem, she answered. "Hey."

"Hey, he said. "Any word from Mason?"

"No, but he's not due to call yet."

"Okay. I wanted to tell you we got a lead on Rain Montes. We found an old girlfriend, and she had an address on him. We got there, though, and he's not there."

Hopeful, Mikey sat up. "Did the girlfriend say anything about him?"

"She wasn't very inclined to talk. We only got the address out of her because we agreed not to say where we got it."

Mikey deflated. "At least that's something."

"She knew Lenora Rodriguez, though."

Mikey straightened again. "What did she say?"

"That Rain had a strange obsession with Lenora. He wouldn't leave her alone. And when she got out of rehab, Rain went looking for her."

Mikey gripped her phone. "Seriously?"

"The girlfriend was seeing Rain at the time, and he left when he learned Lenora was out, saying he was 'finally going to get that girl to listen to him'." Rem paused. "Lenora was dead the next day."

"My God," said Mikey. "Would she testify to that?"

"Don't count on it. Daniels and I had to do some careful coercing to get that much out of her. She's scared of Rain and wants nothing to do with him."

"You think you'll find him?"

"We'll find him. The question is what will he say when we do?"

"He'll lawyer up."

"Maybe not," said Rem. "Guys like Rain are arrogant and think they know better. He's so used to getting away with stuff, he might say something stupid. It's a long shot, but we might be able to push his buttons." Mikey heard a shuffle and Rem's voice muffled when he said something to someone and came back on the line. "We've got a car at his place keeping an eye out, so when he shows, we'll know it."

"Just remember what you said to me. Don't get cocky," said Mikey. "I'm already worried enough about Mason. I don't need to worry about you, too."

"Between Margaret and Rain, I think Margaret wins. She'd reduce Rain to tears. I almost wish she were around to interrogate him."

"Be careful what you wish for."

"No kidding. Call me after you hear from Mason, or if you don't."

"Believe me, I will. And thanks for the update."

"You got it."

Rem hung up, and Mikey leaned against the couch cushions, wondering about Rain, his connection to Gina and Lenora, and Ruben's involvement. Could Ruben be as dangerous as his son? Or was Rain as dangerous as his father?

Checking the time again, Mikey said another prayer for Mason.

Chapter Thirty-Two

MASON SAT THROUGH A difficult session with Hamlish. He'd almost skipped it after finding the notebook, but he'd missed group the previous day and knew Hamlish would come looking if he missed another session. Mason told himself to get through it, then he would go to his room and read the notebook.

He'd flipped through the pages before leaving Storm's stall. It contained numerous handwritten notes, and he'd caught a few names he recognized, but reading it in the stall was a risk, so he'd tucked it into the back of his jeans, said goodbye to Kessler, and left. He'd quickly returned to his room and shoved the notebook under his mattress. Then he sat, trying to think. Was Kessler the source, since he'd basically just told Mason where to find Carla's notes? Or had Kessler found the notebook and hidden it? Or had Carla asked him to hide it?

Mason had debated leaving Windhaven right then. If the notebook contained what he'd hoped, it could be the smoking gun that would bring Windhaven down. But it would need corroboration. Anyone could write what they wanted, but without proof, it was worthless. A good attorney could effectively neutralize whatever information Carla had discovered. Mason needed more.

Now, sitting through his therapy session, his mind wandered. If Kessler was the source, he would have to come forward, but would he? And if he wasn't the source, did Kessler know who was?

"You seem distracted today," said Hamlish.

Mason focused and shifted in his seat. "I guess so. I'm still a little sore after my fall yesterday."

"Did you let Tracy know?"

Mason shook his head. "No, but that's okay. I don't think she'd be eager to see me." Impatient, he was ready to get some answers. "She caught me snooping through her lab yesterday."

Hamlish stilled. "Her lab?"

"Yes. The one connected to her clinic." He chuckled. "I thought it was the bathroom. Silly me."

Hamlish frowned. "What did she say?"

Mason noted Hamlish didn't act surprised that there was a lab at Windhaven. "She kicked me out." He lowered his voice. "You'd think she was doing secret experiments or something."

Hamlish chewed on the end of his pen.

"Why does Windhaven have a lab, anyway? It seems odd." He cocked his head and crossed one leg over the other. "You guys are supposed to inhibit drug usage, not make more of them, right?" He told himself to go slow and not scare Hamlish, but then he asked the big question. "We're not guinea pigs, are we?" He laughed casually as if telling a joke.

Hamlish's face lost color, and he scoffed. "That would be funny, wouldn't it?" He chuckled but didn't look happy. "Can you imagine?"

Staying relaxed, Mason rested his hand on his knee. "No, I can't. The risk would be enormous, and the ramifications immense. People would go to jail...for a very long time."

Hamlish bobbed his head up and down, and his fingers tightened on the armrest of his chair. "Let's hope we don't get caught."

Mason narrowed his eyes. "Let's hope."

Hamlish cleared his throat. "All kidding aside, I don't know why we have a lab, or if it's even used. Probably used to be here before this place became Windhaven."

Mason chose not to mention the lab equipment and numbered test tubes he'd seen in the refrigerator. Hamlish was sweating enough. "Probably."

Hamlish checked his watch. "You know, I think we're good for today. Since you're still recovering, why don't you go rest, and we'll pick it up at group this afternoon. Sound okay with you?"

Mason couldn't wait to get back to his room. "Sounds great. I think I will lie down before I have to head to lunch."

Hamlish stood. "Then I'll see you this afternoon." He headed toward the door. "Enjoy your nap."

Mason nodded. "I will."

Hamlish exited, and Mason followed, happy that he had an excuse to disappear for a bit. Checking the time, he saw he had an hour before he needed to contact Trick and go to lunch. That would be the perfect amount of time to read the journal and decide whether to leave Windhaven now or continue to do some digging. After entering his room, he grabbed the journal, rested against his pillow on the bed and started to read.

Forty minutes later, he sat up, dismayed and shocked. Carla had indeed come to the same conclusions as Mason. Windhaven was using its patients to test drugs. Carla hadn't determined why they were doing it, or what drugs they were using, but her source had confirmed Tracy, Manolo and Hamlish's involvement. She'd also suspected Ruben, with his family's help, had instigated the testing but couldn't prove it. She hadn't come out and named her source, but in the journal, she'd referred to whoever it was as Alpha, likely to protect Alpha in case the journal was found.

Nothing in the notebook gave any clues as to Alpha's identity, but Mason had to assume it was Kessler or Candace. In the notes, Carla had implied that Candace, while aware of what was going on at Windhaven, had been pressured to keep the secret and may have been threatened. And Carla had referred to Kessler as a man who didn't want to rock the boat and chose to look the other way. Carla had also suggested that Kessler had allegedly had an affair with one of the staff at Windhaven, although he would never confirm or deny it.

Thinking it through, Mason made his decision. He would call Trick and stay until six o'clock, his primary intention being to locate Alpha. If it was Candace or Kessler, he would do his best to get them to come forward. Without them, his ability to bring the guilty parties to justice and find Carla's killer would be much harder.

Mason set the journal aside just as there was a knock on the door. "Mason? You okay?" He recognized Candace's voice.

He quickly put the journal back under the mattress, smoothed his hair, and answered the door. "Hi, Candace. Sorry. I must have dozed off."

Candace smiled softly. "Dr. Hamlish told me you were still recovering from your fall. I just wanted to be sure you were feeling all right."

"It's nothing serious. I just wanted to rest. I'll head to lunch soon. I just need to clean up a little first."

Her smile fell, and she nibbled her lip. "About that. That's another reason I stopped by. Ruben has invited you to lunch in his suite. He asked me to escort you there."

"Escort me?" Mason sensed her anxiety. "He's not eating in the dining room?"

"Not today. It can cause a stir when the patients see him. He usually eats alone but asked for your company today." She paused. "It's rare for him to do that, especially in his private suite."

Mason debated his options. Why would Ruben want to have lunch with him, and today of all days? He needed to find Alpha. "Can we do it tomorrow?"

Candace shifted on her feet. "No, unfortunately. Ruben is leaving tonight, and I'm not sure when he'll return." She hesitated. "He insisted you join him today."

Mason glanced at the drawer where he'd hidden his phone. "Okay, then. Can we meet in thirty minutes?" He considered that this could be an opportunity to dig deeper into Ruben's connections to Windhaven and his family's business.

"No, I'm afraid." She smiled nervously. "Sorry. Ruben is ruthless with his schedule. You either come now or don't come at all." She wrung her hands. "But I suggest you do as he asks."

Mason noted the fine lines at her eyes and forehead. Her cheery demeanor had not returned since his last talk with her. A thought occurred to him. "Does he threaten you, Candace?"

She set her jaw and looked down the hall. "Ruben can be an intense man. My advice is that you come with me, because if you don't, well," she lowered her voice, "it could be a problem."

Mason assumed from her look and tone that the management at Windhaven was seriously suspicious of him. Did they know he had the journal? Were Kessler, Tracy and Hamlish talking? What did Ruben want to talk about? If they were on to him, then his opportunity to find the source was gone. They'd close ranks to protect themselves, and he could end up like Amelia, August, Chauncey and Carla.

Seeing the fear on Candace's face, Mason did a quick calculation in his head. Trick and Mikey were expecting his call in fifteen minutes. If he didn't call, Mikey would contact Rem and Daniels, and they would arrive soon after. Mason determined he had maybe thirty minutes before the cavalry swooped in and found him. Hoping he had time to get something out of Ruben and stay alive, Mason shut the door behind him. "Then by all means, let's go to lunch."

Candace led him down the hall, and Mason guessed they were heading to Hamlish's private office where they could access the secret suite. Before arriving there, though, she stopped at a door marked *Maintenance* and opened it.

Mason wondered where they were going. "I figured Ruben would prefer a bigger room."

She stepped inside the small space. Mason followed and saw shelves of various supplies but stopped in surprise when he noticed a portion of the far wall was open. Beyond it stretched a long corridor much like the one he'd seen outside of Hamlish's closet. "What's this?"

"I think you know," said Candace.

Unsure of what she meant, Mason didn't respond but walked behind her as she headed down the sparse walkway. Her heels clicked against the cement floor, and the single bulb above them provided minimal light. Mason figured the hidden corridor he'd found must connect with this one since they looked similar.

Candace went to the end and turned. She walked down another hall and turned again. She stopped at a door, waved a card in front of a metallic eye, and Mason heard a click. She opened the door and walked in. Mason entered a large living area and squinted at the bright light. Cushioned oak furniture filled the space, and big windows looked over expansive wooded grounds. A wide glass back door featured two marble statues on either side of it, each a smaller version of their famous counterparts. One was Michelangelo's *David*, and the other was the *Venus de Milo*. Across from a large-pillowed couch was a brick fireplace, and on the opposite side was a square dining table with candlesticks and a bar area with glass shelves. Beside the bar was a well-equipped kitchenette and a hall, which likely led to a bedroom.

Candace gestured toward the long couch. "Make yourself at home." A coffee table with a newspaper and a magazine casually laid on it was in front of the couch, and two large armchairs sat on either side of it.

"So, there is a secret suite," said Mason. He walked to one of the picture windows and looked outside. He didn't recognize this section of the grounds. Seeing a tall wooden gate, he assumed they were outside and away from the residential section. A small, manicured yard with a vine-covered portico, a water fountain and outdoor furniture was situated just outside the back door. The woods extended just beyond the portico. Mason guessed the grounds he was familiar with were just beyond the trees and outside the gate. "Ruben doesn't kid around when it comes to spending money."

He heard the door click behind him and turned. He was alone in the room. "Candace?" He walked toward the door and tried the knob, but it didn't open. He looked around, wondering why they'd locked him in, and where was Ruben? His heart thudded, and he explored the space. He followed the hall and saw a bedroom with a massive bed and headboard. The room was tidy, and there were no personal items in the closet or bathroom. Wondering what was going on, he returned to the main room when the door clicked again and opened. An attractive woman with dark, smooth, shoulder-length hair entered, holding a leather briefcase. She wore a narrow-cut red suit that emphasized her trim waist. He didn't recognize her, but there was something familiar about her eyes. "Who are you?" he asked.

She smiled. "Hello, Mason." Holding her briefcase, she approached the couch and set the briefcase down. "I'm Mallory. I'm glad we've finally met."

Mason glowered at her. He didn't like where this was going, but the name sounded familiar. "Do I know you?"

"No. Not formally." She sat on the couch. "Have a seat. Get comfortable."

Mason eyed the door and then Mallory.

"The door's locked, so you might as well relax. I know you have questions you'd like me to answer."

Mason reluctantly sat across from her in one of the chairs. "How do you know me?"

She smoothed her skirt. "Your friend, Trick. He reached out to me when you needed help. I arranged for your stay and your scholarship at Windhaven."

Mason dropped his jaw. "You're the reason I'm here?"

"I am."

Some pieces clicked into place. "You work for Ruben, don't you? You find the test subjects at Windhaven? Is that what you do?"

Mallory adjusted the cushion behind her and relaxed against it. "Oh, Mason. I'm a multitasker. There are a lot of things I do around here." She crossed her arms. "And I work for myself."

He snorted. "I bet you do."

Mallory blinked, and Mason sensed the true threat wasn't Ruben.

After a hard stare, she stood. "Where are my manners?" She walked to the kitchenette, where she filled a kettle with water. "Would you like some tea?"

Mason didn't know what to do. Should he run for the door? Try to get out? He thought again of his missed phone call. Help would arrive soon, so why not ask a few questions? "Tea sounds good."

She set the kettle down on a burner and flipped it on. "It shouldn't take long for the water to heat." She grabbed two ceramic cups from a cabinet, spoons, napkins, and a jar of honey and brought them to the coffee table, where she set them down next to a small box of tea bags. "We have a lot to go over. You've been causing quite a stir around here." She sat, reached for her briefcase and clicked open the latch. "Shall we begin?"

Chapter Thirty-Three

MIKEY RAN HER HANDS through her hair. "He's late. He should have called."

Trick eyed the phone that he'd placed on the table in front of the couch at SCOPE. He debated whether to give Mason more time. Had he been delayed?

"Two more minutes," he said.

"That's two minutes too long. He wouldn't make us wait." She held her head. "Something's wrong."

A heavy cloud of worry descended over Trick, and he sensed Mikey was right. He grabbed his phone. "Call Rem."

Mikey cursed and pulled out her cell.

Trick stood, put on his hat and found his keys. "Let's go. Call while you walk. We're going to Windhaven."

Holding the phone to her ear, Mikey picked up her purse and, following Trick, ran out of SCOPE.

Mason watched as Mallory pulled out a folder from her briefcase. "What are we going to talk about?" he asked.

She set the folder beside her and put the briefcase down. "You want to know about Windhaven, don't you? Well, now's your chance."

"Where's Ruben?"

She crossed her legs. "Ruben doesn't handle this side of the business. He won't be attending."

"I thought we were having lunch."

"Food is the least of your problems, Mason." She rested an elbow over the back of the couch. "You know, when I brought you in, I thought you were the perfect addition to the program. I wondered how you'd do on the protocol."

Mason told himself to play this cool. This lady was obviously a big player in whatever conspiracy he'd been trying to uncover, and he'd stirred the waters enough to get her attention. Although she was willing to talk to him now, it was what she planned to do with him after that had him on edge. "What protocol?"

She spoke flatly. "I think you already know. You're a perceptive man. More perceptive than I would have expected. Maybe I should have considered that your ghosts might provide more information than I liked. Guess I should have been less skeptical."

"My ghosts help, but they suck at detail. Maybe you could provide more."

"Happy to." Smiling, she slid a tendril of her silky hair through her fingers, and barely paused. "Windhaven is at a critical juncture in the advanced research of a new drug that would revolutionize addiction therapy. If we succeed with our objectives, it could prove behavioral treatment obsolete, and facilities like this," she waved her hand, "will no longer be necessary. We can turn this place into a spa and turn a better profit."

Mason tried to catch up. "You're testing some miracle drug on the patients without their knowledge? I don't care how life-changing you believe it might be. It's unethical and illegal."

"You're missing the bigger picture."

Mason couldn't believe what he was hearing. "I think you are. People have died. Did your miracle drug kill them?"

"We've had a few hiccups. Not everyone responds in the way we expect. But that's the nature of testing. Some experience...unwelcome side effects. We're still working on getting the kinks out, but it's a delicate and time-consuming process. We're closer, though, than we've ever been."

Mason's shock rippled through him. "Getting the kinks out? These people are dead."

"You're assuming they wouldn't be dead, anyway. If anything, their lives were prolonged by coming to Windhaven."

"And you're assuming they wouldn't still be alive without your drug? Maybe therapy would have worked."

She leaned in. "This comes with the territory. Every trial has its failures. Thankfully, it doesn't happen often, but we occasionally lose test subjects."

"How can you call them that?"

She smirked. "Don't be so uptight. You're one too, you know. You've responded well to the regimen. So much so that we would have gone to phase two, but that won't be happening now, which is a shame."

Mason glared. "What's phase two?"

"At six weeks, we increase the dosage for two weeks, and then taper off for the last four weeks of your stay. By the time you're ready to leave, you're officially through the treatment and ready to return to your life, only you'd no longer have the triggers and cravings you once did. Booze and drugs would have the appeal of a stick of gum or an apple. You'd be free from your addiction. It's really quite amazing."

Mason couldn't begin to utter all the problems with her statement. "How do you know it works long term?"

"We keep tabs on our subjects after they leave. They've been doing extremely well. But we're prepared in case we see signs of remission after a certain point."

"How'd you know I'd be a suitable subject?"

"You fit all the criteria. I almost jumped up and down when your application came through." She paused. "Your reaction to the testing was interesting at first, though. I thought you were going to be a wash. You hated the food."

Mason's shock was only replaced by his need for more information. If he got out of here alive, he'd need it. "It was terrible."

"I'm aware. Our subjects' reaction to food is our first sign that the drugs are working. When we first started, we recognized more sensitivity to certain types of additives, so, for those on the protocol, Manolo made it blander. Less salt. Less sugar. Fewer spices. You, however, took longer to adapt. Usually, once the drug is introduced, it only takes a day or two for the subject to show signs of progress. We had to increase your dosage and hope it worked. Thankfully, it did. Within twenty-four hours, you couldn't speak highly enough about Manolo and his chicken salad." She unbuttoned her jacket. "You provided helpful data."

"Glad I could help." He had to hold back from strangling this woman. "What about the others? The patients who died? Did they provide data too?"

"They certainly did." She picked up the folder and opened it. Mason saw sheets of paper, and Mallory read from one. "Chauncey Pendleton. A very unfortunate casualty, but one of many whose death provided invaluable insight on how to treat patients based on their varied drug usage. Chauncey had been a heavy user. He didn't respond as well, so we adjusted, but he only got worse. His heart couldn't take it." She looked up from the paper. "Our drug works best with people like you, Mason. The moderate, functional user. Hardcore users have too much damage."

"One of many?" asked Mason. "How many are there?"

Not answering, she tossed the paper down, and Mason saw a form with various filled columns and tables, along with a picture of a young man Mason assumed was Chauncey.

Mallory read from the next sheet. "August Delroy. Sweet man. He was a better fit and responded well but had other chronic health issues. We chose to take him off the protocol to see how he would do. It may have been too much, too soon. He exhibited personality changes and relapsed on release. He taught us how important it is to gradually reduce the medication, especially with a history of other medical issues."

She set the paper down, and Mason caught a picture of August. It was the man with the crazy hair who'd visited him in Hamlish's office.

"Amelia Iverhart." Mallory sighed. "She was almost on her way. We thought she was a big success. She'd made it through the program with ease, had shown no signs of difficulty or even desire for another drink. We'd reduced her dosage in gradual steps prior to her exit with minor issues. She did show some signs of paranoia, but that's one of the side effects, along with occasional bleeding from the nose or ears. She'd started telling people there were secrets at Windhaven, not understanding how true that was. Her symptoms diminished, though, as they do for most, so we weren't too concerned. Unfortunately, though, on her last day, Amelia had a seizure. We tried to bring her back. Tracy even gave her an extra dose to see if it would help, but it made her worse and she died."

"But her death was ruled an overdose," said Mason, alarmed and disgusted by what he was hearing.

Mallory squinted. "You've learned a lot for a man who's been in therapy."

"Secrets don't stay secret forever, Mallory."

"We'll see about that." Mallory lowered her papers. "We had to make Amelia look like an overdose. We couldn't risk a closer examination." She shook her head. "Tracy never should have given Amelia that additional dose." She glanced back at Amelia's form. "Live and learn. But Amelia also offered critical information. Age is a factor." She dropped Amelia's paper on top of August's.

"This is unbelievable."

"It's also a lot of work, but it will all be worth it." She flipped through several other papers. "What you don't see are the successes. The ones who've walked out of here as healthy as they've ever been, with no relapses. Not even an urge for a drug or a drink. They're paving the way to a world without drug addiction, Mason."

"That depends on the drug. The illegal ones might suffer, but I suspect you'll have no qualms with the public discovering and using your new miracle treatment." He paused. "Is the Montes family bankrolling this?"

"That's not your concern. I'm only here to explain what you've been so damn determined to find out." She waved the remaining papers. "This is a billion-dollar opportunity. Addiction will be a thing of the past. If you get hooked, no more therapy is required, unless you want it, of course. But your doctor could simply prescribe medication and in ten-to-twelve weeks, you're cured."

Mason didn't know what to say. "If it's so great, why not go through the normal testing channels? Get people involved who want to be involved. Do it the right way."

"That takes years. This is faster."

"But your data is flawed. The F.D.A. would never approve your fast-tracking anything."

"Which is why we fudge the data. Nobody has to know we moved things along."

"You can't fudge something like that."

She put the papers on the table and sat up. "Yes, you actually can. This isn't our first rodeo. We know what we're doing." The kettle whistled, and she stood. "Let's get some tea."

Mason could only stare while Mallory picked up the kettle. She brought it over, poured hot water into each mug and set the kettle on a napkin on the table. She gestured toward the box of various teas. "Help yourself. I believe you're an Earl Gray man. Am I right?" She returned to her seat on the couch.

Mason froze, realizing then why her eyes had seemed familiar. He recalled the woman with no makeup and her hair pulled back who'd brought him his tea and had cleared his plate the last night he'd talked to Carla.

"You're Serena," he said.

Mallory picked up a napkin and set it across her knee. "I am."

"You pretended to be a staff member?"

"I do what I have to do to protect my investment. I knew Carla was sniffing around, and when she started talking to you, I became concerned." She ran a hand over the napkin. "Nobody pays much attention to a server. When I watched you two together, I knew I had to act."

Mason thought back to that night with Carla. "Did you set off the proximity alarm?"

"It's a great tool when you need to clear an area fast." She gestured. "Have some tea, Mason, before the water cools."

Mason debated telling her to shove her tea in a delicate place, but he was acutely aware of the passage of time. He needed enough of it for Rem and Daniels to find him, and he was under no illusions that Mallory would let him walk out of here alive after all she'd revealed. He reluctantly picked up an Earl Gray packet, opened it, and dunked his bag in the water. "Something like this requires big investors. Whether you choose to admit it or not, it's not a big leap to guess that Ruben's family business is your meal ticket."

"They're one of the biggest pharmaceutical companies in the country for a reason." Mallory grabbed a hibiscus tea packet, opened it, and added the bag to her hot water. "I'm glad I got to talk with you. There were a few who thought we should have just taken care of you yesterday after Storm tossed you."

Mason's stomach tightened. "That wasn't an accident?"

"Sorry about that, but some felt you needed a warning." She left her tea bag in the water, added some honey and stirred. "Thankfully, you survived, and you and I got the chance to meet. I was curious about what you knew and how you knew it. I realized that you and Carla were friendly. I just didn't know how much she'd told you. Plus, I wanted her notes, and nobody could find them. We had her laptop, but I knew there was more."

Mason stilled at the mention of the laptop. "You killed her?"

"I didn't, but it was arranged. She was getting too close. We should have clued in sooner, especially when she checked in a third time. To be honest, though, I was curious why the drug hadn't worked on her. Now we know, though. She was faking her addiction those last two times at Windhaven."

Mason held his breath. This was almost too much to take. "If you had her laptop, then why do you need her notes? It's just scribbles on a page."

"True, but they could still do damage in the wrong hands." She dunked her tea bag some more and took a sip of her tea. "The more important issue was to find her source. Someone was talking to her, and I wanted to know who."

Mason finally understood. "You were hoping I'd lead you to Alpha."

Mallory frowned. "Alpha? Is that what you call him or her? How mysterious." She took another sip.

"I didn't find the source, though." Mason forced himself to breathe. He had to keep her talking. He sat back with his tea and sipped from his cup.

"No. You didn't. But this will help." She set her tea down, reached into her briefcase and pulled out Carla's red notebook. "Maybe once I read it, I'll get some ideas."

Mason gripped the handle of his mug. "I guess I shouldn't be surprised."

"We searched your room the moment you left it. It didn't take long. We found the phone too, by the way. You're a sneaky fellow, aren't you?" She put the notebook on her lap. "Did Trick get it to you with Mikey's help? Smart."

Mason froze. "They don't know anything."

"I know they don't. Not enough to do any damage at least." She paused. "Theories and speculation won't get them very far. Ask Gina Rodriguez."

Mason tried not to react, so he drank more tea, trying to stall as much as possible. "What about Gina?"

"Didn't Mikey tell you during one of your secret phone calls? Gina's sister Lenora suffered an unfortunate overdose. Gina is certain it wasn't accidental. Thankfully, law enforcement didn't agree."

"You're responsible for Lenora?"

Mallory reached for and flipped through more of her papers. She pulled out a sheet and read from it. "Lenora Rodriguez. An unexpected mistake, and one that could have been very detrimental."

"Mistake? That's what you want to call it? What about Rain Montes? What did he have to do with it?"

She peered up from the paper. "I'm so glad we're having this conversation. You know about Rain?" She rolled her eyes. "I suppose I shouldn't be surprised. He's a loose cannon, and that stupid tattoo doesn't help. You can recognize him from a football field away. He's like his father. He loves attention, women, and spending money." She sighed. "He fell for Lenora and got her hooked on the parties and drugs. Then, when he saw she was in a bad place, he tried to give her the meds we were testing without having knowledge of what he was doing. Did anybody try to stop him? No."

Mason's hands shook, and he sipped more tea to hide it. "What happened to her?"

"Rain screwed up. Lenora got out of rehab, with or without the help of the medication, it's hard to know. But Rain had to talk to her, to see her. He wanted her to listen to his plan of how they could be together. She rebuffed him, though, which was unwise on her part. Rain doesn't take well to rejection."

"He murdered her and made it look like an overdose."

She touched a finger to her temple. "Such a mess. Ruben was furious. But, like father, like son." She dropped Lenora's paper on the table. Mason got a look at the picture and a chill ran through him. It was the woman from his room who'd pointed and had told him to listen. Now he knew why. She hadn't been asking Mason to listen. She'd been repeating what Rain had said to her before her death. "Rain is obviously dangerous. How do you know he won't kill again?"

She picked up her tea. "Oh, he will." Her eyes twinkled, and an icy chill ran up Mason's spine. The door clicked and opened, and Mason's fear spiked when a tall, well-dressed man with a snake tattoo on his temple entered the room.

Chapter Thirty-Four

TRICK STOPPED AND PARKED in front of Windhaven just as Rem and Daniels pulled up behind them. Two patrol cars with their lights swirling joined them.

Trick and Mikey jumped out and met Rem and Daniels on the front steps.

"Anything?" asked Rem.

"Nothing," said Mikey. "He hasn't called."

Two officers walked over, and Daniels pointed. "Ferguson. Mathers. You stay out here. Nobody leaves or enters. Anybody gives you shit, detain them. Charge them with evading an officer if you have to. You got it?"

Both men nodded.

Two other uniformed officers, one a man and the other a woman, jogged over.

"Fuentes and Gilbert," said Daniels. "You're with us."

"What are we looking at here?" asked the female officer. Her name tag identified her as Fuentes.

"We believe one of the patients here, Mason Redstone, is in danger," said Rem. "Our primary goal is to find him, ensure he's safe, and get him out of here."

Fuentes nodded.

Rem eyed Mikey. "Any chance you two will stay out here while we take care of this?"

"None," said Trick.

"Not a chance in hell," said Mikey.

"I figured," said Rem. "Then stick close to me and Daniels. Let us do the talking." He spoke to Daniels. "You ready?"

"As I'll ever be," said Daniels. "Let's go find Mason."

They entered the facility and approached the front desk, where a woman other than Gloria sat. She was older, wore heavy red lipstick, and her name tag read Rebecca. Seeing them, she widened her eyes. "Can I help you?"

"You bet you can," said Daniels, holding up his badge. "We need to see one of your patients. Mason Redstone."

Rem held his badge out, too. "We believe his life may be in danger."

"His life?" asked Rebecca. "In danger?"

"Your hearing is excellent, Rebecca," said Rem. "How about you get on that phone and have Mason brought here. Right now."

Watching the exchange, Mikey stepped up. "Brought here? We need to go back there and find him."

"She's right," said Trick. "If he's being held against his will, they'll stall, and we'll be too late."

Rebecca sputtered. "Held against his will? What are you talking about?"

Mikey erupted. "We're talking about my brother's life. Windhaven is dangerous, and Mason knows it." She scowled at Rebecca. "Maybe you do, too."

Rebecca widened her eyes more.

"If that's true," said Daniels, "then you better think long and hard about your next move, Rebecca. Because if it's the wrong one and Mason gets hurt, you could be charged as an accessory."

Rebecca paled. "Let me make a phone call."

"Make it fast," said Rem.

Mikey raised her voice. "We're wasting time. Why don't we go to his room? Or just start searching?"

"As much as we hate it, they have to be careful, Mikey," said Trick. "They go in without a warrant and find Mason eating lunch or in a therapy session, it could subject the city to a lawsuit. The people here have an expectation of privacy."

"But that won't happen," said Mikey, her fear growing. She sensed they were running out of time. "Mason's in trouble."

"Which is why I can go in if they can't," said Trick. "I can deal with a lawsuit or even an arrest."

"How's it going, Rebecca?" asked Rem. "Any progress?"

Rebecca looked up, the phone to her ear. "They're looking."

"Looking?" asked Daniels. "They don't know where he is?"

"Oh God," said Mikey. Wringing her hands, she did her best not to dodge past Rem and Daniels and dart down the hall, screaming Mason's name. She stared in that direction, prepared to bolt, when she caught someone peering around the corner. She recognized Candace immediately.

Candace saw her and pulled back, but Mikey didn't let that stop her. "Candace," she yelled. "Wait." Mikey ran over.

Candace hesitated but didn't leave. Her usual perky nature had vanished, though, and her wide eyes conveyed her worry.

"Where is he?" asked Mikey. "Where's Mason?" Trick, Rem and Daniels, and the two officers came up beside Mikey.

Candace tried to act casual. "He's somewhere on the grounds, I'm sure. What's wrong?"

Mikey felt the lie in her bones. "You know where he is, don't you?"

"Is he in trouble?" asked Trick.

"I...I..." Candace stammered. "I'm sure he's fine."

"Listen, Candace," said Rem. "We know what's going on. Mason's been investigating whatever Windhaven's been doing to its patients, and he got to the truth. But somebody's onto him. Do you know who?"

Candace gave an anxious laugh. "What do you mean?"

Mikey got up close. "Stop bullshitting us. Where is Mason?"

Daniels aimed an ugly glare at her. "If he dies, and you could have prevented it, you'll end up in prison."

"And your son will visit you there," said Trick.

Her face turned white. "But I didn't do anything."

"But you know where Mason is," said Mikey.

"She...she just wanted to talk to him," said Candace. "He...he'd... found something."

Mikey put a hand on Candace's wrist. "Did he find Carla's journal?"

"I...I don't know. Maybe." She rubbed her forehead. "I'm not sure what to do."

"Tell us the truth," said Trick. "Aren't you sick of lying? And hiding? While people die?"

"I didn't...I couldn't...they threatened me." She put her hand over her mouth, and tears sprang into her eyes.

"Candace," said Rem, softening his voice. "It's over. Nobody's going to hurt you or your kid, okay? But we can't help you or anybody else until you take us to Mason."

Wiping a tear away, she choked back a sob. "I'm sorry."

"Apologize later," said Trick. "And get moving."

"O...Okay." She nodded and held her chest. "This way." Mikey sighed in relief as Candace turned, and they followed her down the hall.

Mason stared in disbelief as Rain Montes walked into the room. "Mason Redstone," he said. "How nice to meet you." He slid his hands into the pockets of his neatly pressed pants. His dark hair reached his shoulders, and his eyes studied Mason as if he were prey.

Mason knew then he was out of time. He set his cup of tea down. "I didn't know you cared." He straightened in his chair, prepared to flee. "How do you even know me?"

He sneered. "My dad talks about you. He likes you." He stepped closer. "But I think your friendship will be short-lived."

Starting to sweat and with his mind racing, Mason eyed Mallory. "That's your plan? I die from an overdose, too?"

Mallory leaned forward, her eyes sad. "I'm sorry, Mason. We considered kicking you out but knew you wouldn't let it end there. You'd keep digging, and we couldn't take the risk you might find Alpha and convince them to talk. It's better this way."

"If your patients keep dying of overdoses, you'll create suspicion without my help." Mason glanced toward the door, wondering if he could get to it. His lips and fingertips tingled.

"Haven't you heard?" asked Mallory, setting her cup and napkin on the table. "Overdoses are up around town." She nodded toward Rain. "Crazy as he may be, Rain here serves a purpose. Our drug doesn't do much without customers. Rain here ensures the public supply is easy and cheap, and when we're approved and ready to sell, we won't lack for sales." She put her hand on her knee. "You'll just be an unfortunate casualty. Don't forget we found an unauthorized phone in your room, and you broke into our lab after a nasty fall from a horse. You've made it easy for us."

Sweat trickled down Mason's neck. "It won't work. The police will investigate."

"We'll have to take the risk." Mallory picked up the notebook, tucked the papers back into the folder, and returned them to her briefcase. "But you were obviously searching for drugs." She made a tsk, tsk sound. "It's such a shame you found some." She clicked the briefcase closed. "They'll find you in your room after you don't show up for lunch. It will be devastating, especially to your family."

The tingling sensation spread from his lips to his chin and cheeks, and from his fingers to his hands. He touched his skin, wondering what was wrong.

Mallory stood. "Is it hitting you yet?"

Rain smiled. "I think so."

Terror rushed through Mason, and he stood, but his legs felt funny, and he wobbled. He eyed the tea.

"Your Earl Gray is hallucinogenic," said Mallory. "It's amazing what Tracy can do in that lab of hers." She straightened her jacket. "I think you drank enough to let Rain do what he came here to do."

Rain pulled a pill bottle out of his pocket. "A couple of these is all it will take." He shook it, and Mason heard the rattle. "Fentanyl is a nasty drug."

Mason shook his head, and his vision swam. He blinked and stepped away from his chair. "I'm not taking that." He stumbled toward the back door and tried to open it, but it was locked.

"In a few minutes," said Rain. "You'll think it's candy. I'll have to hold you back from swallowing the whole thing." He chuckled.

"Well, gentlemen," said Mallory, buttoning her jacket. "I'll leave you two to your business. Mason, it was nice to meet you. Sorry I can't stay." She picked up her briefcase and walked toward Rain. "You got this?"

"I got this," said Rain.

Mason shut his eyes and opened them. The tingling spread through his whole body, and he knew he had to get out of that room. "Killing me won't help. It will only make it worse." He grabbed the wall beside the glass door to stop himself from falling over.

Mallory glanced at him. "You think I haven't dealt with worse, Mason? This is child's play. You're a drug addict. I know you think you're special, but nobody will think twice when you die from an overdose."

A wave of dizziness hit him, and he fought to stay upright. More tingles raced through him, and a woman materialized in the room. He recognized her long hair and bloody nose. It was Lenora. He blinked again, unsure if it was him or the drugs causing the vision.

Mallory headed for the door. "Do yourself a favor, Mason, and take the drugs. Don't fight him." She shot a last look at Rain before she walked out, and the door clicked behind her.

Rain and Lenora watched Mason and, feeling helpless, Mason pushed back against the glass, realizing there was nowhere to go.

Rain shook the pill bottle again. "Ready to take your medicine?"

Chapter Thirty-Five

CANDACE LED THEM DOWN a long hall, away from where they'd had their family visits and toward the rear of the facility. Trick recalled the blueprints and expected her to take them to Hamlish's office, but she stopped in front of a door marked *Maintenance.*

"Where are we?" asked Mikey.

"You better not be leading us on a wild goose chase, Candace," said Rem.

Trick eyed the hall, seeing Fuentes and Gilbert behind him, but no one else. He wished his partner would step out and tell them he was all right, but Trick knew that wouldn't happen. His stomach tightened in worry. "Why is Red in the maintenance closet?"

"He's not." She opened the door, and they got a look inside. It was a small room with cleaning equipment, a vacuum and shelves of supplies.

"Looks like a closet to me," said Trick. "Where the hell is he?"

Candace's face fell, and she walked to the wall and touched it. "This is a door." She banged on it.

Rem and Daniels entered. "Doesn't look like a door." Rem pushed on it. "How do you open it?"

Candace shook her head. "I don't know. It was open before."

"Think," said Mikey. "How do we get back there?"

Her face stricken, Candace sputtered. "I...I don't know. It should be open." She put her hands on her head. "I don't have access."

"Look around," said Daniels. "Maybe there's a way to open it." He checked behind the shelves, and Rem searched the wall.

"Hamlish's office," said Trick, recalling the blueprints and Red's recounting of finding a secret corridor. "Where is it?"

Mikey's eyes widened. "That's right." She faced Candace. "Take us to his office."

Rem stopped searching, and Daniels waited. "How do we get there from here?" asked Daniels.

"His...his...Hamlish's office?" Candace asked. "But why?"

"Just take us," yelled Trick, his patience at a breaking point. "We're wasting time." He hated to think that Candace was purposely stalling, but the mere consideration enraged him.

Candace jumped. "It's...uh...this way." More tears fell, but she raced out of the closet and turned down the hall. Rem and Daniels followed with Mikey and Rem behind them and Fuentes and Gilbert at the rear.

Candace stopped at a nearby closed door, and Rem swung it open. Hamlish sat at his desk, holding a pen, with a folder and papers in front of him. He dropped his jaw and stood. "What the hell is going on here?" He closed the folder. "Candace? What's wrong?"

Candace stood outside the door. "They're looking for Mason."

Rem walked to the closet door and opened it. Daniels joined him, and Trick and Mikey watched them enter the dark space. "Nothing," said Rem.

"In my closet?" asked Hamlish. "Why would Mason be in there?"

"Look for a button," said Mikey. "That's how he said he'd opened it."

"Opened what?" asked Hamlish. "This is outrageous. I'm calling security." He reached for his phone.

Fuentes and Gilbert approached his desk. "We're the police, sir. We believe a man's life is in danger. We suggest you let our detectives do their jobs."

"A man's life?" asked Hamlish. "Who? Mason?"

"I took him back there," said Candace, her face a mask of anguish. "I didn't think he'd be hurt...I thought..." She put her hands on her cheeks.

Hamlish paled. He picked up the file on his desk. "I'm sure Mason's fine, Candace. Although why they're looking in my closet is—"

"Found it," said Daniels. He pressed something, and Trick heard a click. A sliver of light appeared at the back, and Rem stuck his fingers in the crevice and slid a panel back. Trick could see a hallway with a single light bulb and a cement floor.

"Oh, my God," said Mikey.

"That's exactly what Mason described," said Trick.

"What in the...?" Hamlish walked around his desk and stared. "That's in my closet?"

Daniels stepped out. "Gilbert. Fuentes. You stay with the doctor and Candace. Nobody leaves this room." He pulled out his weapon and checked it.

"And nobody touches those files." Trick pointed at Hamlish's cabinet. "Got it?"

Hamlish gasped. "You can't—"

"We can," said Trick.

Still in the closet, Rem pulled his own weapon and peered down the gloomy hall. "Trick?"

Trick stepped up beside Mikey. "I'll stay with her." He reached down, pulled up his pant leg and took out his own weapon. "Mikey, you stick with me. Any shooting starts, and you run for the hills, got it?"

"Shooting?" she asked. "You think they'll shoot?"

Rem and Daniels, guns raised, stepped into the quiet hall.

"Get behind me," said Trick. "Although I'd rather you stay with Fuentes and Gilbert." He stepped in front of her and followed Rem and Daniels. "Any chance you might consider that?"

Mikey stuck to his back. "No way," she whispered.

Trick entered the corridor. "Then let's go find your wayward brother."

With his back to the glass, Mason felt along it and tried the door handle again, but it wouldn't budge. The tingles coursed faster through his body, and he shook his head to clear it, but it only made it worse. Everything swiveled and twisted, and he closed his eyes.

"Relax, Mason. This doesn't have to hurt."

Mason opened his eyes to see Rain advancing. He swallowed, but his throat stuck. His fear racing, he told himself to stay calm. He eyed Lenora, who remained in the room. "Lenora?" he asked. "I need your help."

Rain stopped. "What did you say?"

Mason looked around, desperate to find anything to use as a weapon. "Lenora. She's here."

Rain held still, but then smiled. "That hallucinogen is kicking in." He raised the pill bottle. "Want some candy?"

Mason bit his lip. The pain helped him focus. "It's her. She...she has something to tell you." He didn't know what Lenora wanted but hoped her presence would slow Rain down. "She blames you." He recalled what Mikey had told him about Rain's psychokinesis. If that were true, Mason had no chance of escape.

Rain scoffed, and his gaze hardened. "She should have listened to me. If she had, she'd still be alive." He took another step. "And you should have minded your own business. You and Lenora are both too stubborn for your own good."

Lenora turned toward Rain. When Rain mentioned how she should have listened, she drifted closer.

Mason sensed her agitation. "You killed her. You told her you loved her, and you murdered her. You're a monster."

Rain raised his voice. "That bitch learned her lesson. I told her she should have listened to me." He patted his chest. "I knew what was best for her."

Lenora glared. Mason tried to catch his breath. "You should have left her alone. Then she'd still be alive."

Rain gripped the pill bottle and held it out. "When you join her, you can give her my regards. Tell her I was right. She was a waste of space." He opened the bottle. "Let's get this over with."

Her face a mask of fury, Lenora rushed at Rain, a bellow of rage erupting from her.

Rain flailed and dropped the bottle. The pills spilled out, and Rain fell back onto the floor.

Lenora spoke to Mason. "Break the glass," she said, her bleeding nose dripping down her gown. He heard her clearly and assumed Rain did, too.

"What the hell—" Rain scrambled backward on his butt until he hit the far wall. "Lenora?"

She shrieked at him, and he yelped in fear and raised his hand. "Get away from me."

Mason eyed the *Venus de Milo* near the picture window, and without thinking twice, he grabbed it, picked it up, and, trying not to stumble, hurled it at the glass. It shattered in a hail of shards and collapsed. Trying to stay on his feet, Mason dropped the statue and ran.

Rem and Daniels walked slowly through the corridor, their guns pointed down the hall. Mikey stuck behind Trick, whose gun was also out, but aimed at the floor.

The only sounds were their breathing and soft footfalls on the cement. Mikey tried to stay calm but was failing. She thought of Mason and prayed they'd get to him in time.

Reaching the end of the hall, they stopped. Rem peered around it and swiveled, and Daniels stayed beside him. Trick approached and turned, and Mikey joined him, seeing another long hall.

"Where the hell are we?" she whispered.

"I don't know," whispered Trick. "But we've got to be close."

Rem passed through an intersecting hall. "Maybe that connects to the maintenance closet."

Daniels peered down it and nodded. "Probably."

They kept going, and Mikey saw another intersecting corridor. "It's got to be down there."

"It better be," said Trick. "We're running out of—"

A loud crash echoed down the hall and bounced off the walls. Mikey shrieked.

Rem moved fast to the corner and disappeared around it. Daniels followed, and Trick reached the edge of the wall and turned. Mikey joined him and saw Rem and Daniels disappear around another corner.

Trick ran to catch up, and Mikey stuck to his back, her heart racing so fast she feared she'd pass out. She wanted to call out to Mason but made herself stay quiet. Trick peered around another corner, and Mikey did the same, seeing Rem standing beside a nearby closed door. Daniels stood on the other side of it. Trick jogged over and stopped next to Rem. "Mikey," Trick whispered. "Stay back."

Mikey plastered herself against the wall. "Don't worry about me. Just get Mason."

Rem tried the knob and shook his head at Daniels. Daniels pounded on the door with the butt of his gun. "Police," yelled Daniels. "Open the door."

Mikey waited, praying no one would shoot. She held her chest in a futile attempt to calm her beating heart. Where was Mason?

"Nothing," said Trick.

Rem lowered his gun, turned, and kicked the door hard. Daniels held his weapon as the wood held but splintered. Rem hit it again, and it cracked, gave way and swung open.

Daniels rushed inside as Rem raised his gun and followed. Mikey heard nothing, and Trick slid to the edge of the door and swiveled. He stood for a moment, waiting.

Mikey heard Rem and Daniels yell "clear," and Trick entered. Mikey went in after Trick and saw a living room with heavy furniture, enormous windows, and a fireplace. Rem and Daniels walked toward the back, where a window had been shattered and glass littered the floor and crunched beneath their feet. A marble statue lay on the ground just outside the window.

Trick walked up and Mikey, after looking around, sensed Mason's lingering presence in the room. "He was here."

Trick stooped down and picked up what looked like a pill. "Hell." His gaze scanned the outside. "They're after him."

Rem and Daniels, still holding their weapons, stepped through the broken window. "He's probably headed for a way through the fence," said Rem.

"That's the only way out." Daniels spoke to Trick and Mikey. "Stick close, but be careful."

Trick nodded, and Mikey looked for Mason through the woods but didn't see anything or anyone. "We've got to hurry," she said.

They raced onto the grounds.

Mason made it to the trees without even glancing behind him. He suspected Rain would recover quickly from his shock and wouldn't be far behind.

He knew the woods wouldn't provide much protection, and he had to find cover. He ran toward the fence that led to the residential side of Windhaven and looked for a gate or another way in. The fence morphed into a black gaping hole, and Mason stumbled backward, terrified. He told himself it was the drugs and raced back toward it. The fence became a fence again, and Mason held onto it, trying to catch his breath. His body shook with chills, and he hoped he could stay conscious. His vision spotted, and he put a hand out to support himself. Looking behind him, he expected to see Rain approaching, but he didn't.

He spotted a bench instead, sitting in a cleared area beneath a tree. Mason darted toward it. Thankful it wasn't large, he picked up one side, and it lifted easily. Dragging it, he almost fell when his balance wavered, and he had to stop briefly before he could pull it to the side of the fence. Taking a second to center himself, he took a deep breath and although his vision blurred, he stepped on the bench, pulled himself over the wood and, losing his grip, fell to the ground hard on the other side and gasped when his breath left his lungs.

"Give it up, Mason." Mason recognized Rain's distant voice. That got him moving, and he pushed himself up with a groan and ran. He wasn't even sure where he was going. His limbs were so heavy, he struggled to stay upright. Everything around him morphed into strange shapes, and the wind pounded in his ears. He giggled for no reason and closed his mouth to stay quiet. In the distance, he saw a castle and a moat. It made little sense, but he ran toward it. Maybe someone inside could help. He wanted to yell but was worried Rain would hear him and follow.

Reaching the moat, he almost didn't cross it, fearing he'd fall in the water and drown. But he told himself he'd rather drown than have Rain kill him, so he gathered his courage and darted across it, surprised he didn't fall in. He made it to the castle, stumbled and fell, hitting his head against something hard. He touched the castle wall, but his hand fell through the slats into liquid, and he pulled back in fear. Where the hell was he? What had happened to him?

He heard a shuffle and a snort, and scrambled away through the dirt, not sure where to go. His vision continued to trick him, and he held his head, but his whole body trembled, and he couldn't make sense of anything.

"There you are," said a voice.

Mason tensed and scooted back toward the liquid wall. His back hit something solid, and he felt dirt beneath his hands. Blinking fast, he saw a man approach. A large snake slithered across his face, and Mason raised his hand. "Don't."

"Too late." The man stood over him. "You're a pain in the ass. They should have taken care of you sooner." He reached into his pocket and pulled something out. "You hungry?"

Mason had a second of clarity, and his vision cleared. Rain stood over him, his fingers curled around something. "I've got a special treat that's going to help you feel a lot better," said Rain. "No more running. No more fear. I promise."

Mason tried to think, but his brain wouldn't work. All he wanted was rest. His mouth was dry, and his tongue felt swollen in his mouth.

"I bet you're thirsty," said Rain. "You take this, and I'll get you some water."

Mason pushed harder against whatever he was leaning against. Inherently, he knew it wasn't a castle. "I'm tired." Rain's face swirled, and Mason squinted when Rain became his mother. "Mom?" He sucked in a breath. "Is that you?"

The vision nodded and smiled. "It is, son. I'm here. I'm right here." His mother squatted beside him. "I want to help."

"He's after me," said Mason, his emotions swirling. "I can't...I can't..."

His mother patted his arm. "It's okay. Take this. It will help with everything." She held out her hand. "You'll feel so much better, and no one will hurt you. I'll be with you, and you can stay with me."

Mason ached to be with his mother. He'd missed her so much. "I screwed up. I'm sorry."

"Take the pills, son. Take them now. Then, you and I can talk."

Mason saw the pills in her hand. He wanted so much to speak with her, and to tell her how he felt. He reached for them.

"There you go," she said, putting them in his palm. "Swallow them, Mason."

Mason moaned, his body tingled, and a strange sensation nudged at him. Something wasn't right. "Mom. Is that really you?"

"Take the damn pills, son. Now."

Her tone struck him. His mother would never speak to him like that. "What's wrong? Are you mad at me?"

His mother grabbed his throat. "I said take the damn pills."

Mason's mother vanished, and Rain came back into view. Mason gasped as Rain squeezed. He dropped the pills into the dirt and gripped Rain's wrist, who squeezed harder. His airway closed, and he fought to get away, but he had no strength.

Rain got in his face and leered. "When you see Lenora, tell her to go fuck herself," he said in a whisper. "You son of a bitch."

Mason kicked out, trying to get away, but Rain's strength outmatched his and, worse, Mason's body betrayed him. He had no leverage and, fighting for air, he saw spots.

Rain grinned and cackled at him, and Mason, his body weakening, began to give up when a knight wearing armor appeared behind Rain. The knight swung an ax and hit Rain hard. The excruciating hold on Mason's neck released, and

Rain buckled and collapsed on top of Mason. Mason gasped and coughed as air whooshed into his lungs. His body still tingled, and his vision still swirled, but he could breathe.

"Mason," he heard someone say. "Mason?"

Mason coughed some more and blinked, seeing the knight. He hoped the knight wouldn't hit him next.

"Mason? Are you okay?" The knight shook him and then rolled Rain's limp body off of him. "Just breathe."

Finally able to move, Mason pushed up and leaned back against the castle. Getting a solid lungful of air, he sputtered and coughed some more. "Where am I? Who are you?"

Still holding the ax, the knight frowned at him. "It's me. It's Kessler. You're behind the stables."

Mason tried to make sense of it. "The stables?"

He heard a shriek in the distance. A woman's voice yelled his name. Kessler turned toward the sound. "Looks like help is here."

Mason blinked several times and finally focused. The knight became Kessler, who was holding a shovel. Rain lay on the ground beside him and moaned. Mikey ran up to Mason and went down on her knees beside him. Trick was with her along with Remalla and Daniels. "Mason, are you okay?" She patted his face. "Talk to me."

Rem and Daniels searched Rain and cuffed his hands behind his back.

"Red?" asked Trick, squatting beside him. "Talk to us."

"I think he's on something," said Kessler. "Look at his eyes."

Mason held his throat. "Mikey? Is that you?" His voice was rough, and his vision continued to swirl. He closed his eyes when Trick morphed into a giant fly.

"It's me," said Mikey. "What's wrong?"

Mason moaned. "Trick's a fly."

He heard a chuckle and a response. "I've been called worse."

"The police are here," said Mikey. "It's over. We'll get you to a hospital."

"What'd they give you, Red?" asked Trick.

Recalling Mallory, Mason cracked an eyelid open. "Something in the tea." He grabbed Trick's arm. "Mallory. She's leaving. You have to stop her."

"Easy. Take it easy," said Trick. "Who's Mallory?"

Daniels had his phone to his ear, and he lowered it. "Is she wearing a red suit?"

Mason did his best to focus before his vision and brain betrayed him again. "Yes. She's got a briefcase. Stop her."

Daniels nodded. "They detained her out front. She's mad as hell, but she's not going anywhere."

Overwhelming relief coursed through Mason, and he slumped back against the barn. "We got her."

"You got her, partner," said Trick. "Nice job, only you didn't have to scare the hell out of us."

Daniels hung up. "Ambulance is on its way. Just sit tight, and we'll get you out of here."

Rem gripped a cuffed Rain by the shoulder and yanked him up. "Come on, soldier boy. Time for you to pay the piper."

Blood streamed down the side of Rain's face, but he was conscious. He stumbled but sneered at Mason as Rem led him away. "Till we meet again."

"Only if I visit you in prison," said Mason.

"C'mon. Move it," said Rem, leading Rain back toward the facility. Two police officers ran up, took Rain by the elbows and led him off. Rem returned, watching Rain being taken away. "So much for psychokinesis," he said. "Thank God."

"No kidding," said Daniels.

Mikey dropped her head on Mason's shoulder. "I'm so glad you're okay." He heard the shakiness in her voice.

Mason squeezed her arm. "I'll live." His throat hurt, but he could breathe easily. More tingles raced down his arms and despite his blurry focus, he saw Carla appear behind Mikey. He sighed, happy to see her, and she winked at him.

"Thanks, Cowboy," he heard in his head.

"You're welcome," whispered Mason.

Mikey raised her head. "What?"

"I think he's still seeing things," said Trick.

"Tell Mom I said hello," said Mason. "And thank Lenora for the help."

Mikey widened her eyes and glanced behind her. "It's not the drugs."

"I already did both." Carla grinned. "And your mom makes a hell of a margarita. We're going to celebrate."

Mason smiled, and as Carla faded from view, he rested his head back, held onto Mikey, and closed his eyes.

Chapter Thirty-Six

MASON SAT ON THE park bench, admiring the gently lapping lake with the quacking ducks. Nearby, in a grass-covered field, teenagers threw a frisbee, and children shrieked as they ran around in the playground.

He took a deep breath, grateful to be home. After leaving Windhaven, he'd spent three days in the hospital where they'd monitored him for any adverse effects from the hallucinogenic and whatever drug he'd been given during his treatment. He'd spiked a low-grade fever and had felt lousy for two days but had quickly recovered. During his stay, he'd learned that Hamlish, Tracy, and Manolo had been taken into custody. Candace had been questioned but released, and Rain and Mallory had been arrested on a variety of charges. All of them had been provided expensive representation. Windhaven had been shut down, the police had confiscated Hamlish's files, scoured Tracy's lab and Manolo's kitchen, and the patients had been offered medical check-ups. Those who had been given the drug were taken to the hospital for supervision, and those who had not had been moved to other facilities. From what Mason had heard, those coming off the drug had experienced some negative effects, but no one had died.

Within days of Mason's rescue, though, the F.B.I. had taken over the investigation. Windhaven was only the tip of the iceberg. The Montes family's pharmaceutical ties to illegal drug testing and unethical business practices spanned several states, and they'd been under federal investigation for some time. Rem and Daniels had been required to turn over all their evidence but could continue their prosecution of Rain Montes for the murders of Lenora Rodriguez and Laura Dunn, and the attempted murder of Mason. After searching Rain's home, they'd found Laura's laptop, plenty of illegal drugs, and pictures of Lenora. They'd wished Rain's attorneys well and had told them to prep Rain for a long prison stay.

After his discharge, Mason had returned home. He'd planned to research new therapy treatment centers, but the next morning, Mikey, Trick and Valerie, who'd returned from Texas during his hospitalization, had sat him down and told him about his sister Margaret's escape.

Mason's stomach flipped at the memory and at the possibility his psychotic sister could be watching him now. He wouldn't put it past her. Scanning the area, he saw nothing suspicious, but kept his guard up. He'd been outraged and furious that no one had told him earlier, but once he'd calmed down, he'd realized why they'd done it. Although he didn't have to like it.

He'd discussed possible therapy options with them, and a few days later, he'd chosen an outpatient program where he could safely continue individual and group sessions three to four times a week. The family sessions would also resume. It would allow Mason to stay home, start working again, and keep an eye on his loved ones. Trick had returned to his apartment, but Mikey remained at Mason's, and Mason had an alarm system installed. He would do whatever it took to keep himself and Mikey safe.

Hearing a child's laughter as he slid down the slide, Mason smiled. He'd been home a week and hadn't experienced the slightest desire for a pill or drug despite his near death at Rain's hands, his hospital stay, and the revelations and worries about Margaret. He had to wonder if it was because of his hard work or the drug he'd been given at Windhaven. He had no way of knowing.

A dog barked, and Mason watched as a woman walked by with a Chihuahua on a leash. Eyeing the time, he figured he should return to SCOPE. He'd had an intense session that morning with his new doctor, Tarina Phelps. She was tough but smart, and Mason had liked her from the start, but she didn't let him get away with anything. His first appointment with the family was scheduled for the next day, and Max would be present. Mason already suspected it would be a rough hour.

He was happy, though, to be back at work with Mikey and Trick and thrilled to see Val, even though Margaret's presence loomed. He prayed his sister would be caught before she instigated whatever plans she'd planned, and Mason had no doubt she had something in mind. Margaret never remained idle for long.

Hearing a yell, he saw one of the teenagers miss the frisbee and run across the grass for it. Sensing he'd had enough decompression time, Mason figured he ought to go before Mikey called, wondering where he was. He started to stand when a man spoke from behind him.

"You mind if I sit?"

Hearing the familiar voice, Mason turned to see Ruben Montes standing beside the bench. Behind Ruben, about ten feet away, stood a burly man in a dark suit and sunglasses, and beyond him, in the parking lot, sat a gleaming four-door expensive vehicle with tinted windows.

Mason didn't know what to think. Ruben hadn't been seen since Windhaven's downfall. Before the F.B.I. arrived, Mallory had refused to talk, and Rain would only yell expletives at the detectives. Mason guessed the F.B.I. had found and questioned Ruben, but obviously, he'd been released. The Montes family and their company, though, were scrambling, and Mason expected that several federal indictments would soon be served. Whether Ruben would be included, Mason didn't know.

Recalling his first meeting with Ruben in Windhaven's library, he gestured to the side of the bench. "Feel free." He imagined Rubin wanted to speak with him due to Mason's involvement in bringing down his family's pharmaceutical empire. Although Ruben had so far escaped the law, Mason knew he'd been involved and had likely been Mallory's boss.

Ruben unbuttoned his sleek navy jacket, revealing a silky shirt beneath. His pressed pants and shiny shoes revealed a similar taste in clothes to Rain's. Father and son were indeed alike.

He sat, tucked his sunglasses into a jacket pocket, and smoothed his hair back. "How are you, Mason?"

Mason glanced at him. "Doing well, no thanks to Windhaven."

Ruben crossed his legs. "No beating around the bush, I see." He sighed. "That's fine. I have little time anyway. I've got a jet to catch."

"Heading to a country with a non-extradition treaty?"

Ruben smiled. "I'm not worried."

"Only because nobody's talking. You've trained your people well."

He rested a hand on his knee. "I told you I valued loyalty above all else. And they know I'll take care of them."

"While you're on a beach somewhere, reading the latest bestseller?"

Ruben watched the teenagers play frisbee. "You make a lot of assumptions."

"Am I wrong?"

Ruben shifted to face him. "I'm a philanthropist. There are more people to help. That won't stop because of this mess with my family."

"Are you trying to tell me you're innocent?"

"I don't think it matters what I tell you."

Hearing more laughter, Mason looked back at the playground. "No. It doesn't." He swiped at a leaf on his shirt. "Why are you even here?"

"I thought we should talk."

"You could have called." Mason paused. "Or were you worried I'd wear a microphone? So you surprised me?"

"You can never be too careful, Mason. I know how the government works. They want me. They'll come after my family to do it, but I don't care. I haven't made it to where I am without knowing what I'm doing." He adjusted the sleeve of his jacket. "Did they ask you to reach out to me? To try to get you to spill my secrets?"

Mason recalled a recent visit from a federal agent, asking him to consider that very thing. Mason had declined, knowing Ruben would be too smart for that. "I told them no."

"Good. It would be a waste of time." He paused. "Besides, there's nothing to say."

"Not if Mallory spills what she knows. And Alpha's out there somewhere."

"Alpha? You mean the source?" He took his phone out, glanced at it, and put it back in his pocket. "That's hardly a concern." He rested his elbow on the arm of the bench. "I hear Kessler spoke to the F.B.I. and now he's disappeared. I suppose he's in protective custody. There'd been a rumor that Tracy was sleeping with him." He shook his head. "Tracy had an Einstein brain but a Jane Austen heart. Mallory missed the clues, which is unusual. She doesn't miss much."

"You and Mallory obviously had a working relationship, if not more. You sure she'll remain loyal despite facing years behind bars? What if the government offers her a deal?"

Looking amused, Ruben chuckled. "Mallory will be fine. She's tougher than most. And any deals or protection provided by the government are only as reliable as those who offer them, which Alpha will soon learn. Without his testimony, her potential years behind bars may dwindle. I wouldn't underestimate her." He glanced at Mason with a gleam in his eye.

Mason didn't want to know what that meant for Kessler. He hoped the government had hidden him well.

Ruben eyed the park. "I'd say Mallory and your sister Margaret share similar traits. They always land on their feet."

Mason tensed. "What do you know about Margaret?"

"I make it my business to know about my friends…and enemies."

Mason held his breath. Was Ruben threatening him? "Am I your enemy?"

"I don't know." Ruben held his gaze. "Are you?"

Mason set his jaw. "What do you want from me?"

Ruben stared. "If only I could say. Unfortunately, I don't think there's much you can do. But it will be hard to forget that your meddling resulted in Windhaven's demise, the end of some promising and lucrative drug trials, and my son's incarceration."

Rain, thought Mason. *He's here about his son.* "Rain is where he belongs."

"I'm under no illusion that my son isn't impulsive. He acts first and thinks later. He inherited my penchant for fun, and my ruthlessness, but doesn't have the mind of a businessman, no matter how much I've tried to instill it in him." He smirked. "He got that from his mother."

"I wish I could empathize, but your kid's a murderer," said Mason. "Are you trying to say he should have covered his tracks better?"

Ruben tipped his head. "There are many things I wish he'd done better. I can't blame it all on you, Mason. To be honest. It's my fault he is where he is."

"At least you're honest." Mason recalled Rain's involvement with Lenora. "Since we're talking openly, without microphones, has Rain ever exhibited unique abilities?"

Ruben scoffed. "You mean spending exorbitant amounts of money, using and selling dangerous drugs, dating crazy women, and ignoring whatever I say? I wouldn't call that unique, but yes."

"Not that," said Mason. "I mean the woo-woo kind." He paused. "Specifically, telekinesis."

Ruben stilled and squinted. "How did you know about that?"

"He used them on Lenora's roommate." He studied Ruben's reaction. "But I suspect that wasn't the first time."

"You never cease to impress me," said Ruben. "You sure you don't want to join my staff?"

"I'll pass."

"Probably for the best."

"Probably." Another dog barked in the distance, and Mason spotted a golden retriever chasing the Frisbee.

"If we're speaking frankly," said Ruben, "and off-the-record…"

"We are," said Mason.

"...then Rain is, in some ways, responsible for the drug trials at Windhaven, and perhaps Mallory's and my family business' downfall."

Curious, Mason rested an elbow on the back of the bench. "Does this have something to do with Victor D'Mato?"

Ruben offered him a smug look. "I believe you've had some experience with him."

Mason chose not to answer. "Have you?"

Ruben nodded. "He was an interesting, but fascinating man."

"That's one way to describe him."

"I believe you and Victor were friends?"

"My history with Victor has nothing to do with you."

Ruben relaxed against the bench. "Maybe not, but it's amazing how people's lives can intersect."

Mason waited. "Well?" He checked his watch. "You're taking your time for a man who has a jet to catch."

"The jet will wait." Ruben stared off toward the lake. "Rain was a troubled child from the start. By the time he got to tenth grade, he'd been kicked out of several schools. I arranged for homeschooling to get him into college, but once he was there, it only got worse. He disappeared into a world of drugs and alcohol that even all my money couldn't stop. He took absurd risks, bought obscene amounts of clothes and jewelry, and was violent with women and men. Without drastic measures, I knew he would either kill or be killed. Not to mention that, as my son, he was a target for anyone thinking they could get money out of him or me. But he didn't care."

Wanting to know more, Mason let Ruben talk. "Didn't you behave the same when you were young?"

"I did for a time, but you know where that got me, and I learned fast. I understood the road Rain was on and where it would lead." He hesitated. "So, as Rain spiraled out of control, I did what I do best. I took matters into my own hands. My family was in the damn pharmaceutical business, so I used those resources. The family disagreed, but I dove into finding something, anything, that would help Rain break free from his dangerous cycle of abuse. It took time, but with shortcuts, a drug was created. I called it Sun since it was the antithesis of rain. Plus, you can discuss the sun all day without people thinking twice about it."

"Clever. Did you give Rain this Sun?"

"Yes. I took that chance. If something terrible happened, it would be on me. I expected it to fail and thought it had. For a few weeks, nothing changed. Rain took the drug, but it was like candy to him. I was about to scream at our well-paid scientists and bring it back into the lab when I noticed a difference. Rain's behavior changed. He started attending classes. His grades improved, and he went to fewer parties. Soon after, his drug usage decreased. He became easier to deal with, and we could talk. We finally developed a father-son relationship."

Finding Ruben's story hard to believe, he kept up the conversation. "What went wrong?"

"Who says it went wrong?"

"Your son's in jail on murder charges. Two people are dead at his hands, and I was almost the third. Obviously, you missed something."

Ruben's face hardened. "Isn't he innocent until proven guilty?"

"That's a conversation for you and Rain's attorney." Mason crossed his arms. "What happened to Rain?"

Ruben glanced back at the lake. "Other than the obvious, there were other unexpected side effects. He could move things without touching them. It began with insignificant items. A pen here. A paper there. He'd pull a chair out and slide it back. It scared him at first, and me, too. Neither of us understood it, or how to control it, or why it was even there."

Mason began to understand. "That's why you sought Victor?"

"I did my research. Victor was a man who attracted those with varied abilities and used his charisma and natural charm to control them."

"He'd created a cult."

"Call it what you want, but if you had those types of gifts or wanted to meet others who had them, Victor was your man. I declined his parties, but I got to know him, and when I told him about Rain, he pointed me toward Gina Rodriguez." Ruben smiled. "A lovely woman with remarkable gifts, and I'm not referring to just the woo-woo kind."

Mason thought of Mikey and gave thanks that she and Ruben had not crossed paths. "What did you do with Gina?"

"You really want to know?" Ruben grinned.

"Only regarding her abilities. You can keep the rest to yourself."

"Pity." Ruben straightened the cuff on his shirt. "I inquired about them. Rain and Gina were similar, but she could only use them when she was angry, but when she was, watch out. She could be dangerous when she wanted to be." Ruben paused. "It was then that I realized the gold mine I was sitting on. Not only did I have a drug that could potentially reduce or end drug abuse, but it also could stimulate startling changes in the brain and body chemistry. The scientists suggested it somehow switched on a dormant gene that produced remarkable results, at least for Rain." Ruben narrowed his eyes. "Victor was onto something. He understood the power of the mind. But what I had was a way to produce and mold that power. Victor could attract the gifted masses, but I could create them."

Mason could see Ruben's cheeks flush with color. "Did you honestly think that would work? Is power that alluring?"

"It almost did work."

Mason simmered with disgust. "No, it didn't. Look at the damage it's done."

"Some see damage. Others see progress."

Mason didn't wish to argue the point. "If Rain's so powerful, then how is he in custody? Why didn't he throw me through a wall or shove the detectives away with his mind?"

"Because all progress comes with setbacks." Ruben tapped a finger on the arm of the bench. "During my association with Victor, Gina offered information about her skills, but I knew I needed more. I gave Gina a substantial sum of money to draw some of her blood. I wanted to study it to see if I could continue what I'd started and understand how Rain had been affected. I hoped that Sun could become the hoped-for miracle drug, but maybe lead to even greater discoveries. Gina took the money, left with a man, and got married. I didn't see her again. Rain had become quite adept by then. His drug usage had never fully stopped, but he'd managed it and the urges no longer controlled him. Eventually, though, his telekinetic abilities diminished. I considered finding Gina, but remembered she had a sister. I figured if Gina had abilities, maybe Lenora did too." He stared off. "I regret that decision to this day."

Mason made some assumptions. "Rain met her and fell for her."

"He did, and worse, whatever the drug had initially done for him was wearing off rapidly. He could still use his gifts, but only during moments of heightened emotion, like Gina. His previous drug usage resumed, although not to the degree as before. But Lenora was a different story. After meeting Rain, she went downhill quickly."

"Did Rain use Sun on her?"

"He did, despite my disapproval. Lenora didn't develop any telekinesis that I know of, but when she straightened out and got clean, she didn't want Rain anymore."

Considering all that had occurred since, Mason sat in disbelief. "You knew he'd killed her, and you protected him."

"He's my son."

"And you kept testing this drug. Only on people who had no choice."

"That was taken out of my hands."

"The hell it was," said Mason. "You just found a middleman." His anger spiked. "Nothing happens without your knowledge, Ruben. You're as culpable as all the rest. And what happens to Hamlish, Tracy and Manolo? And Candace, too? What about their families?"

"Don't feel too sorry for them." Ruben's tone sharpened. "They saw dollar signs. They knew the risks."

"Which includes what will happen if they talk?" Mason sat up. "Did you threaten Candace's son at the same time you were protecting yours?"

Ruben's eyes flared. "Candace's son was never in any danger. And be smart, Mason. Don't fall for Candace's act. She's not as innocent as she pretends to be. Ask her who paid for her kid's private school and how she could afford that nice car she drives." Ruben leaned in. "Nobody's above a payday." Irritated, he sat back. "The people at Windhaven who took Sun? Most them still benefit to this day. Strangely, none of them exhibited the startling abilities Rain did, but they're leading full lives without their addictions." He glared. "What would you have done three months ago for a pill? You were on Sun for several weeks. You've benefited from that drug, no matter how much you want to curse it."

Mason swallowed his anger. "I'm not on it now."

"Let's hope the effect holds." Ruben held Mason's gaze. "I'd hate to see you relapse."

Mason told himself to stay calm. "There is such a thing as healing all on your own."

"Keep telling yourself that, but we all know how rare that is."

"Don't worry about me, Ruben. I can take care of myself."

Ruben glanced behind him. He nodded at the man in the sunglasses, who nodded back. "I hope so, Mason." He looked back. "In fact, I'm counting on it."

Mason heard the car in the parking lot start. "Guess your jet is ready to go. Have a pleasant flight."

"I will." Ruben stood. "And you enjoy your recovery."

Mason stood too and faced him. "Recovery is my strong suit."

Ruben offered a slight smile. "Mine too." He stared for a second. "I'll let Margaret know how well you're doing. Maybe when Rain is acquitted, I can arrange for a chat between you and her."

An ice-cold spear of shock raced through Mason's gut. "What did you say?"

"Gina's not the only lady I became acquainted with during my visits with Victor. Margaret and I have stayed in touch." He leaned closer and whispered. "Your sister's a hellion, by the way. I wonder if your other sister is the same?"

Hot rage bubbled up. "You go near Mikey, and Rain will never see the light of day again, whether he's in prison or not." Mason lowered his voice. "I'll make sure of it."

Ruben offered him a wide grin. "I do like you, Mason." He buttoned his jacket. "There aren't many who stand up to me, and when I meet them, I prefer to keep them around." He paused. "To find out what their weaknesses are." He softened his tone, but the threat remained. "I look forward to seeing you again soon."

Mason bit his tongue, wanting to lash out, but all he could do was watch as Ruben slid on his sunglasses, turned around, and walked away.

A Note from J.T.

I LOVE TO HEAR from my readers about their experiences with my books, and I'd love to know what you thought about *Lost Chances*. At this point, I'm fully locked into the Redstones. I love their crazy family, their complicated past, and all the issues they endure. I include Trick in that mess, as well. He's as big a part of the Redstones as anybody. When I wrote *Of Breath and Blood*, Mason and Mikey just sort of showed up, and boy, I'm glad they did. They allow me to indulge in more of my paranormal pursuits. Daniels and Remalla books allow that, too, but their stories lean more to mystery-thriller-detective stuff, which is also tons of fun to write. So, I get the best of both worlds.

I think the thing I like most about the stories I write is the relationships. Whether it's Mason and Mikey as siblings, Trick and Mason as best friends, Rem and Daniels as partners, or Rem and Mikey as potential lovers, it's all a thrill. It's what grabs me as a reader, too. I want to know what happens next! (Even as the writer, I don't always know. Sometimes I think I do, but then the characters decide otherwise.)

And I like writing the Redstones and Daniels and Remalla as two series that cross over each other. I can focus on one particular group at a time while still following an overarching story involving all the characters. It's risky, especially if a reader has only read one or the other, but my hope is that once you read one, you'll want to read the others, too. (I'm crossing my fingers.)

For newer readers, though, I expect it could get complicated, so I've started adding a list of my books in chronological order to the back matter of my books. It's included here as well. I hope that helps.

Reviews are a huge plus and a big help for an author and potential readers. I would love it if you could please take a couple of minutes to leave a quick review for *Lost Chances*. And if you'd like, please leave a few comments, too.

As always, thank you for your time and readership. It is deeply valued and appreciated.

Now, on to the next book!

Books in Chronological Order

Although recommended but not required, in case you prefer to read in order...

Acknowledgements

ANOTHER BOOK IS COMPLETE, and again, I have many to thank. This doesn't happen alone, and I am indebted to family and friends for their help, support and encouragement. It is truly appreciated.

And a big thank you to my proofers, beta readers and ARC team. You guys are a big part in making my books great. I appreciate all your guidance and advice.

I love writing about the bonds between loving family, deep friendships and the ties that hold them together. Plus, my fascination with the unknown thrown into the mix makes for a satisfying story and hopefully, adds a little more thrill for my readers.

I especially want to thank my fans. Hearing from you and knowing that you're enjoying my books makes all the hard work worthwhile. None of this would matter without your tremendous support. If I can help you escape from this crazy world for a short period each day, then I've done my job.

Here's to more stories, more fun, and more time for yourself. If you can have a little of that each day, you're on the right track.

About the Author

Award-winning author, J.T. Bishop, is a writer of mystery thrillers with a paranormal edge. Growing up, she read Stephen King, Mary Higgins Clark, and Dean Koontz, devoured every episode of the X-files and watched plenty of TV shows with great partnerships that leave you wanting more. She loves tangled relationships, unexpected twists and turns, heart-stopping love stories and the complications that come with all the above. Throw in a little supernatural fun and she's hooked. Her evil plan is to hook you, too.

She's the author of The Red-Line Trilogy and its sister series, The Fletcher Family Saga, which features touches of urban fantasy, light sci-fi, and paranormal romance. She's also happily writing mystery thrillers featuring two charismatic detectives who may occasionally encounter a supernatural villain or two, and a crossover series which follows the exploits of a gifted, but troubled, paranormal P.I. and his spunky sister.

All the above keeps her busy, but in her spare time, she loves good movies, tasty food, an unfortunate sugar addiction, and traveling.

Enjoy an excerpt from Lost Hope, Book Four in The Redstone Chronicles

THE CRICKETS CHIRPED, A soft, cool breeze blew, and the city lights twinkled in the distance. Appreciating the view, Jag sat by himself on a bench at the overlook. After leaving work at two a.m., he'd come here because he knew he'd have the place to himself. As a bartender, he could sleep in, and he liked the quiet of the early morning hours. Needing to decompress before returning home, he would frequently come to this spot in the hills, where he could look down on humanity and feel some distance from it. His job, while entertaining, also exposed him to the seedier side of life, and not wanting to take it home with him, he'd stop at the overlook, where he'd go quiet, relax, and focus on the positive. That wasn't always easy since he was broke, his girlfriend had broken up with him, and his attempts at making it big as a singer had so far failed. He'd left L.A. because he couldn't take the rejection anymore and his friend had offered him a job. It had seemed like a reasonable alternative at the time, but now he wondered if he needed to return to L.A. and try again. Maybe he'd licked his wounds long enough. And after tonight, maybe the universe was giving him the signs that his luck was turning.

He eyed the time and wondered if his new friend would show. Thinking back on his shift, Jag smiled. He'd met a woman at the bar, which wasn't unusual. Women gave him their numbers all the time. It was his job to schmooze and flirt to get them to buy more drinks, and he was good at it. Listening and smiling were attributes that served him well. He rarely acted on any of the interest though, mainly because he'd had a girlfriend and also knew the women were drunk and would likely forget about him the next day. Tonight, though, had been different.

A woman had arrived around midnight, had sat at the bar, and ordered a gin and tonic. He'd made her drink, and they'd started talking. The bar had been slower than usual, and he'd had more opportunity to talk. She'd introduced herself as Eleanor and had an easy laugh and a pretty smile. Her hair was up in a bun and loose tendrils framed her face. She'd told him how she'd left her boyfriend and family in Ohio six months earlier and had come to San Diego to start a new life. Jag had told his story, too. They had an easy camaraderie he rarely found in others. Since breaking up with his girlfriend, he hadn't made much of an effort to date, but Eleanor made his stomach flutter, and he'd told her about his spot, where he'd come at night to overlook the city. When the bar closed, he'd invited her to meet him out here. She'd hesitated, and he'd promised he wasn't a stalker or serial killer. After a thoughtful moment, she'd told him a firm maybe, and she'd left.

Jag didn't know whether she'd join him or not, and she hadn't given him her number, so if she didn't show, he might never see her again. He understood. Few great romances were born in bars between a bartender and a patron, although it would be a cool story if they did.

Deciding he'd wait a few more minutes, he settled back on the bench and enjoyed the peaceful panorama, telling himself that no matter what happened, it would be for the best. Thinking about L.A. and what was next for him, he contemplated his future when he heard a car approaching. He turned and squinted at headlights that turned off the road and saw a car pull into a rocky space and stop.

His heart thumping, he waited. The car turned off, the door opened, and he grinned when he saw her step out. She smiled and closed the door.

Jag stood from the bench. "Glad you could make it."

Taking a deep breath and blowing it out, Eleanor walked over to him and widened her eyes at the view. "You weren't kidding. It's beautiful."

"It's one of my favorite places," he said. "Most people hang out here during the day or evening, but I like it when it's just me."

She set her purse down on the bench. "I can see why." The breeze blew, and the tendrils around her face fluttered.

"What made you decide to come?"

She shrugged. "I knew I wouldn't be able to sleep. And you seemed like a nice guy, and I haven't met many of those." She glanced sideways at him. "And you're cute."

Jag felt his cheeks warm. "You're pretty cute yourself."

She sat on the bench. "Thank you."

"You're welcome." He sat beside her.

They didn't talk for a minute, and Jag enjoyed the moment. He pondered whether his great love story would start with serving a pretty lady in a bar.

"How long do you normally stay out here?" she asked, draping an arm over the back of the bench.

"I don't know. Depends on the night. Thirty minutes? By then, the fatigue sets in and I go home to sleep."

"You ever bring your ex here?"

He shook his head. "No. She's in L.A. Had no interest in coming to San Diego. She's still hoping to hit it big as an actress."

"Good for her. That's a tough gig."

"It is, especially since she's terrible at acting. Can't remember lines to save her life. She got fired from her waitress gig because she couldn't remember the menu."

Eleanor giggled. "Oh, dear."

Jag shifted to face her. "I know."

Eleanor crossed her legs. "Maybe she'll get lucky. Some do, you know."

He nodded. "Some do."

They stared for a moment, and she turned slightly toward him. "You hoping you might get lucky, too?"

Jag chuckled. "It crossed my mind."

She smiled and scooted closer. "It crossed my mind, too. I just don't want you to think I'm the kind of person who meets and makes out with strangers every night."

"Definitely not." His heart thumped faster. "Maybe just once a week."

Her smile grew. "More like once a month."

Jag moved closer. "I can live with that." He looked into her eyes and saw her gaze travel to his mouth. He lowered his head and let his lips graze over hers. The sensation was electric, and he heard her take a breath. "I really like you," he whispered.

"I really like you, too," she whispered back. She pressed her lips onto his, and the kiss deepened.

He felt her hand on his thigh, and he brought his to her cheek, where he cupped her jaw and moved his lips over hers, slow at first, but then the pace picked up. He opened his mouth, and their tongues touched. His whole body tingled, and he told himself to go slow, but Eleanor was picking up speed. She slid her hand up his leg and nipped her teeth against his lips. She moved her body closer, and her other hand slid into his hair.

Trying to catch his breath, Jag slid his lips down her cheek, trailing a path to her jaw. He heard her moan, and his body responded to the sound. He moved his hand down to her shoulder and then cupped her breast. She gasped and gripped his hip, pulling him closer.

She dropped her head back, and he nibbled her ear and kissed her soft skin. "You taste so good," he said between kisses.

Eleanor grasped his hair and pulled him away. She raised her head and stared into his eyes. "I bet you do, too." She kissed him hard, swiveled, and slid her leg over his until she straddled him on the bench. The move thrilled him, and he put his hands on her thighs.

She moaned and rocked her body against his, lowering her mouth from his lips to his throat, where she teased him with her tongue. His heart was thudding so fast, he hoped it wouldn't stop from shock. She ran her hands over his chest, and up to his neck, where she nibbled him. "I want you," she said against his skin.

"I want you, too," he said, although he could barely speak. Everything was happening so fast. He cupped her buttocks with his hands, wanting to yank her clothes off, when she abruptly shot away from him just as he heard an ear-splitting shriek from behind. It penetrated his hazy senses and frightened, Jag stood as she jumped up. A man, bellowing and holding a wicked knife, had swung at them, the blade barely missing Eleanor's head and Jag's face.

Terrified and shocked by the unexpected attack, Jag froze, realizing how close he'd come to dying, and realizing he still might.

The man stood beside the bench in jeans and a dirty t-shirt, holding his long knife and glaring. His muscled shoulders and arms bunched beneath the fabric, and his dark and menacing eyes bore into Jag's. Jag didn't know what to do. He was too scared to move. Eleanor stood still and didn't speak or scream. She simply glared back.

Jag raised a hand. "Lis...listen. We don't want any trouble. Ju...Just leave us alone." His breath came in quick gasps.

The man took a step closer, and Jag stepped away. Eleanor didn't move. "Go," said the man, in a gravelly voice.

Jag assumed he spoke to Eleanor. "Run to the trees. I'll try to fight him off while you get help." He didn't think for a second he could defeat this man, but he wouldn't sacrifice Eleanor to save himself.

"He's not talking to me," said Eleanor.

The man waved his free hand toward Jag. "Go. Now. And don't return."

Jag looked between the man and Eleanor, not understanding. "What?"

"I said go," screamed the man, his face stern.

His tone and volume broke through Jag's fear, and since Eleanor made no effort to do anything but glare, Jag ran.

His adrenaline propelled him down the dusty road. On his right was the steep embankment, and on his left was the pebbled road that led from the street, where he'd parked, down to the overlook. If he could get up and back to his car, he could call for help if he could stop shaking long enough to use his phone. Running as fast as he could, he debated going back. He'd left Eleanor all alone with a crazy man and his knife. She would be murdered, and Jag would be the loser who'd let it happen. For a second, he almost slowed and turned around when he heard a guttural yell, which morphed into a shriek, and then a terrible gut-wrenching wail that abruptly stopped.

His terror ramping up further, Jag forced himself to run faster. The loose rocks made his feet skip and slide, and he almost fell. Gasping for air, he could see his car and raced toward it.

Hearing a scraping sound and what sounded like rapid footsteps behind him, he had the horrifying feeling he was being followed. Something was chasing him. Too terrified to look behind him, he scrambled up the small hill, praying to get to his vehicle in time. His feet slid, and he fell forward but righted himself. Desperate, he heard whimpering and realized it was him.

Reaching his car, he felt a small kernel of hope that he might survive this, when something slammed against him from behind. His body was thrown into his car with a hard thump, and another blow sent him over the hood. His mind and body went numb. After hitting the pavement, his vision spun. His legs wouldn't move, and although he wanted to scream, nothing emerged. And then it was on him, and helpless to stop it, he was dragged into the brush.

Enjoy an excerpt from Of Power and Pain, Book Five in Detectives Daniels and Remalla

NOTE: *OF POWER AND Pain* follows the events of *Lost Chances*.

Rem pulled up and parked at the curb, seeing the various police cars parked in front of a small one-story house with two large trees in the front yard. He turned off the ignition and sat in the car, thinking. Anticipating the crime scene, he wondered what he was about to walk into. Eyeing the time, he noted Daniels would probably be another few minutes. Tapping his fingers on the steering wheel, he took a deep breath to prepare himself, and opened the door.

He slid out of the car and stared at the house. A patrolman stood outside the front entry, and a crime scene van was parked in the driveway. He closed his door, stepped onto the curb and ducked beneath the crime scene tape. An officer approached him, he flashed his badge, and the officer nodded. Rem walked across the grass and jogged up the steps to the concrete patio.

He recognized the patrolman. "Hey, Smithers. How's it going today?"

Smithers, a younger officer who'd been on the job a few years and had a wife and kid that Rem had met at the annual picnic, nodded. "Afternoon, Detective. Sorry you had to come in on your day off."

"Lozano said he wanted us on this one. I'll be curious to find out why." The front door was ajar, and Rem peeked inside the house. He spotted a crime scene technician taking photos. "Have they been in there long?"

Smithers shook his head. "No. Not very."

"Ibrahim on this one?" asked Rem.

"Yeah, he is." He glanced inside. "I think he's checking the body now."

Rem looked at his watch. "Daniels will be here soon. I'll wait while they finish." He noted Smithers' pale features. "Who called it in?"

"The mother contacted nine-one-one asking for a welfare check. Apparently, a friend was supposed to meet the victim for lunch. When she didn't show or respond to messages, the friend called the vic's mom, and the mom called us, demanding someone check on her daughter." He tipped his head toward a patrolman on the sidewalk. Rem spotted Smithers' partner, Hendrix, who was talking to a man in a jogging suit. "I think that's the neighbor."

"What was your reason for going in?"

"We almost left when she didn't answer. But Hendrix wanted to check the back, and we looked through the window."

"What did you see?" asked Rem.

"A woman lying on the floor in the kitchen. We'd hoped she was unconscious, but when we got inside, we realized she wasn't."

Recalling his own days as a young officer, Rem could empathize. "Was it bad?"

"From what I can tell, she'd been strangled." Smithers looked like he'd eaten food way past its expiration date.

"I wish I could tell you it gets easier," said Rem, "but it doesn't."

Smithers ran a shaky hand through his hair. "She looks like my wife, you know? It just kinda hit me."

Rem swallowed, thinking of Jennie. "It happens. It's hard not to think of our own loved ones when something like this happens."

A man stepped out of the house wearing a blue jacket with identification around his neck. His wire-rimmed glasses rested on his forehead, and he slid them down to his nose. "Hello, Detective. Where's your better half?"

"Hey, Ibrahim." Rem checked the time again. "He should be here any minute. What have we got?"

"Female. Probably around thirty years old. Strangled. Been dead about twenty-four hours." He glanced back inside the house. "My guys should be done in a few minutes."

Rem nodded. "That's fine. I'm waiting for Daniels, anyway." He crossed his arms. "That way we can both be horrified together."

Ibrahim pulled off his glasses and cleaned them with the hem of his shirt. "It never gets easier, does it, Detective?"

Rem eyed Smithers. "No. It never does." He wondered why Lozano had sent them to the scene. "Lozano told Daniels he wanted us on this one. Any reason why?"

Abraham put his glasses back on. "I have an idea. But I'll let you and Daniels decide for yourselves when you get inside."

His interest piqued, Rem was about to ask about Ibrahim's cryptic comment but held off when he spotted Daniels pull up to the curb and park behind Rem's car. Rem watched as his partner left his vehicle, approached the crime scene tape, flashed his badge to an officer, and jogged across the grass up to the patio.

Daniels tucked his badge into his pocket. "I didn't expect a welcoming committee."

"We just couldn't wait to see you," said Rem.

"Marjorie tells me that all the time," said Daniels with a smile.

Rem smirked. "Even when you forget to bring dinner home? Like the other night?"

Daniels face fell. "She told me something different then." He held up his index finger. "But in my defense, I was helping you finish a report."

Rem shook his head. "Don't blame me, sport. I suggested you stop and get some Taco del Fuegos when you left. Remember?"

Daniels scowled. "That's probably why I forgot. You made me lose my appetite."

Rem pointed toward the house. "Speaking of losing appetites, we've got a body inside. I was waiting for crime scene to finish." He gestured at Ibrahim. "The Doc here won't tell me what's got Lozano all worked up."

Ibrahim shrugged. "I told him you two could sort that out for yourselves. Check the kitchen counter, though. I think you'll find it interesting." He peered inside the house. "I think you guys can go in now. I'm going to grab something from the van. I'll be back in a second." He pulled coverings out of his pocket and held them out to Rem. "Make sure you wear these."

"Thanks," said Rem, taking the shoe protectors and gloves. He handed some to Daniels. "You ready?"

Daniels took them. "As I'll ever be."

They slid the protectors over their shoes, put on the gloves and entered the house.

Rem followed a narrow hall down to a modest living room with a small, worn couch and end table. A TV hung on the wall, and a wooden coffee table sported a large pink crystal in the middle of it. Rem saw the legs of the victim extending into a square dining area beyond the kitchen tile. A technician had left the kitchen and was taking photos of the rest of the house. Rem walked to the body, seeing a pretty lady in a yellow sleeveless dress lying on her back on the kitchen floor. Her dress had been smoothed to lie flat, and her limbs had been straightened. The only thing that marred her appearance was her bruised neck. On her right bicep was a symbol written in black marker. Rem determined it was either the number eight or the infinity sign. Daniels walked up beside Rem. "She looks posed," said Daniels.

"She does," said Rem. "It almost looks like she's sleeping." He squatted next to her. "Look at her hair and clothes. They've been intentionally arranged."

Daniels nodded. "There's no way she fell backward like that. It's almost like the killer wanted her to be comfortable." He squinted. "What's that mark on her arm?"

Rem looked closer at the strange symbol. "Looks like the killer is telling us something."

Daniels turned toward the circular glass dining table. "That must be her purse." He spoke to a technician who walked through the room. "You guys get a picture of this?"

The technician nodded. "Yes. Feel free to look through whatever you want."

Daniels walked over and went through the purse. He pulled out a wallet. Rem entered the kitchen.

Daniels read from a driver's license. "Her name's Stella de la Rosa. Age thirty-two."

Rem opened some kitchen cabinets and drawers. "Anything else that will tell us a little more about her?"

Daniels opened a pocket. He pulled out what looked like business cards and read from one of them. His eyes widened. "Interesting."

Rem walked back and looked over Daniels' shoulder. "What is it?"

"Guess what Stella does for a living?" He read from the card. "She's a psychic masseuse."

Rem tried to imagine what that was. "What the hell is a psychic masseuse?"

Daniels shrugged. "My guess? She gives massages and psychic readings. Possibly at the same time."

"Seriously?"

"Guess what her motto is? Rest, recoup, and get the scoop." He lowered the card. "Catchy."

Rem found it hard to believe. "How is it we always catch these cases?"

Daniels returned the license and put the wallet and cards back in Stella's purse. "Maybe that's why Lozano asked us to investigate. He knew something we didn't."

"How would he know that she's a psychic masseuse? You think he was a client?"

"I doubt it," said Daniels with a chuckle. "But Lozano has surprised us before."

Ibrahim returned. "You guys see what you need to?" He gestured toward the counter. "Did you note the items the killer left behind?"

Rem glanced toward the far counter. "Haven't gotten that far yet. We're learning about Stella's occupation. She was a psychic masseuse. Ever heard of that?"

Ibrahim shook his head. "Can't say that I have. But I think you two will be far more interested in what's been left on the counter."

Rem walked to the far corner of the counter, and Daniels followed. A piece of lined notebook paper with words written in black marker sat beside a black bow tie. Rem read the note, and a chill ran up his spine. "Hell," he whispered.

Daniels read it out loud. "Four more days." Beneath that was written *For Margaret*. Next to that was the infinity sign.

Rem almost grabbed the counter for support. "You don't think...?"

Daniels appeared to read the note again. "That our killer is referring to Margaret Redstone?" He eyed Rem. "Now I think we know why Lozano sent us."

"Maybe it's a different Margaret," said Rem, hoping and praying it was.

Daniels frowned. "What's your gut tell you?"

Ibrahim nodded toward the body. "You notice the same symbol was on her arm?"

"We did." Rem's gaze returned to the note. "I wonder what that means." Imagining Margaret Redstone's frenetic blue eyes and loud cackle, Rem's heart skipped. "You think Margaret Redstone has something to do with this?"

Ibrahim raised an eyebrow. "She's the lady who escaped the psychiatric ward, right?"

"Yeah. Three months ago," said Rem, feeling as if it had been three years. "There's been no trace of her, and no indication of what she might be up to, until now."

"The question is, what is Stella's connection to Margaret?" asked Daniels. "Why was Stella a target?"

"Maybe Stella didn't have a connection," said Rem. "But obviously the killer does."

Daniels sighed. "We need to learn more about our victim. Maybe she can give us a few clues about why she was murdered."

Ibrahim pointed toward the back of the house. "There's a bedroom, plus an office and massage room down the hall. If I were to guess, she saw clients in her house."

Daniels glanced in that direction. "If that's true, then maybe one of Stella's clients killed her." He shot a look at Rem. "Maybe this has nothing to do with Margaret Redstone at all."

Something told Rem that was wishful thinking. "Let's go find out."

"I'll bag these," said Ibrahim, pointing toward the items. "We'll check them for prints and DNA. Once I have my initial report, I'll send it to Lozano."

"Thanks," said Rem. He followed Daniels through the living room and into the hall. Daniels peered into a doorway on his left, and Rem poked his head into another on his right. Rem saw an open massage table, and various shelves cluttered with crystals, candles, and pictures. It smelled of incense, and Rem stepped inside. "I got the massage room."

"This is the office," said Daniels. "I'll check it out."

Rem studied the walls around Stella's massage table. There were two framed diplomas. One was a certificate of completion for a massage therapy course from three years earlier. Next to it was a diploma from a local community college for a bachelor's degree in kinesiology. He moved to the shelves and eyed the various colored crystals and rocks amid bottles of oils. A shelf above held various books about meditation, stress relief, massage techniques, essential oils, and general well-being.

"I've got a laptop in here," said Daniels from the other room. "We'll have to get our tech guys to look at it."

Rem glanced at another shelf, seeing an array of framed photos. Some were of Stella at what looked like various seminars, sitting cross-legged with her eyes closed. In another photo, Stella was lying on the ground with two people sitting near her head with their hands on her temples. Other photos showed Stella with friends or maybe family. They were all framed except for one picture. It was propped against a framed photo of Stella in front of the Grand Canyon. Rem studied it. Stella was with two smiling men on either side of her, her arms around each of them. Recognizing one of the men, Rem froze. A shockwave rippled through him, and he stepped back. The blood rushed through his ears, and his vision briefly swam. Trying to keep his balance, he bumped up against the massage table and sat back against it.

Daniels entered the room. "I asked Ibrahim to grab the laptop while he's here. He said he'd bag it and bring it with him."

Rem took a steadying breath. His vision cleared, and he blinked.

"What's wrong?" Daniels stopped beside him. "You don't look so hot."

Rem held his stomach. "The photo...." He shook his head to clear it. "I wasn't expecting it."

"What photo?"

Rem's belly churned, and he wished he'd skipped breakfast. "On the shelf. Above the rocks and books."

Daniels eyed Rem for a second. "You okay?"

Rem centered himself. "I'm fine. The urge to puke is easing."

"I hope. Ibrahim won't be too happy if you mess up his crime scene."

"I'm well aware." Rem swiped at his brow.

"You need a trashcan, let me know." Daniels watched a second more and then turned toward the shelf. His gaze traveled over the pictures, and he stopped at the unframed one. His breath caught. "Is that who I think it is?"

His shock abating, Rem stood and approached the shelves. He eyed the one that had set his teeth on edge. "If you're thinking of Victor D'Amato, you're right. Stella knew him." Rem closed his eyes, trying to shut out the swirling memories of his abduction and the knife at his throat. He recalled the note on the counter and opened his eyes. "Which means Margaret Redstone is likely the Margaret in our killer's note. She hasn't gone far, and whatever she's planning, it's just getting started."

www.ingramcontent.com/pod-product-compliance
Lightning Source LLC
Chambersburg PA
CBHW072127250626
47159CB00007B/2593